G.R. EVANS is Professor Emeritus of Medieval Theology and Intellectual History at the University of Cambridge. Her many books include *Belief: A Short History for Today* (2006), *The Church in the Early Middle Ages* (2007), *The University of Cambridge: A New History* (2009) and *The University of Oxford: A New History* (2010), published by I.B. Tauris.

'It may seem that the question of human origins has never been more controversial than today. But in this informative and elegantly written book, G.R. Evans shows how there have always been competing narratives of how the world began and about the significance of human existence. With wide-ranging scholarship and an engaging style, she offers an intriguing and thought-provoking exploration of a set of perennial questions.'

Peter Harrison, Director, Centre for the History of European Discourses, University of Queensland, formerly Andreas Idreos Professor of Science and Religion at the University of Oxford, editor of *The Cambridge Companion to Science and Religion*

'In *First Light* G.R. Evans offers a lively survey of scores of explanations of the creation of the world across periods, continents, and disciplines. She covers Eastern as well as Western religions, "primitive" myths, scientific explanations, and philosophical assessments. She continually shows unexpected similarities. But she finally gives a reluctant "no" to the question whether, as Eliot's character Casaubon in *Middlemarch* asked, there is a single "key to all mythologies". This is a delightful work.'

Robert A. Segal, Sixth Century Professor of Religious Studies, University of Aberdeen, author of *Myth: A Very Short Introduction* and *Theorizing About Myth*

FIRST LIGHT

A History of Creation Myths from Gilgamesh to the God Particle

I.B. TAURIS

LONDON · NEW YORK

G.R. Evans

Published in 2014 by I.B.Tauris & Co. Ltd
6 Salem Road, London W2 4BU
175 Fifth Avenue, New York NY 10010
www.ibtauris.com

Distributed in the United States and Canada
Exclusively by Palgrave Macmillan
175 Fifth Avenue, New York NY 10010

ISBN: 978 1 78076 155 8

A full CIP record for this book is available from the British Library
A full CIP record is available from the Library of Congress

Library of Congress Catalog Card Number: available

Typeset by JCS Publishing Services Ltd, www.jcs-publishing.co.uk
Printed and bound in Sweden by ScandBook AB

Contents

Illustrations

Humans dream of their beginnings and imagine their ends.

(Boethius, *Consolation*, II, Prose 1)

All are but parts of one stupendous whole,
The body Nature is, and God the soul.

(Pope, *Essay on Man*, IX.267–8)

Preface

In *The Hitchhiker's Guide to the Galaxy*, the supercomputer Deep Thought spends seven and a half million years calculating an answer to 'life, the universe and everything'. The answer is '42', but this is not felt to be entirely satisfactory.[1] So Deep Thought creates the earth, a device able to frame the question to which 42 is the answer. In this venturesome tale, the earth comes to an end just before the question which belongs to the answer emerges. So there still seems to be room for discussion about the beginning of the universe and human origins within it.

Edward Casaubon in George Eliot's *Middlemarch* has become a by-word for the scholar who wastes his energies in a hopeless inquiry:

> He had undertaken to show . . . that all the mythical systems or erratic mythical fragments in the world were corruptions of a tradition originally revealed. Having once mastered the true position and taken a firm footing there, the vast field of mythical constructions became intelligible, nay, luminous with the reflected light of correspondences.[2]

He may have gone about it in the wrong way, but he rightly recognised that any exploration has to grapple with the fact that the world is full of tales about how the world began and some of them coincide. The difficulty is to draw from their coincidences any ultimate resolution to humanity's recurring questions about where we all came from and why, indeed why there is a universe at all.

Isaac Newton (1642–1727) was no fiction, and he thought the truth could be unearthed as a matter of 'history' from beneath the fleeting 'correspondences'. While he was founding much of modern physics and helping to design modern scientific method, he also spent decades on comparative research into the *Chronology of Ancient Kingdoms*.[3] James Frazer, who published *The Golden Bough* in 1890, was also eager to find myth-patterns which might allow a glimpse of a lost original unifying 'truth' about creation which human beings 'know' if they could only remember. So there are questions which have seemed legitimate to a series of influential thinkers about what can be learned about the origins of the universe from mythologies.

In the first half of the twentieth century the psychoanalyst C.G. Jung (1875–1961) attempted to apply a variant of this approach to the understanding of the relationship between the interior life of the individual mind and the 'collective' unconscious 'shared knowledge' of all humanity. This was a period of active scholarly interest in the study of mythologies and many texts were being published for the first time. Jung began to make a collection and to read his way into the subject, writing enthusiastically to Sigmund Freud (1856–1939) in late 1909 about his discoveries in the field of symbolism. He said he was beginning to feel he was actually living among a crowd of mythical creatures, centaurs and satyrs; it was as though he was listening to a patient telling him of his recollection of some former life while he strove to understand the meaning of the belief. Then he discovered Mithraism and the mystery religions and the oriental religions.[4] He studied theories of primitive tribes and the way they thought. He connected memories of his childhood games with the Australian practice of locating a god-protector in a stone (*churinga*). Patterns of mythical interpretation, astrology, alchemy, all had validity for him and all fitted together into an immense body of related notions. It began to seem to him that the individual contains a miniature evolved history of the past of all humanity. People are microcosms of their race, embodying a profound 'knowledge' of its beginnings.

There has been resistance to such comprehensive synthesising from a number of points of view. Religious explanations of how the world began have typically relied on the evidence of 'sacred texts' such as the Bible and the Qur'an and the Upanishads: 'It is the fundamentalists who promote the unnecessary either-every-word-of-the-Bible-is-literally-true-or-none-is dichotomy.'[5]

'Fundamentalist' readers of sacred texts may vigorously reject the possibility that a conjunction or coherence of understandings may be glimpsed by comparing them or by reading them in the context of other theories, for example, those of modern science. ('I had a parent come in and basically said I was going to spend an eternity in hell, if I taught her kids about evolution.')[6] Then there have been the attempts of philosophy to find answers by 'thinking' alone, though that has usually involved a good deal of traceable borrowing from one another.

Modern physical science takes a different approach again. It attempts to identify a mechanism or event which launched the universe into existence without resort to the possibility that there was an actual Creator bringing the world into existence by an act of will. It asks how the world began (with a 'big bang' or in some other way?). It looks for evidence (with telescopes and experiments and mathematical calculations involving fundamental particles). It may postulate a Higgs boson to explain how anything can have 'mass'.

There may be no more convincing answers to be found in the pages that follow, but there is much to be gained from approaching the questions in an attempt to see how all this has fitted together over the centuries and through contact with rival explanations.

1. Large Hadron Collider element

Introduction

The beginning of what 'world'?

How did we get here and who or what are we? This is going to be a book about a question everyone sees differently and no one can answer. It is not going to be a tidy book. The reader will be invited to open a series of doors giving different views of the scene. But that does not mean it cannot offer a stimulating glimpse of the attempts human beings have made to answer this question at different times and in different parts of the world.

The problem of fixing on a definition of the 'world' whose origins need explaining is not straightforward. The term 'world' (*mundus*) can be confusing, says Peter Comestor (d. *c.*1178). 'World' can mean the whole cosmos (*empyreum celum*), or the 'world about us' the senses perceive when we gaze at the heavens (*sensilis mundus*), or the earth under the moon, on which we can walk about. A human being too is a 'little world' or microcosm, 'for he bears the image of the whole world in himself' (*quia in se totius mundi ymaginem representat*), 'the world contracted, and abridged into man'.[1] Mythologies commonly leap between the cosmos and immediate local interests and local needs. So 'the beginning of the world' as this book explores it will include the whole cosmos, within which lies the earth, and on it the places where people live.

The different sorts and sizes of 'world' have interacted in the way tales have been told and explanations devised. In the Greek legend of Jason and the Argonauts, the travellers pass from familiar territory to supernatural and magical 'worlds'. They:

> knew that they were come to Caucasus, at the end of all the earth: Caucasus the highest of all mountains, the father of the rivers of the East. On his peak lies chained the Titan, while a vulture tears his heart; and at his feet are piled dark forests round the magic Colchian land.[2]

Creation stories often have fuzzy edges like this. As in this story, the enquirer comes to the ends of the earth and sees beyond into other dimensions of reality. There is rarely an uncrossable line where one order of created thing encounters another; natural and supernatural worlds are not quite distinct.

> Through worlds unnumber'd though the God be known,
> 'Tis ours to trace him only in our own.

The human observer standing on the earth has always been at a disadvantage when it comes to trying to understand how the world began. Even modern science can observe only from an earth-bound standpoint, though there have been a few missions by spaceship which have, with varying degrees of success, made it possible for instruments to take pictures and readings and measurements from the moon and from nearby planets in Earth's own solar system. Getting outside our limited sphere of observation has been mainly a matter of speculative thought, 'modelling' and imaginative jumps.

It would take a being able to see much further and travel much more widely to do better, one:

> . . . who through vast immensity can pierce,
> See worlds on worlds compose one universe,
> Observe how system into system runs,
> What other planets circle other suns,
> What varied being peoples ev'ry star,
> May tell why Heav'n has made us as we are.[3]

We were not able to take notes when creation began

> So even nature could have a memory, could it? Just as she has a memory, of what she thought she was meant to become and where.[4]

History records memory. Yet no human observer was there with a notebook at the beginning of the world to write down what was happening. For many centuries it was believed that Moses was the author of the first five books of the Old Testament, yet it struck commentators that he could not be reporting from observation when he wrote the opening of the book of Genesis. So the problem of the limited human vantage-point extends into remote time too.

That has not prevented historians from beginning their narratives at the absolute beginning and making calculations to arrive at the age of the world. Conceptions of the reliability of admissible historical evidence have moved a long way since the Venerable Bede (672/3–735) had the challenging idea of checking his facts with eyewitnesses. And in the case of a history of creation no one could do that. The Greek '*historia*' means something much closer to 'story' than to its modern sense. Until the nineteenth century 'history' could legitimately include 'story' going far beyond the sort of 'evidence' historians would now accept as reliable.

There are innumerable creation stories across the world which have been handed down orally. If they are not records of 'historical' fact, what are they? It will not do to call them 'myths' and then dismiss them. A myth is not simply a fictionalised tale, nor is it necessarily in some sense 'false' or 'misleading'. It can be a way of seeking to express what cannot be described in any other way. A tribe or people may regard its myths as preserving its 'tradition' and as sacred.

The world's creation stories sit so loosely to modern requirements about historical evidence partly because of the difficulty of dating many of them or mapping the influences which were woven into them. Migrations and invasions, even trading, may explain the similarities among creation stories. Swahili creation stories are strongly marked with explanations closely resembling those in Genesis, because they are derived from Islamic influences and the Qur'an, so they cannot be older than the arrival of Islam in the relevant parts of Africa. But creation explanations resembling other archetypes may have appeared locally without the need to postulate such links in influence or borrowing.

Creation stories throughout the world use narratives in which time-scales and dimensions have little reference to time and space in their familiar dimensions. Many mention an earlier long-lived or gigantic race. Genesis speaks of giants (Genesis 6:4). The Old Testament has its Methuselah figures. Among the ancient Greek creation myths are stories of the vast 'powers' referred to as demiurges, the Greek proto-gods the Titans (such as Saturn, a primordial giant god).

The need to envisage something vast may have been prompted by the fact that the world of lands and seas seems to the uninstructed observer to be huge; above it stretches a still-bigger sky. It is therefore necessary to explain what could be big or great

enough to make or organise this vastness. A favourite explanation
involved getting chaos under control. The Greek writer Hesiod
describes how a semi-personified Chaos gave birth to the Earth
(who covered herself with the Heavens and brought forth the
Seas), and to an Underworld and also to Eros, who set up from
the outset the erotic tensions in the universe that have caused
trouble ever since. Heaven and Earth gave birth to the Titans, the
combative primitive gods. They in their turn are the parents of the
familiar gods of the Greek pantheon, such as Zeus the king and
Poseidon the ruler of the seas. So this approach could produce a
pantheon of gods as well as a 'narrative' of origins.

This is one way of saying that things were not always as they
are now. It allows for the possibility that creation was potentially
a continuous process rather than a moment of divine invention
or a 'big bang'. But there are many other implications and
interconnections, which will be explored in the chapters which
follow.

Some early attempts at explaining things

'Among the ancients there were no end of philosophical systems.'
'All of them got up fictions of worlds at will,'[5] said Francis Bacon
(1561–1626). Has any one explanation proved more satisfactory
than another? The important question may not be which has
stood up best to testing and analysis, but which has had most
influence for other reasons, perhaps just because of the way in
which it was carried round the world by the politically powerful,
the intellectually impressive, the currently fashionable or the most
assiduous travellers and migrants. This dimension of dissemination
and influence will emerge as an important strand in later chapters.

A 'founding myth' is a special kind of creation myth, explaining
the origins of a people or a nation in the context of the beginning
of the world or at some time after it. The poet Virgil (70–19 BC)
told the tale of the founding of Rome in his epic the *Aeneid*. He
begins from the period described by the much earlier Homer in
the *Iliad*,[6] in which the gods play an active part in initiating the
story of the Trojan War. In the course of the journey in the *Aeneid*,
in Book VI, Aeneas goes down into the Underworld and returns.
So even narratives about the beginning of one people on the
earth may overlap into a supernatural dimension and into worlds
beyond this.

Syncretism

The influence of the ancient Romans, and through them the Greeks, has been very significant. Rome conquered Greece about 146 BC. It went on to dominate other parts of Europe, and in extending their Empire after the collapse of the Roman Republic in the first half of the first century BC, the Romans conquered most of modern Europe. They adopted a general policy of merging their own polytheism with that of conquered races, matching the gods where possible (Jupiter with Zeus; Juno with Hera, and so on). Syncretism is tolerant. It does not cling to one system or one god as the only truth. It can offer a synthesis.

Educated Romans travelled, and sometimes settled, across their Empire. The 'higher education' of the day – for which the sons of wealthy Romans were often sent to Athens – made them familiar with Greek philosophies and philosophical systems. Writers were often keen to compare views across the known world of educated men and philosophers. Clement of Alexandria (c.150–215) wrote in his *Stromateis* (*Miscellanies*) about the way the most famous of Greek philosophers, such as Pythagoras (who respected Zoroaster the Persian) and Plato (who says he had visited Egypt and borrowed from Egyptian studies) had got their ideas from the 'barbarians': philosophers of Babylon and Arabia and India, too, even the Celts and the Druids seem to have proved useful sources for Greek thinkers.[7] The Armenian Moses of Khorene (fifth century) is thought to have used the work of Ptolemy, Eratosthenes and Strabo when he wanted to write on history and geography.

Syncretism could be a two-way process, with the conquerors assimilating religious notions of the conquered. When the Romans arrived in Britain they found, as they had in other parts of their growing European and African Empire, a paganism in which people worshipped sacred groves and springs. There was also awareness of the influence of ancient druid practices and the strong position the druid priesthood seems to have still held among the Celtic peoples. Diodorus Siculus wrote of the animal sacrifices of the Celts, where their priests presided, and priestly prophecies based on the observation of birds in flight. He even suggests that there was sometimes a human sacrifice, which enabled the priests to observe the thrashing of the dying victim, draw inferences and foretell the future. So syncretism could work both ways. It could influence the ideas of the dominant culture which was seeking to absorb the religion of a conquered race.

As a conquering race, the Romans were pragmatists when they encountered strong worshipping cultures with particular preferences. They saw the social advantage in allowing conquered peoples to persist in their religious practices. It was always their habit to try to identify local gods individually with gods of their own pantheon, without being too fussy about an exact match. In this way, local people did not feel resentment at being deprived of familiar comforts, but at the same time they were 'integrated' into the large-scale arrangements of the Empire. But if necessary, odd local customs might continue.

The Romans generally approached this process of integration and 'inculturation' practically in other respects too. They made room for the 'mystery religions' which did not quite fit. And the intelligentsia enjoyed philosophical discussions in which they could be supremely dismissive of simple-minded paganism without wishing to purge it from the Empire.

Rome's Empire eventually became enormous in relation to the known world of its time, but it did not encompass the Americas or sub-Saharan Africa or penetrate far into Asia. It is possible that rumours of distant polytheisms reached the Empire; Manichaeism was able to make its way from China. But the Polynesian and Antipodean beliefs cannot have reached so far or the conviction that no one lived in these parts of the world could not have remained so strong.

However, circumstances made it more difficult to carry the ideas of some systems of belief elsewhere. Hinduism is very ancient but it has no founder or prophet or single great first leader. Nor does it have a strong doctrine of a single originating creation, tending as it does to the 'repeating cycle' theory of the universe's creation and destruction. Hindu believers had limited contact with the mainstream Western philosophies of the ancient world during the centuries when they were comparing notes. So Hindu input into a consolidated 'world collection' of creation theories came relatively late.

There remain world religions which cannot easily be absorbed into an all-purpose single system because their foundation ideas are so utterly different. In the Chinese belief-systems, Taoism and Confucianism and Buddhism all include the idea of a dualism of Yin and Yang, female and male principles. These made the Ancient One (P'an Ku). He shaped the landscapes of the earth and eventually fell exhausted upon the earth. His body became five mountains. His blood flowed to form the rivers. His hair spread out and became the plant kingdom. Gautama, the Buddha, who founded Buddhism, probably lived in the fifth or fourth century BC. According to legend, he set out to lead an ascetic life but came to believe that this was too extreme. The right way to live was moderately, seeking enlightenment through meditation. In this way, he attained enlightenment. Enlightenment was the realisation that suffering is a result of attachment to things desired. The ultimate liberation from attachment comes only with the state of Nirvana, when the soul is free from greed and hatred and ignorance. A soul in that state no longer experiences the boundaries of its individuality or selfhood. The Buddha came to believe he should teach this system; he acquired disciples, and Buddhism spread. One of its implications was that conventional ideas of godhead and divinity became irrelevant.

A sense of proportion: how important are we humans in the cosmos anyway?

> Ask for what end the heav'nly bodies shine,
> Earth for whose use? Pride answers, ''Tis for mine:
> For me kind Nature wakes her genial pow'r,
> Suckles each herb, and spreads out ev'ry flow'r[8]

Explanations of creation have often tried to 'vindicate the ways of God to man'.[9] The defence of human dignity is often noticeable in a given explanation, not least in the assumption that the world exists for man. In his *Holy War*, John Bunyan (1628–88) describes a City of God which he calls Mansoul:

> In my travels, as I walked through many regions and countries, it was my chance to happen into that famous continent of Universe. A very large and spacious country it is: it lieth between the two poles, and just amidst the four points of the heavens. It is a place well watered, and richly adorned with hills and valleys, bravely situate, and for the most part, at least where I was, very fruitful, also well peopled, and a very sweet air.

In this 'Universe' is the human soul, which Bunyan depicts as though it were a town: 'Now, there is in this gallant country of Universe a fair and delicate town, a corporation called Mansoul.' It was built by its creator 'for his own delight':

He made it the mirror and glory of all that he made, even the top-piece, beyond anything else that he did in that country. Yea, so goodly a town was Mansoul when first built, that it is said by some, the gods, at the setting up thereof, came down to see it, and sang for joy.

And the builder of the town gave it 'dominion over all the country round about':

Yea, all were commanded to acknowledge Mansoul for their metropolitan, all were enjoined to do homage to it. Ay, the town itself had positive commission and power from her King to demand service of all, and also to subdue any that anyways denied to do it.[10]

We shall come back to this question of the 'human microcosm' of the universe's macrocosm in Part I, Chapter 1 (iv).

A sense of scale: how big, how many, for how long?

Will and Lyra exchanged a look. Then he cut a window, and it was the sweetest thing they had ever seen. The night air filled their lungs, fresh and clean and cool; their eyes took in a canopy of dazzling stars . . . Will enlarged the window as wide as he could . . . making it big enough for six, seven, eight to walk through abreast, out of the land of the dead.[11]

Certain questions hover behind the cosy small-scale creation stories of local tribes as much as behind the ambitious debates in the Western intellectual tradition. It occurred to those framing such explanations that the world has to 'be somewhere', to have a context which might set a scale greater than had been imagined, even open onto other universes.

Could there be a cosmos with our world only a part of it, one of a number of worlds or even universes, so that there is here and there 'a different world', 'a different universe', perhaps many?[12] Augustine of Hippo (354–430) wrote about these matters to meet the criticisms of educated Romans who had arrived indignantly in North Africa as refugees as the barbarian tribes invaded the Roman Empire. They tended to complain that the Christian God did not seem to be protecting what had been for nearly a century his officially 'Christian' Empire:

> For, as they demand why the world was created then and no sooner, we may ask why it was created just here where it is, and not elsewhere. For if they imagine infinite spaces of time before the world, during which God could not have been idle, in like manner they may conceive outside the world infinite realms of space, in which, if any one says that the Omnipotent cannot hold His hand from working, will it not follow that they must adopt Epicurus' dream of innumerable worlds?[13]

John Donne (1572–1631), in the seventeenth century, was still exploring the puzzle of the mismatch between the enormous scale of even the recently discovered extent of the earth and the small amount of information available in Genesis, where 'Moses sets up in a few syllables, in one line, *In principio*':

> That Earth, which in some thousands of years, men could not look over, nor discern what form it had: (for neither Lactantius, almost three hundred years after Christ, nor Saint Augustine, more then one hundred years after him, would beleeve the earth to be round) that earth, which no man, in his person, is ever said to have compassed, till our age; That earth which is too much for man yet, (for, as yet, a very great part of the earth is unpeopled) that earth, which, if we will cast it all but into a Mappe, costs many Months labour to grave it, . . . All that earth, and . . . that heaven, which spreads so farre.[14]

To Donne, 'the whole world', this 'All', was still staggeringly big, although he could be reasonably confident that his own generation had satisfactorily explored it at last. At the same time, he believed that the beginning of the world was in one sense quite simple. God made it and the record of that making could be read in Genesis. It simple 'began'. The hugeness of the world and the absolute power of the god who made it came together to form a satisfactory explanation.

Joseph Butler (1692–1752) came at this question from another vantage-point. He envisaged the possibility that there could be beings able to take an overall view of the universe in a way that we cannot:

Nor is there any absurdity in supposing, that there may be beings in the universe, whose capacities, and knowledge, and views, may be so extensive, as that the whole Christian dispensation may to them appear natural, i. e. analogous or conformable to God's dealings with other parts of his creation; as natural as the visible known course of things appears to us.[15]

Others have speculated, as C.S. Lewis (1898–1963) did, that there may be parallel universes, and they could contain beings unimaginably different from us:

The eldila are very different from any planetary creatures. Their physical organism, if organism it can be called, is quite unlike either the human or the Martian. They do not eat, breed, breathe, or suffer natural death, and to that extent resemble thinking minerals more than they resemble anything we should recognise as an animal . . . They themselves regard Space . . . as their true habitat and the planets are to them not closed worlds but merely moving points – perhaps even interruptions.[16]

An all-powerful Creator for an enormous universe? Little people, local places?

Monotheistic religions usually explain creation as the work of an immensely powerful or omnipotent Creator:

O tell of his might, O sing of his grace,
Whose robe is the light, whose canopy space;
His chariots of wrath the deep thunder clouds form,
And dark is his path on the wings of the storm.[17]

The 'big' explanation with its all-powerful Creator has been beyond the intellectual reach of a large proportion of the human race for much of human history. For many centuries most people lived a local life in a small community and had no way of understanding how big the world is.

A corregidor, leader of a local South American tribe, early in the period of European conquest of South America, was reported as saying to the Portuguese governor of Buenos Aires, 'This land, our children say, only God gave it to us . . . only our hands have worked it.'[18] In cultures and civilisations which had a limited sense of the physical scale of the world and not much contact by trade to enable them to expand their ideas, it was not easy to envisage the sheer scale of the task of creation as it appears from our larger modern vantage-point. For such peoples the 'world' as directly known, lived in, travelled over, has consisted of a relatively limited local area, with the existence of something more extensive a mere guess. Their interpretation of what they see has been conditioned by – and conditions – the 'explanation' they devise when they ask how the world began.

The modern explorer of these 'local' explanations faces a problem. It is now difficult to explore the beginning of the world without being influenced by the heritage of Western Christian and 'philosophical' thought, partly because so many of those who have written about the problem have formed their ideas in that context. John Milton (1608–74), in *The History of Britain*, was keen to show that Britain had been part of Biblical history, and not a remote and isolated place lying outside that story until its people were converted to Christianity. 'That the whole Earth was inhabited before the Flood, and to the utmost point of habitable ground, from those effectual words of *God* in the Creation, may be more then conjectured,'[19] he proposes. Then eight persons were saved from Flood, and 'the giant Noah' partitioned the earth to be peopled by his sons and their offspring.[20] That must include Britain, he insists.

The modern anthropologist who tries to go directly to the tribes and peoples who made up their own explanations will also find it difficult to do so without taking some of that baggage with him. And unless the peoples in question can be shown to have lived in complete isolation until the anthropologist arrives, there may be borrowed ideas, a cross-infection of beliefs, already among them. Without written history and secure knowledge of 'contacts', that isolation may be hard to establish.

Some mythologies have become interconnected with the dominant classical and European framework of explanation. The Greek myths have probably benefited most of all down the ages from the attentions of poets and writers who have made them beautiful and interesting in the retelling. In the plots of these stories with which generations of European children began their classical education, the gods are constantly interfering in the affairs of men. They come and go on earth as they please, suddenly appearing and giving instructions or warnings, in sequences of events where their wishes always prevail. Though the Roman poet

Virgil wrote at the beginning of the sixth book of the *Aeneid* that 'the descent to the underworld is easy but the way back is hard,' the land of shades where the dead dwell was visited by mortals, who even – in exceptional circumstances – returned from there. So travel between 'worlds' is reported in both directions.

The interfering habits of the deities drive the plots of the myths. Human or heroic characters show stupendous courage and persistence but their successes often depend on the goodwill of these interventionist deities. The equivocal character of their behaviour is nicely expressed in a poem on the god Pan by Elizabeth Barrett Browning. Pan decides to make himself a flute. He cuts a reed and thoughtlessly damages the plants by the river and upsets the balance of life there. But when he plays the flute, living things are transfixed:

> Sweet, sweet, sweet, O Pan!
> Piercing sweet by the river!
> Binding sweet, O great god Pan!
> The sun on the hill forgot to die,
> And the lilies revived, and the dragon fly
> Came back to dream on the river.

The difference between him and the 'true' gods is that he cares nothing for the harm he does, while gods who care as they should about creation, grieve for the bruised reeds and the death it cost to create such beauty:

> Yet half a beast is the great god Pan.
> To laugh as he sits by the river,
> Making a poet out of a man.
> The true gods sigh for the cost and pain –
> For the reed that grows nevermore again
> As a reed with the reeds in the river.[21]

Against the caprice of a 'don't care' god has to be set the intentness of the gods when they have destructive purposes they will not allow to be thwarted.

There is often transforming 'journeying' in myths. Aeneas was to become the legendary founder of the city of Rome, and the goddess Aphrodite had her plans for his adventures towards that end.[22] When Troy fell, Aeneas lost his wife. As he searched frantically for her, her shade rose before him, a vast ghost, who calmly reassured him. 'These events do not occur without the will of the gods. It is not the will of heaven that I should bear you company in your flight. There is a long period of wandering before you, over the sea and over the land, and you will meet with many dangers and difficulties.'

Odysseus (Ulysses) is another traveller of Greek legend whose lengthy journeyings after the Trojan War were supervised by supernatural powers for their own ends. Again the story moves between this world and the world where only spirits dwell, and gods, demi-gods and men meet and talk and act in a dance of events. He encounters the beautiful goddess-sorceress Circe, described in some stories as the daughter of the sun god. Circe has changed some of his sailors into pigs and is keeping them in a sty. Hermes (Mercury) appears and provides him with a herb to hold, which will prevent the same fate befalling him when he meets her. Circe is impressed, identifies him as Ulysses, whom fate has long decreed for this achievement, and falls in love with him. She smears the pigs with magic ointment; their bristles fall off and they are his sailors again.[23] Ulysses is now sent on an errand to Hades by Circe. There he is to ask some questions of the prophet Teiresias. He sets sail 'and when the sun had set they came to the utmost border of the ocean, . . . being compassed about with mist and cloud. Never doth the sun behold' those who dwell here. Ulysses makes a sacrifice and various shades come to drink the blood, including that of his dead mother. When he makes to embrace her she explains to him that that is impossible, that the dead 'have no more any flesh and bones . . . but their souls are even as dreams flying hither and thither'.[24]

It is impossible to tell in the reading of these stories where or when creation began and ended. It is treated as a process, a journey and an interaction of creatures and creators. In myths, journeys often pass through times and places and among different kinds of being. Charles Kingsley, telling the story of Perseus, describes how he walked out of Greece to the 'bleak north-west . . . till he came to the Unshapen Land, and the place which has no name'. He went on 'till he came to the edge of the everlasting night', and there by the freezing sea, he found the three Grey Sisters, who had one eye and one tooth among them. Perseus explains that he has been sent by the gods of Olympus to ask them how to find the Gorgon. 'There are new rulers in Olympus,' says one, 'and all new things are bad.' Another says, 'We hate your rulers, and the heroes, and all the children of men. We are kindreds of the Titans, and the Giants, and the Gorgon, and the ancient monsters of the deep.'[25]

The twelve Titans, the proto-gods of the Greeks, who were overthrown by the gods of the classical pantheon such as Zeus the king and his queen Hera, were bigger and fiercer and cruder in their emotions. They were the children of Uranus and Gaia, the ancient Heaven and Earth. They represented the primitive basic powers of the universe, its great abstractions, Ocean, Time, Sun, Moon, and so on. Uranus and Gaia produced a race of giants too, some the product of a terrible crime by Chronos, the youngest Titan, instigated by his mother Gaia. He castrated his father and the spilled blood and cast-aside testicles gave rise to various beings of ill-intent, including the Furies.

These old divinities did not vanish with the Olympians' 'conquest'. They remained in key positions in the cosmos and had children, sometimes by unorthodox methods, including cross-breeding with mortals; these crop up in the myths and take part in events. Greek heroes are not gods but they may be the children of the gods. The hero Hercules was sent to bring three apples from 'the Garden of the Hesperides, although no mortal knew where the Garden was'. Hercules is a son of Zeus but he is mortal. He enquired and was told to ask 'Nereus, the old sea-god . . ., for he knows everything, both in earth and heaven'. He tricks Nereus into giving him directions (the gods are frequently disobliging) and travels on towards the ends of the earth until he comes to the giant Atlas, the Titan who holds up the vault of heaven to prevent it falling down upon the earth. In return for Hercules taking this task for a while, Atlas offers to fetch the apples for him, because the nymphs, the Hesperides, who look after the Garden, are his nieces. He duly brings them back, but it is only by another trick that Hercules is able to persuade him to take back on his shoulders the weight of the world.[26]

These active beings playing their parts in universal events can be classified on a line from 'god' to 'creature', but they do not necessarily stay in one state; they climb in and out of one another's lives and change into one another, acquiring immortality or losing it in the process; they pass from natural to supernatural and back again. So creation in these stories is dynamic, and in many respects disorderly, a vigorous combat of powers and preferences.

But this gives us only the Greeks. What of all the other mythologies, the great complex of explanations in which Jung and others glimpsed a single shared human story of the beginnings of a race? We shall come back to that puzzle later.

PART I

The universe begins

1

Disagreements about first principles

1. WHEN DID THE WORLD BEGIN?

When did the world begin? There seems to be no agreement. A modern cosmologist might accept the Big Bang theory that the universe began with an explosion followed by a continuing expansion of a pre-existing 'dense hotness'. The cosmologist might calculate that the explosion happened about fourteen or fifteen billion years ago and the expansion and cooling-down is still going on, according to the laws of sub-atomic physics. He or she might place the forming of the earth much more recently, say four and a half billion years ago.

The cosmologist might point out that he or she was not talking about the 'creation' but about the 'beginning' of the universe, which is quite different. A religious believer might reply that it is definitely a matter of 'creation': divine power and a divine initiative was required.

A Biblical fundamentalist who accepted the literal truth of everything in the Bible, the Christian sacred writings collected as the Old and New Testaments, might count up the generations and ages given for the people mentioned in the Old Testament, add two thousand years since the death of Jesus, and come to a period of less than ten thousand years.

A less strict believer in the literal truth of the Bible might concede that perhaps the earth is older than the Bible dates indicate, but still resist the suggestion that any creature came to exist other than by the first act of the Creator as described in Genesis. He or she might say that the existence of fossils does not show that these were once creatures in an earlier process of evolution; he or she could prefer the view that the geological 'record' was all thrown together at the time when Noah's Flood covered the earth and then subsided. He or she might argue that fossils are not lost or extinct species at all but were specially created to be found in the geological formations of the earth.

A philosopher might ask what 'begin' means and how 'when' can be fixed before there was any time. He or she might take the cosmologist back to what must lie behind the 'explosion' hypothesis and ask from where and from when was there 'density' or 'hotness' or 'explosiveness' or anything to explode?

The relationship of time to space has frequently been discussed in connection with the difficulty of knowing how to use the words 'when' and 'where' in connection with the beginning of the universe. There were problems here about the idea of 'dimension' too. The notion that time might be a fourth 'dimension' (*temporis dimensio*) already appeared in an eleventh- or twelfth-century treatise attributed to Garlandus Compotista.[1] His assumption and that of his contemporaries was that just as space is composed of parts such as points and lines, so time is made up of instants and, in its 'linear' form, it proceeds from past to present to future. Points become lines if they are drawn out across a spatial dimension, and instants become hours in the same manner if they are extended through time.

Both Samuel Clarke (1675–1729) and Leibniz (1646–1714) wrestled with the question whether time and space ultimately form a single whole.[2] Leibniz says that in that case God could have no 'reason' to chose a time and place to create the world. There would be no 'reason' to 'locate' creation any particular 'where' or 'when' in this homogeneous whole.[3] It would follow that asking when the universe began is nonsense. If God created it, he did so before there was any time to create 'at'. But the world does exist. So God must have created it in eternity, he suggests, and therefore the world is eternal. Samuel Clarke's response is that all that was needed was that the Creator should will the making of the world. That was 'reason' enough. He just chose or fixed or made a 'place' and 'time', and created the world 'then' and 'there', so asking when the universe began is perfectly sensible.[4]

Emboldened by this argument, Clarke suggested that the world we live in could be one of a series of experiments. The Creator could have made other worlds before and after. These could be 'in time' and in some sort of sequence, perhaps getting better and better towards perfection as God 'practised'? But 'before' and 'after' might have no meaning if this experimentation itself was done outside time, for then there need be no lapse of time between the existences of these universes.[5] The Creator could be running several 'simultaneous' experiments, except that if there is no time there is no simultaneity.

In science fiction these philosophical knots can provide the basis for a good story. H.G. Wells (1866–1946) published 'The time machine' in 1895. Its hero is the Time Traveller. He too claims that time is merely a fourth 'dimension' and it is possible to travel through it just as one can travel through space. In the story he is challenged to prove it. He comes back to tell the story of what he found when he went forward towards the end of the world. Humanity seemed to have changed, grown more 'evolved' in the direction of over-refinement. One of the creatures he met seemed fragile:

> He struck me as being a very beautiful and graceful creature, but indescribably frail. His flushed face reminded me of the more beautiful kind of consumptive – that hectic beauty of which we used to hear so much.[6]

Eventually the Time Traveller vanishes on one of his journeys and he does not return. In the Epilogue to the tale, Wells speculates that this 'time' he has gone backwards in time :

> Will he ever return? It may be that he swept back into the past, and fell among the blood-drinking, hairy savages of the Age of Unpolished Stone; into the abysses of the Cretaceous Sea; or among the grotesque saurians, the huge reptilian brutes of the Jurassic times. He may even now – if I may use the phrase – be wandering on some plesiosaurus-haunted Oolitic coral reef, or beside the lonely saline lakes of the Triassic Age.

A member of a primitive tribe might not understand the question 'when' for quite different reasons from a philosopher or a modern novelist or a believer relying on a sacred book or a cosmology, having no clock and no calendar and no way of measuring the passage of time except in terms of the broad rotation of the seasons.

So it is not easy to bring these approaches into a single 'place' for comparison. It grows more difficult still when we look at the many different understandings on which these various approaches have been attempted.

The difficulties of designing a 'scientific' approach to dating

Modern science and modern philosophy were for the most part, despite philosophical borrowings from Egypt and from Asia, creations of the intellectual tradition of Western Europe. This tradition began with the Greeks and Romans, whose literature, including philosophy and science, was the foundation of education for a millennium and a half after the Roman Empire ended in the fifth and sixth centuries. The same intellectual tradition became part of the development of Judaism, Christianity and Islam, one after the other.

Francis Bacon attacked the whole apparatus of inquiry and study which had grown up in the West during the last thousand years; he thought it had taken a wrong turning. It relied on a set of authoritative writings, mainly from the ancient world, with a succession of commentaries, and it mainly consisted in commenting on them again and trying to reconcile differences of scholarly opinion. He said there should be:

> no more of antiquities, citations and differing opinions of authorities, or of squabbles and controversies, and, in short, everything philological. No author should be cited save in matters of doubt; and no controversies be introduced save in matters of great moment.[7]

Writings of his own times, including descriptive and narrative accounts and 'natural histories of descriptions and pictures of species, and the ingenuity lavished on their differences',[8] which had been prompted by the recent discoveries of the New World, were also of no little scientific value in their current forms, said Bacon. What was needed, he suggested, was something much more 'wide' in 'range' and 'made to the measure of the universe'.

'The intellect should be opened up to take in the image of the world as we really find it.' 'Everyone philosophises out of the cells of his own fantasy,' was Bacon's criticism. In his *Instauratio Magna* (*Great Renewal*), he criticises those who attempt to resolve only the familiar questions and seek 'fruitful' (*fructifera*) rather than 'illuminating' (*lucifera*) results. Bacon's theory was that the familiar concepts of modern science's predecessor 'natural philosophy' are 'worthless' when they are discussed as they had been among classical philosophers. Aristotle (384–322 BC) discussed concepts such as generation, corruption, increase, decrease, alteration and local motion. Bacon would prefer to see thinkers asking about the machinery and the processes, about 'attraction, repulsion, thinning, thickening, dilatation, astriction, dispersal, maturation and the like'. These should be treated as phenomena of observed behaviours in the physical world rather than as philosophical concepts.[9]

This revolutionary talk did not go as far as to agree with our 'modern cosmologist' if he or she says the beginning of the world had nothing to do with a Creator. Bacon took it for granted that it did. He wrote about 'God's order which created light alone on the first day, giving the whole day to that and not to producing any of the material works which he turned to on the days following', as though the story in the book of Genesis could be included alongside plain scientific evidence.[10] He wanted close observation and the testing of evidence but resting on a set of assumptions about the truth of the story of the Creation in Genesis:

> We plainly set the seal of our own image on the creatures and works of God rather than carefully examining and recognizing the seal that the Creator has set upon them.[11]

Even if Bacon's own *Phenomena of the Universe* swept away 'no end of philosophical systems' (*valde numerosa*) among ancient philosophers and their more modern counterparts, he insisted that 'humility towards the Creator' should lead us to learn from his creation rather than to pursue our own favourite ideas.

Accordingly, he divides the inquiry about the beginning of the world into five parts, each involving a section of the created universe, working from the 'top' down. The first stage concerns 'ether' and heavenly bodies or stars and planets; the second, passing meteors and 'the tracts from the Moon down to the Earth's surface'; the third, the Earth and sea; the fourth, the four elements; fifth comes natural history, the study of species of creatures.[12] This cosmic division borrows more from the earlier systems he rejects than he might have liked to admit but he clearly saw it as an advance on earlier efforts.

Francis Bacon got credit in later centuries for instigating the fundamental change of mindset which led eventually to the birth of modern science,[13] but he was not the only thinker exploring in this direction. The seventeenth century became an age of mixed endeavour at the boundary between science and philosophical speculation. The French philosopher Descartes also put forward views in areas of scientific inquiry: for example, whether there was a universal 'ether' and, if so, what its characteristics were. Isaac Newton, author of significant modern scientific advances and discoveries, wrote over many decades on topics in the remoter fringes of theological, astrological and alchemical speculation. So even these prominent newcomers with their 'fresh approaches' trailed with them strands of residual assumptions from long-past discussions about how the universe began.

Voltaire (1694–1778) wrote a letter in which he compares the two approaches, the Cartesian and the Newtonian:

> A Frenchman who arrives in London, will find philosophy, like everything else, very much changed there. He had left the world a plenum, and he now finds it a vacuum. At Paris the universe is seen composed of vortices of subtile matter; but nothing like it is seen in London. In France, it is the pressure of the moon that causes the tides; but in England it is the sea that gravitates towards the moon; so that when you think that the moon should make it flood with us, those gentlemen fancy it should be ebb, which very unluckily cannot be proved. For to be able to do this, it is necessary the moon and the tides should have been inquired into at the very instant of the creation.

Voltaire had realised that the proto-scientific explanations which were being tried out tended to take the inquirer back again and again to the way the world began.

> According to your Cartesians, everything is performed by an impulsion, of which we have very little notion; and according to Sir Isaac Newton, it is by an attraction, the cause of which is as much unknown to us. At Paris you imagine that the earth is shaped like a melon, or of an oblique figure; at London it has an oblate one. A Cartesian declares that light exists in the air; but a Newtonian asserts that it comes from the sun in six minutes and a half. The several operations of your chemistry are performed by acids, alkalies and subtile matter; but attraction prevails even in chemistry among the English.

Voltaire criticises Newton for abandoning scientific method when it comes to dating the universe and thinking it acceptable to mingle historiography with the observations. 'It appeared in general to Sir Isaac that the world was five hundred years younger than chronologers declare it to be.'

Voltaire is equally biting about the achievements of the European 'academies' of scientists which had been forming alongside the newly-founded Royal Society in England (1660 but meeting earlier):

> all the Transactions of the several academies in Europe put together do not form so much as the beginning of a system. In fathoming this abyss no bottom has been found.[14]

Early experimental science found itself embattled, then, and far from achieving a clear set of agreed principles on which scientists could establish an answer to the question when the world began.

Fixing the Bible's chronology down the ages

Those who tried to date the beginning of the world from the account in the Bible had no better luck. Like many other medieval historiographers, the Anglo-Saxon Aethelweard (d. c.998) wrote a chronicle which opens with 'the beginning of the world'. 'As we write history we can progress with enjoyment from digression to digression' (*Quamvis per anfractus ludere quimus historiographizantes*), he admits, but he thinks there is no harm in giving a few dates. He states the periods of time: from Adam to Noah (2,242 years), from the Flood to Abraham (942 years), from Abraham to Moses to Exodus (505 years), from Moses to Solomon and building of Temple (478 years), then till the birth of Christ (1,022 years).[15] This gives a total from the beginning of world until Christ of 5,495 years. Short times to the modern eye could perhaps look long times to the Anglo-Saxons, but Aethelweard's calculations emphasise the difficulty for early chroniclers of getting any sense of the real timescales involved in the passage of centuries since the beginning of the world.

It is instructive to set Newton's attempts at calculation beside these, for he tried to adjust the Bible's timing by cross-reference to classical historians as well as mythology, in an attempt to unite all known explanations in a single system. *The Chronology of Ancient Kingdoms Amended* (London, 1728) was a late revision, which he made close to the end of his life, of a very substantial body of work on which he had been engaged for decades. It seemed to Newton that by the 'Light of Nature' much ought to be clear to the inquiring mind, if it had not been confused in its thinking by the

'Worship of false Gods'.[16] He read discursively in search of *origines* among the classical authors and patristic writers mentioned in this study, who had themselves tackled the problem of the creation of the world but without a clear sense of what was and what was not (from the point of view of later scholarship) going to turn out to be secure ground on which to build.

Newton took astrology and numerology and prophecy seriously. He considered historical cause and effect to include divine wrath as well as human agency. He tried as hard to trace these sequences as he did to calculate cause and effect in physics, as though the types of causation involved were the same in all studies and all sciences. The title of one of his chapters in the *Theologiae Gentilis Origine Philosophicae* sums up nicely the all-embracing way he approached the task he had set himself, and which continued to engage him for decades:

> That Gentile Theology was Philosophical and referred primarily to the Astronomical and Physical Science of the world system: and that the twelve Gods of the ancient Peoples were the seven Planets with the four elements and the quintessence of the Earth.[17]

With the same obsessive care he tried to demonstrate that the gods of ancient paganism were 'deified' versions of the human forebears named in the Bible, such as Noah. Noah had three sons; Saturn has three sons. Ham, Noah's son, became Jupiter or Zeus. His four Biblical sons are four identifiable gods of the Greeks or the Egyptians. All systems can be reduced to one. The names of real human ancestors were also used to name the stars. Newton adopted the theory that the Greeks 'despoiled the Egyptians' (Exodus 12:35–6) in forming their own theology and philosophy.[18]

With events in the Old Testament, Newton mingled episodes in Greek mythology; for example, in the year 1039 BC, Ceres, whom he depicts as 'a woman of Sicily', came to Attica in search of her daughter 'who was stolen' and taught the Greeks 'to sow corn', for which she was 'deified after death'. His 'short' preliminary chronicle begins with the flight of the Canaanites into Egypt, and the first date he gives is 1125 BC. He did calculations which suggested that the chronologies arrived at by estimates of generation-lengths 'have made the Antiquities of Greece three or four hundred years older than the truth'. 'As for the chronology of the Latines, that is still more uncertain.' The 'Gods or ancient deified Kings and

Princes . . . have been made much ancienter than the truth,' including those of the Chaldeans and Assyrians. He attempted to create a chronological table which will 'make Chronology suit with the Course of Nature, with Astronomy, with Sacred History, with *Herodotus* the Father of History, and with it self'.[19]

Philosophy and the world that always was

> As I understand it, all the past still exists and it's merely a matter of choosing your point of view.[20]

One of the great puzzles in discussions about creation has always been the one just examined: how to 'place' a creation in which things have measurable dimensions in a 'now' as experienced by observers, and against a state of things in which there may have been no 'here' or 'now' because they had not been invented until the world began.

Some early philosophers said that that was such nonsense that the answer to the question of when the world began was that it did not begin. It always was. Aristotle put this view forward in his *Physics*, arguing from the unsatisfactoriness of the fact that otherwise it seems that we have to postulate an infinite regress. He argued that the matter which makes up the world as we know was always 'there' and the world must therefore always have existed.

The hugely influential Augustine of Hippo grappled with the same problem, partly at the prompting of those philosophical refugees arriving in North Africa who wanted to know why the Christian God seemed unable to protect an officially Christian Empire. Genesis describes an act of creation. Why did the Creator choose to create the heavens and earth when for eternity he had been complete and supremely happy and had no need to make any change? Augustine is well aware that some of those who ask this are determined to show that the world is eternal. They are mad, he says. It could not just always have been there. The way the world looks tells a different story. It is so beautiful that it bespeaks an actual Creator of supreme beauty and greatness who stamped his chosen characteristics upon it.[21]

In Augustine's view it is better not to try to comprehend infinite stretches of time before the world began or an infinite beyond space as we know it. Some agree that the world had a Creator but they have difficulties about the time of its creation,

and also about the 'place' where creation was put. Augustine
gave up the attempt to answer. But he pointed out that the fact
we cannot grasp something so huge does not mean that it is
not real, nor that it is not capable of rational explanation if our
minds could stretch to it.[22]

Augustine insisted that time and space began when the world
was made. To ask why God did not make the world sooner is
nonsense because before there was time there was no 'sooner'.
There is no change in God, and the world he has made is eternally
'now' to him.

> For in the [six days of Genesis] days the morning and evening
> are counted, until, on the sixth day, all things which God then
> made were finished, and on the seventh the rest of God was
> mysteriously and sublimely signalized. What kind of days these
> were it is extremely difficult, or perhaps impossible for us to
> conceive, and how much more to say![23]

Augustine had not read Plato (he confessed that his Greek was
not good enough), but he understood contemporary 'Platonism'
very well and found himself in sympathy with it. It included the
belief that the Creator's motivation for making the world was
sheer generosity. His goodness overflowed.

This leaves us little further forward in pursuit of a date for the
beginning of the world, because all these approaches turn out
to be asking different questions, or the same question in ways so
different that they cannot be satisfied by the same answer.

II. IS THE UNIVERSE 'REAL'?

Tribes and civilisations which invented myths about a world
resting on the back of an enormous tortoise, or hatching from
a giant egg, did not expect to have to show the actual tortoise
supporting the world or the shell-fragments of the cosmic egg.
They were not making that sort of 'truth-claim'. So in what sense
can we say with confidence that the universe is 'real' or that any
explanation of how it came to 'exist' is 'true'? These questions
will hover over everything which follows, as we move in and out of
the shadowlands of attempts to describe a process of creation no
subsequent commentator was present to see.

For practical purposes, the great traditional distinction between 'physics' and 'metaphysics' and that between 'material' and 'spiritual' have often been treated as amounting to the same distinction. If the 'real' is defined by whether it can be measured with physical instruments, the metaphysical and the spiritual must be equally 'unreal'. Yet 'creation' theories and modern cosmology alike face the difficulty that this does not seem to be a hard line when it comes to discussing the beginning of the world. Modern astrophysics and the search for fundamental particles employ experiment and calculation and also speculation, because they are working at the boundary where physics meets metaphysics.

Perhaps the problem lies in the limited capacity of the human mind to grasp reality, however defined? 'Trace science then, with modesty thy guide,'[24] suggests the satirist Alexander Pope. As he describes it, to angels human efforts to understand seem no more impressive than would those of a chimpanzee:

> Superior beings, when of late they saw
> A mortal Man unfold all Nature's law,
> Admir'd such wisdom in an earthly shape,
> And showed a Newton as we shew an Ape.[25]

From nothingness to something: what is everything made of?

> She stood, . . . as the Stone sank slowly through her whole presented nature to its place in the order of the universe and that mysterious visibility of the First Matter of creation returned to the invisibility from which it had been summoned.[26]

In Charles Williams' mid-twentieth-century novel the well-worn question of where the first matter came from is given a twist in a fresh image. He links that starting-point with the equally familiar question of how that matter became so many different things. If 'stuff' has to be postulated as the substance from which specific created things were formed, was it like a big block of modelling material which could be shaped, or of a different order of reality from the 'created things' it 'became'? Was it perhaps the Higgs boson and was the first stuff not 'matter' but 'mass'?

The starting point must be whether there was anything before there was something. Genesis (1:2) says that at the beginning everything was 'without form and void?' What was the nature of this nothingness, if it was nothingness? Most creation accounts, whether they are myths or attempts at philosophical or even scientific explanations, envisage some sort of 'stuff', a primordial matter, whether solid, liquid or gas. The Big Bang explosion seems to rely on there being 'something' to explode. Even if it was recognisably 'stuff', could a modern physicist have measured primordial matter or described it or done experiments with it, as was attempted in the CERN Collider experiments of 2011–12 which set out to find a Higgs boson? Or if samples could be retrieved, would it turn out to be beyond 'analysis' by scientific methods?

The conventional distinction of 'stuffs' for many centuries lay between the 'material' and the 'spiritual' or 'intellectual abstraction' which cannot be weighed and measured and tested by the senses. But this remained an indistinct line in several important and influential discussions. For example, when Aristotle listed four kinds of cause, final (ultimate), formal (shaping), efficient (making things happen) and material (the 'stuff' out of which things were made), he did not see the fourth as so different in kind as to take it into category of its own as an entirely different *kind* of cause. It seemed to him logically satisfactory to list this

2. Head of Ptah, the Egyptian creator god of Memphis

physical 'stuff' alongside his more metaphysical causes. Descartes and Newton discussed 'ether' in terms which leave it uncertain whether it was to be regarded as metaphysical or physical.

Creation by 'saying' is implied in the opening passages of St John's Gospel which described the Word of God bringing the world to being in that way. That would count as a meta-physical ('beyond physics') process. But would the activities of the deities and powers described in the innumerable creation stories of polytheist explanations count as physics or as metaphysics? These entities mutate from one state to another, and beget other divinities and also creatures, without resorting to the usual machineries of procreation, yet they often move in and out of physical being as they do so.

Ancient Egypt had different theories of creation, emerging in its different centres of population. They exemplify very well this difficulty in separating physics and metaphysics in the thinking of various systems. The people of Heliopolis favoured the idea that the god Atum or Ra brought himself to 'being' out of the primordial waters. From him emerged (but how?) eight divinities with supervisory tasks and powers: Isis the mother; Osiris, the god of fertility, and so on. The sun god Ra was important everywhere in Egyptian mythology. The Egyptians of Hermopolis also thought the first 'stuff' took the form of primeval waters. They identified eight characteristics of these waters, which they regarded as eight divinities. So 'stuff' which seems definitely physical is somehow differentiated into dedicated forms and purposes as well as into 'divinities'.

The early Greek author Hesiod (c.750–c.650 BC) suggested that instead of primitive 'stuff' there might have been a great emptiness, a void or chasm. But this too seems to have been able to make a transition to material or substantial being by way of begetting and birth, without Hesiod suggesting that that is inexplicable. 'First there was Chasm, then broad-breasted Earth.' 'From Chasm, Erebos and black Night came to be; then Aether and Day came forth from Night, who conceived and bore them after mingling in love with Erebos.' 'Earth first of all bore starry Sky, equal to herself, to cover her on every side,' then, 'having bedded with Sky, she bore . . . Ocean' and various gods and goddesses.[27] In the stories, the children of these very early beings have a tendency to be fearsome.

These accounts raised and continue to raise all sorts of questions. *Are* these emergent entities so manifestly involved in a creative process 'beings' and if so what sort of beings and what are their powers? Are they spirit and do they engage with matter, entering into it and even adopting material 'being' themselves, if it is so different in kind to the philosopher's and scientist's eye which distinguishes physics from metaphysics?

Sorts of something: the 'elements' and the atoms

The idea that primordial matter resolved itself into four 'elements' seems to have been widespread globally, over many centuries, sometimes with 'ether' as a fifth or 'quintessence'. The traditional four are earth, water, air and fire, which can also be understood as solid, liquid, gas and some sort of 'energy'.

What, then, is meant by calling them 'elements'? Are they stages of the primordial stuff or, like modern chemical elements, irreducible *kinds* of stuff? They seem to have been conceived more as 'states' of matter than as 'elements' in the modern sense of chemical elements. There was no real clarity about all this among alchemists, who resisted the idea that the different kinds of matter were fixed in their kinds and tried to find ways of turning base metals into gold. Alchemy still seemed academically respectable and in keeping with the laws of nature in the lifetime of Newton and beyond.

How do the 'elements' sit with the theories put forward by Democritus (*c.*460–*c.*370 BC) that everything is made of atoms? Democritus envisaged tiny but highly individual particles in a soup of nothingness. Each had its little grappling-hooks, which allowed it to bond with others of the same kind to form materials of different sorts. This notion raised further questions about the 'soup'. If the activity of the atoms involved bonding, it must mean they could move, and to move they had to have a vehicle or space or void to move in. Parmenides (early fifth century BC) said the problem with that was that a void is nothing and by definition a nothing cannot exist.

Atoms have long been accepted in the explanations of modern science, now joined by sub-atomic particles, whose behaviours seem sometimes to depart from the laws of Newtonian physics. Finding a consistent explanation of the building blocks of the material universe did not turn out to be on its way to completion once there was a modern 'table of elements' based on the weights of the atoms of different elements. The Higgs boson began as a postulate whose hypothetical existence might explain the origin of 'mass' in the particles which are – for now – considered to be the fundamental constituents of the universe. But there are other 'bosons' and also 'fermions' whose existence depends on their conformity with two distinct sets of modern calculations or schools of thought. These may not be the end of the story.

Solid matter, refinement, ether and abstraction

In some explanations of creation the traditional elements have been described as forming the structure of the cosmos simply by being the kind of thing they are. The earth is 'earth', solid matter. It is surrounded by water, liquid matter, then by air, gaseous matter, with an encircling empyrean of fire, and all four elements are then in position to form the grand overall shape of the universe. Beyond and above and further out was postulated an 'ether' which is not an exactly an element, but a 'quintessence' in which the stars and planets hang.

Philosophers and even early scientists of the seventeenth century confessed to great difficulty in being clear in their own minds about the nature of an ethereal 'substance', and whether it was substance at all. For is not a non-substance a void? Augustine admitted he had long thought of the spiritual as made of very fine particles of material. The same difficulty arose with the ethereal. Descartes still held to the view that everything in the universe must be some sort of material stuff, in very fine 'corpuscles' which moved about to fill any threatened vacuum. There could, he suggested, be no absolute emptiness or absence of any substance at all. This adjusted Democritus' atoms-moving-in-nothingness and allowed the atoms to fill all space.

The newly 'experimental' scientists of Descartes' time were busy testing the possibility of creating a vacuum. In 1643 Evangelista Torricelli (1608–47) invented a mercury barometer, which contained a space which was a vacuum. He framed the idea that though the earth lies under its surrounding cushion of air, that air grows less and less dense at higher altitudes, on its way to becoming a vacuum ultimately.

Robert Boyle (1627–91) and Robert Hooke (1635–1703) worked together on some experiments with air to see what happens when a vacuum is actually created by pumping out air from an enclosed space until it grows more and more rarefied and is ultimately not there at all. And what happened, they wondered, if air is made more and more rarefied by pumping it out of a sealed chamber containing living things until it approaches a vacuum. Boyle published his discussion of the results in *New Experiments Physico-Mechanicall, Touching the Spring of the Air, and its Effects* (1660). It was observed that pressure changed when the volume of air was altered, and also that living creatures collapsed and died when denied a normal volume of air, though at different rates depending on their species.

This realisation that it was possible to confirm some of the ideas of earlier ages about the layering of the universe and the place of the elements in its construction was also encouraging interest in the forces which held everything together - what kept the planets and stars in their positions and what kept things on earth and prevented them flying off into space. Galileo (1564–1642) had made some tests by dropping different things from a height to test the possibility that gravity is a force which acts consistently on all objects, whatever their weight. Isaac Newton tried out the idea that gravity does not operate only on the earth but is a force effective throughout the universe, keeping the stars and planets in their places and paths of movement.

Newton's theory started a train of thought which led eventually to Einstein's general theory of relativity. This abandons the concept that gravity is a force and seeks an explanation in terms of movement relative to the curvature of time and space. That takes us back into terrain where concepts may outstrip what can be tested experimentally and where mathematical and philosophical reasoning and the definition of terms become necessary again.

The Creator himself as primordial substance

We have not finished with the problems about primordial 'stuff'. If there was always 'stuff', and the 'stuff' is therefore 'uncreated', was the Creator himself this first 'matter' or was he separate from it? If he was something different from the 'matter', was he always there, alongside it? Was anything else 'always there'? And what do 'there' and 'always' mean in a primordial context anyway?

Plato (424/3–348/7 BC) explored these questions in the *Timaeus*. This was one of the small proportion of his writings well-known in the Latin-speaking West before the fifteenth-century revival of the study of the Greek language. It proved to be a stimulating influence because his arguments conflicted with the Christian belief that the only thing that was 'always there' was the Creator himself, and he made the matter and anything else needed as a basic ingredient, from 'nothing'.

Plato reasoned that the primordial matter was not itself differentiated into the elements but was capable of 'receiving', perhaps being stamped with, the characteristics of such elements:

> In the same way space or matter is neither earth nor fire nor air nor water, but an invisible and formless being which receives all things, and in an incomprehensible manner partakes of the intelligible.[28]

It was also apparent to reason, thought Plato, that a particular structure would have had to be adopted, so that 'as the world was composed of solids, between the elements of fire and earth God placed two other elements of air and water, and arranged them in a continuous proportion'.[29]

In some creation stories the originator or Creator was himself the first cosmic material. He was broken into pieces and from those fragments the component elements of the world as we know it sprang – plants and animals as well as the rocky fabric, all held together in a system by their origin in a single being.

Is the creation then more than a piece of modelling clay in which the Creator himself takes shape, or which bears the recognisable imprint of the Creator's thumb? Does the Creator make himself apparent by a sort of reflection in the created world, or is he actually 'in' creation, in its very fabric? Could the Creator be immanent, actually present in the created world and if so how? In the world's creation theories there are many versions of this idea that a Creator might linger in his creation or somehow form part of the world he made, perhaps even be himself the very primordial matter.

The Creator as the 'soul of the world'

Some have suggested that it is more accurate to call the Creator the world's 'soul'. Some of the philosophically-minded ancient Greeks entertained the idea of the world as itself a living being, with a body made of matter and a 'soul of the world' 'indwelling' it and giving it life to the matter. But this talk of an *anima mundi* (as Latin writers called the 'world soul') displeased those thinkers – generally Platonists – who considered that it would degrade a supreme spiritual being to involve himself so closely in matter. So there emerged the idea of a hierarchical trinity, in which the *anima mundi* came lowest, while above was the Word (*Logos*) or rational principle, which could speak to the World Soul and direct the way it shaped matter. Above that was a Supremeness so high as to be above being itself.

It was this hierarchical trinity which Christianity reshaped when it formed the doctrine of the Trinity. In the Christian version, one god is three persons: Father, Son (the Word) and Holy Spirit. They are coequal and coeternal and, although the Son is begotten of the Father and the Holy Spirit proceeds from Father (and the Son, said the Christian West), there is held to be no sequence or subordination. In the Christian Trinity the Holy Spirit is not the soul of the world, but true God. And the reluctance of the Creator to involve himself directly with the created world vanishes in the doctrine of the Incarnation, in which the Son of God became human in order to rescue mankind from the fatal error of its ways.

It is possible to see the struggle to articulate this crucial difference being worked through in the writings of Origen, at a date when much in Christian doctrine had not yet been clearly articulated. Origen (184/5–253/4) wrote *Against Celsus* as a counterblast to the opinions of the second-century pagan philosopher Celsus. Celsus had been attacking Christianity and defending the beliefs of pagans and pagan philosophers. Origen took a Platonist position on the essential superiority of spirit and mind to matter. He seems to have argued that God first made souls, which were rational beings, spirits with reasoning powers. These came to be thought of in later Christianity as angels. Their creation is not mentioned in Genesis, so it was sometimes suggested that they are obliquely referred to in the statement that God separated light from darkness.

Easier to fit into the Genesis story was Origen's hypothesis that some of these spiritual beings became discontented or restless or simply bored with gazing adoringly at their Creator, and turned away. These became the devils of Christian theology and the serpent who tempted Eve was identified as their leader. The mention of the fall of Lucifer (Isaiah 14:12) provided some Biblical warrant for this idea.

Origen held, however, a different version from what became the orthodox Christian view of the way this had resulted in the creation of human beings. One spirit, he suggested, remained in perfect love with God. He became the Logos. In support of this view could be cited Proverbs 8:22–31 (NIV):

> The Lord brought me forth as the first of his works, before his deeds of old; I was formed long ages ago, at the very beginning, when the world came to be. When there were no watery depths, I was given birth, when there were no springs overflowing with water; before the mountains were settled in place, before the hills, I was given birth, before he made the world or its fields or any of the dust of the earth. I was there when he set the heavens in place, when he marked out the horizon on the face of the deep, when he established the clouds above and fixed securely the fountains of the deep, when he gave the sea its boundary so the waters would not overstep his command, and when he marked out the foundations of the earth. Then I was constantly at his side. I was filled with delight day after day, rejoicing always in his presence, rejoicing in his whole world and delighting in mankind.

Origen suggests that those spirits whose love of the Creator had cooled to an even greater degree than that of the 'fallen angels' dropped to the level where they became trapped in matter. These were to be humans, souls in bodies. Souls which had fallen furthest became the lowliest of humans, and the least culpable became the greatest humans. So it is not unfair that there should be social differences. Human beings have essentially chosen their earthly status by their own behaviour.

Origen suggests that this situation may be retrievable if individual human beings love God enough, for then their souls may be reconciled with him and they may be restored to the relationship of happy love for which the Creator intended them.

The immovable principle in Origen's mind is that the Creator is so high above all we know, so remote from the material part of his creator, that to suggest he had in any direct sense a 'hand' in it is to demean him. He is one and spirit and changeless and eternal and infinite. In him goodness and truth and beauty are one.

Yet this Logos, Christians taught, became incarnate as Jesus and was born of the Virgin Mary. He became a man. And thus Christianity established a fundamentally different position on the acceptability of a Creator getting his hands dirty by involving himself with material things and creatures with bodies.

So what of reality?

We are left then, with the task of defining 'reality' in the face of a range of notions of what is real which have proved difficult to resolve over many centuries and in the context of a variety of approaches to explaining origins.

III· WHAT IS THE LAYOUT OF THE COSMOS?

A map-maker is wise to assume that there is a stable layout of the world to be depicted. A map may be used to find one's way about the part of the world it depicts only if the geography stays the same. It has been suggested that even maps in primitive rock art seem to include attempts to depict a relationship of heaven to earth with a world of the dead below.[30] If that is so, they could represent an early attempt to still the spinning chaos of the guessed-at first beginnings we have been considering, for creation myths often describe chaotic change and enormous shifts of shape and identity. 'Mapping' sits oddly with an idea of a created world in which there can be decay and change and regrowth and one thing or place may become another.

What is a map and what is it for? The local peoples who had distinct 'tribal' ideas about the way they came to find themselves where they were – for example, in Africa – did not necessarily keep to their localities. They might migrate again. Yet, as a rule, migrating early tribes did not make maps, either of their localities or of their journeys. Beyond telling a story about it they neither recorded how they had got to where they were now, nor sought to provide guides for those who might wish to take a similar journey.

Each created thing in its proper place: the cosmic frame changes

In H.G. Wells' story 'The star', the motion of the planet Neptune becomes erratic and it gradually becomes apparent that the disturbance is being caused by the arrival in the solar system of a new giant globe.[31] In accounts of creation which take in the whole cosmos the tendency has been to assume that in its main features the cosmos, once made, stayed as it was. No new heavenly bodies would suddenly appear in the sky overhead.

3. God as geometer, from the frontispiece of a Bible Moralisée

4. Virgo, Libra and Scorpio, from *The Wonders of the Creation and the Curiosities of Existence* by Zakariya 'ibn Muhammed al-Qazwini

Western thought had long tended to accept the Ptolemaic plan of the universe, in which the earth hung at the centre of a system of concentric spheres, though there was some disagreement about the details of this arrangement. It was the work of a Greek-speaking Egyptian and Roman citizen, Claudius Ptolemaeus (AD 90–168). At first, as admirers of Greek philosophy, the Western and Arabic thinkers who were its heirs tended to accept this geocentric view.

Yet the Qur'an, the sacred book of Islam, speaks of the 'Lord of the Worlds'. This led some Islamic scholars to suggest that the universe we see may be only one of thousands, some perhaps – who knew? – even bigger and more impressive. Among the leaders of this line of questioning were the mid-thirteenth-century astronomers of the Maragha observatory in Iran and others in Damascus and Samarkand. In Damascus, Ibn al-Shatir (1304–75) also challenged the Ptolemaic picture. These medieval inquirers were busy measuring, and they worked out the mathematics of the movement of heavenly bodies as observed, as Andalusian Islamic astronomers had attempted before them.[32]

The habit of measuring and observing persisted. Copernicus (1473–1543) published a different and more radical challenge to the Ptolemaic convention in 1543, just before he died. In the *De Revolutionibus Orbium Coelestium* he proposed the revolutionary idea that the cosmos did not rotate round the earth at all, or have it at its centre. It seemed to him more likely that it was the sun which stood at the centre. His death saved him from the backlash of persecution which was to be experienced by Galileo (1564–1642), who, as a mathematician and an astronomer using an early telescope – and thus an observer of the cosmos in motion – came to the same conclusion.

Galileo knew how controversial it would be to suggest that the earth is not at the centre of the universe. In 1616 he wrote to the Grand Duchess Christina of Lorraine to suggest that this new structure for the cosmos – with the sun at the centre – need not be taken to conflict with the Bible if the Bible was interpreted figuratively, though it certainly involved discarding Ptolemy's universe and the views of Aristotle. Condemned by the Inquisition and instructed to think differently, Galileo continued his work on the underlying mathematics.

The new heliocentric cosmos eventually took hold as the accepted view, and early modern thinkers had to decide what else they would have to discard in the old cosmic hierarchical arrangements as a result. The English philosopher John Locke

(1632–1704) suggested that perhaps the hierarchy which involves government or dominion could be regarded as a particular dispensation or disposition of the Creator and not something built into the very fabric of the created universe. That might conveniently allow for the assumptions of a hierarchical social order to continue while the physics was adjusted.

Cosmic maps, cosmos diagrams

For students of the created cosmos in the late antique and medieval worlds, the cosmic 'map' remained mainly that of Ptolemy, and an actual set of maps or diagrams was drawn to depict it.

The first need to be met was for a 'cosmic orientation', to give a sense of where the observer stands, not just on the earth but on an earth in a universe. Such a diagram-map 'placed' the familiar earth in a framework of moon and stars and planets. This exercise was attempted by a series of influential authors, mainly Western, some of them classical 'secular' philosophers and some Christian or Islamic, often relying on one another. They all came to similar conclusions.

An important influence on Western cosmic mapping was John Holywood (Sacrobosco) (c.1195–1256), whose *Sphere* was widely-read and used. He used a geometric approach to persuade his readers that the cosmos must be a gigantic sphere, containing all of creation inside it. He offers three reasons for believing the cosmos to be a sphere, not a disk. One is that the 'archetypal' shape of the universe must be that which has no beginning and no end. This is the shape of God himself. Secondly, the sphere is the most capacious 'isometric' container geometrically available. And thirdly, any other shape would leave empty corners.

As proof, he drew attention to what could be learned from observation of the horizon. The horizon is curved. This can be proved by a simple experiment. Set up a signal on land which can be seen by someone standing on the deck of a ship. Let the ship then sail further away until the signal cannot be seen. Climb the mast and the signal will become visible again.[33]

Having established to his own satisfaction that the earth itself is not flat, but has the form of a ball – a matter by no means uncontroversial, as we shall see in a moment – Sacrobosco moved on to describe how this ball was positioned by the Creator in the surrounding cosmos. As a Christian map-maker, he took it for granted that Jerusalem was naturally to be placed at the centre of the earth. It was equally obvious to him that Jerusalem must also lie at the centre of the universe.

This reasoning encouraged the design of a diagrammatic representation of the universe. It is more like a 'tube' or 'metro' map than an Ordnance Survey or street map. It maps an idea. It does not have to be to scale. Its purpose is to place the elements of creation in their proper relationship to one another by means of a visual device.

In Sacrobosco's version of the cosmos there is an outer sphere, which is fixed. Within it are more spheres, arranged concentrically about the earth. Seven bear the planets, including the moon, and the eighth is the earth itself. The classical heritage had more to contribute here. Anaximenes (d. 528 BC) suggested that the sphere or ring carrying a star or planet was formed of some sort of invisible 'essence' (the fifth element, or quintessence) with the stars and planets, eternally burning, somehow embedded in it and rotating with it. Anaximander, his teacher (sixth century BC), envisaged an original great ball of cosmic fire which had developed layers and sub-structures. He thought individual spheres or rings were made of fire, but partly hidden behind a dark mask facing the earth. This had holes in it through which the fire showed, so that it appeared as small round planets or stars to the observer on earth.

In Sacrobosco's diagrammatic map of the earth itself, the equator is an east–west axis round which the planets spin, and it marks the hottest part of the earth. The Arctic to Antarctic pole runs so as to intersect the equator. The ends mark the positions of the coldest regions of the north and south. At an angle of 23 degrees to the equator slants another axis, on which ride the signs of the zodiac, a circle of the heavens which Sacrobosco believes governs the activities of all living things. (He includes astrology in this astronomical diagram, with no thought that he is moving into another realm of ideas.)

The music of the spheres

> Eternal Ruler of the ceaseless round
> Of circling planets singing on their way.[34]

This mapping and diagram-making slides effortlessly into a theory of creation in which there is living participation at the highest level in the continuing story of the unfolding of creation. Planets and stars have not always been treated as mere cosmic objects. They have often been depicted as players in a cosmic dance.

Cicero, the Roman philosopher and statesman (106–43 BC),was one of the popularisers and transmitters of this idea that the heavenly bodies are alive and involved in the affairs of mankind. In his book *On the Republic*, written to brace the Roman citizen with a sense of his high calling, he explains that humans may dwell on earth (*qui tuerentur ullum globum*) but they have souls[35] which are fragments of the stars, little pieces of the eternal fires (*ex illis sempiternis ignis*) spinning in the heavens.[36] The message is that human beings too should seek to maintain the wonderful unity of soul and body and not on any account consider taking their own lives and breaking that link by leaving their bodies. It is their duty to stay at their posts until the supreme god ends their lives. They should seek to live according to high principles of justice and piety, for that is the way to heaven.

In *Republic*, Book VI, Cicero describes a dream. In it he says he saw the Roman hero Scipio Africanus, who was one of his ancestors and who had defeated Hannibal in the Second Punic War and helped to save Rome from invasion. He had gone to North Africa to try to bring a rebellious Carthage under Roman control once more.

In the dream, which came to be known as the 'Somnium Scipionis' ('The Dream of Scipio') and acquired a literature of its own, Scipio gives Cicero lessons in cosmology as well as in how to achieve the sense of political proportion a statesman needs to cultivate. The sleeping Cicero seems to be snatched up high into the heavens, from which he is able to look down on the earth. He sees the beauty of the universe, its amazing size and how tiny the earth looks from above.[37]

He can see that the universe is made up of nine spheres, with heaven on the outside containing all the rest.[38] This fixed sphere is itself god, the supreme being. Revolving within this heavenly sphere are seven more, which turn in the opposite direction. Six of these are the spheres of Saturn, Jupiter, Mars, the Sun, with Venus and Mercury as its attendants forming spheres still further in. Within this arrangement of concentric spheres is the sphere of the Moon. The moon marks the boundary between the eternal and the sublunary, which is the mortal and destructible creation – destructible, that is, except for the souls which belong to human

beings who live there. Last is the sphere of the Earth, which forms
the ninth sphere and is the centre of the universe.

Cicero can hear music. Scipio tells him that this is the music
of the spheres, which they make by their movement, for it is
mathematically harmonious. The outermost heavenly sphere gives
out the highest note and the moon the lowest with the others
sounding proportionately between. Human music as we enjoy it is
founded on these harmonies and imitates them.

Scipio shows him the zones of the earth, the cold zones near
the poles and the heat of the equatorial zone. Between these lie
two temperate zones, the habitable part where Cicero lives and
its counterpart, the Antipodes, with which it is impossible to have
any connection because the equatorial heat would kill anyone
who tried to cross to the southern hemisphere from the north.
Moreover, the island of land which makes up the landmasses that
Cicero knows is surrounded by a great ocean, the Atlantic, which
dwarfs it in size. On this landmass even the most famous names
are known in only a limited way. Roman celebrity does not extend
to the Ganges or the heights of the Caucasus. And anyway, of what
value are the tiny voices of these little figures in the universal scale
of things, or the universe's time-frame? Set your mind on what
matters, on high and worthwhile things, he tells Cicero.[39]

Lifted up in imagination so that he can look down on earth and
its affairs, Cicero gains a new viewpoint and a better perspective.
He can see new stars and he realises that up there the stars look
bigger than they do from earth, while the goings-on below are
reduced to the pygmy scale of importance they have for the gods
gazing down. For Scipio draws Cicero's attention back to the earth
and points out how thinly peopled it is, what extensive tracts of
land are uninhabited and uncultivated.[40] What value can be placed
on human accolades arising from down there, when they are seen
in their true perspective from above?

Some of these ideas appeared again in the *Natural History* of
the elder Pliny (AD 23–79), where the universe, within its ever-still
outer sphere, is ceaselessly spinning, with circling planets also
revolving in orbits and making music.[41]

The cosmology in Cicero's story of the dream was of great
interest to the late Roman philosopher Macrobius (395–423).
He wrote a commentary on the 'Dream of Scipio' which became
something of a textbook on cosmology for the Middle Ages in its
own right. It includes prototypes of the diagrams Sacrobosco drew.

The 'zones'

In Sacrobosco's *Sphere* 'zones' are drawn across the two-dimensional representation of the earth as a ball. The notion of 'zones' was another borrowing from classical literature. It had been suggested by the Roman poet Ovid (43 BC–AD 17/18) in his *Metamorphoses*, where he says that 'many zones are marked on earth.'[42]

Zones were thought to reach further out, too. Sacrobosco also quotes Virgil:

> Five zones possess the sky, of which one is ever
> Red from blazing sun and ever burnt by fire.[43]

Pierre d'Ailly (1350–1420), a very influential late medieval writer, also took the view that the earth is a sphere. In his *Imago Mundi* (1410) d'Ailly helped develop the diagram-map of the earth further still. His version shows the axis joining the earth's Arctic and Antarctic poles as a line which, when produced, stretches out to the edges of the universe. His earth too has tropical zones on either side of the equator and it clearly shows the emptiness of the southern hemisphere.[44]

Attempts to depict zones and climates in the medieval accounts had also been partly prompted by Eratosthenes (*c.*276–195 BC), whose ideas were picked up and transmitted to the Latin-reading West by Pliny in his *Natural History*. Pliny describes the *circuli* or *paralleli* into which the earth can be divided, by taking measurements by sundial gnomons at midday at the equinox. The first of these runs south from a line running through India, Arabia and the Red Sea and across to the Atlantic at the Pillars of Hercules. Others can be drawn northwards, with Rome in a sixth circle and Milan in a seventh. Further north still run more lines, in the last of which is Ultima Thule, where the year is divided into a day lasting six months and a night lasting six months.[45]

Beyond the Pillars of Hercules is the circumambient ocean, believed Herodotus. 'The Greeks say that it flows round the whole world, from where the sun rises, but they cannot prove that.'[46] Macrobius, who included 'zones' in his world-picture in the 'Dream of Scipio', thought the stream of ocean flowed round the back of the world, keeping to the same temperature zones. Sacrobosco drew on this heritage when he set the zones out in detail.

Round or flat?

If it turned out that the earth was flat, how would that affect the
great diagram of the cosmos and the ideas about the spheres?
Plutarch (*c.* AD 46–120), wrote against the spherical view in his *De
Facie in Orbe Lunae* (*On the Face in the Moon*).[47] The sixth-century
writer Cosmas (*c.*535–47) remained an advocate of a flat-earth
view, but with cosmic modifications. Cosmas had travelled a good
deal as a merchant in his youth, reaching Abyssinia and India. In
his *Topographia*[48] he tried out a picture of the earth as lying flat
under a curved lid, which is the heavens. Cosmas says that first in
the order of creation came earth, which forms the base. There
is water above it, then air above that, then fire. Cosmas suggests
that this is a model given some authority by the Old Testament
description of the Tabernacle carried by the Jews as they fled from
Egypt, whose details he describes.[49] It looked, he suggests, a bit like
a model of the cosmos shaped on his hypothesis of a flat earth.
(This prompted the question whether the rims of heaven and
earth must be glued together round the edges and, if not, what
might lie through the gap.)

In his view, cosmic movement and activity on earth under the
dome of the heavens takes place by angelic agency rather than
through interaction of the sort we would now call chemical or
physical. It is their positive action at the Creator's command, not
some rotating system of spheres, which keeps things as they are, in
Cosmas' opinion.[50] There is no need to postulate a great system of
rotation within a fixed outer sphere.

Even in Cosmas' day, not everyone was a flat-earther. John
Philoponos (*c.*450–*c.*570) did not agree that the earth was flat. And it
was generally accepted in European thought by the seventh century
that the earth is spherical (*mundus est figure sperice seu rotunde*).[51]

Yet even if the earth is not flat, a map is. For those trying to
depict the layout of the earth, it was not easy to represent a ball
on a two-dimensional surface, a page or a sheet of parchment.
The 'sphere' hypothesis made the geometry of mapping much
more complex because it became a three-dimensional task which
had to be carried out in two dimensions. From a mapping point
of view, this is challenging. The earth was always conventionally
represented in this tradition in a flattened way as a disk with the
equator running across its middle.

There remained the further difficulty of finding a way to show
what happens behind the area which can be seen on the page. An

encircling ocean is shown on maps. Gerardus Mercator (1512–94) tried using a cylinder as a means of projecting all this in his nautical map proposals of 1569 and the device became common for its advantages as a practical aid to the sailing of a ship.

Can a map of the earth show heavenly or historical places?

All sorts of questions were prompted by these discussions. Was it possible to sail round behind what we can see of the surface of the earth? Is this out-of-sight area just water? Is this the reality hinted at where the Bible says the waters were gathered together?[52]

Some postulated a counter-balancing landmass on the back instead.[53] Could this be Paradise? Another practical question for map-makers was whether to include places 'known' to exist because they were mentioned in an authoritative source such as the Bible, but not necessarily accessible by normal travelling arrangements.

Throughout the Middle Ages 'Jerusalem' meant to the popular imagination both the actual city and the 'heavenly city'. So when the Crusades began in the late eleventh century there were undoubtedly some who thought that in travelling to Jerusalem they were also travelling to heaven, 'earthly Jerusalem, the image of celestial Jerusalem'.[54] Pope Urban II made a recruiting speech at the Council of Clermont in 1095 which is reported by several chroniclers:

> That land which as the Scripture says 'floweth with milk and honey', was given by God into the possession of the children of Israel Jerusalem is the navel of the world; the land is fruitful above others, like another paradise of delights. This the Redeemer of the human race has made illustrious by His advent, has beautified by residence, has consecrated by suffering, has redeemed by death, has glorified by burial. This royal city, therefore, situated at the centre of the world, is now held captive by His enemies, and is in subjection to those who do not know God, to the worship of the heathens. She seeks therefore and desires to be liberated, and does not cease to implore you to come to her aid. From you especially she asks succor, because, as we have already said, God has conferred upon you above all nations great glory in arms. Accordingly undertake this journey for the remission of your sins, with the assurance of the imperishable glory of the kingdom of heaven.[55]

So travelling to Jerusalem could also be understood as travelling to another reality, outside space and time. When the first Western crusaders set out at the end of the eleventh century to capture Jerusalem, they could be forgiven if they were confused about their journey's end. Were they going to Jerusalem on earth or the new Jerusalem in heaven? Baldric, archbishop of Dol, spoke of 'earthly Jerusalem, the image of celestial Jerusalem'.[56]

One of the fundamental assumptions of the thought of earlier centuries in many places and many traditions was that although there is a clear distinction between the 'natural' and the 'supernatural' worlds, the line could be crossed – in dreams, in imagination, perhaps even on one's feet, though it might not be easy to find the direction. Many early map-makers in Europe apparently thought the Garden of Eden could be travelled to. At least they placed it on their maps as though it could, where it may be found at the eastern point of the world. There Asia, Europe and Africa, the three continents then recognised, were thought to meet. Sometimes they had to find a place for it elsewhere, where the design of the map allowed room, but 'where' seems a relatively elastic notion in early map-making. So in this confidence that the supernatural as well as the physical cosmos can be mapped, early maps show the 'location' of the Garden of Eden as well as the shape of known local lands. Thus both a continuity across spaces, physical and metaphysical, and a continuity across time came to seem mappable, and the making of early maps included game attempts to make it possible.

Even at its most primitive, a map is a sophisticated device. It requires the acceptance of conventions for representing huge distances in a small space, and depicting the ups and downs of landscape on a flat sheet. A map needs ways of showing scale and proportion. The distinction between diagram and 'miniature reality' may not be clear or consistent. Medieval map-makers saw no objection to including 'portrayals' of a variety of different kinds of things – ideas or theories, notes of the spiritual or fictional, the relative positions of things which did not necessarily have physical location. They could determine the position of something represented on a map by its importance, and that importance did not necessarily have to be geographical. It could be historical or religious or even mythical.

Accordingly, the medieval world-picture map, relying on the assertions in the book of Ezekiel, places Jerusalem at the centre of the world.[57] Traditionally, in early European maps, the east is put at the top, creating a different conventional orientation from that which now places the north at the top. Genesis (2:8) says the Garden of Eden was in the east, so the Garden of Eden is placed there, though it is not a 'place' which can now be visited, as Christopher Columbus acknowledged:

> Holy Scripture testifies that Our Lord created the Terrestrial Paradise . . . I do not find and have never found any Latin or Greek work which definitely locates the Terrestrial Paradise in this world, not have I seen it securely placed on any world map.[58]

(Columbus himself floated the idea that the earth might be pear-shaped with the earthly paradise at the stalk.)[59]

There were other Biblical mentions which needed to be accommodated in a map of the world.[60] Where should God and Magog be placed (Genesis 10:2; Revelation 20:8)? Where were the cities of the Medes and the Persians (2 Kings 17:6)? Where exactly did the Magi come from (Matthew 2:1–12)?

Paulino of Venice saw the value of maps in their broadest sense, including diagrams and pictorial aids, as assistances to theological understanding:

> I think that it is not just difficult but impossible without a world map to make [oneself] an image of, or even for the mind to grasp, what is said of the children and grandchildren of Noah and of the four Kingdoms and other nations and regions, both in divine and human writings. There is needed moreover a twofold map, [composed] of painting and writing.[61]

Protestants too took maps seriously as theological aids. Luther claimed that the very geography of the world as it had originally been created had been altered by the Fall and the Flood.[62] Maps appeared in printed Protestant Bibles first in Zurich in 1525, which contained a map of the journey described in Exodus. By the later sixteenth century, four maps were used in the Geneva Bible of 1559: the Exodus journey again, and the division of Canaan among the twelve tribes of Israel, plus Palestine in the time of Christ and the journeys of St Paul. Pictures of the Garden of Eden became topographical in the Geneva Bibles, though not in German Lutheran ones. Town maps depicting Jerusalem mutated from 'plans' which might be reproductions of real towns into the designs for an improved 'new town' – a 'New Jerusalem' – found in some German Bibles.[63]

'Mapping' the hemispheres?

The limited 'three-continent geography' of a Christianity which recognised only Europe, Asia and Africa before the sixteenth century, and which had no notion of the way Africa stretches southwards into another hemisphere, imposed a further limit on mapping.[64] Early map-makers drew Africa much smaller that it is now known to be, with a southern line cutting off the continent at the bottom of the Sahara roughly at the level of the Horn of Africa. The Indian Ocean may be shown as a landlocked sea with a land link between India and Ethiopia.

To the modern eye, it seems obvious that the limited scope of the three known continents should have presented a challenge to the curious. For example, what happened where Africa ended to the south? No one in Europe really knew. Although there was trade, no one seems to have gone south across the Sahara expressly to see how much of Africa there was, or west until the end of the Middle Ages and the period of the discoveries, though there were tantalising early hints that there might be something to be found in that direction. *Navigatio S. Brendani* (*The Voyage of St Brendan*) speaks of an Atlantic full of islands. Brendan (*c.*486–575) saw these as the islands of the Promised Land. To the east there were journeys which hinted that there was more to see. Marco Polo (*c.*1254–1324) said there were 7,459 islands in the waters south of China. Yet the theory that God made and caused to be populated only three continents seems to have dominated Western thought as well as Western exploration.

All the zoning in the diagrammatic maps is focused on the northern hemisphere, because that was thought to be the only inhabited region of the earth. Cicero had explained in his *Republic* that both hemispheres were in principle habitable (*duo sunt habitabiles*), but the southern was not connected with the northern from a travelling point of view because the hot equatorial region was deemed to be impassable.[65] The hypothesis that the equator forms a burning barrier so hot that nothing could cross it and live was widely shared, and therefore whether anyone dwelt below the equator remained a matter of speculation. Cicero did not rule out the possibility that there might be places to live south of the equator or that someone might live in them. Those who dwell in the south are, he thought, in some way a mirror image of those in the north (*adversi*). Cosmas challenged this theory. No Antipodes could be possible, he said. If people walked backwards, they would keep treading on snakes which they would fail to see because they were gazing always behind.[66] Pierre d'Ailly reviews different opinions on the habitability of the southern parts of the earth and whether it is counterpart to the northern earth.[67]

With a world-map such as this, the 'three-continent' northern European conception of the world left the puzzle of an empty southern hemisphere. Matthew 18:19 says the apostles were sent to preach to all nations. The medieval 'Beatus' manuscripts preserve attempts to map the missions of the apostles, as described by Beatus of Liébana (d. 798) in his commentary on the Apocalyse. If no one can get to any southern lands which may exist past the boiling hot equator, the Bible must therefore be telling us that there are no 'nations', no peoples to be saved, living below the equator.[68]

Daniel Defoe (1659/61–1731) was still thinking about this in 1725–6, long after it was known that there were other continents and that they had people living in them. When he published his *General History of Discoveries and Improvements* he notes that it:

> has been the occasion of much dispute among the Learned Geographers and Historians, as well of the present, as of the past Ages . . . namely, How and when the great Continent of America came to be peopled with Inhabitants, and from whence? A difficulty which has been thought so great, that some . . . would have us put God Almighty to the Repetition of a particular Creation of the species, both of Man and Beast, for the supplying that part of the World . . .
>
> I shall in the pursuit of this undertaking shew how easy it might have been for all the kinds of living creatures which were found in America, except Man, to arrive there without the help of Navigation.[69]

His suggestion about the navigation is that America could have been reached from the west side of Africa and that the Carthaginians once 'possess that coast', so it is perfectly possible that humans exposed to the preaching of the Gospel could have made their way to America.

The continuing life of the notion appears in William Carey's *An Enquiry into the Obligations of Christians*.[70] He mentions Christ's commission to the disciples. Does that commission extend to the missionaries of the present day, or are those who 'to this day, are lost in ignorance and idolatry' to be left to end in hell?

IV. IN GOD'S IMAGE?
WAS THE WORLD MADE FOR OUR BENEFIT?

The peopled cosmos

In 'The crystal egg', one of H.G. Wells' science fiction stories, is to be glimpsed the planet Mars, with its creatures not designed on any known plan.[71] In many mythologies there are such creatures at a transitional stage of early creation, when one thing becomes another in a sea of violence and destruction. The fluidity with which one thing turns into another in many creation legends sets the scene for a hierarchy of created beings in which all may not be as it seems – or not for long. In some systems there is respect for all creatures. In Brahmanism, for example:

> Each day we must perform what we call the five great sacrifices. The first is to Brahma, the world spirit. We recite to him from the vedas. Later we make a libation of water to our ancestors, while to all the gods we pour ghee onto the sacred fire. Next we scatter grain for the animals, birds, spirits. Finally we worship man by offering a stranger hospitality.[72]

Yet the Judaeo-Christian understandings of the hierarchy of creation, which have become so widespread down the centuries as European influence has spread, are built on the assumption that the world was made for man.[73] The creation of mankind is the most important creation 'event'. For human beings were made in God's image (Genesis 1:26). In token of their status in God's eyes, in Genesis human beings are given dominion over all other creatures.

This optimistic elevation of human beings does not make it easy to fit in the angels. Genesis does not give any detail on their creation, but there emerged an understanding that they were created as purely spiritual rational beings, whereas humans are spirits in bodies. They remain eternally as they were created. Pseudo-Dionysius wrote in the fifth century about the existence of orders of angelic beings in the heavens in an attempt to provide a more complete hierarchy of the universe.[74] Seraphim and cherubim are highest, because they gaze directly on the Creator in adoration. Archangels and angels are lowest, because they have messages to carry and interact with human beings.

This idea of a hierarchy of merit and social structure can provide a framework for the universe, as in Dante's *Divina Commedia*, where the heavens and the circles of purgatory and then of hell reach ever downwards as a series of lodging places for human souls. But hell and purgatory raise further questions about the Creator's intentions which must wait for later chapters.

Cosmas believed that the angels keep the universe in order for human benefit until the world ends, when all the stars will fall from their places.[75] The angels, theologians such as Anselm of Canterbury later suggested in his *Cur Deus Homo* (*Why God Became Man*), live to help human beings to get to heaven, where the angels will be pleased to receive them, so that they can fill the gaps in the perfect number of heavenly beings which were left by the fall of their companion angels. Angels, having no bodies, do not breed. So they could not fill the gaps themselves.

The 'world-picture' of the sixteenth century[76] still owed a great deal to this early Christian and medieval conception of a human-centred cosmos. Man was made in God's image. Man was a microcosm of the macrocosm. Man had a place in a hierarchy appointed by the Creator; amongst human beings too there was a social hierarchy planned and approved by God.

These assumptions still seemed fundamental early in the seventeenth century when Sir John Hayward (1560–1627) described a human being:

> Thou art a mark, endued with reason and understanding, wherein God hath engraven his lively image. In other creatures there is some likeness of him, some footsteps of his divine nature; but in man lie hath stamped his image.

Hayward included a brief version of the traditional hierarchy of created being, in which all creatures resemble God if only in 'being', such as stones; some more closely, in having life; some more closely still in having higher modes of life and activity. But among creatures with physical existence, only human beings have powers of understanding and a capacity to reason and it is in this that they are truly made in God's image:

> Some things are like God in that they are; some in that they live; some in their excellent property and working. But this is not the image of God. His image is only in that we understand.[77]

This is an idea not far removed from the way Dorothy Sayers put it in the mid-twentieth century: 'As soon as the mind of the maker has been made manifest in a work, a way of communication is established between other minds and his.'[78]

John Milton took it as a certainty that the Creator gave humanity this special privilege:

> Let us make now Man in our image, Man
> In our similitude, and let them rule
> Over the Fish and Fowle of Sea and Aire,
> Beast of the Field, and over all the Earth,
> And every creeping thing that creeps the ground.
> This said, he formd thee, Adam, thee O Man.[79]

Alexander Pope knows it is the general view of his contemporaries that the world exists for man.[80] He hints ironically that this view may be mistaken:

> Of systems possible, if 'tis confest
> That Wisdom infinite must form the best,
> . . . 'tis plain
> must be somewhere, such a rank as man:
> And all the question (wrangle e'er so long)
> Is only this, if God has plac'd him wrong?[81]

Adam's being created, suggests John Locke, should be separated from his being given dominion, but that does not mean he was not created to have that dominion. The creation of the first human being 'was nothing but his receiving a being immediately from omnipotency'. Adam:

> was created, or began to exist, by God's immediate power without the intervention of parents or the pre-existence of any of the same species to beget him, when it pleased God he should; and so did the lion, the king of beasts before him, by the same creating power of God.

So 'bare creation gave him no dominion'. 'It was God's appointment [which] made him monarch.' This took place by a 'positive grant' recorded in Genesis 1:28, 'The original grant of government, . . . not being until after the Fall, when Adam was somewhat, at least in time, and very much distant in condition from his creation.'[82] Human supremacy was all a matter of the

Creator's wishes, then. It was not an unavoidable consequence of the structure of the universe:

> What such necessary connection there is between Adam's creation and his right to government, so that a natural freedom of mankind cannot be supposed without the denial of the creation of Adam, I confess for my part I do not see.[83]

Uphill from primitive man?

> Suppose that God could not, in the first instance, create anything better than a Bosjesman or an Andaman islander, or something still lower; and yet was able to endow the Bosjesman or the Andaman islander with the power of raising himself into a Newton or a Fénelon.[84]

As the globe was gradually explored, many tribes were discovered by more 'civilised' travellers to be living primitive lives, in which some critics claimed they were little better than animals, ruthless, murderous, without law or order. Others spoke of the 'noble savage'.

Jean Jacques Rousseau (1712–78) began his *The Social Contract* (1762) with the statement that men are born equal but are everywhere in chains;[85] a political statement not a comment on a natural 'physiological' hierarchy. Until the eighteen century it was not controversial to regard humans as born to places in a hierarchy or overarching social structure, from which it did not behove them to try to escape. In his first letter to the Corinthians, Paul explains that in the 'body of Christ', made up of the members of the Church with Christ as their head, each member has a function and a place. The hand and the ear and the eye cannot dispense with one another's help and none of them can take over the work of the others.[86] This view that places and roles in society are a created thing and not a mutable human construct had a far wider reach than the Christian community and some notion of the 'body politic' appears in many cultures.

This raised questions. Are humans all at the same level or are some created to be better or higher is the cosmos, like the 'orders' of the angels? Are some people more fully human than others? How much variation is possible before a creature would cease to be human?

5. God resting after creation, Byzantine mosaic in Monreale

Cosmic progression

The belief that a human creature may progress up and down the cosmic hierarchy according to the way it behaves entered the equation from the Hermetic tradition (see Chapter 4 (i)). Behave like a beast and you become a beast. Imitate God and you rise towards a higher state than the human. It was adaptable. Sir John Hayward put the idea in terms of the Christian belief that human beings are made in the image of God:

> Seeing then that thou art of so noble a nature and that thou beaten in thine understanding the image of God, so govern thyself as is fit for a creature of understanding. Be not like the brute beasts, which want understanding: either wild and unruly or else heavy and dull. Certainly of all the creatures under heaven, which have received being from God, none degenerate, none forsake their natural dignity and being, but only man. Only man, abandoning the dignity of his proper nature, is changed like Proteus into divers forms. And this is occasioned by reason of the liberty of his will.[87]

Is this human or not? The creation of monsters

> Pushmi-Pullyus are now extinct. That means, there aren't any more. But long ago, when Doctor Dolittle was alive, there were some of them still left in the deepest jungles of Africa; and even then they were very, very scarce. They had no tail, but a head at each end, and sharp horns on each head. They were very shy and terribly hard to catch. The black men get most of their animals by sneaking up behind them while they are not looking. But you could not do this with the pushmi-pullyu – because, no matter which way you came towards him, he was always facing you. And besides, only one half of him slept at a time. The other head was always awake – and watching. This was why they were never caught and never seen in Zoos. Though many of the greatest huntsmen and the cleverest menagerie-keepers spent years of their lives searching through the jungles in all weathers for pushmi-pullyus, not a single one had ever been caught. Even then, years ago, he was the only animal in the world with two heads.[88]

Stories of monsters abound in all mythologies, some benign and some fearsome. They are monsters because they do not comply with the requirements for a creature of a recognised kind. What becomes of human positions in a hierarchy if we cannot be certain whether a creature is human or not?

The enthusiasm for collecting cabinets of 'curiosities' displayed by young men on their travels during the Enlightenment of the European eighteenth century was nothing new. The Greeks and Romans were at it too, millennia earlier. Herodotus in his *Histories* takes the reader on a tour of the lands where peoples of strange but distinctive customs dwell. He describes the Gamphastes, who wear no clothes and live without violence, and the Blemmyae, who have no heads and see and talk through eyes and mouths in their chests. He writes of the Arimaspians who live in northern Scythia (possibly the Urals) in an enduring struggle with the Griffins who guard the gold which is to be found near the cave where the north wind arises. He describes one-eyed people, the Arimaspoi, and cannibals, the lawless Androphagi.[89] Herodotus may be reporting stories which have some basis in fact, perhaps in the struggles of tribes in an area north of the Black Sea where Persians penetrated, and he mixes groups with physical oddities and groups with startling customs. But what matters for our present purposes is the insouciant way he mixes the genres of human and non-human, creatures seen and creatures only told of, and assumes that near the edges of the known world certainties fade and categories of being blur.

The Roman naturalist Pliny was a source of later Western knowledge of much of this monster-lore insofar as it described sheer oddities.[90] Pliny, relying on Herodotus and his own ideas, offered quite a list of monsters, including not-quite humans and humans who were simply 'different' because they lived in remote places, such as the Berber *garamantes* of North Africa. Some had startling and unusual customs. Augiles worshipped the lords of the underworld. Others departed from human norms. The Thibii have two pupils in one eye and in the other eye they have the outline of a horse. Satyrs are an extreme case, with the ears and feet of goats. Some 'people-eaters' drink out of human skulls. Some of the cannibals in the region of Scythia wear human scalps on their chests like napkins.[91] Some monsters, such as the Manticore, were said to be composite, made up of parts of known real ordinary animals. Images of Egyptian gods with dog heads made the concept of Cynocephali familiar to Greeks and Romans.

These fantastical beasts reappear in accounts written during the Middle Ages. One of the questions for Christians was whether the birth of the monsters is a consequence of the Fall. Would there have been monsters if there had been no Fall? Were they in God's original plan? Are they Cain's descendants[92] or human 'thistles', a result of the detrimental changes which took place in the world after the Fall? Isidore, bishop of Seville (*c.*560–636), writes of giants, pygmies, cyclops, hermaphrodites, dog-faced men. William of Auvergne (1180/90–1249) believed that monsters still lived outside Christian Europe and were to be found at the edges of the created world – for example, in India.

Curiosity accompanied the fifteenth- and sixteenth-century discoverers on their travels. Syllacio wrote to the duke of Milan on 13 December 1494. Syllacio was lecturing at University of Pavia and had a friend on Columbus' second voyage (1493–6). This was Guillermo Coma of Aragon, who was sending Syllacio news of his progress.[93] He described encounters with *anthropophagi*, also called the *Canaballi*, man-eating savages of the Caribbean. The information suggested that these man-eaters might be reformed: 'being intelligent, sharp-witted and shrewd, they could easily be led to adopt our laws and our manner of life, when they realise . . . that our way of life [is] more civilised than theirs.'[94]

Monstrous races were always seen as distant, remote, 'other' by reason of where they lived as well as because it could not be certain that they were truly human.[95] The theory that no human beings could live south of the equator gave rise to debates. Did it mean that the Creator had put other kinds of creature there, or even creatures made the reverse way round, with their feet pointing backwards, for example (*antipodes*)?[96] Do monsters have souls? remained the question for Christians. And did God save the monsters?

PART II

Why it is difficult to agree

6. Adam and Eve with the Serpent, by Hans Baldung Grien

2

What is the evidence?

Sources: sacred books and the 'book of nature'

It was long believed that Moses wrote Genesis, the first book of
the Old Testament, the 'sacred text' which provided Judaism and
Christianity with their creation stories, and on which the Qur'an
later also drew. But Moses does not claim that he saw creation
happen. Creation had no other human observer except Adam and
Eve, and even they were not there until near the end of the 'six
days' of creative work as it is described in Genesis. Moses did not
need to be present if the Holy Spirit told him about it afterwards,
suggested John Donne, dean of St Paul's Cathedral in London:
'The holy Ghost hovered upon the waters, and so God wrought;
the holy Ghost hovered upon Moses too, and so he wrote.'[1]

Donne's younger contemporary John Milton, puritan and
revolutionary, began his epic poem *Paradise Lost* by calling on
the inspiration of the 'heavenly muse', the same Holy Spirit, to
help him tell this same story of events which had no eyewitness
historian to record them:

> Sing Heav'nly Muse, that on the secret top
> Of Oreb, or of Sinai, didst inspire
> That Shepherd,[2] who first taught the chosen Seed,
> In the Beginning how the Heav'ns and Earth
> Rose out of Chaos.[3]

Alongside the traditional explanation that the Creator himself
imparted the creation story to Moses ran another strong tradition.
This was the argument that creation, or the natural world, will
'reveal' all the inquirer needs to know. It tells its own story. When
Paul of Tarsus wrote in his letter to the Romans that, 'since the

creation of the world God's invisible qualities – his eternal power and divine nature – have been clearly seen, being understood from what has been made,'[4] he was providing the Christian world with an 'authority' for this view.

Even so, it was clearly recognised that 'you only have to look' did not work for the whole of the Christian faith. Hugh of St Victor (1096–1141) distinguished the 'work of creation' from the 'work of restoration' on this principle. He says that creation was a form of revelation, showing forth what the Creator is like; but for the story of the incarnation and crucifixion and redemption the inquirer must rely on the narrative of events to be found in Scripture. Robert Kilwardby (c.1215–79) among other medieval theologians accepted the same traditional set of assumptions.[5]

Thomas Aquinas (1225–74) argued in his *Summa Theologiae* that for this reason theology has something to add to philosophy.[6] Philosophy is simply the product of human reason. Theology includes what God has revealed, which human reason would not otherwise know about. The proofs of the existence of God put forward by Thomas Aquinas in his *Summa Theologiae* rest upon observation of the created world and on reasoning about it. It is but a step, he suggests, from treating observed phenomena as evidence of the Creator's deliberate revelation of his creative activity, to the view that they also say something about the Creator himself. The arguments brought together by Aquinas mostly turned on the assumption that anything so big and complicated and beautiful as the world and its contents must have had an initiator, and an initiator about whom certain things could be guessed. He or it must have been very powerful, perhaps all-powerful, also very clever; and he or it must have taken seriously the importance of making something beautiful (though he or it would have had to create the idea of the beautiful too).

Roger Bacon (c.1214–94), one of the more radical thinkers of the Middle Ages in the West, also struggled to work out the relation of philosophy and 'revealed' theology.[7] The Bible, he says, reveals the 'final' (ultimate) cause of creation, the Creator himself, but the rest has to be worked out by philosophy, and philosophy has not succeeded yet. Philosophy, he notes, has had help from the theology developed in the Christian tradition. It would be wrong to think of philosophy as confined to the secular thinkers of the ancient world or merely thought up by the 'heathens' who lived before the Christian era. There are indications that the patriarchs benefited from philosophical instruction. Josephus (AD 37–c.100) says Noah and his sons taught the Chaldeans; Abraham taught the Egyptians; Isis and Pallas were contemporary with Jacob and Esau; Prometheus and Atlas were contemporary with Moses; Hermes was a grandson of Atlas; Asclepius was taught by Atlas or Apollo.[8]

The thrust of all this was to try to bring together the strands of rational and 'revealed' routes to discovering about creation with an acknowledgement that from an early period thinkers were actively comparing notes. Interest in these questions did not die away with the Middle Ages. It was still a matter of active controversy in the early modern period. Matthew Tindal (1657–1733) wrote *Christianity as Old as the Creation* partly to discuss this contemporary moment in a long-running controversy down the centuries. He accepts in the traditional way that Christianity has its 'revelation' in the Bible and that the creation itself can be counted as an act of revelation. He insists that God gave his creatures from the first all they needed to know.[9]

Richard Bentley (1662–1742)[10] suggests that the alternative to the Christian view of creation as an act of revelation by the Creator is an atheism which says that 'all about us is dark senseless Matter, driven on by the wild impulses of Fatality; that Men rose out of the Slime of the Earth, and that what is called the Soul, perishes by Death.'[11] His argument is partly that religion is more comfortable and keeps society in better shape, but he grapples with the atheists' philosophical contention that mind can be explained in terms of matter.

The controversial central assumption here is that nothing is needed – or even possible – beyond experimental verification of observations by way of explanation of how the world began. If 'the Brain is but Body' is Mind anything more? If 'no Motion in general superadded to Matter, can produce any Sense or Perception . . . or any Degree of it . . . beget Cogitation,' what is thought and what is feeling? No hypothesis about 'fine particles' can explain Mind, Bentley claims. 'Concussions of Atoms can never be capable of begetting those intrinsical and vital Affections, that Self-Consciousness, and other Powers that we feel in our selves.' 'Sense and Perception can never be the product of Matter and Motion.' The atheists ask why there are only five senses. If there is a God why did he not give us more? Bentley responds by inquiring what more could there be? Do his questioners have any ideas?[12]

The Age of Reason and natural theology

During its 'Age of Reason', the eighteenth-century West returned for a time to the question of what can be learned by reason and from 'revelatory' nature. This was a period of intense scrutiny of what could be inferred from 'scientific' observation. It was also a time when some leading thinkers wanted to strip the Christian religion of its complexities and postulate a plain, impersonal, machine-making deity whose operations could be assessed rationally and by observation of the evidence. The 'deism' of the seventeenth and eighteenth centuries was a European phenomenon in which a new simplified monotheism was proposed by the forward-thinking, in what remained a predominantly Christian culture.[13] (Although Zoroastrianism won the approval of some writers of the Enlightenment, such as Voltaire, because they said it was – being apparently a form of Deism – more rational than Christianity.) David Hume (1711–76) sneers at:

> superstitious atheists [who] acknowledge no being, that corresponds to our idea of a deity. No first principle of mind or thought: No supreme government and administration: No divine contrivance or intention in the fabric of the world.

Deism not only questioned the need for detailed structure of the by now quite complex theology of the Christian faith; it also despised comfortingly particular and manageably small gods of polytheistic paganism:

> Our ancestors in Europe . . . believed, that all nature was full of . . . invisible powers; fairies, goblins, elves, sprights; beings, stronger and mightier than men, but much inferior to the celestial natures, who surround the throne of God.

Experimenting a little with the study of 'comparative religion', Hume describes the highly interactive relationship some peoples have with their small gods and idols:

> 'The CHINESE, when their prayers are not answered, beat their idols. The deities of the LAPLANDERS are any large stone which they meet with of an extraordinary shape. The EGYPTIAN mythologists, in order to account for animal worship, said, that

the gods, pursued by the violence of earth-born men, who were their enemies, had formerly been obliged to disguise themselves under the semblance of beasts. The CAUNII, . . . resolving to admit no strange gods among them . . . beat the air with their lances . . . to expel the foreign deities.[14]

It seems to him obvious that these 'imperfect beings' are simply not worthy of respect as potential Creators. 'To ascribe the origin and fabric of the universe to these imperfect beings never enters the imagination of any polytheist or idolator.'[15]

Hume pointed to what he claims to be a general conviction of 'mankind' that there must be 'intelligence' in the being or beings who created and rule the world.

The only point of theology, in which we shall find a consent of mankind almost universal, is, that there is an invisible, intelligent power in the world: but whether this power be supreme or subordinate, whether confined to one being, or distributed among several, what attributes, qualities, connexions, or principles of action ought to be ascribed to those beings; concerning all these points, there is the widest difference in the popular system of theology.[16]

The thrust for simplification takes him back to the discussions of Greek philosophers. 'The common people were never likely to push their researches so far, or derive from reasoning their systems of religion':[17]

Even at this day, and in EUROPE, ask any of the vulgar, why he believes in an omnipotent creator of the world; he will never mention the beauty of final causes, of which he is wholly ignorant: He will not hold out his hand and bid you contemplate the suppleness and variety of joints in his fingers, their bending all one way, . . . with all the other circumstances, which render that member fit for the use, to which it was destined . . . he will tell you of the sudden and unexpected death of such a one . . . [which] he ascribes to the immediate operation of providence.

Hume, with a mind formed in the classical tradition, remained convinced that the origin of the world should still be treated as a philosophical rather than a theological question:

It was merely by accident, that the question concerning the origin of the world did ever in ancient times enter into religious systems . . . The philosophers alone made profession of delivering systems of this kind; and it was pretty late too before these bethought themselves of having recourse to a mind or supreme intelligence, as the first cause of all.

He means by this that while a philosophical approach will take the inquirer into essentially theoretical questions of causation, a polytheist can be seduced into worshipping everything he does not understand:

Whoever learns by argument, the existence of invisible intelligent power, must reason from the admirable contrivance of natural objects, and must suppose the world to be the workmanship of that divine being, the original cause of all things. But the vulgar polytheist, so far from admitting that idea, deifies every part of the universe, and conceives all the conspicuous productions of nature, to be themselves so many real divinities.[18]

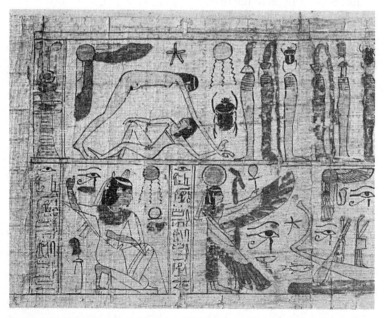

7. Detail of the creation of the world, from a funerary papyrus of Serimen, priest of Amon

Intelligent design

In the chaotic myths of polytheism a guiding intelligence is not a necessary postulate. To Western minds, which were mostly monotheistically inclined after the end of the ancient world, the best clue that a single powerful intelligence made the world became the argument from its 'design'. This argument was framed definitively for the early modern world by William Paley (1743–1805) in a vivid image in his *Natural Theology* (1802):

> Crossing a heath, suppose I pitched my foot against a stone, and were asked how the stone came to be there: I might possibly answer, that for any thing I know to the contrary, it had lain there for ever: nor would it perhaps be very easy to show the absurdity of this answer. But suppose I had found a watch upon the ground, and it should be inquired how the watch happened to be in that place; I should hardly think of the answer which I had before given, that for any thing I knew, the watch might have always been there. Yet why should not this answer serve for the watch, as well as for the stone? why is it not as admissable in the second case as in the first?[19]

His answer is that while a stone has a look of chance about its shape, a watch does not. Its form bespeaks its purpose and explains the way is has been made to serve that purpose:

> For this reason, and for no other, viz., that when we come to inspect the watch, we perceive (what we could not discover in the stone) that its several parts are framed and put together for a purpose . . . This mechanism being observed . . . the inference, we think, is inevitable, that the watch must have had a maker; that there must have existed, at some time, and at some place of other, an artificer or artificers, who formed it for the purpose.[20]

No rational mind could believe that the watch itself was a mere accident. Does it follow that there was a Creator or that he was divine? John Stuart Mill (1806–73) seems to take a cautiously positive position in his *Theism:*

> The signs of contrivance are most conspicuous in the structure and processes of vegetable and animal life. But for these, it

is probable that the appearances in nature would never have seemed to the thinking part of mankind to afford any proofs of a God.[21]

The argument from analogy

Another seminal idea of the eighteenth-century West was that of Joseph Butler (1692–1752). Butler had an unusual education for an Englishman of his time because he was sent to a 'dissenting academy'. These were schools for the children of families which were not practising members of the 'established' Church of England, lack of conformity with which meant loss of certain civil and legal rights. These schools combined a high academic standard with practical education for boys who would have to earn their living in trade. The master in charge of this particular academy was Samuel Jones, himself a former student at the University of Leiden. He introduced Butler to John Locke's *Essay Concerning Human Understanding*. Butler fell into correspondence with Samuel Clarke, whose Boyle lectures given in 1704 had prompted much fresh speculation on the existence of God and how (if at all) God can be in 'space', or have had a hand in the creation of the universe. Butler became an Anglican in 1714 and was then permitted to go to Oxford University (1715–18).

His *Analogy of Religion* was published in 1736. It is a moral as much as a cosmological work and it had an enormous influence for more than a century, becoming a set book in the two English universities, alongside Paley and the long-established classical textbooks. Butler saw a convincing link between what could be observed by way of evidence that the world is

> governed, and the nature of the God who runs it, so that one may argue from such facts as are known, to others that are like them; from that part of the divine government over intelligent creatures which comes under our view, to that larger and more general government over them which is beyond it.[22]

This observer, 'postulating a natural Governor of the world, . . . will argue thence for religion'.[23]

In Butler's view, other people's explanations are unsatisfactory. Some 'form their notions of God's government upon hypothesis', some 'indulge themselves in vain and idle speculations, how the world might possibly have been framed otherwise than it is', some, the Deists, particularly offend him. Much better, much stronger, he feels, is the argument from analogy.[24] Resemblances and parallels may be taken as proofs as strong as anything to be derived from experiment, and themselves analogous with such proofs:

> Let us then, instead of that idle and not very innocent employment of forming imaginary models of a world, and schemes of governing it, turn our thoughts to what we experience to be the conduct of Nature with respect to intelligent creatures; which may be resolved into general laws or rules of administration, in the same way as many of the laws of Nature respecting inanimate matter may be collected from experiments.

In fact, the possibilities do not stop there:

> And let us compare the known constitution and course of things with what is said to be the moral system of Nature; the acknowledged dispensations of Providence, or that government which we find ourselves under, with what religion teaches us to believe and expect; and see whether they are not analogous and of a piece. And upon such comparison it will, I think, be found that they are very much so: that both may be traced up to the same general laws, and resolved into the same principles of divine conduct.

The plans of Providence must be proportioned to the vastness of the universe. 'As the material world appears to be, in a manner, boundless and immense; there must be *some* scheme of Providence vast in proportion to it.'[25]

Paley's and Butler's arguments were taken up in succeeding generations but not uncritically. John Stuart Mill was less keen on 'analogy' than on 'design'. He thought that it would be naive to infer that any resemblance or analogy between nature and its Creator is a reliable guide to what he is like and what he has done. What counts is 'the special character of those resemblances'.[26]

Baden Powell (1796–1860), father of the founder of the Boy Scout movement, was a theologian with scientific interests, writing during the period when the British Association for the Advancement of Science was being formed, and when a classical education was still just sufficient as a qualification, especially for writing on those aspects of science which overlap with philosophy and theology. He died just before he could take part in the debate in the Oxford Museum where he would undoubtedly have defended Darwin's ideas.

The confident assumption that a thinker was free to move amongst discoveries in wholly different areas of research and intellectual endeavour without having to declare them 'not his subject' lasted little beyond his generation, but he could remark on the 'tendency and progress of discovery towards a coalition and combination of different trains of research'.[27] He cites work on 'the action of magnetism on light' and 'the relations of chemical to electrical action'.[28]

Baden Powell saw force in arguments from analogy:

> the source of inductive certainty, that certainty beyond the mere limits of sense, that superstructure larger than any foundation of facts, is accounted for by natural and acknowledged processes. It arises in the first instance out of the power of abstraction, . . . by whose aid the mind creates what are indeed new conceptions, yet formed only out of materials already furnished . . . the process derives its whole force from the discovery and acceptance of sound and well-framed analogies.[29]

But he was writing at a date in the mid-nineteenth century when consciousness of the need to define scientific methodologies was at a height. Baden Powell was himself involved in the early development of the British Association for the Advancement of Science. Science, he thinks, involves 'the application of a higher reasoning to the mere facts of observation which essentially constitutes *science* . . . mainly effected by the application of . . . systems of abstract and necessary mathematical truth'. Scientific 'principles are themselves . . . derived from experience.'[30] In short, the traditional distinction between abstract philosophical reasoning by which explanations of the origin of the world might be deduced and the method of induction from observation and experiment is not as sharp as had been thought:

> The very notions of a body in uniform rectilinear motion, or of forces acting on it, are essentially ideas of experience, and certainly could have no application without reference to the real existence of matter and force.[31]

The evidence?

Within the parameters of the grand options identified down the centuries, whether to believe the text of a sacred book, think the matter through by pure reasoning or make inferences from observation of the universe, there has proved, then, to be a good deal of room for manoeuvre and changes of fashion. Has there been progress?

3

The great rival religious theories

1. POLYTHEISMS

> Lo! the poor Indian, whose untutor'd mind
> Sees God in clouds, or hears him in the wind;
> His soul, proud science never taught to stray
> Far as the solar walk, or milky way.

When he wrote this, the satirist Alexander Pope was playing with an assumption: that educated Westerners were capable of taking a more advanced view of the difficult questions about the origin of the universe than those of less 'civilised' races. His 'Indian' is content with 'an humbler heav'n', less cosmic, less abstract, more local. 'Some safer world in depth of woods embrac'd':

> He asks no angel's wing, no seraph's fire;
> But thinks, admitted to that equal sky,
> His faithful dog shall bear him company.[1]

Innumerable explanations of the way the world began were offered by those who worshipped many gods or powers, especially local ones. In myriad stories these entities come into existence – who can say how – change from one kind of thing to another, motiveless or variously motivated as rivals or as collaborators. It is all very dynamic, also chaotic. Whether the Creator was omnipotent; whether creation was a single act or a continuous process; whether it had to be repeated; the irreconciliability of good and evil: the questions philosophers wrestled with, and which we shall come to later in this book – these questions simply did not arise if created things were thought to emerge in a thousand ways from a busy interaction of relatively minor players.

Yet in its conceptually undemanding way, polytheism offered a flexible and adaptable way of making sense of the beginning of the world and the origins of life. It adapted itself to large-scale and to small-scale explanations. At the level of the local and domestic, a variety of entities and objects, people (especially ancestors) and even concepts could be regarded as having power to create, and then to affect one's daily life. That power was a reassurance if it was on one's side, and a reason for fear if it was hostile and could not be won over by worship or bribery. People naturally tried to placate what they feared, and to enlist 'power' on their side in the vicissitudes of life, by offering gifts or sacrifices.

Was this all polytheistic variation derived from a single primal 'knowledge' in which is a 'key to all mythologies'? On the face of it this seems unlikely, despite the confidence of *Middlemarch*'s fictional Mr Casaubon and his real-life successors that there is a 'key to all mythologies' to be found. Polytheistic systems have arisen independently in different parts of the world. Deities could be firmly linked to a particular place, where a mountain or a rock might be worshipped as 'god' or 'goddess'. Or they could 'travel' and be identified relocated in other scenes. The gods have many names, and often only an oral and local tradition to explain who or what they are and what they can do.

Part of the difficulty is that, as we shall see in Chapter 5, knowledge of mythologies throughout the world was brought together for purposes of modern study only piecemeal, as Europeans 'discovered' new parts of the earth from the end of the fifteenth century. With that process of discovery went intrusion, and few polytheisms can have remained unaltered.

Cold northern polytheism encounters Christianity

An example of the way encounters could eventually modify mythologies is the story of the beliefs devised by peoples of the far north. The primitive ancestors of the Inuit or Eskimo peoples probably arrived in North America from the European–Asian landmass. This was a hunting culture. Although animals were essential food, the Inuit believed they had 'souls' and when they killed an animal the people respectfully acted out a ritual to send its soul on its way. Sea and land animals were clearly distinguished for religious purposes, as were the gods of sea and land and air. Beings regarded as gods included Sedna, the Sea, who ruled the creatures which lived in the sea, and deities representing sun and air. Religious rituals such as masked dancing involve the representation of animals.

Among the creation legends of these peoples, the cluster relating to Sedna is especially important to the polytheism of these northern lands. In some versions she is a giantess, the daughter of Anguta the Creator. After a family quarrel her angry father paddled her out to sea in his divine kayak and threw her overboard. She clung to the sides of the boat with her fingers but he chopped them off and she and her fingers fell deep into the water. There she became the goddess of the sea and her giantess-sized fingers became creatures that live in the sea, such as the seals and whales and walrus hunted by the Inuit.

In another version she is an ordinary girl who refuses to enter an arranged marriage with any of the men selected by her father. He too takes her out to sea and throws her overboard, and her clinging fingers freeze and drop off, again giving rise to sea creatures, while she becomes the goddess of the sea. Other versions of the story involve her marriage to a hunter (who bribes her father with fish to win her hand). The hunter turns out really to be a great raven. He carries her off to a clifftop nest and when her father tries to rescue her the great bird mounts a storm and her father throws her into the sea to try to save her. In yet another version she is thrown into the sea by her father to try to appease the bird-god and a sea-spirit he has enlisted on his side. In all versions she loses her fingers and goes to live in the sea, sometimes transformed with a fishtail.

These stories assume something which is a commonplace in polytheistic versions of a creation story. This is the facility with which humans, gods and animals move in and out of one another's worlds and are transformed from one kind of being to another. There is often violence and brutality and a transference of powers and forms and modes of beings whose mechanisms are not made clear. In the spirit of such flexible transformation and transmutation, the Inuit believed in some form of reincarnation, to the point of giving a newborn child the name of someone who had recently died.

There is evidence of a Norse 'discovery' of America in the Norse Sagas. Norse peoples show genetic evidence of some Mongoloid intermingling but their arrival in modern Scandinavia and their genetic heritage seems to be Indo-European and historically shaped in part by their place at the far fringes of the Roman Empire. Norse gods formed a different pantheon from that of the Inuit. They stood for warfare and conquest and were useful to skiers, where the Inuit ones were predominantly fishing assistants.

In the Saga of Eric the Red (*c.*1000), the Norsemen set sail into unknown seas where for many days they were surrounded by icy fog and could not see where they were going. When at last the sun broke through they were able to work out from the positions of the heavenly bodies where they might be; they hoisted sail and went on. Then they saw land, with forests on it, but they were not sure whether this might be Greenland. More land appeared, but still they were not sure. They went on once more and at last they came to land with high ice mountains, and there they landed.[2]

The Norsemen brought their own pagan beliefs to this new land and the sagas described them as living there for a time, but no one seems to have seen a need to sit down with the people already there and attempt a conflation of their respective

8. Carving of Thor

creation legends. Tidiness, consistency and coherence did not seem important. Nor was there apparently an attempt to impose a 'superior' religion of the conquerors upon the invaded and conquered people already there.

Olaus Magnus (1490–1557), a Swedish Roman Catholic priest to whom such a requirement came more naturally, wrote a 'Description' of 'northern peoples' known to him, including those in 'the very farthest part of the North, which most men think uninhabitable because of the intense cold'. He comments on the pagan belief of some of the pre-Christian northern peoples known to him: 'During the time of paganism these Lithuanians, as long as they were held by the error of heathendom, revered three main divinities, fire, woods, and serpents.'[3]

Tracing these encounters in northern polytheism is manifestly difficult on several levels: ethnic, chronological and attitudinal.

Syncretism and synthesis

One way of bringing together so much that seems disparate has been the practice of syncretism, which simply merges the gods encountered elsewhere with gods familiar at home. This can be done even where the god has a local manifestation. Often a god has been located in a statue for purposes of worship. Statues and other depictions of gods might have characteristic features (an 'iconography') to give a clue which god or goddess is intended. For example, the Greek goddess Pallas Athene might be portrayed with an owl as a symbol of her special responsibility for 'wisdom'. No difficulty was felt about regarding such statues as the actual god or goddess. Yet it was accepted that the god might also live in other statues claiming to be the same divinity. That allowed the merging and adaptation of the pantheons of conquered peoples – the syncretism successfully practised in the imperial expansion of ancient Rome. Such elastic belief systems have proved immensely durable, often continuing under the surface when an officially approved monotheism took over. Augustine of Hippo relates with affectionate disapproval his own Christian mother's habit of treating the shrines of the saints much as pagans treated the shrines of local gods, pouring libations and praying for assistance.

Another method of synthesis has been to mingle more and less sophisticated levels of understanding and belief. Hinduism (a term used by European merchants from the late eighteenth century to describe the religion of India) is a particularly comprehensive and accommodating form of polytheism with very ancient origins, into which have entered sophisticated philosophical traditions and various abstract ideas.

The Upanishads, the sacred texts which give a framework of belief to Hinduism, were composed at intervals across the centuries, the earliest of them before Buddhism arose in India. Their oral transmission means that they were subject to modification after they had first been composed. One of the oldest is the Aitareya Upanishad. It describes creation in this way. First there was Spirit and the Spirit was the whole universe. The Spirit 'thought' of making worlds from his own being. He made light, which is space. He made 'waters'. He made death and creatures able to die, to dwell on earth. He made creatures to dwell in the lower 'waters' under the earth. The heavenly or ethereal waters he placed above.

Then he made a guardian for the world by brooding over him until he was born like a hatchling from an egg. His birth produced a speaking mouth and from that speech came fire. Nostrils appeared, which breathed, and then there was air. The eyes emerged and with them sight and from sight came the sun. From the skin came plants. From the heart came mind and from mind the moon.

So were made the gods, sun and moon, air and fire and so on. In the ocean into which they fell the gods were hungry and thirsty. They demanded somewhere to live and food to eat. They were offered horses or cows but they found those unsatisfactory. They were pleased when they were offered human beings to dwell in. Fire entered the mouth and became speech, air the nostrils and became breath, the sun sight and entered the eyes and became sight and the moon entered the heart and became mind. Habitation was thus provided for the gods and they began to be drivers of human behaviour.

Hinduism has proved to be a characteristically Indian form of polytheism. Hindus now live all over the world but the religion did not spread by mission or conquest, though commerce helped diffuse it. (Indian traders brought Hinduism to Malaysia and its archipelago in about the first century AD.) A vast range of beliefs and texts and practices can now be called Hindu. There is a Brahmin tradition. There is a 'philosophical' Hinduism based on the Upanishads. There is a Yogic branch of Hinduism. There is Hinduism which has its focus in *dharma* or right living. There is a Hinduism which concentrates on worship. Yet there is still at 'folk'

level in Hinduism a simple polytheism where the gods remain
local deities.

The Hindu pantheon takes various forms. Above the little local
gods some Hindus would set no supreme being. Others identify a
spirit, Brahman, the ground of all being but not himself existing,
certainly not in a material sense. Others, following the Bhagavad-
Gita, might say that he is also all material substance, so that all
creation derives from him. He is then rather like what Aristotle
would call the 'material cause'. Some Hindu philosophers
attribute properties or characteristics to him, some say he can
have nothing of the sort but is some form of infinite bliss or
world consciousness. Brahman can therefore be seen either as a
transcendent or as an immanent reality, in a range of ways which
affect the understanding of the way the world came into being
from or through him.

In trying to describe creation, Hinduism is as comprehensive
as it is possible for any religion to be. It has its busy productive

9. The Hindu god
Vishnu

and squabbling gods. It describes various ways in which large and small creatures came to be: from eggs, from seeds, from the wombs of other creatures, by sweat or effort. In Hindu mythology a great tortoise supports the four elephants on its back, which in turn support the earth. Or the Great Cosmic Tortoise is taken as a framework for the cosmos, with its undershell the earth and its domed shell above forming the heavens. More abstractly, Hinduism recognises the idea of elements or elemental substances, earth, air, water, ether and fire (or 'shining').[4]

Synthesis and transformation of creation mythologies have taken sophisticated modern shapes in novel genres. Rudyard Kipling (1865–1936) was born in India and although he was sent to England for his education, like many other children of British parents who served in British India in Victorian times, he returned to India in 1882 and worked as a sub-editor on the *Civil and Military Gazette*. His father had taught architecture in Bombay and was able to help procure the post for his son. Kipling stayed there for more than six years. When he returned to London in his early twenties, he began to write and publish, including *The Just-So Stories*, with its tales of the origin of various creatures. The stories render something of the essence of what he knew of India, with its mythical stories of the primitive and creation-relations of man and beast and the endless potential of things as they were first made to turn into things as they are now. He is able to treat them as moral tales for Victorian Christian children. But their potential as satire for adults was not lost on George Orwell when he wrote *Animal Farm*.

Bertrand Russell (1872–1970) tried out the elephants and the tortoise in the context of the discussion about the nature of causation, which had been going on at least since Aristotle, and found it wanting:

> If everything must have a cause, then God must have a cause. If there can be anything without a cause, it may just as well be the world as God, so that there cannot be any validity in that argument. It is exactly of the same nature as the Hindu's view, that the world rested upon an elephant and the elephant rested upon a tortoise; and when they said, 'How about the tortoise?' the Indian said, 'Suppose we change the subject.' The argument is really no better than that. There is no reason why the world could not have come into being without a cause; nor, on the other hand, is there any reason why it should not have always existed.

There is no reason to suppose that the world had a beginning at all. The idea that things must have a beginning is really due to the poverty of our imagination. Therefore, perhaps, I need not waste any more time upon the argument about the First Cause.[5]

Moving up and down the ladder of being: the Hermetic tradition

> Plac'd on this isthmus of a middle state,
>
> . . .
>
> He hangs between; in doubt to act, or rest;
> In doubt to deem himself a god, or beast;
>
> . . .
>
> Created half to rise, and half to fall.[6]

An important and philosophically more sophisticated version of the free transitions from one kind of thing to another which mark the polytheistic systems is the idea that a human being can be transformed and move higher or lower in the hierarchy of being. This was one of the beliefs attributed down the centuries to Hermes Trismegistos (Hermes the 'thrice-great'). The origins of this system of belief are probably now impossible to retrieve. He may have been a cultural blend of the Greek messenger god Hermes and the Egyptian god Thoth, as some have suggested.

A body of writings known as the Corpus Hermeticum survives. This was probably written in the early Christian era, and is certainly not of great Egyptian antiquity, as Renaissance Europe thought. Marsilio Ficino (1433–99), who translated most of the Corpus Hermeticum into Latin and launched it on the Renaissance world, claimed that 'Hermes' was older than the Greeks.[7] Giordano Bruno (1548–1600) was one of the most enthusiastic Renaissance adopters. His mistake too was to think Hermetic tradition was the pristine one and not the debased early Christian period stuff it actually seems to be. The contemporary admiration for Egypt was a factor in giving this material its seductive attraction for Renaissance authors. The notion became widely known and a useful literary conceit, as in Sir John Hayward's *David's Tears:*

> And as every kind of beast is principally inclined to one sensuality more than to any other, so man transformeth himself into that beast to whose sensuality lie principally declines.[8]

One of the documents in the Corpus Hermeticum has the title 'Poemandres'. It tells the story of the 'descent' of man to a sinful or 'beastly' state. The story is told by the author as having been revealed to him when, in an experience of something like rapture, he found himself lifted out of his body to a great height. There he heard the voice of a being of huge dimensions who asked him what he would like to know. This Being was Poemandres, the shepherd of men.

The author answers that he wants to know God and to understand the universe and its creation. He is allowed to see all things bathed in light, but then darkness descends and turns into a 'moist stuff' which belches out smoke and groans an inarticulate cry of pain. Then from the light comes a Word, the Logos, which brings the familiar four elements out of this agonised chaos. This light is God the Creator and it is prior to all things; it is Mind and the source of the Word and it is Life.[9]

The author is now able to see that there is a cosmos in the embrace of the all-powerful Creator. He realises that he

10. Unusual depiction of Tara, Bodhisattva of compassion

understands this through the Logos which is Reason. This is the archetypal Form of the cosmos. He sees that Nature, worked upon by the Word, was able to copy the archetypal Form of the cosmos and make a world out of her self.

So, he learns, the frame of things was set, with plain unreasoning matter below. Whatever in the natural creation which was capable of doing so, rose up to be united with the formative mind. The formative mind set the spheres spinning and down below the elements gave rise to the things which are without reason, fish in the water, birds in the air, the animals that walk on the earth. The division of hermaphrodite creatures into male and female pairs followed, and then came the instruction to 'be fruitful and multiply'. Seven planets or Archons act as fates.

Man was the special direct creation of Mind; he is Mind's equal and is in the image of God. Man is able to show the divine form to the rest of creation and creation responds with love. Man alone of all creatures is both mortal and immortal. God loves him.

Poemandres explains how human beings can learn to know themselves and reach the Good, or bend their desire upon their bodies, and then they live in darkness and face death. What does a creature have to do to merit death? Simply to move down towards resembling the original raw matter:

> To this Man-Shepherd said: When the material body is to be dissolved, first thou surrenderest the body by itself unto the work of change, and thus the form thou hadst doth vanish, and thou surrenderest thy way of life, void of its energy, unto the Daimon. The body's senses next pass back into their sources, becoming separate, and resurrect as energies; and passion and desire withdraw unto that nature which is void of reason.
>
> And thus it is that man doth speed his way thereafter upwards through the Harmony.[10]

The 'Sacred sermon', another work in the collection, tells much the same story, again with the personification of powerful abstractions: for example, 'Darkness that knew no bounds was in Abyss, and Water [too] and subtle Breath intelligent; these were by Power of God in Chaos.'[11]

Yet another of these documents, 'To Asclepius', a dialogue between Hermes and Asclepius, discusses the idea of the Creator as Prime Mover, that which moves all things which are moved, and which must logically be more powerful and greater than the things it moves. Again, philosophical reasoning is applied to a deification of abstract ideas. The cosmos is a huge 'body'. But that which moves it and that in which it moves must be unimaginably more vast. Yet space cannot, it seems, be a body, for bodies must be able to move about in it. Air *is* a body, for although things do move in the air, the air can blow in the form of winds and act as a sort of solid. If we think of space as a spiritual substance, or as an energy, or even as a world consisting in thought, or as God himself, it becomes possible to imagine how bodies can move in it, or in him.

The Prime Mover cannot itself move. Other things, the spheres of the planets, move in relation to this supreme fixity, and in relation to one another:

> 'Tis Mind and Reason (*Logos*), whole out of whole, all self-embracing, free from all body, from all error free, unsensible to body and untouchable, self stayed in self, containing all, preserving those that are, whose rays, to use a likeness, are Good, Truth, Light beyond light, the Archetype of soul.

> Asclepius: What, then, is God?
> Hermes: Not any one of these is He; for He it is that causeth them to be, both all and each and every thing of all that are. Nor hath He left a thing beside that is-not; but they are all from things-that-are and not from things-that-are-not. For that the things-that-are-not have naturally no power of being anything, but naturally have the power of the inability-to-be. And, conversely, the things-that-are have not the nature of some time not-being.
> Asclepius: What say'st thou ever, then, God is?
> Hermes: God, therefore, is not Mind, but Cause that the Mind is; God is not Spirit, but Cause that Spirit is; God is not Light, but Cause that the Light is. Hence one should honour God with these two names [the Good and Father] – names which pertain to Him alone and no one else.[12]

Versions of 'To Asclepius' and the 'Perfect sermon' were translated into Latin in the ancient world, possibly by Apuleius (*c.*125–80 BC), the author of *The Golden Ass*, which is full of tales of amusing transformations. The Christian author Lactantius (*c.*240–320), himself a North African, mentions Hermes, and Asclepius' 'Perfect sermon', in connection with the idea that demons can enter statues and inhabit them.[13]

This North African connection may be a route by which Augustine of Hippo learned of the Hermetic ideas, for Apuleius too was a North African, from Madaura. It is this old Latin translation Augustine quotes in *The City of God*. He describes what Hermes Trismegistos said about demons. Apuleius says the demons are not gods but have a position in the cosmos midway between gods and men. Hermes says some minor gods are made by the Creator and some 'made' by human beings, who make statues and invite spirits to come and live in them. Augustine suggests that these may have been evil spirits. These evil-spirited statues then mislead their worshippers into adoring them instead of God and into wrongdoing to please them.[14]

A sermon in the Corpus Hermeticum on how the unknowable God may be known contains the Hermetic 'argument from design'.[15] It describes how the wonderfulness of created things can teach the observer about the Creator. Renaissance scholars were tempted to conjure with notions their orthodox Christian

11. Detail of the relief of the 'Tomb of the Harpies' from Xanthos, Turkey

faith would frown on.[16] This all had extensive potential for making polytheism's creation stories and several branches of dubious 'science' look respectable in the Western intellectual tradition. When Isaac Newton dabbled in astrology and alchemy he was a late follower of this Renaissance fashion[17] which had borrowed from Hermetic influences and which included briefly included magic in the catalogue of respectable studies for that reason (for more on magic and mystery, see Chapter 6 (iii)).

II. MONOTHEISMS

Judaism is a religion of a particular people, and of their laws and culture. This discouraged any missionary activity. The coming of missionary-minded early Christianity, which adopted the Old Testament as part of its own sacred literature, inevitably brought the Jewish creation story into Christianity. There it was subjected it to Christian interpretations and given a wider dissemination, as is apparent throughout this book. Christianity and Judaism both stood out in the early Christian period because they would not compromise the oneness of God, and that led to their persecution by the civil authorities, who required worship of the Roman emperor. Islam began after the collapse of the Roman Empire so it did not face the same challenge. Christianity and Islam, but not Judaism, were missionary religions from their very beginnings.

In the religions which regard the Old Testament as a sacred text the story recorded in Genesis is the starting-point for thinking about the origins of the universe and the creation of the earth and its creatures. Judaism, Christianity and Islam developed and interpreted the Genesis story of creation in different ways. The huge influence of these three religions and their common Old Testament creation-story heritage in the history of thought and belief throughout the world make them of immense importance to the history of explanations of creation.

The creation story of Judaism and Christianity

The book of Genesis was probably written between the eighth and the tenth centuries BC. In the story as it is told in the first chapter, the Creator, here called Elohim, 'makes' the world by 'saying so',

over six 'days', and he does it sequentially step by step. On the
first three days the cosmos is divided and the earth given its broad
arrangement. On the first day darkness is separated from light;
on the second day air and water are separated, on the third day,
land and sea. The heavenly bodies are positioned on the fourth
day. Then on successive days creatures are brought into being, to
dwell in each element-area of the earth.[18] On the fifth birds are
made for the air and fish for the sea; on the sixth, the land is filled
with animals and the final creatures made; of these, the highest is
mankind. Then Elohim rests for a seventh 'day'.

In the story as told in the second chapter of Genesis, the
Creator is called Yahweh. This Yahweh is a fierce and jealous
Creator, always consistent, making laws which must be obeyed, and
exacting a terrible penalty if they are not. A hierarchy of creatures
is described. They are created in sequence, with human beings last,
and highest. The other creatures are made for the service and use
of humankind. Yahweh makes man from the earth and breathes
life into him. Woman is made from the rib or side of the first man,
created to be his companion. The man and the woman are given
the Garden of Eden to live in. The first man, Adam, names the
animals[19] and is put in charge of them upon the earth. There are
rules these first people must obey, namely not to eat the fruit of a
particular tree. When they do so, they are punished, driven out of
the garden. The whole world is altered by their sinning. Thorns
and thistles spring from the earth. They themselves will in future
have to work for a living. Their innocence is irretrievably lost.

Judaism and Christianity followed this disaster through in
different ways in their account of what the Creator did about it.
In Judaism, the Creator made a covenant with his creatures, and
obeying his law became of central importance to pleasing him.
According to the Christians he sent his Son, the Logos, to make a
supreme sacrifice in order to put things right.

The creation story in Islam

The book of Genesis provides a creation story from which Islam
also drew, in the Qur'an. The Qur'an is not prescriptive about the
'days' of creation and what happened on each. It mentions two
and four, though it also says there were six (41.9–12). The Creator
was Allah, with no Logos or Christ-figure and no Holy Spirit or
World Soul involved. The Qur'an describes the creation of human

12. Adam and Eve and their
thirteen twins, from *Zubdet ut
Tevarih* by Lokman

beings from a lump of matter (23.12–14) and describes Adam and
Eve as being created in heaven (2.36), or possibly in a Garden
like the Garden of Eden, and then moved to earth as a form of
banishment. Jesus is a created being in the Qur'an (3.59).

The Creator's forming of the cosmos with its stars and planets
proved to be an area of particular interest to Arab astronomers in
later centuries. Abu Nasr al-Farabi (*c.*870–950) was one of the Arabic
scholars who were translating and studying the ancient Greek
philosophers centuries before the Latin-speaking West had direct
access to Plato and to much of Aristotle in the original language.[20]

The objective of this Islamic scholarship was to reconcile
Greek thought with the teaching of the Qur'an, especially with
belief in one God. For, they found, Greek philosophy at its most
sophisticated was monotheistic too, and Greek thought had plenty
to say about the idea that the one God was the cause of all things.
Islam responded positively to a number of these Greek ideas.
Al-Farabi lists some of them, emphasising that there is common
ground in the idea that the Creator remains essentially detached
from matter, and that he works by 'intellect'. 'The First is not

in matter and has itself no matter in any way whatsoever.' It is 'actual intellect'. 'The First is that from which everything which exists comes into existence . . . by way of an emanation.' Matter is inferior stuff in creation. It exists only to give body to forms. 'Matter exists for the sake of form, and if there were not form in existence, matter could not exist.'[21]

Al-Farabi also warmed to the idea that the Creator did not create the world out of neediness. 'But the First does not exist for the sake of anything else and not in order that anything else should be brought into existence by it.'[22]

Adopting a classical Greek cosmos, al-Farabi describes the world above the moon and the nine planetary spheres, the 'sublunary bodies', the 'elements', 'minerals . . . plants . . . animals including those which have speech and thought'.[23]

As for human beings, they are created as animals, but as animals with the distinction of being reasonable. 'Once man comes to be' he first eats, then feels through the senses and then becomes rational.[24]

Creation in Sikhism

Sikhism was in principle a missionary religion from the first but it really began to spread only in the nineteenth century, as Sikhs emigrated from Punjab to work in other countries. Then it began to attract converts. Sikhism is a monotheism whose God is infinite and omnipresent and eternal. Before the world was created he was.[25] Creation was an act of his divine will. Sikhism came relatively late to the world religious stage.

In fifteenth-century Punjab the young guru Nanak Dev Ji had a moment of revelation which led him to claim that neither of the religions then general among his people, Hinduism nor Islam, was teaching the truth. Other gurus followed him, the last of whom died in 1708, and the 'ten gurus' became the authority-figures of the new religion. The Guru Granth Sahib created by the guru Gobin Singh became the authoritative scripture of Sikhism and itself the tenth guru.

Sikhism is a religion of right conduct. The believer should live a life of faith in which meditation plays an important part, because it allows the believer to develop an inner eye, 'communicate' with God and grow towards enlightenment. Inwardness is all. Outward rituals are of no value, though the Sikh should practise charity and work for the common good. Salvation consists in achieving union with God.

The Sikh is to pursue the truth and live truthfully. It is a truth that all human beings are equal and Sikhism teaches tolerance of other faiths. It does not require asceticism or self-denial, though attachment to worldly things is thought to get in the way, because it promoted the five 'evils' of greed, attachment, inappropriate longings or lust, egotism and anger. The human being who fails to achieve enlightenment and union will be reincarnated. The body is a mere vehicle.

III. DUALISMS

That peculiar gnostic hate of the world and of creation.[26]

Dualist beliefs about creation embody what are essentially 'two-power' theories. Instead of a single Creator, two are envisaged, with opposing preferences and objectives. They are potentially equal. Either could 'win' control of the universe. The believer is invited to prefer one to the other and to support what is almost a 'team' or an 'army' struggling for a victory which will determine the future of the universe. Creation is therefore regarded as a battle, from its inception to the present time, for the believer still has a part to play in deciding the outcome.

The Christian doctrine of the 'fall of Satan' presents a variant. Satan is depicted as an angel, a creature of the one God and sole Creator. He and certain of the other angels have 'fallen' by opposing their wills in some way to the will of the Creator. A common version has them aspiring to be more like the Creator than they possibly can be since they are mere creatures. The Creator punishes them by casting them from his presence, or they punish themselves, turning their backs on God. Satan, disguised as a serpent, tempts the first woman, Eve, and the first man, Adam, to disobey the Creator's command.[27] So sin comes to earth. Resentful fallen angels still try to seduce human beings into joining them, setting themselves against the Creator in the same way. In this version of the dualist story the rebels cannot win but the consequential damage to Creation is great and lasting.

The tradition that matter is bad and spirit is good – and that spirit mingles with matter only reluctantly – is found in many cultures.

This mingling is always to the detriment of the spiritual because the soul is tugged into bad habits by fleshly lust. Various forms of what was essentially the same explanation have been offered down the centuries. Good and evil, light and darkness, spirit and matter have been paired and opposed, with good, light and spirit always on the same side, or even treated as interchangeable.

This primordial polarisation of spirit and matter at the creation is also linked in many creation stories with the separation of light and darkness. For example, a Zoroastrian version of the creation story emphasises the duality of light and darkness, good and evil. Zoroaster, founder of Zoroastrianism, who gave his 'revelation' to the peoples of Central Asia, taught that Ahura Mazda is the uncreated Creator, the good, truth, light, and he counters forces in the universe pushing the other way. Mithraism, a religion probably derived from Hinduism, with its origins in Persia, associates light with the good, Azda is a god of light, a god of truth, a god not in the ancient Aryan pantheon, a quite different sort of god. As light he prompts growth and health; he promotes peace and spirituality. These effects are in fundamental opposition to darkness, barrenness, suffering, vice, impurity.[28]

The war of good and evil

Dualist explanations of creation have varied in their details, but they have had certain things in common. They have all taken it that there is a bad as well as a good power. One of the most important repeating themes in many cultures is the idea that the universe is the scene of a war between good and evil, which are fighting for ultimate control of the universe. In the Gnosticism and the Manichaeism of the early Christian period and the Catharism and Albigensianism of the Middle Ages, even in the witchcraft of early modern times, occur stories of cosmic battles. What is witchcraft, but the view that if there is war between good and evil and evil might win, Satan's followers may have an enjoyable time being wicked in his service and ultimately be the victors?

In this war, the disciple or believer must take sides and can contribute to the outcome by his or her personal behaviour. This durability and persuasiveness of 'dualist' explanations of the way creation occurred can partly be explained by the way it helps explain the 'divided' feeling many people (and peoples) have described, in which their good intentions (spiritual) seem to be

frustrated by their bodily appetites (material). On the assumption
that matter is evil rests the idea that abstinence from bodily
pleasures in general is virtuous, or morally beneficial. Asceticism
was highly respected in the late antique world. Porphyry, in *On
Abstinence from Animal Food*, written late in the third century AD,
assembled the arguments for and against as they stood in his times.
He himself favours vegetarianism but he knows that nomads and
troglodytes, who eat nothing but meat, can be nice people and live
good lives.[29] Sexual abstinence entered into Christian monasticism
in the form of a vow of chastity.

There were dualist 'scriptures' – for example, those of the
Manichaeans[30] – but no single authoritative text emerged which
could form a point of reference for a dualist 'orthodoxy'. Perhaps
there were too many characters moving in and out of the plot
for consistency to be expected, and in any case mythologies have
always tended to set little store by consistency.

The cosmic beings who were characters in the battle stories
could relatively easily be identified with figures in a local pantheon
or in more abstract terms, as concepts in a philosophical system.
In some versions of the creation story, the 'good' is identified as
a cluster of powers, a 'side' in the war, or a 'team'. In this team
there was a great father-figure. There were five intellectual aspects
of his greatness: personified versions of 'reason' or *nous*, mind,
intelligence, thought and understanding. There were a primal
spirit, a mother, personified elements who could be regarded as
sons of the father (water, fire, light, ether, wind) or as a composite
being or son or self.

This first creation process is then followed in some tales by
another. The second creation was to determine whether the world
was to be run for the benefit of the sons of light or the sons of
darkness. Immense forces are invoked, holding things in their
right or 'good' position in the form of gods or heroes who hold
up the heavens or support worlds. The Greek Atlas is an example.
In the world of light, then comes a third creation, in which a
Christ-figure is sent to rescue Adam and Eve, the endangered first
humans, and bring them to the light. Meanwhile in the world
of darkness, there is a king, with under him powers ruling five
kingdoms which are the counterpart of the five intellectual goods.
This king also has a son. There are anti-humans in this dark world
too, and fallen angels. Polytheistic elements are mingled in this
partly Christianised tale. There are twelve signs of the Zodiac, or
virgins. There is a just outcome and the good triumphs.

Gnosticism is a collection of beliefs, probably drawing on several oriental religions and emerging as a contemporary influence about the time when Christianity began. Especially important may have been Mazdaism, with its concept of the war of good and evil, though most of the surviving 'gnostic' texts have links with Alexandrian Egypt.

Still other creation myths try to explain how the world came to be riven with disputes and full of dangers. An epic of creation survives from Mesopotamia which describes a war of good and evil among the gods; in this the goddess of the sea is the villainess. She is defeated and torn into two parts, one of which becomes the earth and the other the heavens. The victors then put order into the universe, giving the planets and stars their places and pathways and establishing a human society as a counterpart to the kingdom of the gods in heaven.

One leading idea in all these stories was that they help to account for life's pain and suffering. Disciples naturally wished to escape this discomfort, and some thought they could do this through magic or through astrological devices; some thought there was a saviour.

Mani and the Manichaeans

One historically important strand of dualism providing Gnosticism with a clear focus came from Persia, where its prophet was known as Mani (c. AD 216–76). Manichaeism, like Zoroastrianism, was a cult with a drama. A cast of cosmic beings fought on behalf of good and evil; light and darkness, spirit and matter were at war, and here too the fight was for ultimate superiority in the universe. This battle was itself a great creative act, for it would determine what kind of world there would be and who would control it.

Manichaeism became widespread from the fourth century. It penetrated into the Far East, where Manichaeans could still be found in the fourteenth century. It spread towards the western end of the North African coast, where it captivated the young Augustine, later bishop of Hippo, and held his interest and respect for nearly ten years.

Augustine gives us an idea of the content of Mani's 'Epistola fundamenti' ('Fundamental epistle')[31] in the extensive writings he poured out against the Manichaeans once he fell out of love with their ideas and became a Christian. His disillusion set in when the great leader Faustus arrived in North Africa and Augustine, who had long waited for his arrival so as to learn the answers to his own burning questions, discovered that he himself was cleverer than Faustus.

This 'Fundamental epistle' was one of the candidates for a 'holy book' because some saw it as an 'authoritative text' from a prophet of the movement. Augustine describes Mani's account of the birth of Adam and Eve, 'whether they were produced by a word or from matter'. He mocks his claim that there was a great battle 'before the framing of the world'. Mani claims that in the beginning the father was eternal light and good and wisdom.[32] How does he know? Augustine enquires.

One of the most important shifts of fundamental position Augustine helped to bring about in Western Christian thought was to rearrange the elements in the dualist explanation. For the Augustine who in 386 became a converted Christian, there could be only one God, the supreme God, who created everything which exists from nothing. That includes matter, which is therefore not a 'bad' thing, and bodies, which are therefore also no longer to be regarded as inherently 'bad' in contrast with spirits (good) – though Augustine had his lingering reservations about the tendency of sensual appetites to lead into sin – and even darkness.

This left Augustine, and the Cathars, Bogomils and Albigensian dualist 'heretics' who appeared at intervals down the medieval centuries, with the problem of evil. If God is all-powerful and all-good and nothing exists which he has not made, what is evil and where does it come from? We shall come to that problem in more detail in Chapter 6.

New turnings in the dualist maze?

> The Authority, God, the Creator, the Lord, Yahweh, El, Adonai, the King, the Father, the Almighty – those were all names he gave himself. He was never the creator. He . . . was formed of Dust . . . and Dust is only a name for what happens when matter begins to understand itself. Matter loves matter. It seeks to know more about itself and Dust is formed.[33]

Even this modern attempt by the novelist Philip Pullman to propose a fresh possibility is not really so new. In the seventeenth century John Donne discusses 'what this Action, which is . . . called a *Moving*, was', 'whether it was a stirring, and an awakening of a power that was naturally in those waters, to produce creatures, or whether it were an infusing a new power, which until then those waters had not, hath likewise been disputed'.[34]

Before Donne, in the fifth century, Augustine had tried to find a way to put substantially the same question. Donne approved Augustine's view[35] that 'all was embowelled, and enwombed in the waters' but preferred the view that this was the moment of the 'creating of nature' and that

> the Spirit of God produced them then, and established and conserves ever since, that seminall power which we call nature, to produce all creatures (then first made by himself) in a perpetuall succession.[36]

Was Pullman's Dust-with-curiosity the same thing as primal matter or Chaos? It seems to be 'without form and void' until it begins to ask questions about itself and becomes (perhaps) conscious. It does not seem to be much of a person.

4

Choosing an approach

I. CLASSICAL PHILOSOPHY

The gods of Egypt took an interest in supervising the conduct of the human race as part of their follow-through of creation, says Diodorus Siculus (or Diodorus of Sicily, fl. 60–30 BC). Osiris made people give up cannibalism. He and the goddess Isis provided fruit and vegetables to eat instead. Diodorus explains that Egyptians commemorate all this in their harvest festivals and tell local stories of the contributions of other gods. The god Hermes gave language to mankind; invented writing; designed the mathematical rules which give harmony to music and made musical instruments; invented reasoning and taught people to discuss and debate. Here was a god of wisdom and prudence. All the arts and activities of humanity are thus turned into divine gifts, for which the generous god in question deserves thanks and respect.

These gods did not restrict themselves to Egypt and its affairs. Osiris (the originally 'human' Osiris who became a god) went through Ethiopia and Arabia into India and took up hunting elephants. So a world sphere of influence is established. And these are gods with stories – often archetypal stories – woven into the commemoration of all sorts of events, including battles in which rival powers find their places in the great scheme of things. They are gods eager to participate in human affairs, not gods who, having made the world, sat back.

In Diodorus' day, the modern subject-divisions of 'philosophy', 'science' and 'theology' did not exist. Though it had its departments and specialist areas, knowledge formed a continuum in which these different methods of study were not formally distinguished in any consistent way. Diodorus could tell his tales using colourful stories as a garment in which to wrap quite demanding arguments

about the need for intellectual effort in understanding how the
world began and how it is run. No one would accuse him of being
'unscientific' or 'unorthodox' if he used such illustrative devices.

Nevertheless, authors who have written about the creation and
running of the world down the ages have tried to establish what
kind of account they are giving. Are they appealing to people's
beliefs or to their love of beauty or amusement, or to their powers
of reasoning, they wonder? Are they offering hard evidence
or spiritual or even emotional satisfaction? Are they seeking to
comfort or to frighten, to inspire awe or a sense of familiarity, to
scale creation up or down as a phenomenon?

Philosophical discussions about the beginning of the world in
classical Greek and Roman philosophy brought certain topics to
the forefront. These philosophers say they had drawn some of
their ideas from Eastern philosophies and religions, so this was
not in its origins just a European set of explanations. Themes were

13. The Ancient
Egyptian goddess
Bes

tossed from hand to hand, mind to mind, never finally resolved and always ready to crop up again in discussion.

They became frequent topics for dinner-party conversation, as Plato's *Symposium* and Macrobius' *Saturnalia* illustrate. Plato's *Symposium*, set in *c.*400 BC, describes a drinking party, at which those present make speeches about love. The first speaker, Phaedrus, explores the idea that Eros, the god of love, is the very first of the gods and had no parents. In the *Saturnalia*,[1] which pretends to be an account of a fifth-century AD dinner party held on the Roman feast of the god Saturn, the guests begin in Book I by trying to show that all religions derive from sun worship, and from there they go on to talk of many things.

The earliest Greek philosophers: the mathematical approach

John Milton draws a vivid picture of the Creator as geometer, drawing a vast circle in the void to set the bounds of the universe and then those of the earth within it:

> He took the golden Compasses, prepar'd
> In Gods Eternal store, to circumscribe
> This Universe, and all created things:
> One foot he center'd, and the other turn'd
> Round through the vast profunditie obscure,
> And said, thus farr extend, thus farr thy bounds,
> This be thy just Circumference, O World.
> Thus God the Heav'n created, thus the Earth
> He is not clear about the origin of the 'matter':
> Matter unform'd and void: Darkness profound
> Cover'd th' Abyss.
> He is clear that the mathematics is fundamental:
> And Earth self ballanc't on her Center hung.[2]

From the first, Greek philosophers seem to have been interested in how the world began and they tended to see it in mathematical terms. Later writers reported the views of those who left no written legacy. Thales (*c.*611–545 BC) – of whose actual words nothing survives – was credited by Proclus (AD 412–85) with the invention of geometric theorems and an emphasis on the fundamentally mathematical character of the structure of the universe. Even the notions of infinity and eternity are understood as the absence of bounds and measures, and therefore in terms of mathematical assumptions. Anaximander (c.610–c.546 BC) seems to have been the first to suggest there might be infinity at the 'beginning' of things and that the beginning was actually not a beginning at all because that which has no boundaries cannot ever have had a beginning (though the fragment of his writing which has come down by report tries to describe this in terms as much poetic as philosophical).

Pythagoras (c.570–495 BC) was the focus of many ancient legends, some of which said he was taught by Egyptians, some by the Greeks. The Neoplatonist Porphyry wrote a *Life of Pythagoras*[3] in which he is described[4] as studying with the Egyptians and also with the Arabians and Babylonians (where he conferred with the Chaldeans) and learning their theories of the world and nature and its origins. None of Pythagoras' writings survives, but he too gained a reputation for establishing a number of mathematical principles as fundamental to the way the world was formed and continues.

Anaximenes was another 'pre-Socratic' philosopher of whose work only fragments survive. He seems to have tried to explain how things began by looking for some all-purpose 'stuff' from which everything in creation might have come. The answer seemed to him to be air. Air can be more or less dense, he suggested. Rarified, it becomes fire. Dense, it is wind or cloud, or, progressively growing denser, water or earth or rocks. This description of a possibility of change did not include an explanation of why change might take place or by what mechanisms or at what promptings. But it allowed him to visualise the earth as a disk of denser air floating in the general surrounding air.[5]

Empedocles (b. c.490 BC) was a Sicilian, a believer in the four elements of earth, air, water and fire as the ultimate ingredients of everything in the physical world. He took the universe to be a sphere, but a sphere in continuous cyclical change as Love and Conflict strove for dominance, and the way things were was reversed and then reversed again.

These tantalisingly fragmentary reports suggest that the fundamental questions which were being asked as philosophical thought on the Greek model evolved had already identified themes which were going to reappear generation by generation. These first philosophers were interested in what there was before there was anything, what sort of stuff was needed to make a world, whether the process was governed by rules, especially mathematical rules.

Aristotle

With Aristotle (384–322 BC)[6] we are on firmer ground of record because of the number of his surviving writings, even if some of them read like the untidy lecture notes they probably were. He held that there must have been some primordial stuff, for there could, he argued, have been no creation from nothing. In his *On the Heavens* Aristotle starts from the foundation principles of Pythagorean mathematics, with its ideas about the nature of number (that is, multitude) and of magnitude, and their implications for an understanding of the way things must be in the universe.

On these foundations he builds his claim that the 'primary body' must be eternal, and incapable of growing or shrinking or altering in any way. He cites in further evidence the common experience of all mankind. All seem to have a conception of 'deity' as something which is higher than humanity and immortal; and all recognise that history seems to show that the heavens have always looked the same and appear to be everlasting.[7]

He also finds strong and persuasive the argument that a 'simple' body, as he believes this primal universe must be, must also be 'simple' in its motions. This happy acceptance that what is elegant is likely to be true is characteristic of the classical Greek philosopher. He postulates two and only two fundamental 'motions'. One is circular motion (for the heavens rotate). The other kind of motion is centripetal and centrifugal force: motion to and from a centre. This is all very geometrical, or astronomical, a matter of 'magnitudes in motion', rather in the spirit of Pythagorean mathematics as it was later related by Nichomachus of Gerasa (*c.* AD 60–120) in his book on arithmetic.[8]

In *On the Heavens*, Aristotle goes on to consider whether the universe is an infinite body (which is what he says most earlier philosophers thought). He sets out, again mathematically, the reasons why he thinks it must be finite. Then he turns to whether there can be multiple or infinite universes and again his answer is no. There can be only one.[9] This conclusion was to be questioned, and it still is. The answer is of enormous importance because much of the reasoning from 'nature', much of the argument that the Creator must be thus on the evidence of the print he has left on what we can see, depends on there being only the one world the human observer inhabits. If there could be any number of other worlds, all perhaps unimaginably different, the chains and threads of reasoning break off and fray. Apparent certainties fade.

Aristotle sees things teleologically, in terms of their purposes and ends, as moving to a final fulfilment of the potential that was in their beginning. The Aristotelian theory of causation was also immensely influential in this connection (see Chapter 3 (i)).

The first cause (which is 'final' in the sense of being the ultimate beginning) is the Prime Mover. Behind him is no infinite regress. The Prime Mover alone is self-moving. All other things are moved. With this explanation in the *Metaphysics*[10] goes another in the *Physics*, where Aristotle puts forward the idea of a Prime Mover which is original, the source of all motion, but never itself moved. That need not mean that the creation does not change and move.[11]

In the *Metaphysics*[12] and his writing on growing and shrinking, Aristotle also explores the various possible ways of 'coming to be'. In *On Generation and Corruption,* he also considers the manner in which things decay or cease to be. This imports a dynamic into the discussion of the way things are, which was to be of importance in later thinking about a creation in which the Creator did not simply make the world and leave it to its devices but superintends those 'devices' in some way.

The cosmos, Aristotle argues, has a region beyond the moon and a region under the moon where we live. In our part of the cosmos things are made of the four elements. Beyond the moon, the stars are made of an ether, later classified as a fifth 'element'. This grows ever purer and more refined the further it is in 'outer space' and thus more distant from the earth.

Plato

The thought of Plato gave rise to two influential but essentially different accounts of creation. The first is his own account in the *Timaeus*. The second is a version articulated by 'Neoplatonists' who developed his ideas in later centuries, which will be described later. This is the theory that creation was an overflowing of divine goodness, out of sheer generosity. That is the 'Platonist' explanation of the way anything more than the Creator ever came to be without diminishing his celestial dignity. Otherwise the multiplication of things we know in creation would have to be the result of some sort of inner divine catastrophe, a divine restlessness, hunger and need seeking satisfaction, rather than an act of divine generosity in which there is no neediness.

Plato presents his companion in the dialogue *Timaeus* as an astronomer. Timaeus, says Socrates, 'has made the nature of the universe his special study'.[13] In the *Timaeus* dialogue he is invited to explain how the world began. He begins by distinguishing between those things reason can 'apprehend', which are changeless, and what is known only by sense-perception, which is in a state of perpetual flux. This presents the puzzle whether the world as we can perceive it through our senses – the bodily world – is always there, changeless, or did it have a beginning and enter into a changeable state?

What is must have a cause. Here Plato agrees with Aristotle. But Plato had a higher sense of the kind of supremacy appropriate to a supreme being (and he feared it might be an insult to that supremacy even to speak of him as 'being' in any way we can understand). A Creator able to cause what we see in this world is surely beyond finding by direct inquiry. Or if he could be met with that way, he is surely beyond description. What we can examine and test by sense perception is always, for Plato, at a lower level than that ultimate reality.

Nevertheless, we can reasonably ask what choices the Creator made when he caused things to be in the created world. For example, it was the Creator's choice whether to make the world unchangeable or not. This task Timaeus approaches by asking what was probable. Timaeus assumes the eternal to be better than the short term and finite. If the Creator was good, he would choose to do the best thing and make an eternal world. On the other hand, to be a copy is not to be the original and there are various ways in which the creature may be said to be 'like' the Creator and ways in which it may not. If the creature and the Creator were identical at every point the creature would 'be' the Creator. So the creation need not be changeless and eternal.

Such a world as the Creator makes will tend to resemble him and therefore provide clues to what he is like. It is possible to reason about it and come to some conclusions by analogy about the behaviour of the Creator who made it. 'As being is to becoming, so is truth to belief.'[14] Why did the Creator make the world? He was good. The good are not jealous. The good want to be generous. The best he could do was to share himself, by making a creation like himself and able to enjoy its life or existence, within its creaturely limitations, as he does. So the world as God made it is good, beautiful, a place of truth, justice and mercy, exemplifying all the divine attributes of the highest good himself, which, for the Platonist, become one in him.

Yet Plato's Creator in the *Timaeus* is only an *opifex*, a craftsman. He does not create the universe from nothing. He merely determines the shape a pre-existing primordial matter is to take by applying to it eternal pre-existing forms, patterns or ideas. He casts the matter into moulds. He imposes order where before there was a shapeless jumble and the order is itself a great good. So Plato's story in the *Timaeus* sees the Creator as more like a workman who, when he takes it into his head to make something other than himself, finds pre-existing primordial matter waiting for him and also a convenient set of primordial forms or ideas, ready-made designs and patterns. All the craftsman Creator has to do is to put matter into the mould and there is an elephant or a cabbage or a human being.

Plato adopts certain rules as self-evident truths. One is to deem rational creatures better than unintelligent ones. Another is to accept that reason and intelligence must reside in the soul, so rational beings must have souls, as well as bodies for the souls to live in. Plato agreed with Genesis and the ensuing Christian tradition in seeing the creation of the world as the act of a benevolent and all-powerful Creator, who made it for good reasons. Because these are reasons, they can be understood at least up to a point by rational creatures. Reason is reasonable absolutely and everywhere:

> Why did the Creator make the world? . . . He was good, and therefore not jealous, and being free from jealousy he desired that all things should be like himself. Wherefore he set in order the visible world, which he found in disorder. Now he who is the best could only create the fairest; and reflecting that of visible things the intelligent is superior to the unintelligent, he put intelligence in soul and soul in body, and framed the universe to be the best and fairest work in the order of nature, and the world became a living soul through the providence of God.[15]

Essential to this view of a Creator who could not make anything which was not the best was the orderliness and beauty of creation. This idea and this emphasis was imported into Christian thinking in the first Christian centuries and did not seem to be in conflict with Genesis, though Genesis does not speak in terms of divine rationality. Plato disagreed with Genesis and the Christian tradition and regarded the Creator as a mere craftsman or 'artificer' who takes existing matter and forms it according to an existing pattern ('form' or the Platonic 'idea'). 'All that becomes and is created is the work of a cause, and that is fair which the artificer makes after an eternal pattern':

There is a universal nature out of which all things are made, and which is like none of them; but they enter into and pass out of her, and are made after patterns of the true in a wonderful and inexplicable manner.[16]

Yet this Creator who stands so high in Plato's conceptual as well as physical universe, remained a mere craftsman, for he did not make the world from nothing and he did not control the kinds of things which could be made. Those were dictated by the forms in something of the way envisaged by Charles Williams:

He remembered the Hand thrust out from a cloud in many an early painting to image the Power behind creation, and the hand that lay open before him seemed meant to receive that creation as it came into being. He saw . . . that the Stone no longer rested on the table but that it threw out of itself colour shaped into the table: the walls and furniture were in themselves reflections of that Centre in which they secretly existed; they were separations, forms, and clouded visibilities of its elements . . . The stone quivered with its own intense and hidden life.[17]

This principle he applies to the macrocosm of the world itself as well as to certain of the creatures within it, so that the world itself is a body with a soul, the *anima mundi*. The created world, Plato thought, writing about it in the *Timaeus*, must be 'bodily', made of the four elements and able to be perceived by the senses. It must also be united by harmonies and proportions. It should ideally be symmetrical and unitary and smooth. What form was it appropriate for that world-body to take? The best possible form was a sphere, with no hands and feet needed. God made this sphere and infused it with a soul – which has reason as well as harmony – though not in a sequence, for the soul is a higher and more excellent thing than a body, so it had to be prior to the body. Plato includes a detailed discussion of the mathematics and ratios of planetary motions.

Plato's reasoning took him further. He argued that the 'form' of the world must have been 'the form of the perfect animal' and that was a 'whole', which 'contained all intelligible beings, and the visible animal, made after the pattern of this, included all visible creatures'.[18]

This would have to be a sphere, he thought:

And as he was to contain all things, he was made in the all-containing form of a sphere, round as from a lathe and every way equidistant from the centre, as was natural and suitable to him. He was finished and smooth, having neither eyes nor ears, for there was nothing without him which he could see or hear; and he had no need to carry food to his mouth, nor was there air for him to breathe; and he did not require hands, for there was nothing of which he could take hold, nor feet, with which to walk. All that he did was done rationally in and by himself, and he moved in a circle turning within himself, which is the most intellectual of motions; but the other six motions were wanting to him; wherefore the universe had no feet or legs.[19]

This sphere with its body and soul would have to be a single whole, comprehending all creation. (This also seems to Timaeus an argument against the possibility that there could be more than one world. The elegance of unity and simplicity is strong with his mind.)

Plato also thought that there could be only one created universe. If there was more than one, the plural worlds would be part of a greater world which 'contained' them 'and therefore there is logically, and will ever be, but one created world'.[20]

The creation of each departure in this created world from the one, the eternal, the boundless, is taken to import its own distinctive features. Days and nights and months and years came with time, and time came with movement, for that means there is before and after. Number arrived too, with the sun and moon and five planets, the multiple orbits of the heavens, and also location.

There is also a possibility of created things 'becoming' and thus growing and changing. One of the ways this happens in Timaeus' account is by a process of personification. Hermes and Lucifer appear in the narrative. The moving stars become 'living creatures' with bodies, chained to their paths and orbits. Under the Creator's hand there come to be animals. These are of four sorts, each appropriate to one of the four elements: the gods in the fiery heavens; the birds who live in air; the creatures which live in water; and those who walk on land.

Plato argues that since it is a good thing for the universe to contain all the kinds of creature it ought to contain, all these must have come into being. To his way of thinking, the Creator cannot be changed by the creation. One sort of created thing would be made by the Creator himself, but such a being would be immortal.

His suggestion is that the Creator poured into a vessel the soul of the universe and mingled it with the remainder of the elements. The resulting individual souls were fragments of the world soul, each in a body. These souls were assigned to individual stars and they had revealed to them the laws of destiny.

He reviews the possible kinds of mortal beings which the Creator could have made. To be mortal, he argues, creatures would have to be created by a creature. So each of these stars was entrusted with the making of its own kind of mortal being, by some form of dilution of itself.

Their bodily nature gave these mortal creatures sensations and emotions. The turbulence of these emotions subsides as they settle down after coming into being. If they live their mortal lives well they will be elevated to live in their native stars. If not, they will be reborn as women and if they fail again, as successively lowlier creatures still. (There is a foretaste here of an idea which became controversial in Christian theology down the centuries, that attaining heaven required good behaviour and individual progress.)

Why are humans the shape they are? Tumbling or rotating spheres are a good shape for stars but humans need to be able to walk about on the ground so they need legs for locomotion. The front is better than the back so we move forward and look forwards. We have forward-looking faces in which are all the features we need to minister to the needs of the soul. We have, for example, eyes which let light into the soul.

So far Plato has been talking of the higher forms of created being, in which there is soul and intelligence. But he also discusses the 'essentials', created things which are simply necessary to the whole project of creation. This is a kind of container or context of all else. From it emerge the four elements. It is as though water when condensed becomes earth and air when heated becomes fire, which when condensed and compressed becomes water, and so on.

There is a shift in the reasoning at certain points, from the philosophical – what can be ascertained by pure reasoning on self-evident first principles – to the historical. Timaeus accepts that not all details can be worked out by pure thought. 'We must accept what has been handed down from old times,' what those who claimed to be the offspring of the gods have said. They must know what their ancestors were like. There can be no secure proofs, but it is the custom to accept the accounts of those who speak of their own families.[21]

These ideas, chiefly compounded of reasoning on a set of pre-sumptions archetypically 'Platonic', became influential throughout the ancient world and beyond. 'Neoplatonists' appeared: Porphyry wrote comments on the *Timaeus* which survive as fragments. Proclus (AD 412–87) also wrote a commentary on the *Timaeus*, struggling to articulate what is meant by saying that the Creator creates. How can anything come from so complete a being, which is other than that being?

The Platonic explanation that creation is no more than the result of the overflowing generosity of a Creator who is good did not in itself explain why the overflow was different from the Creator. Brahmanism holds that the cause must have contained the effect in a primordial state. How did the plurality and diversity of a creation which lies *outside* the Creator come about?[22]

Pythagorean mathematics, as Nicomachus of Gerasa explained it, says that there would have to be some 'difference'. An important principle is that there must be some separation of dimension, some 'otherness' before there can be plurality or diversity. Points become lines only if they are located along a 'dimension'. One times one is one. 'Two' is needed before there can be arithmetical calculations which result in plurality. There were discussions down the centuries about whether even 'two' was enough to produce 'number'. Two seemed to some to be merely the 'otherness' needed. Three was the first number, they thought.

Plutarch

Plutarch wrote a *Moralia*, a collection of essays on aspects of practical ethics, in which he includes some reflections on creation, rebutting such extreme scepticism. He tended towards a Platonic account. He thought there must be a second principle, the Dyad, able to involve himself with the muddle of the world in a way the supreme Creator could not. But this principle could also be the source of evil in the world.

The Romans

Greek is a much better vehicle for the discussion of abstract ideas than Latin, though Cicero and later Boethius (*c*.480–524/5) tried to improve its capacities in that respect. The Romans aspired to be Greek in their philosophy, and the educated Roman would study philosophy to equip himself for the public life in which he would need to be able to make speeches. Roman thinkers made few enormous strides to compare with those of the Greeks.

Cicero

Cicero, taking to philosophy in his retirement from a busy and stressful public life, wrote several books gathering together the opinions of philosophers so far. We have already met him in the 'Dream of Scipio' and taking a view on the Antipodes (see Chapter 2, 'The music of the spheres'). Beginning *De Natura Deorum* (*On the Nature of the Gods*), he takes it that the beginning of philosophy and the original prompter to attempt it was *ignorantia*. Philosophers were puzzled and wanted to understand the world.[23]

The question most interesting to philosophers of the past, he suggests, has been whether the gods both created and sustain the world (*regantur atque moveantur*). If gods do not sustain and control, what is the point of prayer and offerings and all religious practice?[24] (Support on backs of tortoises could be a matter of sustaining too.)

If you take away sanctity and religion (*sanctitas et religio*), says this former public servant, society crumbles (*perturbatio vitae sequitur et magnae confusio*). Some say divine control is orderly, dignified, benevolent, and must thus be regarded as providential.[25] In all this Cicero speaks to the Roman mind with its civic sense, in terms which would have been less congenial to the Greeks.

Cicero was also drawn to the more abstract ideas of the Greeks. In the *Timaeus* the Creator is craftsman or maker (*opifex*) and builder of the world (*aedificator mundi*), he explains. But Cicero's summary of the views of earlier philosophers tends to be scathing. If the world itself is a living being, he asks, what shape is it and why? That rotating sphere of Plato – how could it be steadfast of mind or happy if it was eternally spinning round? Would this Creator-world be too hot in the parts of him that are desert, too cold in cold regions of the earth? A god who is pure mind without body is hard for us to grasp. Pythagoras' idea of a 'soul of the world' (*anima mundi*), with our individual souls mere fragments of world soul, is all very well, but Pythagoras does not seem to see that that makes the Creator a broken thing.[26]

He sides with those who question the possibility of the eternity of the universe. On the other hand, he sees that to deny it raises a question. If the world was created at some point, why did the Creator suddenly wake up after ages of slumbering and decide to create the universe (for time could have been passing even if nothing was happening)? What desire could lead the Creator to take a fancy to decorate the firmament? And what does 'after' mean in eternity?[27] How can anything which has 'come into being' be eternal? It is true that for there to be measurable ages there would have to be rotation of the heavens. But it is not conceivable that there was ever a time before time existed.

Cicero is also interested in the way the machinery of creation could work, though again he does not think much of the suggestions made so far. Mockingly he writes of the absurdity of the suggested mechanisms, the method of engineering proposed, involving tools, levers, derricks and workmen as agents.[28]

He conjures with the idea of Providence as a capricious fortune-teller in quite the spirit of Boethius who was later to write about Fortune's Wheel in his *Consolation of Philosophy*.[29] The Epicureans are very sure of themselves, Cicero reports. They deride the *volubilis deus*, the rotating sphere of burning fire. They do not think much of Plato's *opifex* or artisan deity. They sneer at Providence (calling her an old hag of a fortune-teller). They too ask sceptically what machinery was used in creation: tools, levers, derricks?[30]

In the *Academica*, Cicero suggests that the most important point in dispute is whether the gods are idle and do nothing, or both created and now keep in motion the world as we know it. He also asks about the elements, whether they can be regarded as first principles, as forms of prime matter without species and quality underlying everything from which everything is formed. As Gore Vidal comments:[31]

> It is the view of the Jains that the cosmos is filled with atoms. I use the word that Anaxagoras invented for the infinitesimal bits of matter that make up creation. Yet the life monad of the Jains is not exactly the same as an atom.[32]

Cicero reports that Democritus (*c.*460–370 BC) says that everything is made of atoms, whose collisions and connections make the world (*ex quo efficeretur mundus omnesque partes mundi quaeque in eo essent*). A fiction, he cries.[33]

Lucretius

Lucretius (*c.*99–55 BC) wrote an epic poem *De Rerum Natura* (*On the Nature of Things*) to encourage a friend of his to stop worrying about death. In it he sets out the views of the Epicureans. Death is the end, for, without a body, the soul cannot go on. So there is no reason to fear death if one will know nothing after it. There can be no more suffering.

If, suggests Lucretius, 'the nature of the gods' is:

> . . . so subtle,
> So far removed from these our senses, scarce
> Is seen even by intelligence of mind.

The gods can hardly take an interest in us:

> What may not
> Itself be touched in turn can never touch.[34]

How is it imagined that the gods acquired 'the archetype for [en]gendering the world' or got the idea of making human beings?[35] There are too many flaws in the universe for it to be possible that the creation was properly planned and executed by a divine Creator:

> . . . in no wise the nature of all things
> For us was fashioned by a power divine –
> So great the faults it stands encumbered with.[36]

The world is patchy, with forests and mountains and deserts and seas and areas of extreme heat and cold. Moreover, the world is not eternal. It stumbled into being over many ages by trial and error conjunctions of particles, until there emerged sun and moon and earth and some ether, containing fire, broke away and rose upward and formed the stars.[37]

Ovid
Ovid gives an account in his *Metamorphoses* (*Changes*), in which he tells the history of the world from its creation. His emphasis is on the imposition of orderliness:

> Before the sea was and the lands and the sky which hangs over all, the face of Nature showed alike in her whole round, which state have men called chaos: a rough, unordered mass of things, nothing at all save lifeless bulk and warring seeds of ill-matched elements heaped in one.[38]

There was air but no light (*lucis egens aer*). The Creator put things into order, 'rent asunder land from sky, and sea from land', and 'lodges things in their proper places'. The 'chaotic mass' was resolved into its 'cosmic parts'. Man was made, 'a living creature of finer stuff than these, more capable of lofty thought'. Then came the Golden Age in which 'everyone behaved well and needed no laws. There was order and prosperity, but then the silver age, the brazen age and the iron age followed and with them came evil. They say that the Giants essayed the very throne of heaven, piling huge mountains one on another, clear up to the stars.'[39]

Pliny

The 'natural scientist' Pliny remarks that the universe can reasonably be thought of as a power (*numen esse credi par est*). Its attributes would be eternity, immensity, being unbegotten and immortal. God is not omnipotent if he cannot kill himself. Pliny rejects as absurd the possibility that there could be numerous worlds (*innumerabiles . . . mundos*). He also rejects the idea of the universe as a revolving divine sphere. It cannot be a smooth featureless whole (*lubricum corpus*) when you can see the figures of bear, bull, plough and so on in the stars, and when seeds fall from the sky and generate particular things including monsters. In other words, there is far too much particularity.[40]

He favours instead the idea of a ruler and Creator as *anima mundi*, a world 'soul', or rather as 'mind' (*animum ac planius mentem*) which brings light to drive out darkness. It seems to him foolish to believe in many gods and to personify things and abstractions as gods; this is particularly inappropriate when gods are made of what is vicious and evil. He expresses distaste for the whole business of worshipping such beings in order to flatter and placate them. This could lead to having more gods in the heavens than people on earth (*Maior caelitum populus etiam quam hominum*).[41]

In the same way it is unfitting to have Fortune treated as a deity, to give way to fears of chance, and live in slavery to omens. Pliny sneers at astrology. God does take an interest in his world, at least in governing events, he believes.[42] The view that astrologers 'are impressed by the stars' in ways which are the devil's work and deceitful was to persist strongly, into the Christian Middle Ages.[43]

The Stoics
The Stoics thought the gods would only need to fuss if they were uneasy. A happy and eternal being is tranquil. It has no troubles, experiences no upsets itself and brings no trouble upon any other being; it does not get angry or have favourites: that would be an expression of weakness.[44] This is the essential position of the Stoics.

The Stoics are a late antique phenomenon. Seneca the Younger (*c*.4 BC–AD 65) and Epictetus (55–135 AD) helped to embed certain ideas into Greek and Roman thought, among them an echo of Buddhism – that the aim of life is to cultivate detachment from caring about anything which could cause upset. Being philosophical is being tranquil. This is a philosophy which is also a way of life and in which theology and philosophy are merged.

The Stoics believed that the Creator is a first and rational principle of all things and immanent in his creation, but undisturbed in his supreme tranquillity by the goings-on of his creatures. Nevertheless, he shapes it and its affairs and represents a sort of fate, determining its unfolding. In some versions his action is seen as that of a designing fire or a breath (*pneuma*).

Aspects of this admiration for tranquillity found their way into Christian theology too, in the notion that God feels no distress or disturbance although he is supremely concerned on our behalf.

Seneca the Younger
Seneca knows that people discuss whether the Creator is omnipotent (*quantum deus possit*); whether he made matter or simply used primordial matter; whether forms gave matter its nature or matter dictates the kinds of forms there would be; whether God can do whatever he likes or is restricted by the stuff he has to work with. Thinking about such questions is a good idea. It helps to develop a sense of perspective and proportion. His own view is that the Creator is mind and nothing else (*nulla pars extra animum est*); he is absolute reason (*totus est ratio*). So how can people believe that the universe, which is order, is ruled by chance (*casu volubile*)? Educated people as well as others believe this, but Seneca is confident that the universe is planned. It does not move haphazardly.[45]

He wrote a book *On Providence*, in which he tackles certain perennially awkward questions in a dialogue with Lucilius: 'You have asked me, Lucilius, why, if the world be ruled by providence, so many evils befall good men?'

First, he says, it is necessary to prove 'that providence governs the universe, and that God is amongst us'. Then we can go on to consider:

> Why do many things turn out badly for good men? Why, no evil can befall a good man; contraries cannot combine. Just as so many rivers, so many showers of rain from the clouds, such a number of medicinal springs, do not alter the taste of the sea, indeed, do not so much as soften it, so the pressure of adversity does not affect the mind of a brave man; for the mind of a brave man maintains its balance and throws its own complexion over all that takes place, because it is more powerful than any external circumstances. I do not say that he does not feel them, but he conquers them, and on occasion calmly and tranquilly rises superior to their attacks, holding all misfortunes to be trials of his own firmness.[46]

These classical theories caused endless difficulties for Christian commentators down the centuries for a millennium and a half at least. The problem was that they wanted to regard these authors as 'authorities', not necessarily on a level with Christian authors, and certainly not with Scripture. But certain principles could not be admitted without posing a challenge to the truth of the Bible. Three errors of this sort were briskly despatched by Peter Comestor. Plato thought there was primordial matter and form as well as the Creator, so that the Creator would be a mere craftsman; Aristotle thought the world was eternal as well as the Creator, Epicurus suggested the world began when atoms coalesced into something solid. Only Moses got it right.[47]

II. THE EARLY CHRISTIAN THEOLOGICAL SYNTHESIS

The conviction emerged early on in the history of Christianity that orthodoxy matters. There is only one true faith. Eternal life depends on holding it. It is not a question of exploring alternative philosophical viewpoints and having an interesting debate. It is not acceptable to stir different ideas about creation together into a colourful stew.

That position was not arrived at all at once. The first Christians, Jesus' disciples, were not educated men. It was not until the new religion began to spread that its adherents encountered sophisticated thinkers throughout the Roman Empire, who challenged them to catch up with contemporary arguments and decide where their beliefs fitted in.

Everywhere among Greek and Roman philosophers it was accepted that reason is a high 'good'. Aristotle had said that rationality is a defining characteristic of human beings and distinguishes them from lesser and lowlier animals. To be intelligent is to understand things, and for a thing to be intelligible is for it to be susceptible of rational and consistent explanations. So Christian thinkers began to look for reasoned accounts of creation, why and how it happened and what may be inferred about the Creator from an understanding of the process. They heard about the various ideas the philosophers had been discussing, and continued to discuss, and the contradictory opinions they held: for example, about the eternity of the world and whether God is a spinning sphere, and whether the universe is designed on a mathematical basis, and so on.

Justin Martyr

Justin Martyr (103–165)[48] was born of pagan parents. His early experience nicely exemplifies the contemporary taste for philosophical exploration. As he describes in his *Dialogue with Trypho* (Trypho was a Jewish philosopher), he was educated first in a philosopher's school run by a Stoic.[49] This teacher was unable to give him a satisfactory explanation of the nature of God and the creation of the universe. So he took himself to another teacher, one who presented himself as an Aristotelian or peripatetic philosopher. This teacher seemed to be interested only in his tuition fee. So Justin tried a Pythagorean. This teacher told him he would first have to lay foundations by studying the mathematical subjects of music, geometry and astronomy; he was disinclined to give time to all that. Then he found a Platonist.

Such a wandering review of alternative systems tended to be the way philosophical education then worked. There were 'schools of thought' from which students could choose in selecting the actual school where they would study. Yet there was, as Justin comments in his *Dialogue with Trypho*,[50] much of common interest for all philosophy students. There was difference of opinion about the number of the gods and whether the God or gods care about

individuals and whether the gods punish bad behaviour; the same
questions doggedly recurred.

Before he had settled to mastering the Platonic system, he
encountered an elderly man on a sea-shore where he had gone
for a period of quiet reflection; Justin learned from him about
Christianity and was converted. The assumption was that intelligent
young men would want answers to life's great questions, and the
young Justin found something he greatly respected in the courage
of Christians, who were facing persecution in these early centuries
and could be executed for their faith.[51]

Justin began to travel and teach in his own right. He founded
a school in Rome some time after AD 138 and Tatian (*c.*120–80)
became one of his pupils. Tatian was an Assyrian and his special
interest was in reconciling the Gospels with one another and with
the theological ideas Christians were beginning to explore.

Philo of Alexandria

Philo of Alexandria (20 BC–AD 50) was another Jewish philosopher
who became interested in these themes. He knows that many
educated people say, as Aristotle .had, that the world had no
beginning and is itself eternal, but he himself sees a dividing line
between eternity and infinity on the one hand and the measurable
and quantifiable on the other. So he argues in his *De Opificio Mundi*
(*On the Making of the World*) that time began when the created
world began.

It is God who should be worshipped, not the world he made,
Philo insists. His reasons for saying so derive directly from classical
philosophers. There must be cause and effect and the ultimate
(final) cause is God, as Aristotle says; and this God must be pure
mind or intelligence, higher – as some Platonists would argue –
even than goodness and beauty and truth.

He wrote other explanatory texts too, including, *On Providence,
On the Eternity of the World* and *On the Giants of the Old Testament*. *On
the Making of the World* is partly a treatise on the law of Moses, seen
as the Creator's rules for running the world. These create norms
and order and consistency. They have their force and derive their
reliability from God.

Philo thinks that the ideas or patterns for everything were
eternally in the mind of God, in contradiction of Plato, who

argued in the *Timaeus* that these ideas already existed before the Creator thought them. But he follows Plato in assuming that the 'stuff' out of which God made the world was already there. He did not make everything from 'nothing' because there was already some formless 'something' he could use.

On this elevated understanding of the rationality and intellectual control of the Creator, Philo suggests that creation was carried out over six days not because God could not work faster but because this was the orderly way to do it.

Clement of Alexandria

Clement of Alexandria, head of the school for new Christians which was set up at Alexandria in Egypt, was anxious to place Christian thinking in the educated culture of its time in a way which would establish its intellectual respectability. He accepted that Greek philosophy owes a good deal to the 'barbarians' or secular philosophers. The Greeks could, he thought, be vainglorious about their philosophical achievements. Epicurus maintained that only Greeks would be true philosophers. Yet Pythagoras was not a Greek and Antisthenes came from Phrygia and Orpheus from Thrace. It is widely held that Homer was an Egyptian and Thales from Phoenicia. Pythagoras lived among the Egyptians and studied with them so as to master their mysteries. Plato admits he learned his philosophy from barbarians.[52]

Clement acknowledges that the philosophical sources which have found their way into the minds of the Greeks are very broad, geographically speaking. In his *Miscellanies*, Book II,[53] he points out that even Scripture says the Greeks have stolen ideas from the barbarians. He mentions Brahmins and other eastern thinkers and notes that these were much respected by the Egyptians, the Chaldeans, the Arabs, the Persians. He recalls that Pythagoras was said to be a pupil of an Assyrian thinker and had heard Brahmin teaching too. He mentions Buddhism and Zoroaster, whom he knows to be a Persian.

He discussed the narrative of the creation in Genesis in an attempt to free the Christian from having to take the six days literally. He himself could not see how the Creator could have made the world in a temporal succession of events since time itself had to be created before there could be temporal succession.

Origen

Origen (184/5–253/4), one of Clement's pupils, was also busy reconciling Christianity with classical philosophy in his thinking and writing. He, like Clement, taught and wrote at a time when education was sophisticated, philosophical, aware of the refinements of language and the implications of the way it was used. Origen had that sort of education himself, but his father was also anxious for him to study the scriptures of the Christians. This forced him to think through the task of reconciling the two systems of thought.

He did so at a time when first principles were being established both for the study of holy texts and for the statement of Christian doctrine. It was far from easy to be sure what were the fixed points, the certainties, on which to build. He seems to have become a controversial figure even in his lifetime and he was regarded as holding dubious opinions for centuries afterwards. He was forced to flee from Alexandria in 231 and settled in Caesarea. He appears to have run a school in which the syllabus included the philosophical topics of physics and metaphysics and also ethics as well as the study of the Bible. Only fragments of Origen's commentaries survive, though he quotes them himself in his *Philocalia*.[54]

In *On First Principles*,[55] he lists particular points in the doctrine of creation to be found in the teaching of the apostles:

That there is one God, who created and arranged all things, and who, when nothing existed, called all things into being – God from the first creation and foundation of the world.

Secondly:

That Jesus Christ Himself, who came (into the world), was born of the Father before all creatures; that, after He had been the servant of the Father in the creation of all things – 'For by Him were all things made'. He in the last times, divesting Himself (of His glory), became a man, and was incarnate although God, and while made a man remained the God which He was.

He can be seen wrestling with the task of reconciling Scripture with philosophical assumptions.

I know that some will attempt to say that, even according to the declarations of our own Scriptures, God is a body, because in the writings of Moses they find it said, that 'our God is a consuming fire' (cf. Deuteronomy 4,24); and in the Gospel according to John, that 'God is a Spirit, and they who worship Him must worship Him in spirit and in truth' (cf. John 4. 24).[56]

Basil the Great (Basil of Caesarea)

Basil the Great (329/30–379) was one of a group of contemporaries in what is now central Anatolia who became known as the 'Cappadocian Fathers'. His younger brother was Gregory of Nyssa, and Gregory of Nazianzus was his close friend. Basil and Gregory Nazianzus studied together in Constantinople and Athens and received a thorough grounding in Greek philosophy. Basil set about earning his living in some of the usual ways open to an educated man, as a teacher of rhetoric and as an advocate. But he came from a well-connected Christian family and eventually became a bishop.

Basil is best-known for the series of homilies he preached on the book of Genesis about 370. He was better-placed than Latin commentators of the period to appreciate the fine points of the conflict of the Genesis story with the thought of Plato and the other Greeks who had written about the creation of the world. He also had some respect for the views of Origen. Basil wanted to link what he had to say with ancient learning, to command the respect of pagan philosophers of his time but also to win thinkers who had been trained in that tradition to the Christian faith. So in his first homily he links Moses with Egyptian learning. Moses was adopted by Pharaoh's daughter.[57]

Basil admits that the 'philosophers of the gentiles' have made many attempts to explain creation but he says they could not agree.[58] Some would not allow that an intelligent primary cause lay behind creation. Some said everything was made by the elements coming together. His own view was that the 'six days' must really have been no time at all since there was no time until God made it. He also suggested that the creation of plants and animals was the creation of seeds, which grew to maturity with great speed. Animals were created full-grown.

The Bible, he suggests,[59] settles several of the questions raised by the conflicting philosophers. Genesis establishes that the world had a beginning and was not eternal. The New Testament explains that the world will end (1 Corinthians 7:31 and Matthew 24:35). It follows that it did not coexist with God from eternity.

The world is not itself God. God made the world. He made it from nothing. There was no pre-existing matter. Primordial matter was created, in a subtle and undifferentiated form by God when he made the heavens. Remove the qualities or attributes of this stuff such as blackness, density, coldness and the substance itself is no longer there.[60]

He addresses himself equally robustly to accounts of creation which try to explain why the earth does not fall 'down' by suggesting that it rests on a 'tortoise' or 'elephant' support. If a support is needed, it would itself need a support and so on *ad infinitum*.[61] That is absurd. God is all the support the world needs to stay in its 'place'.

More of the absurdities of rival explanations are exposed in *On First Principles*, Homily II.2. If it were true that matter is uncreated, matter would deserve the same worship as God. Similarly, if ideas are primordial, the forms the Platonists claim that God used to make things from primordial matter, those too would be equal with the Creator. God has these ideas himself. He thought them from nothing.

Ambrose of Milan

These ideas were read with respect by Ambrose (337/40–397), who became bishop of Milan and preached sermons on Genesis himself. In his discussion of the first day, he plunges straight into the question of what was there from the beginning (*ab origine*).[62] Christians believe that God made the world from nothing. Plato and his disciples say that there were three things (*tria principia*) at the outset: God; the forms or ideas or patterns; and the stuff, or primordial matter (*Deus et exemplar et materia*). He knows that there are those who believe the world itself is eternal, uncreated, not made, as Aristotle argues; that some say there is only one world (Pythagoras) but others (such as Democritus) say that there are innumerable worlds; and still others say the world is itself God.

Augustine of Hippo

Ambrose thus provided a learned and compelling reconciliation of Genesis and philosophy, capable of commanding the respect of pagan intellectuals. These sermons were heard by just such a pagan intellectual in the person of the new professor of rhetoric, the Augustine who was later to become bishop of Hippo, and who came to his sermons expecting as an expert in oratory to dismiss them with scorn.[63] He found himself transfixed, and it was these sermons which soon helped to bring about his conversion to Christianity.

The worry which had brought Augustine from his native North Africa to Italy to teach concerned an aspect of the creation of the world which his own work eventually made prominent in Western thought (see Chapter 3 (iii)). For ten years, Augustine had been a follower of the dualist Manichaeans, who had taught him that the universe was under the divided control of two powers, the good spiritual, the bad material. It followed that the whole physical world was evil, a creation of an evil power. This hypothesis threw Genesis into quite another light. The Manichaeans even suggested that the whole Old Testament was the story of the works of the evil power and only the New Testament told of the works of the good God.

Once he had become a Christian, and returned to North Africa, and especially after his speedy translation into a bishop for Hippo, Augustine saw it as his task to defend the truth of the Old Testament and its account of a creation of the material world by the one Creator who also made all things spiritual.[64] Ambrose's sermons and Basil's analysis proved invaluable aids. Augustine wrote on Genesis 'against the Manichaeans', and on the literal meaning of Genesis, returning to the topic again and again over the years. In his treatment of the literal meaning of Genesis, written about 391, he argued that the world must have been made in an instant because there was no 'time' at first to separate the 'days' sequentially. But there was still a sequence of events.

Augustine also discusses creation in his book *The City of God*, in which he tries to set heaven in its cosmic context. There are, he recognises, different ways of understanding the expression 'world without end'. A similar definitional difficulty attaches to talking about a 'beginning'. Why did God suddenly decide to create heaven and earth? He is changeless so he could not have had an idea he had not had before. He must always have had this idea and in the mind of God the world was indeed eternal. Augustine comments that Apuleius believed the world had always existed, and so had the human race. But what does 'always' mean in the context of time? He puzzles over Plato's view that the Creator made the gods. Augustine is not sure whether Plato was speaking of the stars when he said this; and did he really say the world is itself an animal which would live for ever?[65]

Here he visibly struggles with his lack of direct knowledge of Plato's teaching (he admits that his Greek was poor). He depended on ideas he had heard about only at second hand but which were evidently present in contemporary discourse. Augustine nevertheless strove to persuade pagan philosophers who had come to North Africa in flight from the barbarian invasions of Italy that Christianity deserved respect as a system of belief for intelligent people.

Augustine's work had an immense influence in the Latin-speaking West. He wrote towards the end of the Roman Empire, when the language-division between Greek and Latin writers was becoming wider. Partly as a consequence of this estrangement of the two language communities, his influence in Eastern Europe was much smaller.

John Philoponos

John Philoponos (490–570) wrote *De Opificio Mundi* (*On the Making of the World*) against the Neoplatonist Proclus (412–85), with the purpose of demonstrating that there was no truth in the argument that the world is eternal. This seemed to him to be the chief and most powerful anti-Christian argument in the pagan armoury. He relied in part on Basil the Great's work in reconciling Genesis with philosophy, and insisted that matter is a creation of the good God. But he also drew on Aristotle's attempts to explain the sheer machinery involved in creation. He discussed motion and dynamics with a thoroughness which was quite new.

Boethius

In 522 Boethius became a very senior 'civil servant' in the contentious last years of the Roman Empire. It turned out to be a dangerous promotion. He soon found himself under house arrest on charges of treason. He knew he was almost certainly awaiting execution. It made him think.[66] His reflections prompted him to write a book which became a classic throughout Europe for centuries.

The *Consolation of Philosophy* was an attempt to find a world-view which could comfort a man in such extremes. He must have needed someone to talk to, and the natural literary device was to personify Philosophy herself and ask her advice. So the book begins with a sketch of her fearsome person, with its contradictory aspects. She is immensely tall and at the same time no bigger than an ordinary human being. She is of venerable age but young and vigorous. She is dressed in the finest garments but her clothes are tattered and dusty. Through it all, however, shines her keen-eyed intelligence. She arrives to find the Muses sitting with Boethius, composing poems to help him express his grief, and she sends them away with scorn. They are far too emotional.

There follows a bracing discussion. Boethius remembers old times when he has sat with 'Philosophy' in his library 'discussing' the great questions of life.[67] Now he confides in her about his sense of injustice. He lists events and acts to demonstrate that he does not deserve his fate. And now people speak ill of him just because he has been condemned. His reputation is unfairly destroyed.

Boethius seems to have been a Christian, on the evidence of a few brief surviving treatises on what were current problems and disputes about orthodoxy.[68] However, in the condemned cell under house arrest awaiting the politically-motivated execution which eventually befell him, he turned to a personified and goddess-like Philosophy for comfort and advice. He says both Plato and Aristotle thought the world had no beginning and discusses Aristotle's ideas on the eternity of the world.[69]

Gregory the Great

Augustine described the Creator of the visible world, heaven and earth, and of all souls, as giving rational souls blessedness by participation in his own unchanging and incorporeal light.[70] Gregory the Great (540–604) had similar things to say about creation in his *Moralia* (*Morals*) on the Old Testament book of Job. This was written as a result of a period of study of this text with his monastic companions while he was on a diplomatic mission to Constantinople. Job contains some puzzling passages in Book II which describe the 'Sons of God' coming to the court of heaven in which God presides as monarch. Gregory suggests this means the angels. Even more puzzling seem the appearance of Satan among them and his conversation with God, during which God offers to test his servant Job and show that he will remain faithful to God. Gregory is interested by the paradox that the angels who dwell in the presence of God seem to be able to go about the earth too and minister to humans beings at the same time. This he puts down to the 'subtlety' of their nature. They converse with God in an inward and spiritual way. In any case, since God is everywhere, they do not need to leave him in order to go about the earth. Yet it is not like God's power of omnipresence. Angels are bounded by space and although they know and see far more than us they are not omniscient, as God is. And when something is said to happen on a particular day it is not limited in time for God, for whom nothing changes, nothing comes and goes.[71]

Bede

Bede (672/3–735), a monk of Wearmouth and Jarrow in northern Britain, took account of Augustine in his own writing on creation.[72] He also acknowledges a debt to Basil of Caesarea, through Ambrose of Milan, in arriving at his understanding of the opening passages of Genesis. Bede's explanation is that the Creator both made and governs the world (*creavit et gubernat*). The Creator works in four ways. There is that which was not made by the Creator because it always was (*sed a aeterna sunt*), which of course is the Creator himself. There is primal matter which God made by his Word. There is the creation of living things over the six days. And there is the running of the universe as it continues until now.[73]

The Christian creeds

The Nicene Creed was a creation of the Council of Nicaea in 325 and it is first and foremost an attempt to defend the truth against various opinions which the Christian Church had decided to deem heretical. It sets out (among other things) the parameters of a doctrine of the Trinity in which the divinity and equality of the omnipotent Creator, the uncreated eternal Logos and the uncreated eternal Spirit are stressed. It also embodies a Christian position on some of the themes of dualism:

> We believe in one God, the Father, the Almighty, maker of heaven and earth, of all that is, seen and unseen. We believe in one Lord, Jesus Christ, the only Son of God, eternally begotten of the Father, God from God, Light from Light, true God from true God, begotten, not made, of one Being with the Father. Through him all things were made . . . We believe in the Holy Spirit, the Lord, the giver of Life, who proceeds from the Father [and the Son].[74] With the Father and the Son he is worshipped and glorified.[75]

The Apostles' Creed was believed to be the work of the apostles but in reality it seems to have developed through liturgy and in worship, and its form was probably settled in Carolingian times:

> I believe in God the Father, Almighty, Maker of heaven and earth: And in Jesus Christ, his only begotten Son, our Lord: . . . I believe in the Holy Ghost.[76]

Some medieval Genesis commentators

A later medieval author, Robert Grosseteste (*c.*1175–1253), wrote on the six days of creation in Genesis. In his 'Proemium' or 'Preamble' he goes into some detail on the knowledge of earlier mythology by classical and Christian authors. He describes how Pythagoras and Plato made journeys in which they met the Egyptians as Augustine attests. He himself relies on Pliny for his description of India and says he has read in a 'Greek Book' that the Bragmanes live on an island which God gave them to be their inheritance. He is happy to accept that rivers which flow from Paradise reach into the earth as we know it.[77]

He comments on the controversial questions which went on being raised from age to age. The philosophers are mistaken in claiming that the world is eternal. Grosseteste offers a robust rebuttal of these philosophers.[78] 'Beginning' is not a simple notion; *principium* has several meanings.[79] Is the heaven above the firmament? Strabus says, 'The heaven is not the visible firmament, but the empyrean or fiery or intellectual heaven.'[80]

Henry of Langenstein (*c.*1325–97) was still writing in this tradition of Christian rebuttal of pagan philosophical ideas where they conflicted with Genesis, with the same subtle skills in reconciling what could be reconciled, and with a similar but increasingly more advanced interest in the mechanisms involved.

III. Just 'Saying' the World

Firstly, a spirit within them nourishes the sky and earth,
the watery plains, the shining orb of the moon,
and Titan's star, and Mind, flowing through matter,
vivifies the whole mass, and mingles with its vast frame.
From it come the species of man and beast, and winged lives,
and the monsters the sea contains beneath its marbled waves.
The power of those seeds is fiery, and their origin divine,
so long as harmful matter doesn't impede them
and terrestrial bodies and mortal limbs don't dull them.[81]

Virgil here tries to trace the way mind brings matter to life, with more than a nod to the dualist idea that matter is a heavy drag. Could 'mind' do more than that? Could the universe be 'made' by mere thought, or by the expression of thought? 'The words grew sacramental; they had not existed by themselves but as the communication . . . of a stored and illuminated mind.'[82]

The idea that creation could take place in such a way is widespread among the world's creation theories, both polytheistic and monotheistic. Among the Incas are found myths of the creation of particular creatures one by one by the gods, sometimes by the power of thought alone or by expressing the thought in words. As a god had the idea of a creature, so that creature came to be. (Some of these creatures turned out to be disobedient so the gods tried to make creatures from mud or wood in the hope that they would pray to the gods as instructed.) Hindu thinking also makes the Word a creative force.

The Jewish philosopher Philo of Alexandria warmed to the Greek idea of the Logos as a creative Word. Genesis seems to say that the Creation was brought about by 'saying' it. The Christian story of creation is among this group which rely on the idea that creation took place by the Creator's merely speaking the Word, though this idea was properly formulated only with the emergence of Christianity and under the influence of the Greek philosophical idea of the Logos. The idea had a wide appeal to thinkers in the early Christian world that, as Dorothy Sayers put it, with the insight of a writer, 'the mind of the maker is generally revealed, and in a manner incarnate, in all its creation.'[83] Sikhism too envisages creation from nothing by divine will expressed through the word of the Creator.

How would it work?

The idea of creation by thinking or saying has continued to be attractive down the ages, although it lacks visible machinery from which it can be seen how it might work. A question which has caused much controversy is the relationship between the Creator and the Word creatively spoken. Justin Martyr may have derived the realisation that there is a problem from Philo, though it was quite widely discussed.

Justin was inclined to think of this Logos as a being in some way separate from and less than the Creator. He tried to describe some mode by which the Word could come from the unbegotten God.[84] The Logos is perhaps an angel, a messenger who announces to the human creation what the Creator wishes them to be told; the very messenger who appeared as God to Abraham and Jacob and Moses.[85] Origen, too, wanted to protect the separateness of the Creator, and for this purpose the manner in which he might have to deal with the world he had made had to involve some distance, some intermediary. Origen took this Logos to be subordinate or secondary to the Creator for the same reasons as others. Anything else seemed to him to compromise the unity of God.

Tatian was an Assyrian Christian thinker who insisted on the importance of monotheism but tried to protect it in different ways. His idea was that God had all creation potentially within him and that when he expressed his power in words, creation came into its creaturely existence. Tatian also brought the Holy Spirit into his structure or framework. All creatures, he thought, participate in the spirit or *pneuma* which permeates the world. Tatian wrote an *Address to the Greeks* in which he explained the Christian doctrine of creation as he understood it. There is one God who is the ground (*hypostasis*) of all that exists and in him before creation took place was the power of the Word. At God's will the Logos did the work of creation. This was like the lighting of many torches from the first flame. The first flame is not diminished by creating other flames. It is like speech, for when I say something I am not deprived of the power to say it again.[86]

The orthodox Christian position was that the Word is God. John's Gospel begins with a statement about that:

> In the beginning was the Word, and the Word was with God, and the Word was God. The same was in the beginning with God. All things were made by him; and without him was not any thing made that was made. In him was life; and the life was the light of men. And the light shineth in darkness; and the darkness comprehended it not. (King James Version)

This theology of creation by divine 'saying' became the accepted view in Christian tradition, though not without its debated aspects cropping up again and again to cause trouble. In Milton's account the Almighty speaks and the Son, accompanied by the Holy Spirit, gives effect to what he says by speaking to bring about the actual creation:

> And by my Word, begotten Son, by thee
> This I perform, speak thou, and be it don:
> My overshadowing Spirit and might with thee
> I send along, ride forth, and bid the Deep
> Within appointed bounds be Heav'n and Earth,
> Boundless the Deep, because I am who fill
> Infinitude, nor vacuous the space.
> Though I uncircumscrib'd my self retire,
> And put not forth my goodness, which is free
> To act or not, Necessitie and Chance
> Approach not mee, and what I will is Fate.
> So spake th' Almightie, and to what he spake
> His Word, the Filial Godhead, gave effect.
> Immediate are the Acts of God, more swift
> Then time or motion, but to human ears
> Cannot without process of speech be told,
> So told as earthly notion can receave.[87]

5

Going to see

1. OUT OF AFRICA

An important dimension of the question of whether there is a 'key to all mythologies' is the extent to which shared ideas and stories reflect not some original human 'knowledge' but exchanges and conversations in much more recent times. In order to get a picture of the ways in which that could have happened we need to explore the travelling and trade and missionary endeavour which has 'globalised' fragmented human societies.

In 1860 a debate was held in the newly built University Museum in Oxford at which T.H. Huxley (for the scientists) faced Samuel Wilberforce, bishop (for the Biblical scholars) on the subject of Charles Darwin's recently published theory of the origin of species. Although the words exchanged were not noted accurately at the time, the challenge certainly lay between the view that God made the world exactly as it says in Genesis and the evidence that humans developed from earlier primate species.[1] 'Until recently the great majority of naturalists believed that species were immutable productions, and had been separately created,' wrote Darwin in the Preface to the third edition of his *The Origin of Species*.[2] He went on to set out step by step the main published opinions which had appeared before his own book.

One of them was a paper which Dr W.C. Wells had read before the Royal Society in 1813, 'An Account of a White Female, Part of whose Skin Resembled that of a Negro', and published in 1818:

> After remarking that negroes and mulattoes enjoy an immunity from certain tropical diseases, he observes, firstly, that all animals tend to vary in some degree, and, secondly, that agriculturists improve their domesticated animals by selection; and then, he

adds, but what is done in this latter case 'by art', seems to be done with equal efficacy, though more slowly, by nature, in the formation of varieties of mankind, fitted for the country which they inhabit.

Wells applies this hypothesis to his African examples:

Of the accidental varieties of man, which would occur among the first few and scattered inhabitants of the middle regions of Africa, some one would be better fitted than the others to bear the diseases of the country. This race would consequently multiply, while the others would decrease; not only from their inability to sustain the attacks of disease, but from their incapacity of contending with their more vigorous neighbours.

He explores the way characteristics might become more noticeable as a consequence of this 'breeding' process:

The colour of this vigorous race I take for granted, from what has been already said, would be dark. But the same disposition to form varieties still existing, a darker and a darker race would in the course of time occur: and as the darkest would be the best fitted for the climate, this would at length become the most prevalent; if not the only race, in the particular country in which it had originated.[3]

Darwin's own researches drew on another continent and chiefly on non-human and non-primate species, but the overall force of his argument carried the day with the emerging scientific establishment.

It is now widely accepted scientifically, subject to discoveries which seem to challenge this view,[4] that the first humans probably appeared in Africa, evolving from earlier 'non-human' primates. Of the primates' view of all this, we can know nothing. The very first humans appear on the outskirts of recorded history only dimly until there were enough of them for definable groups to be called 'tribes'. It is impossible now to glimpse what the first humans thought about where they came from, or even when and how they became capable of formulating that thought. There is a great unfathomable leap from early humanity to 'talking' humanity. So what do the African traditions have to say about the emergence of human beings and how far did those traditions influence the ideas of human groups of later ages which found themselves far from their African origins?

The answer appears to be that when, comparatively only very recently, humans from Christian and Islamic civilisations 'came home' to the place which saw the origins of their race, they did so with a confident sense that it was they who were the natural teachers, they who had an understanding of 'origins' to bring, and not they who had something to learn. The current early twenty-first-century movement of Chinese trading interests into Africa will be bringing another set of existing religious assumptions into the equation.

Modern science places the first humans in sub-Saharan Africa, south of the great barrier formed by the Sahara desert. North of that barrier, along the North African coast, there was energetic contact with the European and Arabian worlds throughout some of the key periods when ideas about creation were being exchanged, world religions emerging and philosophers exchanging ideas. While all that was going on, from south of the desert there was silence, for these early explorations did not reach so far.

That does not mean, of course, that the peoples living south of the Sahara had nothing to say about their own ideas of creation, but that 'story' could survive only orally in societies without written records; and it was partly obliterated by the effect on the cultures of the indigenous Africans by Islamic and later European traders, and eventually by European missionaries and colonisation.

The sub-Saharan African tribes never mingled in such a way as to develop an advanced civilisation in the way that seems to have happened in South America (see Chapter 5 (iii)). A creation myth can be influenced by contact with others, but where the cultures which meet are not of equal influence and are at a similar stage of civilisation one may easily dominate the other. No sub-Saharan African people arrived independently at a cultural sophistication which influenced others.

There *were* African migrations. On the evidence of the likenesses of local languages, the Bantu-speaking tribes must have spread across much of Africa, probably from the Niger region in the west, but these peoples are of many ethnic groups and their progression cannot be seen as a conquest or the outreach of a single civilisation. Pigmy peoples of the Congo and Central Africa seem to form a genetic cluster, but they remained mostly simple hunter-gatherers. Further south may be grouped indigenous peoples in what is now

South Africa, Zimbabwe, Botswana and Namibia. These bushmen or 'San' also remained largely hunter-gatherers.

Another genetic cluster includes peoples of the Nile region, but the story here is more complicated. While the Maasai people of modern Kenya are a semi-nomadic Nilotic people, the ancient Egyptian civilisation belongs culturally with the ancient civilisations of Greece and Rome. Among the peoples immediately south of the Sahara, the more developed and successful tended to be those such as the Hausa peoples, which had been influenced by Arabic tribes who brought a belief in Islam to join the indigenous religions of the Africans.

For all these reasons, it is instructive to try to trace the historical and geographical confusion which surrounded the attempts down the centuries even to explore, let alone to understand, this cradle of human life.

How did primitive African tribes believe the world began?

A Kalahari bushmen's creation story tells how once people and animals lived beneath the surface of the earth with the Lord of Life, Kaang (Käng). This was a golden age, an age of happiness, when there was no quarrelling or warfare and everything was bathed in a light which did not come from the sun. Then Kaang decided to make a more wonderful world above ground.

He created a great tree whose branches stretched out across the whole world. Under its roots he made a passageway down to the place where people and animals were living comfortably together. Then he led the first man up to the surface, followed by the first woman, and then all the people. After that he brought up the animals, who rushed out eagerly, and some of them swarmed up into the branches of the tree.

Kaang gave them all instructions. They were to continue to live together peacefully, people and animals. He gave especially firm instructions to the people not to build fires. If they built fires evil would come. They promised and he left them to their lives, moving away but continuing to watch over them.

In their underground world it had always been mysteriously light, but above ground the sun set and it grew dark. The people were frightened because they could not see what was happening and, lacking the fur the animals wore, the humans felt cold. Someone suggested building a fire to give light and heat, forgetting Kaang's warning. But the fire frightened the animals, who ran away to live in mountains and caves, and people and animals lost the ability to talk to one another. People and animals now lead lives of mutual suspicion and antagonism and there is no more peace.[5]

What was this story seeking to account for? Hunter-gatherers will naturally think about their relationships with animals. This may be part of the reason that animals play such an important role in the myths. The Bushmen believe that living things, including plants, are animated by spirits which can move between different kinds of being, so that the leopard or elephant one meets might be one's dead uncle.

The frustrations of being unable to talk to the animals were the subject of a children's book by the widely travelled civil engineer Hugh Lofting (1886–1947), *The Story of Dr. Dolittle*. His story is set about 1840, at the time when the exploration of the African interior was beginning in earnest. Dr Dolittle talks to animals. Polynesia the Parrot bewails the general loss of communication between people and animals:

'I was thinking about people,' said Polynesia. 'People make me sick. They think they're so wonderful. The world has been going on now for thousands of years, hasn't it? And the only thing in animal-language that PEOPLE have learned to understand is that when a dog wags his tail he means "I'm glad!" – It's funny, isn't it? You are the very first man to talk like us. Oh, sometimes people annoy me dreadfully – such airs they put on – talking about "the dumb animals". DUMB! – Huh! Why I knew a macaw once who could say "Good morning!" in seven different ways without once opening his mouth. He could talk every language – and Greek. An old professor with a gray beard bought him. But he didn't stay. He said the old man didn't talk Greek right, and he couldn't stand listening to him teach the language wrong. I often wonder what's become of him. That bird knew more geography than people will ever know. – PEOPLE, Golly! I suppose if people ever learn to fly – like any common hedge-sparrow – we shall never hear the end of it!'

There is also a monkey called Chee-Chee, who is able to contribute a creation story as it has been handed down among his own monkey-people:

And many of the tales that Chee-Chee told were very interesting.
Because although the monkeys had no history-books of their
own before Doctor Dolittle came to write them for them, they
remember everything that happens by telling stories to their
children. And Chee-Chee spoke of many things his grandmother
had told him – tales of long, long, long ago, before Noah and the
Flood – of the days when men dressed in bear-skins and lived in
holes in the rock and ate their mutton raw, because they did not
know what cooking was – having never seen a fire. And he told
them of the Great Mammoths and Lizards, as long as a train, that
wandered over the mountains in those times, nibbling from the
tree-tops. And often they got so interested listening, that when he
had finished they found their fire had gone right out; and they
had to scurry round to get more sticks and build a new one.[6]

Lofting was telling a gentle tale, but one informed by an
awareness of the preoccupations of an age.

Christian influence on African ideas of creation: North Africa

The process of establishing contact between a familiar 'old world'
and newly found 'new' one turned out to be especially complex
in Africa because North Africa – the strip along the coast above
the Sahara desert – was already familiar to the ancient Greeks and
Romans. Africa was an 'old world' continent as far south as the
Sahara, sharing the culture and inheritance of the ancient world
– Egyptian, Greek and Roman. Those who wrote about the origins
of the world thought of it as containing far fewer landmasses than
really exist.

Africa as a whole remained a great mystery to the ancient
historians and thinkers of Europe, who had no idea how far down it
stretched beyond the equator and into the southern hemisphere.
In the first century BC Diodorus Siculus wrote of monsters to
be seen there. It was admitted that the interior was unknown.
'Inner Ethiope, is not yet knowne for the greatnesse thereof, but
onely by the sea coastes,' but with emphasis on tradable products
alongside the tales of monster-people and creatures unlike any
that might be met with in the streets of Roman cities. Travellers'
tales had told of Libya's 'horrible wildernesses and mountains,
replenished with divers kinds of wilde and monstrous beastes and
serpents'. African heat seemed 'already halfeway to purgatorie or

hell', a country almost not of this world.[7] This was the territory of an early form of 'science fiction'.

When Christianity began, within the context of the culture of ancient Greece and Rome, North Africa was for a time one of the most significant areas in the development of Christian theology. The great library at Alexandria, which was burnt by Julius Caesar in 48 BC, had long established Alexandria as a centre of high culture. Clement of Alexandria taught in Alexandria and helped to lay the foundations of the synthesis of Christian and Greek philosophical thought. Cyprian, bishop of Carthage (d. 258) took a lead in the 'rigorist' controversy, which imposed an expectation of high standards of conduct on Christian believers, with short shrift for backsliders. The Donatists were Berber Christians who formed a schismatic community in the fourth century after a controversy about the restoration of Christians who apostatised in times of persecution to save their skins. Augustine of Hippo became perhaps the most influential early Christian Latin-speaking writer of all.

So North African ideas about creation absorbed the earliest Christian thinking, and had their own input into it, even before the rise of Islam and the arrival of Arab influences.

The influence of Islam on African ideas of creation

The Islamic conquests which settled the Mediterranean coast of Africa in the first centuries after the foundation of Islam endured as a major influence after the early Christian period and penetrated inland for purposes of trade from the coasts of the Horn of Africa and the eastern coasts of sub-Saharan Africa. Arabs began on their own descriptive world geography about 800, extending as far as China, and they had a much better idea of the real extent of the world than Christians or Jews.[8] The Indonesian peoples of the ocean off the east coast of Africa, animists and Buddhists and Hindus, probably encountered Arab traders and their Islamic belief system in the eighth century. As in North Africa, there was intermarriage with the indigenous peoples and some hybridisation of popular beliefs. Islam arrived in Malaysia in the twelfth and thirteenth centuries and presided over it for many centuries, with a Malacca Sultanate established in the thriving port of Malacca from 1401. Here Sunni Islam was dominant. The older animism persisted, as it tends to do everywhere, and, in Sufism with its mystical slant, it remained active, with some tints of Hinduism.

Some personal viewpoints on the Islamic theory of creation and on cosmology in the context of the beliefs of other religions as they appeared survive in the remarks of travellers. A near-contemporary of Marco Polo (c.1254–1324), the Venetian merchant and Christian traveller into far East Asia, was Ibn Battuta (1304–68). A Muslim from Morocco, he travelled to North Africa, as well as to Eastern Europe, the Middle East, India, South-East Asia and the Far East as far as China, mainly between 1325 and 1356. 'The Chinese are infidels. They worship idols and burn their dead as the Indians do,' he explains. Nevertheless,

> In every city of China is a quarter where the Muslims live separately and have mosques for their Friday prayers and other assemblies. They are highly regarded and treated with respect.[9]

His recorded perceptions of the religions and customs of the peoples he encountered are heavily coloured by his own Islamic viewpoints about the religions he encounters and their practitioners. He notes a variety of religions. In some places, Islam dominates the religious scene. For example, 'the inhabitants of the Maldives are all of them Muslims, pious and upright.'[10] This was not always so, he notes. Once,

> these islanders were infidels and . . . every month there would appear to them an evil spirit of the jinn, coming from the direction of the sea and resembling a ship filled with lights. On seeing him it was their custom to take a virgin girl and, after dressing her in finery, to conduct her to . . . the idol-temple, which was built on the seashore and had a window looking out on the sea.

The girl would be left overnight and would be found the next day raped and dead. Families became reluctant to hand over their daughters and in the end a beardless boy offered to go; he recited the Qur'an and the approaching spirit, hearing this, retreated into the sea. This led the people to want to know more about Islam and they were converted.[11]

In some encounters Ibn Battuta finds things to respect, particularly the practice of austerity, which accords with an attitude which finds matter and love of material things and bodily pleasures distasteful. In South India 'we found a *jugi* leaning against the wall of . . . an idol temple; he was between two of its idols and showed the traces of continuous practice of . . . austerities.'[12]

Creation had, he found, left traces on the land. The footprint of Adam was to be seen in Ceylon, where:

> The Foot of our father Adam . . . is on a lofty black rock in a wide plateau. The blessed Foot sank into the rock far enough to leave its impression hollowed out. It is eleven spans long.[13]

So Islamic influence spread wider and sooner across much of Africa and Asia before that of Christianity. Yet it seems to have been less inclined to seek to impose a unified imperial culture upon the peoples than the Christians who arrived later with missionaries as well as explorers and traders. It was the impression of one of the European travellers that Islam had had a limited influence on African thinking about human origins: 'The great majority of the Bertas have scorned to accept the religion of their conquerors, nor do the Arab Fugara take any pains to convert them,' while 'the unsophisticated pagan negro is of course looked down upon as a very inferior being by . . . the son of the Arab.'[14] Juan-Maria Schuver was rumoured to be planning to travel from Cairo to the Cape in the course of the journey he began in 1881 and which he draws on in this passage. Here he is describing the peoples of the Berta region between the two Niles, and their approach to the Islamic influence of the Arab traders who lived and traded among them and sometimes intermarried with them.

Schuver did not think the Bertas were much interested in theology or philosophy: 'Like every other black tribe I visited, the Bertas, though not devoid of the idea of a Supreme Being, show a remarkable unconcern for the supernatural.'[15]

Yet further on in his journey, he observes 'squatting ghost-dances' in the firelight which turn out to be 'evening schools', where 'Sudanese youth, under the pious eye of one or more clerics, absorbs the forms and prayers of the Koran'.[16]

Christian influence on African ideas of creation: the rest of Africa

Africa long remained mysterious to the Western writers who contributed to the new 'common understanding' of the world which began to develop from the sixteenth century as Europeans 'discovered' new lands. In the late fifteenth and sixteenth centuries, when the Americas were discovered, ships full of would-be traders who were Christians also sailed round the Cape of Good Hope at the southernmost point of Africa in search of the Indies. Only the coasts became familiar in this process. Only later still did European explorers with commercial as well as missionary[17] intentions set off into the heart of Africa (sometimes confusing the two aims).

When Daniel Defoe's Captain Singleton went on his fictional travels in an African interior not yet known to Europeans, he, or rather Defoe himself, could let his imagination range:

> We conversed with some of the Natives of the Country who were friendly enough. What Tongue they spoke, I do not yet pretend to know. We . . . asked them what country lay that way, pointing West with our Hands. They told us but little to our Purpose, only we thought by all their Discourse that there were people to be found of one Sort or other every where; that there were many great Rivers, many Lions and Tygers, Elephants, and furious wild Cats . . . and the like.
>
> When we ask'd them, if any one had ever travelled that Way, they told us Yes, some had gone to where the Sun sleeps, meaning to the West; but they could not tell us who they were. When we ask'd for some to guide us, they shrunk up their shoulders as Frenchmen do when they are afraid to undertake a thing.

There is a hint of the hope that the journey into Africa could take the traveller back towards the beginning of the world:

> For a Day's Journey before we came to this Lake, and all the three days we were passing by it, and for six or seven Days March after it, the Ground was scattered with Elephants Teeth, in such a number as is incredible; and . . . some of them may have lain there for some Hundreds of Years, so . . . they may lye there for ought I know to the End of Time.[18]

When Christian Europe began to understand the extent of Islam's awareness of Africa it could be highly critical. Defoe blamed the 'Turks' for the mess Africa was now in, as he saw it.[19]

Into the interior

Africa's interior remained 'dark' to Europeans until the nineteenth century. The first modern Christian missionaries arrived wherever they landed in the continent with mixed motives, of which the missionaries themselves were perhaps not always aware. They thought they had a duty to bring their faith to primitive peoples and convert them, in the footsteps of the apostles who had been told to take their Gospel to all the earth. William Carey wrote a thoughtful pamphlet in 1792 on the question of whether the duty laid on the apostles to take the Gospel to all the earth extended to present-day missionaries. 'One would have supposed that the remembrance of the deluge would have perpetually deterred mankind from transgressing the will of their Maker'; but so 'blinded were they' by sin that 'gross wickedness prevailed wherever colonies were planted.'[20]

David Livingstone (1813–73) was a self-educated Scot, who worked in a cotton mill from the age of ten, but subsequently qualified as a doctor and offered himself in due course as a missionary. Livingstone was sent by a missionary society to what is now South Africa, where he arrived in 1841. He found that little progress had been made in twenty years of previous missionary effort, and there were still few native Christians there. He decided to try a new approach in another place further north, accompanying a fellow missionary, Roger Edwards.

This began Livingstone's own journeyings and his experimentation with the dimensions of what was to become a process of scientific exploration, trading expansion and European colonisation. He too found it difficult to win converts and he lost faith in the methods of earlier missionaries. His interests moved towards exploration and he began to see advantages in combining mission with trade and the transformation of local customs ('Christianity, Commerce and Civilization', as it was to say on his tombstone). Between 1852 and 1856 he travelled north into the interior of the continent, coming across the great waterfall on the Zambezi which he called the Victoria Falls in honour of the queen of England.

He became one of the first Europeans to cross the interior of Africa from its Western coast to the mouth of the Zambesi. Earlier attempts had been thwarted by European susceptibility to local diseases and the difficulty of keeping pack animals alive, as well as by active hostility from the local tribes. The tribes had, after all, reason to fear from their experience with the Arabs that expeditions of men with white or brown faces might be slave-traders.

Livingstone's widening interests were disapproved of by the society which had sent him out to Africa. It demanded that he concentrate on his missionary work and do less exploring. In 1857 he resigned from the society and sought patronage and funding elsewhere. The Royal Geographical Society helped him win the appointment of consul for East Africa. That took him into areas of activity where the British government had a policy interest and was prepared to provide funding. He was commissioned to lead an expedition to explore the Zambezi River, in search of valuable natural resources. The trip took years (1858–64) and it became apparent that Livingstone was not competent to lead an expedition on this scale. He could be moody and unable to listen to criticism.

But he was indefatigable in his desire to return to Africa. He was back in Africa in 1866 on an expedition to find the source of the Nile, a topic of considerable European interest at the time and the subject of a certain amount of competition. These European expeditions travelled with enormous numbers of local porters to carry supplies – and even, if necessary, their white leaders; Europeans on the expeditions seem often to have become ill and to have had to be carried on litters. Livingstone lost a number of his team on this trip and was reduced to relying on the help of slave-traders travelling in the same direction. He was said to have been treated as a 'show' by natives who kept him in an enclosure and fed him for their entertainment.

Livingstone's last expedition was the one on which he famously became 'lost' and was 'found' by Henry Morton Stanley. Stanley had set off from Zanzibar in 1871 with an expedition comprehensively furnished with two hundred porters. These soon began to desert him, and disease in both human and animal members of the expedition got in the way of progress. He came across Livingstone ('Dr Livingstone, I presume').[21]

For all the faults in human relations which he seems to have shared with other leading explorers, Livingstone took seriously the need to get to know local customs. He tried to learn local languages and set about analysing their grammars. He tried establishing a local school, where the children were to be taught by his new wife Mary, daughter of a fellow missionary, whom he met and married in Africa.

Livingstone records some of the religious notions of the natives he encountered:

A comet blazed on our sight, exciting the wonder of every tribe we visited. That of 1816 had been followed by an irruption of the Matabéle. The most cruel enemies the Bechuanas ever knew, and this they thought might portent something as bad, or it might only foreshadow the death of some great chief. On the subject of comets I knew little more than they did themselves, but I had that confidence in a kind of overruling Providence which makes such a difference between Christians and both the ancient and modern heathen.

And, in an observation which underlines the difficulty of separating worship from creation beliefs in some African cultures, he comments that:

the different Bechuana tribes are named after certain animals, showing probably that in former times they were addicted to animal-worship like the ancient Egyptians . . . 'they of the monkey' . . . 'they of the alligator' . . . 'they of the fish'; each tribe having a superstitious dread of the animal after which it is called. They don't eat their own animal. If you want to know which tribe someone belongs to you ask 'What do you dance?'[22]

The assumption persisted that there was a barrier to cross between an old and a new world of thought. Livingstone talked to Sechele, the chief of the Bakuena among the Bechuana tribes, and when Sechele asked how it was that his people had heard nothing of Christianity before, Livingstone explained about 'the geographical barriers in the north, and the gradual spread of knowledge from the south, to which we first had access by means of ships'. 'And,' he added, 'I expressed my belief that, as Christ had said, the whole world would yet be enlightened by the Gospel.'[23]

African beliefs encounter Europe's 'superior civilisation'

Verney Lovett Cameron (1844–94) was the first European explorer known to have crossed Africa from east to west. His preoccupations were commercial. 'Why are not steamers flying the British colours carrying the overglut of our manufactured goods to the naked African?' He identifies 'hotbeds of corruption' locally preventing this. As to making positive efforts, he thought 'the advance of trade and civilisation into the interior from the southward may be left to take care of itself. Every year the ivory traders push further north.' He was very much aware of the importance of 'the question now before the civilised world . . . whether the slave-trade in Africa . . . is to be permitted to continue'. But he also observes what seems to him the essential dependency of the Africans on the guidance of a superior European civilisation, if they are not to descend into barbarism:

> Many people may say that the rights of native chiefs to govern their countries must not be interfered with. I doubt whether there is a country in Central Africa where the people would not soon welcome and rally round a settled form of government. The rule of the chiefs over their subjects is capricious and barbarous, and death or mutilation is carried out at the nod of a drunken despot.

He warns that Africans are easily influenced. Given the chance of 'throwing off the yoke of their own rulers, [they] soon fall under the sway of the strangers.'[24]

When it came to the 'sway of strangers', the Belgians seem to have behaved especially badly to the Africans they encountered. The Congo remained largely unvisited by Europeans until late in the nineteenth century, when Belgium began to take an interest in it, despite the unhealthy climate, and its natural resources, including mineral resources, were ruthlessly exploited with much loss of life among the native peoples.

Not all European arrivals were so obtuse when it came to respecting differences. Sir Richard Burton (1821–90), served in the Indian army and then travelled in Arabia and wrote about it.[25] In 1854 he set out on explorations of Somalia and beyond, dressed as a Turkish merchant to make himself less conspicuous. Again he published an account, this time of his *First Footsteps in East Africa, or, An Exploration of Harar* (1856). He had conceived the idea of looking for the source of the White Nile. The Blue Nile rises in the highlands of Ethiopia and its course had been traced reasonably fully, but the route of the White Nile remained largely unknown. He gained support from the Foreign Office and the Royal Geographical Society as well as the East India Company. He was given leave for two years, on full pay. He put an expeditionary force together, including John Speke, and they were in Zanzibar by the end of 1856. They believed they were looking for a source in great lakes, which turned out to be correct.[26] Like other explorers, Burton became interested in the languages spoken and the beliefs held by the peoples of the lands they crossed.

He encountered cultural differences. For example, with the expectations of a nineteenth-century Englishman about good manners, he did a good turn and expected polite thanks, which in one case he describes, he did not receive:

> He is thankful to Allah for the gifts of the Creator, but he has a claim to the good offices of a fellow-creature. In rendering him a service you have but done your duty; and he would not pay you so poor a compliment as to praise you for the act. He leaves you, his benefactor, with a short prayer for the length of your days.[27]

But Burton understands the response. This is not discourtesy. It is the 'politeness' of another religion and another culture.

In general, though, the European traveller thought he was bringing to Africa not only the light of truth and the hope of salvation but also a superior civilisation. The title of Joseph Conrad's novel, *Heart of Darkness*, published as a serial in 1899,[28] reflects a not-untypical view of Africa of the period. It has been suggested that the character of Kurtz in Conrad's story was modelled on the real explorer Henry Morton Stanley. Certainly both treated their native African porters as though they were little more than pack animals.

The introduction of European values, coupled with a conviction of the superiority of European civilisation, inevitably changed what it encountered and modified native beliefs about creation. As Kurtz puts it in Conrad's *Heart of Darkness:*

> We whites . . . must necessarily appear to them [the 'savages'] in the nature of supernatural beings . . . By the simple exercise of our will we can exert a power for good practically unbounded.[29]

Mapping Africa but not the myths

There emerged a need to draw together coherently and consistently in a map the new information gained through Livingstone's work and other explorations. The explorers had given conflicting geographical reports and there were in the nineteenth century huge areas still needing 'scientific' European exploration. In preparing his 'Map of Eastern Equatorial Africa' for the Royal Geographical Society, Ernst Georg Ravenstein (1834–1913) set himself a high standard. He worked from explorers' accounts and also used routes travelled by indigenous traders and tried to position tribal areas correctly.[30] Missionary societies wanted maps too, and not only of Africa, to enable them to send missionaries to the right places.[31]

But until the early twentieth-century fashion for collecting myths there was no comparable attempt to map the beliefs of the indigenous peoples of Africa so as to discover whether they could possibly have transmitted reliable information about how they got there and how the human race began.

II. REDRAWING THE WORLD-PICTURE: NEW CONTINENTS

Travel stories of creation

If going to Africa down the centuries did not bring inquirers into contact with the remains of the first humans until the very recent past – and then only in such an untidy manner – is it possible to find out how the world began by exploring the world as a whole? Modern palaeontology thinks so. Modern archaeology thinks so. Modern cosmology, particle physics, astronomy, astrophysics think so.

In primitive societies the opportunities for going on physical explorations to discover how big the world was and how far back it went were limited. There was only the horse, and in some societies only the ox, for transport. There were dangers in long journeys – being set upon by robbers on the way only one of them. Remote places were likely to be dangerous. For many centuries it was believed that the sea boiled at the equator because it was so hot, and a strong disincentive to travelling south to see what might be there was the belief that it was impossible to cross the equator and survive.

In any case, the idea that the way to find out the truth is to go and see, and test by investigation and experiment, is relatively modern. Another way to recapture events is not to replicate a journey by actually exploring, but to tell the story of the original 'journey' from the beginning of the world to where the story-tellers find themselves now. That was what primitive societies often chose to do. In some North American Indian myths the 'local people' describe how they emerged from the underworld or ground or ocean, and then migrated until they settled in their present place. This is a travel story which can take the listeners in imagination beyond the confines of the physical world they know and into extraordinary scenes. The key thing is the way myth-telling makes possible the blurring of the boundary between places it would be possible to reach by travelling to see them and places which cannot possibly be visited except in story and in thought.

Among the first to realise the possibilities of actual travel as a means of inquiry about creation were the discoverers who put together a full picture of the globe of the earth, with the positions of the lands and seas to be found on it. These 'discoverers', exploring mainly from the sixteenth to the nineteenth centuries, and chiefly as Western Europeans, in a sense 'discovered' nothing when they 'found' other peoples and cultures and beliefs in the 'new' lands, because the peoples they found already knew they were there and had their own cultures and explanations of the way they had come to exist. What the discoverers did was to connect this new knowledge with the picture of the world which had grown up in Europe, and to amend that picture accordingly. They and the earlier map-makers were engaged in the enormous task of depicting that part of the cosmos which is 'the earth under the moon' and fitting it to what they (variously) believed about its creation.

Once the old Silk Route to trade with India and China became dangerous with the fall of Constantinople in 1453, and the Ottoman Turks began to threaten overland commercial traffic to and from Europe, the Portuguese started to try to find a way round Africa by sailing south. Africa was discovered to reach much further south than expected, when Bartholomew Diaz got to the Cape of Good Hope in 1488. Though Columbus, too, had partially explored the way by sea down the coast of Africa in the early 1480s, this route became the Portuguese 'way' and the Spanish project became the westward exploration in the expectation of finding India in that direction.

Christopher Columbus goes west

It might be the presumption of those who invented 'mapping' that the contours of the world would not change. But they had to change when it was realised that there were far more than three continents and that one of the known three was much bigger than had been thought by the educated Europeans who had relied on the classical texts. It turned out that the whole appearance of the created world had been misrepresented. The map of the created world had to be withdrawn comprehensively when first a whole new portion of the northern hemisphere and then the continents of the southern hemisphere were 'found' by Europeans. The process of joining up localities as the full extent of the world was 'discovered' ultimately involved a multicultural joining-up of viewpoints, perceptions and assumptions. But at first, the explorers became the conquerors. And Europe imposed its world-view.

Christopher Columbus (1451–1506) did not set sail without doing his research. He did what he could to teach himself what was to be known about the layout of the created world. He seems to have read the travels of Marco Polo and the late fourteenth-century 'travels' of the fictional Sir John Mandeville, both of which were popular reading in translation in several languages by his time. For more theoretical discussions he had Pliny's *Natural History*. Ptolemy's second-century *Geography* had been rediscovered in the fifteenth century and translated about 1409 by Jacobus Angelus. Columbus probably read a copy of the printed version of 1478. This was a source used by Peter d'Ailly in his *Imago Mundi*. Columbus certainly had access to a copy of that, for an example survives with his marginal notes.[32]

Columbus was not looking for a 'new world'. The presumption was still that the apostles, having been sent to bring the Gospel to all the world, had been able to reach it all. So he was expecting to find only an alternative route to the desirable trading grounds of the Far East, which were in the already-known continent of 'Asia'. The voyage west was simply a business venture, a gamble that there might be a quicker route in that direction for those engaged in trade with India and China.

Whatever 'maps of the world' Columbus may have seen would have created expectations that there might be new islands to be found, but not new continents. Columbus's notion of the distance across the open Atlantic which would have to be sailed to reach the Indies was optimistic. He thought it would be less than three thousand miles. He was not far out in terms of the distance to the Americas, but greatly underestimated the distance to Asia, had there in fact been no extra continent in the way. He thought, too, that there were other islands on the way, beyond what are now the Canaries, Madeira and the Azores, where ships might take on water and food supplies. As far as he could discover, the objective seemed achievable.

Columbus was acting as an agent for traders. He had to persuade the 'venture capitalists' and prestigious patrons of the time to back his expeditions. The motivation and the financing for the exploration remained predominantly commercial, with a whiff of imperialism on the part of politicians who lent their support. Patrons could confer political approval and respectability.

Royal patronage was best, if you could get it. Columbus tried unsuccessfully to obtain funding from John II of Portugal in 1485 and again in 1488, for a voyage west into the Atlantic. He tried Venice and Genoa, where commercial sponsors were to be sought, again unsuccessfully. His brother got short shrift from Henry VIII of England when he made a funding bid there. In Ferdinand and Isabella of Aragon Columbus at first found yet another refusal in 1486. Their advisers told them he was over-optimistic about the distance. But he persevered and a package was eventually put together, including funding from private Italian funders. Any profits were to be shared. The politics of the Iberian Peninsula were uncomfortable for Spain at the time, and recent

14. A Native American dressed for war with a scalp, by George Townshend, Fourth Viscount and First Marquess Townshend

war left its rulers eager both financially and politically for a high-profile success. In 1493, he presented a diary of his first voyage to Ferdinand and Isabella.

Columbus's own motivation, however, included something more than a desire for commercial success and possible personal rewards in the form of honours from pleased patrons. It would have been impossible for him not to place what he was doing in a theological context, and it is clear that he did. Late in life, probably with the help of a better-educated friend, Gaspar Coriccio, who was a Carthusian, he compiled a *Book of Prophecies*.[33] These were apocalyptic, anticipating the coming of a New World of the Biblical sort, with the promised fresh creation of the book of Revelation.

Columbus's *Book of Prophecies* was designed as a presentation to Ferdinand and Isabella, to be made between the third and fourth voyages. He could expect them to be interested, for a 'messianic' fervour in the creation of an empire was sharp in Spanish politics. His sources gave him links with Joachimism. (Pierre d'Ailly mentions Joachim of Fiore several times.) Columbus notes that 'the Calabrian Abbot Joachim said that whoever was to build the temple on Mount Zion would come from Spain.'[34] He tied his efforts to the exploration of the world:

> During this time I have studied all kinds of texts: cosmography, histories, chronicles, philosophy and other disciplines. Through these writings, the hand of our Lord opened my mind to the possibility of sailing to the Indies and gave me the will to attempt the voyage.[35]

The conjunction was clear in his mind: 'For the voyage to the Indies neither intelligence nor world maps were of any use to me; it was the fulfilment of Isaiah's *prophecy*.'[36]

Rearranging the old theory

The sixteenth-century Western European 'discoverers' who 'found' the rest of the world and added it to the three continents previously 'known' set out with an 'inner world' of old theories of the shape in which the world had been created, against which they expected to be able to interpret what they saw.[37] The Spanish discoverers placed Atlantis in the Atlantic Ocean, where it had a 'wonderful history . . . almost forgotten in ancient times, Plato alone having preserved it'. 'Plato, in Critias, says that to Neptune's share came the Atlantic Island, and that he had ten sons, Africa, Atlantic, Haiti and so on.'[38]

> By divine permission, and perhaps because of their sins, it happened that a great and continuous earthquake, with an increasing deluge, perpetual by day and night, opened the earth and swallowed up these warlike and ambitious Atlantic men. The Atlantic island remained absorbed beneath that great sea, which from that cause continued to be unnavigable owing to the mud of the absorbed island in solution, a wonderful thing.[39]

A South American flood may now be added to the five floods recorded by the ancients, suggested the Spanish explorer Pedro Sarmiento de Gamboa (1532–92), and he discusses the manner in which the world to the east, and the West Indies, may have been peopled,[40] so as to provide human beings for the missionary endeavour of Christians now that they had found their way there. Peruvian Indians were misled by the devil,

> giving them to understand that he had created them from the first, and afterwards, owing to their sins and evil deeds, he had destroyed them with a flood, again creating them and giving them food and the way to preserve it.

He explains that:

> the natives of this land affirm that in the beginning, and before this world was created, there was a being called Viracocha . . . which means Creator of all things . . . He created a dark world without sun, moon, or stars.
>
> He formed a race of giants of disproportionate greatness painted and sculptured, to see whether it would be well to make real men of that size. He then created men in his likeness as they are now; and they lived in darkness.
>
> [He] ordered these people that they should live without quarrelling, and that they should know serve him. He gave them a certain and precept which they were to observe on pain of being confounded if they should break it.[41]

Then they transgressed and 'some were turned into stones, . . . some were swallowed up by the earth, others by the sea, and over all their came a great flood.'[42]

Thomas More (1478–1535) has one of his fictional characters describe at the beginning of his *Utopia* how he had himself travelled and made discoveries and how he found that:

> Under the equator, and as far on both sides of it as the sun moves, there lay vast deserts that were parched with the perpetual heat of the sun; the soil was withered, all things looked dismally, and all places were either quite uninhabited, or abounded with wild beasts and serpents, and some few men that were neither less wild nor less cruel than the beasts themselves.[43]

Yet these imaginary travellers reported that:

> as they went farther, a new scene opened, all things grew milder, the air less burning, the soil more verdant, and even the beasts were less wild: and at last there were nations, towns, and cities, that had not only mutual commerce among themselves, and with their neighbors, but traded both by sea and land, to very remote countries.

Here were mirrored lands and ships and ways of life known to the inhabitants of the northern hemisphere which provide fictional points of comparison and contrast. There are small touches indicating differences (the southern seafarers did not know the use of the compass, for example).

The story-teller relates 'many things that were amiss in those new-discovered countries' and also 'not a few things from which patterns might be taken for correcting the errors of these nations among whom we live'. And he describes Utopia itself. Here is a civilisation arising in another part of the created world, which a Christian may study and reflect upon and try out challenging ideas, without falling into heresy.

So it was not only actual travellers who took part in the rethinking of the map of the created world in its ultimate context of an ancient 'creation cosmology'. A number of 'armchair travellers' did the same, and not only in works of satire and political comment. Richard Hakluyt (1552/3–1616) became interested in geography as a boy, when he noticed some maps belonging to a cousin of his who was a lawyer acting for commercial trading ventures. Lying with the maps of the world on a table were books on cosmography.

At Oxford in 1570, where apparently he had financial support as a student from the Skinners' or the Clothworkers' Company,

Hakluyt took the opportunity to read about other countries and recent discoveries, in as many languages as possible. He is said to have given lectures on geography, explaining 'both the old imperfectly composed and the new lately reformed mappes, globes, spheares, and other instruments of this art'.[44] He wrote travellers' tales, narratives chiefly concerned with English and French successes in settling the Americas. The French had been concentrating on Canada, and Hakluyt may have read Jacques Cartier's account of his journey of the 1530s.

He attracted the attention of ambassadors and diplomats, who saw him as a useful potential aide in the task of drawing together plans and conclusions about ways in which European nations would be able to profit from the new discoveries and how they might share out the benefits. He was taken to Paris to assist in this work. Partly through his cousin the lawyer, he came to the notice of Sir Francis Walsingham (1532–90), Queen Elizabeth's skilled support in foreign affairs, and adventurers of the time such as the navigator, slave-trader and pirate Sir Francis Drake (1540–96) and the explorer of South America, Walter Raleigh (1554–1618), and was drawn into court circles and dubious but exciting company. There he learned to write to please the queen.

Just as Columbus was able to reflect on creation cosmology from the deck of a ship, so Hakluyt thought about it from the safe distance of a room full of books. Hakluyt's own great work was to be the collection of *The Principal Nauigations, Voyages, Traffiques and Discoueries of the English Nation* (1589). He aimed to include eyewitness accounts, but he travelled only vicariously, through the experiences of others. Nevertheless, Hakluyt's second-hand voyages include expressions of sympathy with, and interest in, other ways of understanding creation from a religious point of view;[45] for example, describing Russian Orthodox monasteries and marriage ceremonies, with emphasis on the many images in the church, relics, healings and miracles by saints:

They have no preachers . . . to instruct the people, so that there are many, and the most part of the poor in the country, who, if one ask them how many gods there be, they will say a great many, meaning that every image which they have is a god . . . their ceremonies are all, as they say, according to the Greek church used at this present day, and they allow no other religion but the Greeks' and their own.

He relates how in Benares in India 'they be all gentiles and be the greatest idolaters'. In their houses the people:

> have their images standing . . . made of stone and wood, some like lions, leopards, and monkeys, some like men and women, and peacocks, and some like the devil with four arms and 4 hands.[46]

He notes that the local people sacrifice to these images. He discusses the role of Brahmins as priests, describing marriage ceremonies involving the holy river and sacred cows. In Guinea are to be found, he suggests, 'a people of beastly living, without a god, law, religion or commonwealth'.[47]

This shift of perceptions as knowledge of the New World was accommodated is also visible in the work of Samuel Purchas (1575?–1626). He was a puritanically inclined Anglican clergyman and theological travel writer who never went more than two hundred miles from Thaxted in Essex himself, but who acquired other people's travel stories and (after 1620) some of Hakluyt's manuscripts. He published the influential *Purchas his Pilgrimes: Microcosmus, or, The Historie of Man* (1619).

He too found it natural to conjoin the account of an expanding geography with questions arising for creation theology. For him man is a microcosm and creation and the story of humankind forms a single tale:

> God which in the beginning had made the world, and endowed man with the Naturall inheritance thereof, whom also he made another, a living and little World, yea, a compendious Image of God and the world together.

Purchas was also well aware of the significance of the belief that the exploration of the world was a Christian duty, first entrusted to the apostles so that they could spread the Gospel.

> He committed to faithfull witnesses, giving them charge to go into all the world and preach the Gospel to every creature . . . Thus we have one Author of the world, of Man, of Peregrinations by men in and about the World.[48]

Purchas includes notes on the range of the apostles' comprehensive journeyings. Philip went to 'Asia superior'; Thomas to the Indians and 'some of the Jesuits have added China also to the labours of St. Thomas'; Matthew went to Ethiopia, 'that namely which adhereth to India, as Socrates writeth'. Nicephorus added the Anthropophagi. But Purchas was capable of scepticism. He thinks some stories are falsifications. He is prepared to believe that the devil 'obtruded on the Credulous world' various false tales, including 'Lives [lies] of the Saints, Histories, yea, Misse-stories, Hisse-stories, by the old Serpent hissed and buzzed amongst superstitious men'.[49]

Faced with the difficulty that the 'whole world' the apostles were sent to as missionaries turns out to be rather bigger, and it is evident that there were places the apostles did not reach, Purchas seeks to answer those who say 'wee have not named all Countries of the World.' Perhaps the apostles were too busy to complete the task? No one in America seemed to have heard of Christ when the continent was 'discovered'. Perhaps they had heard but their descendants had forgotten. 'Time eates up her owne Children, and . . . none can prove that Christ hath not beene there preached in former times, because these are thereof ignorant.' Or perhaps there were no people living there in the apostles' times and these lands were 'latelier peopled then the Apostles dayes'. 'Who can tell that America, and many parts of Asia, Afrike and Europe were then peopled with Men?' It is most likely they were not, for 'how great a part of the World is yet without habitation? How great a part of the World is yet unknowne? All the South Continent is in manner such, and yet in reason conjectured to bee very large, and as it were another New World.'[50]

This tiptoeing into the way other peoples lived and thought, and how they understood the rules as well as the shape of the created world was the beginning of a slow and patchy process of comparison and shared understanding.

Islam considers the New World

When Europeans discovered the Americas they were looking not for a New World but for an alternative route to India. Indeed they called the peoples they found in America 'Indians'. How did the New World's 'India' appear to peoples of the Old World and its India, who learned about it from European travellers' tales?

Hadis-i nev Tarig-i garbi, a 'history of the India of the West', published in 1875, was a reprint of a text already circulating in manuscript, and previously published in 1730, when Islamic and Ottoman printing was a novelty. The subject-matter of the maps was

as known in the sixteenth century and the text was substantially a
composition of the sixteenth century. This is a work which relied on
European writings about the European discoveries, so it contains
no new information about the New World itself. Its interest lies
in the way it attempts to bring together the new knowledge of
lands on which the Qur'an gave no clear guidance with Islamic
expectations. The Ottoman Turks stood near the height of their
power and geographical spread in the sixteenth century. But they
never moved into the New World. Their contemplation of its
appearance remained at a distance.

The Preface includes a review of creation as it looked to
contemporary Islam:

> Magnificent, Omnipotent Creator and Universal Ruler, Who
> compounded the four opposing elements with two words, and
> who arranged in six days without buttress and support the nine
> revolving spheres of heaven. In the gardens of His Omnipotence
> the face of the sun – a fresh rose; in the seas of his Divine Wisdom
> the luminous moon – a solitary water-lily; the crescent written in
> the firmament of the sky; and every reflection seen is an indication
> of the perfection of his power. And the alternation of the four
> seasons is the proof of His endless wisdom in every matter.[51]

If a 'a new world is visible' it must manifest 'the omnipotence
of His Lordship the All-Creator' and its appearance must be
designed to increase the faith of believers. The fundamentals
have not changed. Readers may be confident that the 'Creator,
out of Whose Creativeness the spheres of heaven/Find so many
thousands of forms of expression'[52] is creatively at work.

The Preface goes on to provide a reassuring familiar account
of the cosmos, with its concentric spheres, in which the earth is
also a sphere, its zones, its equator, with a discussion of its size,
citing Ptolemy and reliant on the classical background especially
of Greek thought on which Arabic science had long relied.[53]

III. FILLING THE EMPTY HEMISPHERE

After the discovery of the New World it was not long before the
map of the rest of the globe, including the 'empty' southern
hemisphere, was filled with further discoveries: of the Antipodes

and the Pacific and South America. Antarctica waited until the late nineteenth and twentieth century for exploration, but there, as it turned out, there really were no people to be found already living there, only seals and penguins and skua gulls.

Contact with Europeans

Western discovery of Australian and New Zealand came late in the story of European 'discoveries'. Two sightings of the Australian continent by Dutch and Spanish ships respectively are cited in 1606. The Dutch ship landed at the Gulf of Carpentaria in the north of the Australian continent and Australia briefly became known as New Holland.

Into the Antipodean world of Australian, Tasmanian and Maori peoples sailed Abel Jansen Tasman (1603–59) in search of promising trading opportunities for his Dutch sponsors. He made two voyages and came across Tasmania, New Zealand and the north Australian coasts, but it was not felt that these were worth following up from a commercial point of view.

He was followed by Captain Cook (1728–79) in a journey sponsored by the Royal Navy and the scientists of the Royal Society, and launched in a rather different spirit. Secret 'instructions' were given by the Admiralty commissioners to Cook, dated 30 July 1768. He and his sailors were not to attempt conquest. They were to be pleasant and use bribery rather than force to establish good relations with the peoples they encountered on their journey:

> You are to endeavour by all proper means to cultivate a friendship with the Natives, presenting them such Trifles as may be acceptable to them, exchanging with them for Provisions . . . and shewing them every kind of Civility and regard.[54]

Exploration is approved of as something which will 'redound greatly to the Honour of this Nation as a Maritime Power'. If it proves possible to 'take' lands peaceably and with the consent of those who live there, that is acceptable: 'You are likewise to observe the Genius, Temper, Disposition and Number of the Natives, if there be any', and 'take possession of Convenient Situations . . . in the Name of the King of Great Britain', 'with the Consent of the Natives'.[55] So the leading approved motivation was to benefit what would now be called the 'developing nations'; these European explorers consequently approached any peoples they encountered with an assumption that theirs was the superior civilisation.

The expedition sailed on south into the unknown seas. Some Pacific islands were found and claimed for Britain, with the 'consent' of their inhabitants. There is no mention of mission in the 'instructions'. The natives are not to be converted to Christianity by those on board these ships, though that objective was identified for later voyages. This meant that for the moment the observation of what the 'natives' believed remained incidental to the stated preoccupations of the explorers, though some general impressions were recorded.

Scientific curiosity about the cosmos was an important driver too. There was a transit of Venus across the sun to be observed, due to occur in 1769. (It took place when the expedition was at Tahiti and was duly observed.) There were lands to be located if they really existed, the unknown lands to the south (*terra australis incognita*).

Cook reached New Zealand and mapped the coast for some months. He carried on to find the east coast of Australia, landing at Botany Bay. In the journals kept during this and his other voyages, Cook reflected a little on the peoples he met. He describes the people of 'Caledonia' and notes that 'we have all the reason in the World to suppose ourselves the first Europeans they ever beheld.' He found them benevolent, trusting, anxious to be helpful and, in appearance, 'woolly-headed'.[56]

The blend of commercial, scientific and national expansion objectives proved destructive. Tasmania was first called Van Diemen's Land when it was found by Abel Tasman in 1642, but this expedition does not seem to have 'met' the natives. To begin with, both French and British ships made relatively peaceful contact, though French explorers of the early 1770s exchanged fire with the natives, who used stones and arrows. From the end of the eighteenth century seal hunters began to visit Tasmania in earnest in pursuit of the fur trade. That led to settlements, at least during periods of months, and more active contact between Europeans and the aboriginal Tasmanians, to the natives' detriment. Tasmania's native tribes suffered comprehensively at the hands of the Europeans.

George Augustus Robinson (1788–1866) recorded his experiences when he was the chief protector of aborigines of Port Philip (1839–49). He learned of the shortage of blankets and clothing and destitution generally, murders of women and children by 'some white ruffians', and sketches a general picture of desperate natives raiding white settlers' lands and stealing food. 'I would recommend that native tribes . . . who mix with settlers, be placed under control,' he suggests. 'A religious missionary, a medical attendant, and a schoolmaster, are required. It would be desirable to remove the convicts.'[57] As a consequence of this social disintegration, by the mid-nineteenth century the numbers were dropping and aborigines were persuaded to allow themselves to be moved to Flinders Island. By 1880 they were all dead, and with them their languages and culture and religion.

The original notions of creation held by oral tradition in these tribes faded with the destruction of their way of life. Yet Tasmanians, like Australian aborigines, seem to have been indigenous peoples with a very long history in the lands in which the Europeans 'found' them. There they had developed their own polytheistic and animistic religious system with their own accounts of creation. A Tasmanian creation story tells of a Creator taking earth up to the sky, where he made a man, Parlevar, the ancestor of the original Tasmanians. But the man had a tail like a kangaroo and no knees. This was inconvenient because it meant he had to sleep standing up. A Great Star Spirit took pity on him, cut off his tail and made him knee joints. Parlevar eventually came down to earth by walking down the Milky Way. The original Creator quarrelled with Parlevar's divine rescuer the star god, and was ejected from heaven. He came to live near Louisa Bay. His wife came to live in the sea. Their children came down from the sky in rain. In this way the gods came to earth, where they fought the evil spirits lurking there. The Creator made rivers and mountains and islands in the sea. He did this with the aid of various animals which he also created. The ants helped cut channels into the ground to make beds for the streams. The kangaroos sat, making depressions in the ground which filled with water to become lakes. The Creator God eventually died and became a great rock standing near the sea.[58]

Aboriginal belief systems

Not all the polytheistic peoples' ideas about creation encountered by these further 'discoverers' were so old or so profoundly connected to the places where the 'discovered' peoples lived as those of Australasia. But here, as in the West's slow and confused meeting with sub-Saharan Africa over the centuries, was to be a wasted chance to glimpse the very old beliefs of ancient peoples.

Australian aborigines may have lived on their ancestral lands, generation after generation, for as much as 100,000 years. Their ultimate origins and date of arrival remain uncertain. They are among the peoples best able to lay claim to having had their own origins at the beginning of the world. That did not mean they remained homogeneous. By the time Europeans arrived, these first Australians spoke several hundred languages and many more dialects, among a population estimated at between 300,000 and 750,000.

Their religious beliefs were strong, but localised. Their gods were gods of place, gods of local landscape. Features of that landscape were often explained by events so primeval as to be regarded as part of the very 'creation'. Perhaps an ancestor sat down long ago, and left what is now a dip in the ground, or the slithering passage of a primal snake left a local riverbed. Some of the gods and ancestors and even animals and rocks thus had a key role in creation.

These were functional gods who did orginating acts, which had their results in the world in which the aboriginal believer was now living. The gods did not necessarily cease to act. They still did things

15. The Three Sisters, Blue Mountains, New South Wales

16. Aboriginal rock painting from the Kakadu National Park. The main figure is thought to represent Namondjok, a creation ancestor associated with various myths

'now' to keep the universe running. For example, the Wandjina were believed to bring the rains or thunder and lightning in the wet season in parts of Western Australia, and beings with different names were trusted to do the same in other places.

These ancient aboriginals also shared a belief that once, at the beginning of the world, what are now human beings were animals and plants. Transformations from one kind of creature to another continued. They thought that human beings might still be reborn in such forms when they died. These assorted animal and vegetable beings could all be regarded as 'ancestors', and credited with giving the first instruction to ensure the local aboriginals had the skills they needed to survive, such as hunting and finding food. These skills embodied fundamental fixed rules or laws of life, and might be celebrated by being re-enacted in ceremonies and rituals. So unimaginable antiquity and enormous power were also 'here' and 'now' and easily grasped by each generation.

How far these practices reflected conscious notions among the ancient aborigines themselves it is difficult to say. They amount to 'renderings' of what they seemed to observers to believe. It is one thing to interpret them philosophically, in the categories of

European thought, importing into these apparent 'understandings' abstract ideas of the sort Western philosophers have made familiar. It is another to be confident that this can be accurate.

An example of this difficulty is the fact that the Australian aborigines do not seem to have developed a concept of 'soul'. Yet there is the germ of a 'Platonic idea' in the concept of a 'totem' or emblem, an original animal, plant or object, a representation of which becomes the 'sign' of a group or sub-group within a people. Each person believes himself or herself to be derived from or associated with his or her totem. That would make an individual whose emblem was a particular animal or plant regard others of the same kind as his relatives. So an aborigine might belong to a kin-group of kookaburras. A local landmark might be regarded as the clan emblem.

Polynesia

The Australians and Tasmanians, once settled, were not apparently given to exploring (except perhaps in the 'walkabout' custom of going off to spend time in the bush). Yet much of the southern hemisphere which the Christian West believed to be uninhabited because it lay beyond the impassable burning equatorial regions had already been pieced together by sea by Polynesian adventurers travelling from island to island in canoes. The marks of their journeyings are to be 'heard' in the interrelatedness of the Indonesian languages.

Using boats to get about the Pacific is one way in which creation beliefs could spread, but settlements on separate islands could and did also develop individual versions of the stories. One view found among the islanders was that the gods lived somewhere to the west. Others identified a volcanic area as more probable. In each crater, they thought, lived a being whose power was manifested in smoke and periodic eruptions of red-hot lava. The volcano-dweller sometimes came out to play in the flow. Such gods were a mixture of those who had always been divine and those who had been important human beings who had been translated to divine status at their deaths. Some had roles: for example, acting as columns or pillars in the temple of the gods.

There was another kind of divinity with particular appeal to local people. These looked after or served as mascots for different kinds of craftsmen and traders and those who farmed and fished.

Some presided over particular localities. Some were benevolent, some mischievous, but all responded to human attention in the form of worship or acts of propitiation and they tended to be small-minded rather than cosmic in the scale of their operations.

Worship required some fixtures. There might be nothing more than a little shrine to domestic gods in a dwelling. There were public shrines, containing an image of the god. There were temples, where the god could be thought of as making a home or habitation and which might contain household goods suitable for the deity's use. Some Polynesian temples kept a canoe handy for the god to use.

Europeans' experience of Polynesian religious and creation beliefs was variable. One Hawaiian legend foretold a visit by one of the gods. When Captain Cook arrived in 1778 on his third voyage, the Hawaiians welcomed him as a god on a floating island and treated him with ceremony accordingly. But an early missionary society venture in Tahiti was disastrous. Far from being humbly grateful, the natives met the missionaries with guns and showed signs of wanting to capture any goods the missionaries had with them. Nearly half of the first seventeen missionaries left on the first available ship.

Maori New Zealand

The New Zealand islands appear to have been comparatively late to experience human settlement. The people now known as Maori seem to have set out from eastern Polynesia and eventually landed in what is now New Zealand in the thirteenth century AD. They brought with them belief systems close to those of the aboriginal Australians. They too were polytheists and animists, personifying natural things and natural forces and imputing to them spiritual powers which must be placated. Good order was preserved in daily life partly through a strong system of taboo, which prevented and controlled activities.

Europeans came to New Zealand in 1642 when Abel Tasman's expedition landed and there was a battle with the Maoris. It was 1769 when the British Cook expedition arrived and set about a systematic exploration of the coasts. The nineteenth century brought Christian missions and the conversion of a large proportion of the Maori population from their original religious and creation beliefs.

European encounters with South American polytheisms

When South America first became 'known' to European explorers it tended to be thought of as an outpost of Asia. In a sense it was. Some of the 'Indians' who were 'found' in South America by the early Spanish and Portuguese discoverers from Europe are thought to have come from among the Mongolian peoples of Asia and across the Baring Strait, which was then an Arctic land link into North America. They had not been in South America long, comparatively speaking, though long enough for hundreds of indigenous languages,[59] tribes and customs to have emerged. Some immigrants into South America probably arrived in the sixth century AD and moved southwards from Mexico as nomadic hunter-gatherers, where they encountered peoples already living there. These peoples moving through the southern American continent influenced one another's cultures through trade and contact. Theirs is partly a 'travel' story of their origins.

17. Blanket based on a sand painting design. Two supernatural holy people flank the sacred maize plant, which was their gift to mortals in a creation myth

The Aztec culture may have begun with this sixth-century southward movement of peoples from the north, but it flowered into a characteristic civilisation in its own right during the fourteenth to sixteenth centuries, until its armies were defeated by the Spanish conquistador Hernán Cortés (1485–1547) in 1521. Mexico City was built by the Spanish conquerors on the ruins of the Aztec capital.

The main tribe the Spanish conquistadors encountered when they arrived seems to have been the Tenochca or Toltecs, a people who had apparently come into South America from the northern continent about the twelfth century AD, to live as best they could on poor lands. These were not triumphant conquerors of South American lands, but humble immigrants. Their migration may have been prompted by a rejection by neighbouring peoples in the north of the habits of human sacrifice among these tribes. It perhaps became too uncomfortable to linger in the face of their disapproval. As the Tenochca themselves told the story, Huitzilopochtli, one of their gods, had ordered this move into the area which is now Mexico.

The Toltecs held an extensive hotchpotch of beliefs about creation in which it is possible to glimpse some of the reasons for their practices of sacrifice. In one version the present world was thought to be the fifth attempt at creation, the first four having ended in disaster and destruction. This fifth world remains in being because a small god covered in sores had been sacrificed. He had become the sun. In another story two primordial gods of the sky were horrified when they found they had produced a baby bullock. They cast him out of the skies and as his blood fell in droplets everywhere, innumerable new gods appeared. These new gods did not like being confined to earth and they demanded the power to create human beings. Carrying out this task involved a journey to the underworld, where the necessary ingredients for making humans could be found in the form of the bones and ashes of the dead. Again, sacrifice was needed to make human creation possible. In another story altogether the world is the creation of twins, the gods Texcatlipoca and Quetzalcoatl. One of them lost a foot in the process.[60] In another tale, the creation of a sun able to move in the sky required the death of a god.

In the climate of this way of thinking of creation as involving even the sacrifice of the gods themselves, human sacrifice may have seemed a way of influencing or procuring a favourable heavenly response. It is not hard to see why tribes which did not use such extreme methods of propitiation could find this disturbing. The sacrifice is sometimes depicted in images as a ceremonial act involving the tearing out of the heart of a living person. The murderous regime extended to the exaction of human sacrifice in the course of legal and administrative practice in various areas of life.[61]

The Aztec god Huitzilopochtli had uncertain origins (as a god or a human hero), but in 1487 a great temple was dedicated to him with an enormous festival of human sacrifice. Surrounding peoples were asked to send victims, on pain of military invasion if they refused. Quetzalcoatl, the ancient plumed serpent with origins deep in the wider South American tradition, was a god of less extreme preferences. He accepted sacrifices of small animals but not of people.

Montezuma (1456–1520), leader of the Aztecs in the crucial second decade of the sixteenth century, encountered the Spanish conquerors' style of government in the person of Hernán Cortés not long before his death. Some stories suggest he regarded Cortés as a god, or pretended to do so, offering placatory gifts. He proceeded in a sophisticated way to offer the newcomers hospitality, but he found himself their prisoner and was soon executed.

The Incas, like the Aztecs, practised human sacrifice, including the sacrifice of children. Inca peoples were developing a culture from 1000 BC in the coastal deserts of modern Peru. They considered the mountains sacred because they rose up closer to the heavens where the gods dwelt. On the desert floor they drew pictures so that the gods could see them from the heavens. In the mountains of the Andes they built temples. Sun worship came naturally within this cosmic framework.

They left sophisticated artefacts which tell something of the story of their civilisation. The Incas, like the Aztecs, were mathematically sophisticated astronomers. They also used developed skills of measurement (involving knots in coloured string) to record the affairs of their extensive lands, covering Ecuador, Chile, Argentina, Peru and Bolivia in the period just before the arrival of the Spanish conquistadors.

In the centuries before the arrival of the Spanish and Portuguese conquerors of South America the Mayas had also developed a high civilisation and a written language, and they spoke a variety of languages. They too had a creation story and a cosmology closely resembling the general structure of the one which emerged in

Western European culture. The Mayan cosmos had levels or layers, a heaven above, an earth beneath and an underworld beneath that. The underworld was the realm of the dead and it had its god, just as the heaven had its sun god.

For the Mayas, creation was cyclical. It is easy to observe that the heavens revolve. The world comes and goes and comes again. It does this in a way sufficiently orderly and predictable to encourage the design of calendars. The priests of their religions saw stories in the skies and used rituals to prophesy and also to try to influence events within these cycles at propitious moments. Astronomy (taken to a sophisticated point of mathematical accuracy) and astrology were conflated. On earth the principal Mayan god is Maize, a god who takes the form of a handsome youth.

These are religious ideas designed to make sense of observed phenomena and give identity to concepts or events by the simple expedient of making each a god.

Christianity encounters the South American Indians

In general the effect of the arrival of the Spanish conquerors in the period of the discoveries was to impose on the existing polytheisms of South America a dominant Roman Catholic Christianity. Western 'discoverers' sometimes integrated mythological elements in a diffuse process of 'inculturation'. Patagonians were identified as giants in the fifteenth century ('*Hic sunt gigantes pugnantes cum draconibus*' – 'Here are giants who fight with dragons').[62] But this was probably more by way of travellers' tales than an adoption of the religion of the conquered native peoples.

There were some serious attempts to discover what the natives believed, going far beyond the general tenor of the casual observations described in the case of Europeans in contact with native peoples in other parts of the world. Friar Bernardino de Sahagun (1499–1590) wrote a history of Mexico (finished about 1569) in which he described the beliefs of the peoples the European conquerors had found there.

He explains in his prologue that he had met with the 'prominent men' in a series of major villages, explained what he wanted to do and asked them to find him knowledgeable old men who could answer his questions. He also had a few Indians who spoke Spanish who acted as interpreters. These interpreters were his own former pupils at the College of Santa Cruz de Tlaltelulco.

He himself had acquired a good knowledge of the local language. The explanations were given in pictures and the pictures were explained in words, and then the words were translated into Spanish and recorded.[63]

His *History* begins with a list of gods and their origins and conduct. It goes on to describe the festivals of the year among the pagans, a matter of practical importance where Roman Catholicism was seeking to introduce another sequence of feasts running through the year. The third section considers the origins of the gods. There are stories in which there is passage between divine and human status, such as that of the birth of a child (Vizilopuchtli) who could not be killed, from a mortal mother who had become pregnant in a mysterious way.[64]

There were attempts to ensure that the native people were treated appropriately. The well-meaning but hard to enforce Laws of Burgos (1512) made it unlawful to ill-treat the people and encouraged attempts to convert them to Catholicism.[65] But these laws allowed the creation of legal ghettos (*encomiendas*), with immigrant colonists as masters who imposed tight rules for living and working that were just this side of slavery.

Recorded perceptions of the social realities of South American places visited by European travellers in the nineteenth century may suggest that contact had caused mutual recoil rather than coalescence of cultures:

> In the evening, talking with the 'mayor-domo' of these mines about the number of foreigners now scattered over the whole country, he told me that, though quite a young man, he remembers when he was a boy at school at Coquimbo, a holiday being given to see the captain of an English ship, who was brought to the city to speak to the governor. He believes that nothing would have induced any boy in the school, himself included, to have gone close to the Englishman; so deeply had they been impressed with an idea of the heresy, contamination, and evil to be derived from contact with such a person. To this day they relate the atrocious actions of the bucaniers; and especially of one man, who took away the figure of the Virgin Mary, and returned the year after for that of St. Joseph, saying it was a pity the lady should not have a husband. I heard also of an old lady who, at a dinner at Coquimbo, remarked how wonderfully strange it was that she should have lived to dine in the same room with an Englishman; for she remembered as a girl, that

twice, at the mere cry of 'Los Ingleses,' every soul, carrying what valuables they could, had taken to the mountains.[66]

Charles Darwin, whose reflections these are, had some sympathy with, but limited understanding of, behaviours he observed:

It is impossible to be much surprised at the fear which natives and old residents, though some of them known to be men of great command of mind, so generally experience during earthquakes. I think, however, this excess of panic may be partly attributed to a want of habit in governing their fear, as it is not a feeling they are ashamed of. Indeed, the natives do not like to see a person indifferent. I heard of two Englishmen who, sleeping in the open air during a smart shock, knowing that there was no danger, did not rise. The natives cried out indignantly, 'Look at those heretics, they do not even get out of their beds!'[67]

He made links with preoccupations of his own civilisation:

On the 19th of August we finally left the shores of Brazil. I thank God, I shall never again visit a slave-country. To this day, if I hear a distant scream, it recalls with painful vividness my feelings, when passing a house near Pernambuco, I heard the most pitiable moans, and could not but suspect that some poor slave was being tortured, yet knew that I was as powerless as a child even to remonstrate. I suspected that these moans were from a tortured slave, for I was told that this was the case in another instance. Near Rio de Janeiro I lived opposite to an old lady, who kept screws to crush the fingers of her female slaves. I have stayed in a house where a young household mulatto, daily and hourly, was reviled, beaten, and persecuted enough to break the spirit of the lowest animal. I have seen a little boy, six or seven years old, struck thrice with a horse-whip (before I could interfere) on his naked head, for having handed me a glass of water not quite clean; I saw his father tremble at a mere glance from his master's eye.

Darwin suggests that, contrary to popular belief, this sort of behaviour was worst in Spanish colonies:

These latter cruelties were witnessed by me in a Spanish colony, in which it has always been said, that slaves are better treated than by the Portuguese, English, or other European nations. I have seen at Rio de Janeiro a powerful negro afraid to ward off a blow directed, as he thought, at his face. I was present when a kind-hearted man was on the point of separating forever the men, women, and little children of a large number of families who had long lived together.

Darwin was writing in an era when slavery was under question and had been outlawed under British law but in South America he found it still flourishing and even defended:

I will not even allude to the many heart-sickening atrocities which I authentically heard of; – nor would I have mentioned the above revolting details, had I not met with several people, so blinded by the constitutional gaiety of the negro as to speak of slavery as a tolerable evil. Such people have generally visited at the houses of the upper classes, where the domestic slaves are usually well treated, and they have not, like myself, lived amongst the lower classes. Such inquirers will ask slaves about their condition; they forget that the slave must indeed be dull, who does not calculate on the chance of his answer reaching his master's ears.[68]

So the Europeans who encountered peoples living in the southern hemisphere where they had long believed there could be none, made every effort to spread the Christian Gospel and their 'superior civilisation' among them, but at a huge cost to the continuation of the indigenous peoples' creation beliefs as well as to their cultural independence and general health and welfare.

IV. FACT AND FICTION

The eighteenth century's Western authors tended to think of themselves as rational and enlightened. But they enjoyed a good story about travel as much as the readers of Hakluyt and Purchas, and they were not too fussy as to whether it was fact or fiction. In their tales are to be found instructive reflections of the degree to which 'global awareness' of the creation stories of other peoples and other belief-systems was developing. They also reveal something of the extent to which the influence of Christianity and Islam had already coloured or overlaid the beliefs of the original inhabitants of different parts of the world.

The *Voyage Round the World* of William Dampier (1651–1715) appeared in 1697 and was an instant success. He had kept a vivid diary record of adventures on his own voyages. These adventures were not all of a respectable sort by any means, but they were exciting. He had sailed with privateers and buccaneers. One of the attractions of the book was the controversy it consequently generated. Dampier was obliged to publish a 'Vindication', and a 'pamphlet war' ensued. Nevertheless, his record caught the imagination of the Admiralty as well as of gentlemanly sensation-seeker readers and he was commissioned to make an official voyage.

His stories were written in a homely way, in clear simple language, and offered the reader a rattling good yarn. They were less informative about the way other peoples understood the world and its origins, but obliquely they show a good deal of the interests and expectations of the readers of travellers' tales, where he included some descriptions of the local people and their behaviour and beliefs. On the Mosquito Indians he wrote that there were only about a hundred of them; they were 'raw-boned, lusty, strong' and warlike with the lance. They were excellent fishermen and seamen. 'When they come among privateers, they get the use of guns, and prove very good marksmen.' They married for life and the couple settled on a small 'plantation' which was managed by the wife. 'They have no form of government among them.'[69]

He noticed some of the consequences of native encounters with Islam and Christianity. At Mindanao, 'one of the Philippine Islands', Dampier was told by a friar that 'the natives were Muhammedans', who had trading experience with the Spanish 'but were now at war with them'. The people of Mindanao, he says, wore garments made of plantain fibre. They were 'ingenious, nimble, and active when they are minded', but 'lazy', poor because they could not compete with the dominant European nations in trade, and subject to a 'prince' who ruled them like a tyrant. Dampier's account of their religious observance suggested that although they were all Muslims, they were not 'very strict in observing', except during Ramadan. They 'take care to keep themselves from being polluted by tasting or touching anything that is accounted unclean'.[70] This included swine, which were plentiful in the islands, but when the sailors shot them and took them on board for food, the inhabitants would no longer allow the sailors to enter their houses.

Dampier discusses encounters with native peoples but mainly in terms of their external behaviours, skills and social arrangements, and not their beliefs. In any case, these people had met white men in ships before and could not be guaranteed to represent the original opinions of their races. In his stories of the Philippines he discusses Islamic observances. 'The inhabitants of Condor are idolaters,' he comments, 'but their manner of worship I know not of.' He notes a temple he saw with an elephant and a horse statue in it. In China he set out to see the 'manner of living' but has little to say about Buddhism.[71]

The experience of native peoples in their encounters with Europeans could be more uncomfortable than their encounters with Islam:

> The Dutch, being seated among the Spice Islands, have monopolized all the trade into their own hands and will not suffer any of the natives to dispose of it, but to themselves alone.[72]

Some of the best-sellers of the generation which followed were travel books. In 1718 appeared Daniel Beeckman's *Voyage to and from the Island of Borneo* and Woodes Rogers' *Cruising Voyage Round the World*. The attraction lay partly in the freedom authors felt to set exciting adventures and improbable happenings in distant places where, it could be imagined, anything could happen.

Ambrose Evans' *The Adventures and Surprizing Deliverances of James Dubourdieu and his Wife* is a moral tale. The travellers encounter the noble savage, a favourite eighteenth-century figure, in the form of an unfallen tribe which is incapable of understanding the idea of 'the pursuit of gain and riches' and those who live with the objective of 'having what was more than absolutely necessary'. These people had 'no form of government'. They did not need 'magistrates', for 'there was no ground for contention; there being no property among them but a perpetual and uninterrupted course of a perfect love of one another.'[73] The travellers applauded all this but suggested that their own Christian religion has something more to offer, in the promise of eternal life.

The tribe brought forth a young girl to expound their own religious beliefs, including their theory of creation. She described a Being, who had 'produce'd' by 'infinite power and wisdom, all things that fill the universe', 'infinite and every where', which sustains 'everything that is', without beginning but which 'didst give beginning to every thing else'. 'This great God', she said, 'has planted in us certain laws, which are equally evident and beneficial, and of which reason is our teacher; a teacher who can never deceive us, since this great God has given us no other guide either to him or of our own actions.' 'This great Being has created human kind with a beneficent intention, for eternal goodness could have no other.'[74]

When told the Christian story, these people saw no advantage in it. Their people had, they said, a:

> history that begins before the creation of the world, and reaches down to our separation from the rest of mankind . . . being written on the very first foundation of our nation. By this account the creation of the world is attributed not immediately to God, but to certain spirits made by God of wonderful power and wisdom . . . every one of the stars, as well as the sun, were made by these immortal spirits.[75]

Danel Defoe

A satirist can play fanciful games with reality while making serious points. That is his job. The eighteenth century loved satire. Daniel Defoe's *Robinson Crusoe* appeared in 1719.[76] In it he sets up an experimental environment in which to test the answers to some controversies of the time about the ways in which it is possible to know anything about the Creator and the origins of the world.

Shipwrecked on a desert island, Crusoe acquires as a servant a native – who is, to European thinking of the time, a 'savage' – when he rescues him from his fellow cannibals. Anxious to civilise this individual, whom he refers to as his 'Man Friday', Crusoe teaches him the Christian faith. The only 'authorities' available are the Bible he has with him, saved from the wreck, and what a rational human being can work out from the observation of nature.

Here was a handy test of a fashionable theory of the time that Scripture and revelation provide sufficient information for the enquirer. It is also a test of contemporary theories about the capacity of the 'savage' to learn and accommodate himself to the 'superior civilisation' of the European. (Are savages inherently inferior or merely in need of opportunity to better themselves in learning and conduct?)

In 1720, Defoe published *The Life, Adventures, and Pyracies, of the Famous Captain Singleton*. Singleton goes to parts of the world untouched by Crusoe, to Newfoundland and the East Indies and to Madagascar where he is marooned for a time. He and his companions walk across sub-Saharan Africa, where they encounter beasts and landscapes unfamiliar to a Europe which had not yet made this journey in reality.

The boundaries between travel, science fiction and theological speculation are crossed and recrossed among Defoe's preoccupations. In another of his writings, Defoe has comments to make on the world before the Flood. He asks the necessary preliminary question, 'How do we know what happened when there was no one there to record it?' The answer favoured by contemporaries was that there was an oral tradition, conceivably handed down in the relatively short sequence of generations from Adam to Moses. Oral tradition:

> had so just an Authority, the Authors living so many years to perfect their Posterity in the Particulars of what they related to them, that we have no Reason to doubt the Truth of what was handed down from Father to Son; when MOSES, the first Historian that we know of, was not so remote from the last Days of Noah, as that the Particulars could be lost, but being convey'd from Father to Son, he might be well able even without the help of Divine Inspiration, to write the whole History of things before the Flood, Noah having without doubt made a perfect Relation of them to his Sons.[77]

As to how Moses gained a scientific understanding of the events of creation, Defoe warms to the story of Moses' 'spoiling' of the Egyptians who 'had made Discoveries in many useful Parts of Science'. He explores what happened to the earth after the Flood, noting the Babel episode and the confounding of tongues and consequent mutual unintelligibility which still afflicts humanity.[78] He asks whether the offspring of Ham became the founders of the modern Arabic civilisation. Did Shem go to Assyria and Asia, Japhet to the north and Europe?

Travel and religious understanding including knowledge of origins were readily connected. Mankind had to discover that boats float and could be used as a means of transport. Chapters follow in Defoe's account on how navigation was developed, and it can then be asked 'how they became acquainted with foreign countries'. Defoe links this beginning of a human 'connectedness' with the idea of making and maintaining 'an intercourse or communication of Nations by Water' for that was the 'Original of Trade', and the subsequent attempt by civilised peoples 'to plant their own people in Colonies, and Settlements in remote Countries, which were yet uninhabited, and divided from them by the great Waters'.[79]

Defoe's imitators

Shortly after appeared Jonathan Swift's *Gulliver's Travels* (1726);
he also mentions Dampier.[80] Gulliver travels as a ship's surgeon
and then as a captain to strange places with science fiction
characteristics. In Lilliput, Gulliver finds himself in a country
where the people are tiny. They challenge the conventions
about the size-range the Creator chose for real human beings.
Awakening from sleep, Gulliver finds himself bound with fine
cords by miniature guards. These appear to be human in every
respect except for their size:

> I felt something alive moving on my left leg, which advancing
> gently forward over my breast, came almost up to my chin; when,
> bending my eyes downwards as much as I could, I perceived it to
> be a human creature not six inches high, with a bow and arrow
> in his hands, and a quiver at his back.[81]

The question of what counts as human is therefore implicitly
raised at the outset.

To these little people, Gulliver's size makes him seem a god.
When the nervous natives gather threateningly and even shoot
their tiny arrows at Gulliver, the Lilliputian authorities hand them
over to him for punishment:

> the colonel ordered six of the ringleaders to be seized, and
> thought no punishment so proper as to deliver them bound into
> my hands; which some of his soldiers accordingly did, pushing
> them forward with the butt-ends of their pikes into my reach. I
> took them all in my right hand, put five of them into my coat-
> pocket; and as to the sixth, I made a countenance as if I would
> eat him alive.

Gulliver elects to behave like a benevolent 'deity':

> The poor man squalled terribly, and the colonel and his officers
> were in much pain, especially when they saw me take out my
> penknife: but I soon put them out of fear; for, looking mildly,
> and immediately cutting the strings he was bound with, I set him
> gently on the ground, and away he ran. I treated the rest in the
> same manner, taking them one by one out of my pocket; and I
> observed both the soldiers and people were highly delighted at

this mark of my clemency, which was represented very much to my advantage at court.[82]

There is a further challenge to the concept of what it is to be human later in his journey, when Gulliver finds himself among a people, the Houyhnhnm, who seemed to be horses. To these people he is a 'brute animal'. Meeting him, they 'looked upon it as a prodigy, that a brute animal should discover such marks of a rational creature'.

In speaking, they pronounced through the nose and throat, and their language approaches nearest to the High-Dutch, or German, of any I know in Europe; but is much more graceful and significant. The emperor Charles V. made almost the same observation, when he said that if he were to speak to his horse, it should be in High-Dutch.

These cultured horses find his cultural assumptions surprising: for example, the difference of expectation in the point of naked-ness. To these civilised horses:

my discourse was all very strange, but especially the last part; for he could not understand, why nature should teach us to conceal what nature had given; that neither himself nor family were ashamed of any parts of their bodies.

Gulliver compromises:

I first unbuttoned my coat, and pulled it off. I did the same with my waistcoat. I drew off my shoes, stockings, and breeches. I let my shirt down to my waist, and drew up the bottom; fastening it like a girdle about my middle, to hide my nakedness.[83]

Finding himself next in territory where he is with giants, he discusses the extent of the mismatch of sizes. It is not only the people who are huge. Everything else on this island of giants is correspondingly enormous too, except for the creatures in the seas (because the sea is continuous throughout the world fish must be the same sizes everywhere). For these giants, because 'the sea fish are of the same size with those in Europe,' they are 'consequently not worth catching'. But on land all the rest of 'nature' is also 'of so extraordinary a bulk', and why this 'is wholly confined to this continent, . . . I leave the reasons to be determined by philosophers'.[84]

In Chapter 23 of *Gulliver's Travels*, Gulliver finds himself in a world which goes beyond science fiction into magic. Here he is able to play with the concepts of time as well as those of space, and reach back to the beginning of the world to see things for himself:

> Glubbdubdrib, as nearly as I can interpret the word, signifies the island of sorcerers or magicians. It is about one third as large as the Isle of Wight, and extremely fruitful: it is governed by the head of a certain tribe, who are all magicians.

This governor, he says,

> desired me to give him some account of my travels; and, to let me see that I should be treated without ceremony, he dismissed all his attendants with a turn of his finger; at which, to my great astonishment, they vanished in an instant, like visions in a dream when we awake on a sudden . . . I had the honour to dine with the governor, where a new set of ghosts served up the meat, and waited at table.

He was invited to 'call up' the spirits of any of the dead he would like to talk to:

> among all the dead from the beginning of the world to the present time, and command them to answer any questions I should think fit to ask; with this condition, that my questions must be confined within the compass of the times they lived in. And one thing I might depend upon, that they would certainly tell me the truth, for lying was a talent of no use in the lower world.

He saw Alexander the Great and Hannibal and Caesar and Pompey:

> The governor, at my request, gave the sign for Caesar and Brutus to advance towards us. I was struck with a profound veneration at the sight of Brutus, and could easily discover the most consummate virtue, the greatest intrepidity and firmness of mind, the truest love of his country, and general benevolence for mankind, in every lineament of his countenance. I observed, with much pleasure, that these two persons were in

good intelligence with each other; and Caesar freely confessed to me, 'that the greatest actions of his own life were not equal, by many degrees, to the glory of taking it away.' I had the honour to have much conversation with Brutus; and was told, 'that his ancestor Junius, Socrates, Epaminondas, Cato the younger, Sir Thomas More, and himself were perpetually together': a sextumvirate, to which all the ages of the world cannot add a seventh.[85]

Talking to the ancients is taken further:

Having a desire to see those ancients who were most renowned for wit and learning, I set apart one day on purpose. I proposed that Homer and Aristotle might appear at the head of all their commentators; but these were so numerous, that some hundreds were forced to attend in the court, and outward rooms of the palace. I knew, and could distinguish those two heroes, at first sight, not only from the crowd, but from each other. Homer was the taller and comelier person of the two, walked very erect for one of his age, and his eyes were the most quick and piercing I ever beheld. Aristotle stooped much, and made use of a staff. His visage was meagre, his hair lank and thin, and his voice hollow.

Gulliver realises that the great thinkers know nothing of their later commentators. 'I soon discovered that both of them were perfect strangers to the rest of the company, and had never seen or heard of them before.' A ghost whispers to him:

that these commentators always kept in the most distant quarters from their principals, in the lower world, through a consciousness of shame and guilt, because they had so horribly misrepresented the meaning of those authors to posterity.

Discovering what succeeding generations have said about them, the thinkers are annoyed:

Aristotle was out of all patience with the account I gave him of Scotus and Ramus, as I presented them to him; and he asked them, 'whether the rest of the tribe were as great dunces as themselves?'

But there are more recent thinkers who were more than mere commentators, whose ideas are currently fashionable. Gulliver asks for Descartes and Gassendi to be sent for. He asks them 'to explain their systems to Aristotle'. Aristotle is happy to acknowledge that he had not got everything right, but he also thinks these newer ideas are 'equally to be exploded'. 'He predicted the same fate to ATTRACTION, whereof the present learned are such zealous asserters'.

[New] systems of nature were but new fashions, which would vary in every age; and even those, who pretend to demonstrate them from mathematical principles, would flourish but a short period of time, and be out of vogue when that was determined.[86]

Facing the difficulty of explaining to his readers where all these countries are, Gulliver proposed a revision of the map of the world whose contours and layout had been so recently more or less settled:

I cannot but conclude, that our geographers of Europe are in a great error, by supposing nothing but sea between Japan and California; for it was ever my opinion, that there must be a balance of earth to counterpoise the great continent of Tartary; and therefore they ought to correct their maps and charts, by joining this vast tract of land to the north-west parts of America, wherein I shall be ready to lend them my assistance.

He floats the ever-exciting (is there life on Mars?) possibility that further undiscovered peoples may yet be found:

The kingdom is a peninsula, terminated to the north-east by a ridge of mountains thirty miles high, which are altogether impassable, by reason of the volcanoes upon the tops: neither do the most learned know what sort of mortals inhabit beyond those mountains, or whether they be inhabited at all. On the three other sides, it is bounded by the ocean. There is not one sea-port in the whole kingdom: and those parts of the coasts into which the rivers issue, are so full of pointed rocks, and the sea generally so rough, that there is no venturing with the smallest of their boats; so that these people are wholly excluded from any commerce with the rest of the world.

Sindbad the sailor

Eastern legend includes some parallels with the travellers' tales of the West. Richard Burton's translated *The Book of the Thousand and One Nights* in which Scheherazade sought to entertain her royal husband with stories so that he would not have her beheaded, as he had the habit of doing with any wife who bored him (and they had all bored him up to the point when he married her). Among the tales are the stories of Sindbad the sailor.[87] Sindbad goes on a series of voyages which make him a wealthy man. On his first voyage he lands on a island which is really a whale; on the second on an island where the Rocs lay their eggs; on the third on an island inhabited by a monster who starts to eat the crew; on the fourth on an island populated by naked savages; on the fifth, he is captured by the Old Man of the Sea; on the sixth he is floated away on a raft when he is shipwrecked; on the seventh again he is shipwrecked and floated away on a raft. Each time the adventures which follow involve strange creatures and places and everything turns out well, with wealth and status for Sindbad.

Interpreting what you see in pictures

Thomas Daniell (1749–1840) and his nephew William, and later William's younger brother Samuel, travelled round the world as landscape painters. This was a period when the fashionable painter was a portraitist. They hoped to earn their keep and make their reputations by depicting the exotic scenery of the Orient. Thomas successfully sought the patronage of the East India Company to fund the first stage of the journey, of 1785–8, to India, but he described himself as an engraver. The two continued to China and set sail for England again only in 1794. Samuel journeyed from 1799, going to South Africa and then to Ceylon (Sri Lanka).

The pictures that resulted were prints which appeared in six sets of twenty-four between 1795 and 1808. Samuel's were eventually made into high-quality books of plates which sold for a substantial sum. The works were essentially Romantic landscapes, depicting important buildings both European and oriental, but peopled with figures engaged in the activities of the locality, sometimes in religious observation or worship. They made drawings of local people in costume. They seem to have had only a hazy understanding of the religions whose buildings and sculptures they encountered, confusing a statute of the Buddha with a Hindu god, but they were clearly struck with admiration and respect at some of what they saw. In a cave they found stalagmites which were worshipped by the local people as gods. 'This place is considered a most sacred cavern by the Hindoo and in the month of February at least 10 thousand resort here to pay their devoir to the images.' 'We . . . entered the Brahmin's compound with hope of having a little conversation with him but he kept muttering on in the same style as before and could scarcely get a word from him.' 'He visits the Maha Deos of the cavern once a day we were informed . . . by mere crawling.' 'The building on the Western extremity of the rock is an ancient Hindoo temple, held in great veneration by the votaries of the religion.'[88]

V. CREATED UNEQUAL?

Human but socially inferior?

The early modern European discovery of the rest of the world and the peoples living there raised the question whether these inhabitants were human and, if they were, whether they were 'noble savages' or degenerate and not the equal of civilised Europeans. The 1776 American Declaration of Independence statement that all men are created equal[89] was the product of its political times, concurred with Rousseau (see Chapter 1 (iii)), and went against a steady current of opinion in previous centuries that this was not so at all.

Christian and Jewish apologists had long appealed to the story of the three sons of Noah. This is the first point in the Genesis story where it is possible to show authority for the view that human beings may be racially different and that that difference could justify unequal treatment. The descendants of Ham came to be regarded as black. The Babylonian Talmud links blackness with sinfulness and degeneracy. Conversely, among Muslims, racial prejudice was expressed against fair races as well as the very dark, with the brown skins of Arabs rated highest.

The belief that no beings truly human – and therefore among those for whom Christ died – could possibly live in parts of the world where the sons of Noah could not have arrived and the apostles could not have reached, had its legacies. It follows that if any beings do live in the southern hemisphere, they cannot be truly human. That inference raised questions about the true human status of such beings as it turned out did live in the lands which were discovered from the late fifteenth and sixteenth century, and seemed human on first sight.

Although it became apparent that the equator was not a barrier of such heat that no human could cross it and live, there lingered the notion that these southern dwellers were not really human. It followed either that it was legitimate to treat them like animals and consider their accounts of their origins and the way the world began to be at best childish nonsense with no more than curiosity value, or that there was a Christian duty to seek to convert them to the Christian view of the creation of the world.

There is a long and regrettable story here, as conquering discoverers treated discovered peoples as an inferior creation. It was not confined to those who sailed about the world calling themselves Christians. It had philosophical respectability among the Greeks. Aristotle considered that some races were naturally slaves.

Peter Martyr (1400–1562), in *De Orbe Novo* described the Caribbean. In his *Decades* he mentions it as lived in by Amazons, popinjays, golden pebbles, nightingales and lions. Herodotus wrote about the Amazons, but he places them in the vicinity of the modern Ukraine. Other writers put them in Asia Minor or in Libya. The Amazons took part in the Trojan War, so they cannot have been New World people to the ancient world, let alone Americans or Caribbean dwellers.

Robinson Crusoe's Man Friday in Danel Defoe's novel provides a test case for the proper treatment of 'native' humans.[90] Thomas Coke (1747–1814), a preacher to the North American Indians, saw it as his plain duty to turn them Christian and took a stance against black slavery:

> We have in this state got up to the Cherokee-Indians, who are in general a peaceable people. I trust, the grace of God will in time get into some of their hearts . . . I met with a little persecution on my former visit to this Continent, on account of the public testimony I bore against Negro-Slavery.[91]

Enslaving human creatures

From the seventh century, Arab traders were colonising those parts of East Africa which could conveniently be reached from the Indian Ocean. A few crossed westwards and settled in Arab quarters in African towns. They traded in slaves. The slave trade which took captured Africans to the Americas began in the sixteenth century and continued until the nineteenth. These slaves were captured by African slave-dealers from Central and Western Africa and sold to traders from Europe (Portuguese, French, Spanish, Dutch and British, and also some of the American settlers themselves), who took them across the Atlantic to work in cotton, coffee and cocoa plantations or in the mines or as house servants, to be slaves to the colonising Europeans. Slave-dealing was not new to Africa but this fresh market meant a vast expansion of the trade. The number of slaves taken was certainly in many millions.

Britain had a heavy commercial involvement in this trade. At the end of the eighteenth century a very high proportion of its income from foreign trade was derived from the triangular process by which British products purchased African slaves for shipping to the Americas, where they produced goods such as tobacco and cotton and sugar, which were wanted in Britain. The defenders of slavery were willing to claim that the slaves were lesser humans who could only benefit from lives of slavery.

British Quakers began to protest. They petitioned Parliament in 1783 for an end to the trade in slaves. In the same year William Wilberforce (1759–1833) met James Ramsay, a ship's surgeon, who had seen for himself the conditions in which slaves were transported across the Atlantic, and also had experience of the life of slaves on the plantations. Now that he was back in England he was eager to campaign against the whole system, including the moral attitudes of the plantation owners who bought the slaves.

In 1784 Ramsay published *An Essay on the Treatment and Conversion of African Slaves in the British Sugar Colonies*. This created something of a furore. Responses were written: for example, that of 'Some Gentlemen of St. Christopher' in 1784, accusing him of grossly misrepresenting the position. The Bible approves slavery, they argue; in their island there have been plans long under consideration to make laws to ensure that the slaves are more comfortable, 'of obliging those masters who are inhuman to treat them with more tenderness'. Ramsay makes wild accusations relying on anecdote, they claim, while not at all understanding the way the island runs its affairs. Ramsay's book was influential nevertheless. In 1787, it was given to Wilberforce by Thomas Clarkson, who had won a Cambridge prize for an essay on the slave trade. They formed a lasting alliance. Wilberforce was persuaded to lead a campaign in Parliament for the abolition of the trade as unchristian.

A few freed slaves were able to play an active part, giving lectures and writing publications of their own, to demonstrate their fullness of humanity. Because Wilberforce became ill, it was in the end William Pitt who set in train the process of introducing a Bill to abolish the slave trade in 1789, with Wilberforce himself introducing it in an immensely long speech in 1791. It was not to pass without opposition. The call to end the slave trade was seen as an attack on the existing social order, an encouragement to uprisings by the lower classes everywhere and a route to revolution on the scale currently being faced by France.

In 1792 a new but still unsuccessful Bill came before the English Parliament calling for the abolition of slavery, and again Wilberforce was the driver of the attempt to change the law. A further vote followed in 1793 and again it was defeated, though narrowly. Repeated attempts continued to fail, as long as the abolitionists were associated in the public mind with the dangerous revolutionaries who had brought down the monarchy and the old social order across the Channel in France. There was a near-miss in 1804 when a Bill got through the Commons only to be lost because there was no time in the Parliamentary session for it to go through the Lords. Perhaps Wilberforce was too polite to the powerful, but he grew more astute and some politicking brought him the support he needed and the Foreign Slave Trade Bill was passed in 1806.

The white settlers of the American South, where most of the African slaves found themselves, continued to treat the slaves as human beings of lesser value. The subjugation of the black slaves of America and their descendants, and of the Native American tribes in some areas included denying them the vote and banning intermarriage with whites by law until the 1960s. There were 'Jim Crow' laws, imposing segregation by race and colour. Only in recent generations has the language and the thinking swung round, with the introduction of careful phrases such as 'Native Americans' for the 'Indian' tribes and 'Hispanic Americans' for Mexican immigrants.

Mission to 'inferiors'

The end of the slave trade encouraged a different sort of interference with the lives of peoples in the 'discovered' lands. Sub-Saharan Africa was colonised by European nations mainly in the nineteenth century. The process involved a good deal of individual adventuring and entrepreneurship, but the driving force was Christian mission. This was prompted in part by a new awareness in the European conscience as the realities of the slave trade were brought home to them that the world was full of peoples who had not heard the Gospel. They recognised a duty to preach the Gospel to these peoples, forced to admit that the apostles had after all left some of the world's peoples uninstructed.

Missionary organisations proliferated in the nineteenth century. David Livingstone went out as a missionary, sent by the London Missionary Society (see Chapter 5). Its parent – simply called the Missionary Society – had been founded by evangelical Nonconformists in 1795 to spread the Christian Gospel to Africa and the Pacific. Wealthy subscribers proved willing enough to supply funding and the society was able to send out ships full of missionaries.

The European explorers of the nineteenth century, with their mixed motivation of mission and commerce, might have been more humane than the slavers, but they still felt themselves to be dealing with inferiors who would benefit from being brought up to civilised standards by encounters with a higher and Christian civilisation. Mission included the importation of European culture and governances. Mungo Park, writing on his *Travels in the Interior of Africa* in 1860, suggests that three-quarters of 'Negro inhabitants' of Africa are slaves by social custom and inheritance.[92]

He notes that 'the negroes have no written language of their own':

Appeal to written laws, with which the pagan natives are necessarily unacquainted, has given rise in their palavers to (what I little expected to find in Africa), professional advocates . . . who are allowed to appear and to plead for plaintiff or defendant . . . Mohamedan negroes . . . are not always surpassed by the ablest pleaders in Europe.[93]

He notes the mingling of a residual paganism with the influence of Islam: for example, the:

charms or amulets called saphies which the Negroes constantly wear about them . . . these are prayers, or rather sentences from the Koran, which the Mahomedan priests write on scraps of paper, and sell to the simple natives, who consider them to possess very extraordinary virtues [worn as amulets to protect]. It is impossible not to admire the wonderful contagion of superstition; for, notwithstanding that the majority of the Negroes are pagans, and absolutely reject the doctrines of Mahomet, I did not meet with a man, whether Bushreen or Kafir, who was not fully persuaded of the powerful efficacy of these amulets. The truth is, that all the natives of this part of Africa consider the art of writing as bordering on magic; and it is not in the doctrines of the Prophet, but in the arts of the magician that their confidence is placed.[94]

He is interested in the origin of the Moorish tribes, but as far as he can discover:

nothing further seems to be known than what is related by John Leo, the African, whose account may be abridged as follows:– Before the Arabian Conquest, about the middle of the seventh century, all the inhabitants of Africa, whether they were descended from Numidians, Phoenicians, Carthaginians, Romans, Vandals, or Goths, were comprehended under the general name of Mauri, or Moors. All these nations were converted to the religion of Mahomet, during the Arabian Empire under the Caliphs . . . Many of the Numibian tribes retired southward . . . [I question] to what extent these people are now spread over the African continent.[95]

Attitudes which recognised the full humanity of all human beings and the equal claims of their accounts of creation were slow to emerge.

PART III

The main competing explanations

6

The beginning of the world: a one-off event?

I. ONE CREATION COMPLETE AND PERFECT

How could six days be one event?

The 'six days' of creation described by the book of Genesis took a great hold on the imagination of Christians and European philosophers for the many centuries during which the Bible's account of the beginning of the world was taken literally. One important question was whether these were literal days or metaphorical 'days' in which 'day' stood for a longer period such as an 'age', or perhaps for a 'stage' in creation.[1] But six of anything seems to imply that the creation was not a single instantaneous event such as a 'big bang'.

The need to understand the creation as essentially the single perfect work of an all-powerful God who could not make mistakes or have afterthoughts drove a flurry of questioning and interpretation. What, it was asked, is the significance of the seventh day of 'rest', for such a Creator could not possibly have been tired? And how could 'days' mean anything when the Creator is eternal and may have been acting without reference to time? Augustine asks about this in his book *De Genesi ad Litteram* (*On Genesis Taken Literally*).[2] When God said 'Let there be light' did he speak 'temporally' or 'in the vocabulary of eternity' (*in verbi aeternitate*)? If he spoke temporally he spoke in a way which was mutable. But God is not mutable. So this must be a mode of speaking to help our creaturely understanding.

Robert Grosseteste was one of many commentators who reflected on this problem about time and took a similar approach to explaining the essential unity of the serial story in Genesis. He wrote about the 'six days' with many of Augustine's sensitivities. The order of creation can be grasped only by faith, he suggests. The story is told as it is in Genesis in consideration for human intellectual limitations, 'in order that anyone, even among the uneducated, may be able to grasp a story of this kind easily, through his imagination and through the images of corporeal things'. In other words, we learn better in pictures. Grosseteste, like Augustine, considers that putting the explanation in the form of a step-by-step story with figurative meanings was a helpful way of assisting human stupidity. The 'archetypal world' is Christ, the 'begotten wisdom of the Father'. He is the perfect light, with the created intelligence of the angels coming into being on the second day. Then, on the third day, God brought matter and form into existence, from nothing (*ex nihilo*),[3] and the details unfold from there. But it is put like that, in this serial manner, for our creaturely benefit, to help us understand.

The six days as a row of pegs to hang scientific questions on

As early as the Middle Ages, thinkers whose minds were full of scientific questions were using Genesis as a row of pegs on which to hang their speculations. This amounted to an early attempt to read the creation story as a scientific explanation. Grosseteste's efforts in this direction were supplemented by those of Henry of Langenstein. Questions arising explore, at the boundary between philosophy and science, the range of possible meanings of 'coming to be'. For instance, what is the difference between God's saying 'let light be made' and it instantly is; and his saying to a seed 'bring forth a plant', meaning 'you have a power in your striving for a plant to come to be out of you'? It takes the seed some time to become a plant.[4]

Where Genesis describes the way the waters were gathered together to allow dry land to appear, Grosseteste offers three possible explanations. Perhaps God made low-lying areas of land for waters to flow into; perhaps air did not exist but 'the whole space between the earth and heaven was occupied by vaporous and thin waters as Jerome and Bede thought'; perhaps it is as Augustine suggests, and the matter assembled itself into categories of earth and water. Grosseteste thinks that Basil the Great, in his *Hexameron*, may have provided a satisfactory account of when water got its tendency to flow downwards. It could have been an inherent property of water from its creation to flow downhill; or this property could have been added to it when God gathered waters together in one place. In one case the habit of flowing water was instantaneously created with water itself, in the other it was successive, something added to water as it was at first.[5]

Making the rules: creating and maintaining order

> All forms of polytheism . . . are with difficulty reconcileable with an universe governed by general laws. Obedience to law is the note of a settled government, and not of a conflict always going on.[6]

John Stuart Mill observed. One of the features which most conspicuously distinguishes the chaotic but lively primitive creation stories from more sophisticated accounts is the idea that there are rules. A Creator with a plan, a Creator in charge, a Creator with the power to insist makes arrangements. These include designing a shapely and regular world, usually with a top and a bottom, an up and a down, a heaven above and an earth below. He gives creation laws to run by. They include the idea that things fall into and follow a recognisable order, and that that order remains consistent.

This orderliness and these rules are intrinsic to the single complete and perfect act of creation. Creation is a framework as well as its contents. There are rules of required conduct, with punishment to follow disobedience, as the first humans found.

The first principle of an ordered system has usually been the idea that each created thing 'belongs' somewhere in the system:

> The bliss of man (could pride that blessing find)
> Is not to act or think beyond mankind;
> No pow'rs of body or of soul to share,
> But what his nature and his state can bear.
> Why has not man a microscopic eye?
> For this plain reason, man is not a fly.[7]

The Genesis accounts of creation have built into them several assumptions about the order of things. One of them is the division of kinds of things, genera and species, such as land and sea and different sorts of creatures to dwell in each. Another is that there is a hierarchy of those creatures, with human beings supreme. Not only does each created thing have its proper place in a conventionally 'ordered' creation; it also occupies a fixed place above or below other created things.

Pseudo Dionysius the Areopagite was not, as once widely thought, the first-century Dionysius who was converted by St Paul in Athens (Acts 17:34). He was a fifth-century Greek Christian philosopher who especially emphasised the 'hierarchy' he perceived in the structure of the universe. His idea was that all creatures depend directly on the Creator for their continuing being and are placed by him where he intends them to be in the hierarchy. Dionysius' *Celestial Hierarchy* portrays an ordered universe shot through with divine love and overflowing from its Creator, only to return to him. His ideas had their influence down the ages, through John Scotus Eriugena and Nicholas of Cusa and Lorenzo Valla, who questioned which Dionysius this was, but took the ideas seriously. Ideas of hierarchy have tended to be fixed. Social mobility is a concept which sits uncomfortably in the traditional view of a universe with a single powerful Creator who knew what was best and would never need to change his mind.

The 'chain of being' is described by Sir John Fortescue, the fifteenth-century jurist, in terms of an orderliness which is harmonious as well as hierarchical:

> In this order hot things are in harmony with cold; dry with moist; heavy with light; great with little; high with low. In this order angel is set over angel, rank upon rank in the Kingdom of Heaven; man is set over man, beast over beast, bird over bird, and fish over fish, on the earth, in the air, and in the sea; so that there is no worm that crawls upon the ground, no bird that flies on high, no fish that swims in the depths, which the chain of this order binds not in most harmonious concord.

The differences between creatures include, he says, for each a feature which places it in a hierarchy, and:

> by which it is in some respect superior or inferior to all the rest. So that from the highest angel down to the lowest of his kind there is absolutely not found an angel that has not a superior and inferior; nor from man down to the meanest worm is there any creature which is not in some respect superior to one creature and inferior to another.[8]

His purpose in describing things in this way is to include political and social order in this framework, 'So that there is nothing which the bond of order does not embrace.'[9]

In a hierarchical view of the universe, any creature disturbing the hierarchy by trying to put itself in an inappropriate place disrupts the order. This became a strong idea in the European Middle Ages and continued so until early modern times. It had the advantage of encouraging a calm and accepting atmosphere in a society whose members see no alternative but to know their place. It outlaws social mobility. Anything else can cause cosmic disruption.

The consequences, as Alexander Pope describes them, might be cosmic.

> Or in the full creation leave a void,
> Where, one step broken, the great scale's destroy'd:
> From nature's chain whatever link you strike,
> Tenth or ten thousandth, breaks the chain alike.

The very earth could be flung out of its position in the universe:

> Let earth unbalanc'd from her orbit fly,
> Planets and suns run lawless through the sky;
> Let ruling angels from their spheres be hurl'd,
> Being on being wreck'd, and world on world;
> Heav'n's whole foundations to their centre nod.[10]

Ralph Higden's *Polychronicon* knits things together even more closely:

> In the universal order of things the top of an inferior class touches the bottom of a superior: as for instance oysters, which, occupying as it were the lowest position in the class of animals, scarcely rise above the life of plants, because they cling to the earth without motion and possess the sense of touch alone. The upper surface of the earth is in contact with the lower surface of water; the highest part of the waters touches the lowest part of the air, and so by a ladder of ascent to the outermost sphere of the universe.[11]

The whole created universe is arranged then, on this system of creation, in an orderly and hierarchical way, with each thing or creature in its place and all those places fixed.

II. A SINGLE BUT IMPERFECT CREATION

Is the Creator omnipotent?

Was the Creator of the universe powerful and well-intentioned enough to see the business through and ensure there was a good outcome? Has the ordered system of the first creation 'worked'? These were questions much on the minds of classical Greek and Roman thinkers and their heirs in the early Christian period. It asks not only how things began but how they will end, and where creation is now, in the journey from start to finish. It has never been satisfactorily answered, but that is partly because the way the question is put is itself a product of a way of thinking heavily indebted to ancient Greek thought and the Christian tradition, and to the arguments they exchanged in the first Christian centuries.

The 'stone paradox', which is at least as old as the Middle Ages, puts two stark alternatives. Either God *can* create a stone he cannot lift. Or God *cannot* create a stone he cannot lift.[12] Either possibility seems to means he is not omnipotent, because in either case there is something he cannot do. The question of divine omnipotence arises only in monotheistic systems of belief. If there are many gods there must be many powers shared amongst them.

'Errs not Nature,' asks Alexander Pope when earthquakes or violent storms wreak destruction?

> When earthquakes swallow, or when tempests sweep
> Towns to one grave, whole nations to the deep?

He notes one possible answer: that the Creator made only general rules, allowing events in particular cases to vary :

> No, ('tis replied) the first Almighty Cause
> Acts not by partial, but by gen'ral laws.[13]

Creation stories include various ways in which the creative act of a single divine author goes wrong or seems to go wrong. One is the natural disaster. Earthquakes and tsunamis may be more predictable today, but they still take communities by surprise and cause death and destruction. In earlier centuries they caused bewilderment.

John Stuart Mill suggested that such events are actually 'imperfections' in creation or failures by the Creator to ensure that the machinery would not break down: 'They are like the unintended results of accidents insufficiently guarded against, . . . or else they are consequences of the wearing out of a machinery not made to last for ever.' Imperfections in creation would thus be signs of weakness in the Creator. They would: 'point either to shortcomings in the workmanship as regards its intended purpose, or to external forces not under the control of the workman'.

It seems to Mill possible that:

> the purposes might have been more fully attained, but the Creator did not know how to do it; creative skill, wonderful as it is, was not sufficiently perfect to accomplish his purposes more thoroughly.[14]

In how many ways might the Creator's omnipotence be modified?

An aspect of the traditional belief in the omnipotence of the Creator is the association of several divine attributes with that of omnipotence. One is the completeness of the Creator, the belief that he was not bored or needy when he made the world. He made it for the benefit of the creatures not as a plaything for himself. This idea was already found in Neoplatonist thinkers, who saw it as an attribute of an omnipotent supreme being that he must also be supremely good and true and beautiful, and everything he did and made would necessarily flow from those qualities and reflect them. Generously creating a world was an understandable action of such a being.

> How first began this Heav'n which we behold
> Distant so high, with moving fires adornd
> Innumerable, and this which yeelds or fills
> All space, the ambient Aire, wide interfus'd
> Imbracing round this florid Earth, what cause
> Mov'd the Creator in his holy Rest
> Through all Eternitie so late to build
> In Chaos, and the work begun, how soon Absolv'd.[15]

Matthew Tindal's *Christianity as Old as the Creation* was published in 1730 in a period when European thinkers were returning to the task of trying to work out what could be known by reasoning alone and without reliance on what any sacred book 'revealed' about the creation of the world.[16] In it he argues that when God made the world he built into human nature a capacity to understand how it all began:

> the Christian religion has existed from the beginning; and that God, both then, and ever since, has continued to give all mankind sufficient means to know it; and that it is their duty to know, believe, profess, and practice it; so that Christianity, though the name is of a later date, must be as old and as extensive as human nature; and as the 'Law of our Creation,' must have been then implanted in us by God himself.

He reasons from this presumption that God acted in a completely disinterested way in creating the world. It is:

> demonstrable that the creatures can neither add to, or take from the happiness of that being; and that he could have no motive in framing his creatures, or in giving laws to such of them as he made capable of knowing his will, but their own good.

To suggest anything else is to argue that he made the world because 'he was not perfectly happy in himself before the creation'.

But Tindal seems to see a built-in limit to the Creator's powers here, even if it is self-imposed:

> he, who can't envy us any happiness our nature is capable of, can forbid us those things only, which tend to our hurt . . . and as God can design nothing by his laws but our good, so by being infinitely powerful, he can bring every thing to pass which he designs for that end.

God thus seems to set a rule of disinterested action by which he is then himself bound:

> The difference between the supreme being, infinitely happy in himself, and the creatures who are not so, is that all his actions in relation to his creatures flow from a pure disinterested love; whereas the spring of all the actions of the creatures is their own good. 'We love God, because he first loved us,' and consequently, our love to him will be in proportion to our sense of his goodness to us.[17]

But if he binds himself can he change his own rules? Could an omnipotent God behave out of character? Are there things God cannot do because of the way he is? If he could do anything, might he choose not to? Why would he do that? To make something less than a perfect world when a perfect world was possible seems perverse.

This sort of paradox was of much interest in the early Christian centuries and the Middle Ages. Augustine argues in *The City of God* that it puts no restrictions on God's omnipotence that he cannot die or has to know everything which will happen.[18] It is just that he chooses not to die or to be ignorant of future events. And because that choosing is in accordance with his nature, he will always make those choices. But he remains free and able not to make them.

Anselm of Canterbury (1033–1109) devotes a chapter of his *Proslogion* to the discussion of the paradox that it seems there are many things an omnipotent God cannot do. He cannot lie or behave corruptly. But such actions are not powers; they are impotences, he suggests. He cannot make what is done not to have been done (though that question remained a lively one in twelfth-century discussions of the question whether God can restore lost virginity). So Anselm's resolution of the paradox depends on the definition of the term *potestas*, power.[19]

Thomas Aquinas looked at divine power in the *Summa Theologiae*. His suggestion is that to say that God is omnipotent is to say that he can do all things which are possible. But he recognises that that is to say no more than that God is able to do what he is able to do. So it is necessary to refine the definition of what is possible, extending it to encompass the whole of being and such abstractions as the impossibility of embracing the simultaneous truth of contradictory things. Perhaps God can do that too.[20]

René Descartes tried another approach in his *Letter to Arnaud* in 1648. This was to suggest that God has so designed the human mind that it cannot think outside this box of the possible and impossible. It simply cannot conceive of the possible simultaneous truth of contradictory statements.[21] This is a form of intellectual law which is analogous with the laws of physics as used to explain the material world. But our inability to think beyond is not a sure indicator that there is nothing beyond.

These debates opened up the possibility that things which look to us like mistakes and imperfections could nevertheless be the work of an omnipotent Creator, since such a Creator could have a much bigger set of possibilities than we can begin to understand.

So the common explanation of what appears to be flaw and failings in creation has been the one offered by Alexander Pope: these things only appear to be the case. If we could see it all, as God can, we would find there are no mistakes:

> All chance, direction, which thou canst not see;
> All discord, harmony, not understood;
> All partial evil, universal good:
> And, spite of pride, in erring reason's spite,
> One truth is clear, Whatever is, is right.[22]

Richard Bentley, preparing his Boyle lectures in the series founded by Robert Boyle – lectures which required him to discuss the existence of God – wrote to Newton. The topic of Newton's four letters in reply was God's relation to creation seen in the terms of the discussions which were going on in contemporary physics about the operations of centrifugal and centripetal force on a cosmic scale and most especially about gravity – how it works and what it is.[23]

He described the forces he thought might create a spherical shape:

> It seems to me that if the Matter of our Sun and Planets, and all the Matter of the Universe, were evenly scattered throughout all the Heavens, and every Particle had an innate Gravity towards all the rest, and the whole Space, throughout which this Matter was scattered, was but finite; the Matter on the outside of this Space would by its Gravity tend towards all the Matter on the inside, and by consequence fall down into the middle of the whole Space, and there compose one great spherical Mass.

This possibility seemed to require that space should be finite. It would be quite different if it was infinite. Then the result would be a number of masses spaced out, rather in the way the stars seem to be in the sky, assuming that the matter in which they were located was translucent:

> But if the Matter was evenly disposed throughout an infinite Space, it could never convene into one Mass, but some of it would convene into one Mass and some into another, so as to make an infinite Number of great Masses, scattered at great Distances from one another throughout all that infinite Space

And thus might the Sun and fixt Stars be formed, supposing the Matter were of a lucid Nature.[24]

Another of Newton's correspondents was the German philosopher Gottfried Leibniz. The arguments between Newton and Leibniz exemplify aspects of the change which was in process in European thought and which was repositioning the boundary between the natural and the supernatural.

Newton writes in his *Optics* of the difference between God's mode of seeing and our own, for he sees things as they are and we see only images of their reality. This approach was based on centuries of theory about the way the senses operate to bring things into our minds in the form of images, for that indirect perception is all we can have. But it also postulates that the whole created universe is God's watching and feeling 'space', his *sensorium*, by contrast with out small *sensoriola*:[25]

Does it not appear from phenomena that there is a Being incorporeal, living, intelligent, omnipresent, who in infinite space, as it were in his sensory, sees the things themselves intimately, and throughly [sic] perceives them, and comprehends them wholly by their immediate presence to himself: of which things the images only carries through the organs of sense into our little sensoriums, are there seen and beheld by that which in us perceives and thinks.[26]

A second area of radical disagreement between Newton and Leibniz concerned the need for God to make adjustments in order to keep the world in being. Scientific observation and mathematical calculation had persuaded Newton (in Leibniz's view) that God would have to nudge the universe from time to time in order to maintain its motion; and would have to modify the motion of the planets, which appears to have irregularities, and ensure that the fixed stars remained in their places and did not fall into a huddle. It is symptomatic of the difficulties contemporaries were experiencing in finding unequivocal terms and exact language that it is not always clear to them – or to us – what is meant.[27]

In late 1715, Leibniz wrote to Conti about Newton's ideas:

It is not sufficient to say: God has made such a law of Nature, therefore the thing is natural. It is necessary that the law should be capable of being fulfilled by the nature of created things. If, for example, God were to give to a free body the law of revolving round a certain centre, he would either have to join to it other bodies which by their impulsion made it always stay in its circular orbit, or to put an angel at its heels; or else he would have to concur extraordinarily in its motion. For naturally it would go off along the tangent. God acts continually on his creatures in the conservation of their natures, and this conservation is a continual production of that which is in itself perfection.[28]

Leibniz knew there was disagreement as to whether the Creator had finished work, or even got creation right in the first place. He wrote during this period (from 1706) to Caroline, Princess of Wales,[29] who was hostile to the idea that 'God needs to correct and reanimate his machine.'[30]

Could Creation's apparent imperfections indicate something less than divine omnipotence?

Paley's 'watchmaker' theory may provide evidence that the world had an intelligent designer but it does not show that he was necessarily omnipotent or infallible or always in control or his designs always the best. Better-designed watches may in theory always be possible. The watch found on the ground may not be indestructible; it may be broken and have stopped working. The 'analogy' theory of Joseph Butler is not much help here either. Creatures cannot provide analogues of omnipotence, infallibility and so on, and they obviously make mistakes.

What if the process of creation was nothing but a chance growth or spontaneous generation, as in the image used to describe Dorothy Sayers' hero of her series of detective stories, Lord Peter Wimsey? 'His long, amiable face looked as if it had generated spontaneously from his top hat, as white maggots breed from gorgonzola.'[31] Modern science considers that maggots do not breed spontaneously in that way, but that, like other creatures, they have their rules and laws of existence, which proponents of a theory of divine omnipotence must regard as the best possible rules for maggot life. This possibility too had been actively considered by the Greek philosophers and again in the first Christian centuries. Augustine tried to dismiss the assertion the Epicureans make: that things 'are formed and destroyed by the fortuitous movements of atoms, while [others] hold that they are made by God's hand'.[32]

John Stuart Mill set out challengingly for his own time a number of these long-standing questions about the extent of the Creator's powers. Why would anything remain to be completed, improved or apparently rethought, he asked, if God is all-powerful and all-knowing and all-good? His answers too try to be reassuring (there are good reasons for everything, but they are beyond our comprehension): 'we do not know what wise reasons the Omniscient may have had for leaving undone things which he had the power to do.'

The Creator may have had 'good reason' for doing things the way he did. Postponing completion or arranging for fresh starts might have been part of a better plan which we do not understand.

It was still necessary for Mill to deal with the problem that an omnipotent God could not have found himself in a position where he 'had to adapt himself to a set of conditions which he did not make':

> He must at least know more than we know, and we cannot judge what greater good would have had to be sacrificed, or what greater evil incurred, if he had decided to remove [any] particular blot.

Mill's view is that the argument from design leads to an intelligent Creator but not necessarily an omnipotent or omniscient one or one whose arrangements are always for the best. 'We are not even compelled to suppose that the contrivances were always the best possible.' Why, for example, could human bodies 'not have been made to last longer, and not to get so easily and frequently out of order'.

> Must we resign ourselves to admitting the hypothesis that the author of the Kosmos, though wise and knowing, was not all-wise and all-knowing, and may not always have done the best that was possible under the conditions of the problem?[33]

III· A SINGLE EVENT WITH ERRORS BUT CAPABLE OF MODIFICATION?

'Where ends the virtue, or begins the vice?'[34] The moral complexion of creation

'We now pass to the moral attributes of the Deity, so far as indicated in the Creation; or . . . what indications Nature gives of the purposes of its author,' wrote John Stuart Mill. 'We have not to attempt the impossible problem of reconciling infinite benevolence and justice with infinite power in the Creator of such a world as this.'[35]

He was wrong, of course. We do. The problem has refused to go away, despite the best efforts of thinkers down the ages. Everywhere people have suffered and had bad 'experiences' and struggled to make sense of them. A good Creator who in a single event made a good universe can surely not be responsible for pain and disease and misbehaving creatures.

A frequently asked question has been whether there is a source of all misfortunes, so powerful as to be an origin of all evil. Polytheisms can accommodate the problem of the way evil came into creation with relative ease. We looked at the 'dualist' answer, which requires a single 'evil' power to confront the good, in Chapter 3(iii). But further dimensions of the problem emerge if we ask whether the universe was a creation of a single Creator, who gave it a moral dimension from the first. We then have to ask: are the laws of the universe more than its mechanical processes? Do they include moral or ethical rules?

If, as Greek philosophers and later Christians argued, the ultimate power in the universe makes everything that 'is' and sets all the rules and the standards, that power can do no wrong (because he makes the rules) and can define everything he makes as 'good'. The Creator's moral purposes are then simply what he chooses they shall be. But in that case, what is the meaning of 'good'? Is it anything more than being 'like' the Creator or imitating him?

When he ceased to be a Manichaean, Augustine was left with the problem of explaining where evil comes from if not from a primal power in the universe. He had become certain that the world was made in its entirety by one good and omnipotent God, a God who could not behave out of character and therefore could not be the source of evil. His conclusion was that evil is nothing.

His conclusion was that the Creator did not make evil; we rational creatures did that. But what we made was a vast emptiness or privation: the absence of good. It is a very powerful, dangerous and damaging nothing. Had he known of such things Augustine might have called it a black hole, sucking into itself everything which comes too near and obliterating it in a jumble of confused destruction. For, although it does not exist, evil has comprehensive powers to cause upset in the universe, confusing human thinking and motivation, and prompting wrong actions by rational creatures which, like the butterfly of modern chaos theory,[36] set off chains of events reaching far beyond their starting point of a flutter, leading in the case of evil actions to damage and harm in the form of 'natural disasters' as well as wounds and disappointments.

A moral universe?

One of the implications of the presumption that the universe is dynamic is that living things have to behave properly in order to occupy their proper places in the process. 'Philosophy is the knowledge of things human and divine, linked with the study of the right way to live.'[37] This formula, offered in the sixth century by Isidore and confirmed in the Middle Ages by Robert Kilwardby, preserved a connection which seemed obvious to classical thinkers. Ancient philosophy was moral as well as intellectual, concerned with right living as well as right thinking. Even the maverick Roger Bacon suggested in the thirteenth century that all speculative philosophy has moral philosophy for its end and aim. Wisdom was revealed to the first patriarchs, but knowledge fell away and after that philosophy has had to work hard to retrieve knowledge.[38] Similarly, humankind now has to strive to be good, he says. So, for the Christian student of creation theory, being good means staying away from evil, resisting the suction of that black hole in the universe. It involves right conduct.

These were not questions raised only by Christians. The Hindu idea of *dharma* depends on the belief that the universe has built-in rules which determine both the right way to live and the inescapable consequences of actions good and bad. In the Upanishads, *dharma* is universal law from creation itself; it is harmony; it is order. If creatures live rightly the balance of the universe is preserved. Human right living or good behaviour is important. The Hindu epics, the Mahabharata and the Ramayana,

were written in Sanskrit in the last few centuries before the birth of
Christ and include myths about the first rulers of India and stories
with morals and lessons to be learned and treatises on philosophy
and ethics. The Bhagavad-Gita draws on the Mahabharata and is a
compilation setting out principles of right living.[39]

The Flood: a cleansing second start?

The emphasis on good behaviour was linked in the Old Testament
with the idea that the Creator is angered by disobedience to his rules
of creaturely right conduct. A Creator fiercely 'just' and retributive
appears in the story in Genesis 18, which tells of the destruction of
Sodom and Gomorrah. God and Abraham have many conversations
in Genesis. This is a time when the Creator is recorded as talking
with his creatures. This story tells how three visitors (sometimes later
understood to have been angels, or as representing the Trinity),
arrived at the home of Abraham and his wife. These 'travellers' were
shown hospitality and Abraham went with them to see them on
their way, to a place where they all found themselves looking down
on Sodom and Gomorrah, which were cities of the plain.

God then revealed to Abraham that he intended to inspect the
cities to see whether the rumours which had reached him of the
bad habits of those who dwelt there were true. If he found they
were, he intended to destroy the cities. Abraham, whose nephew
Lot lived there, asked God to spare the cities if some righteous
people were found there. When God agreed, Abraham gradually
reduced the number from fifty to ten, with God agreeing to the
new reduced number step by step.

God sent his messenger to carry out the destruction but Lot was
warned and fled with his family. At the last minute his wife turned
back and became a pillar of salt. This is an ending in which the
Creator is fully in charge, even if he allows his stated intentions to
be modified at a creature's request.

In many creation stories, including the Judaic one, the
Creator destroys the world with a great flood and gives it a new
start, allowing only a selected few humans and animals to survive
in an ark, and breed to populate the world again. The Talmud
(c.200–500 AD) contains the results of some centuries of work
by rabbis, including attempts to explain the practicalities of life
onboard the ark (where was the rubbish kept and how was the
animal excrement disposed of?).

The book of Genesis (6–9) describes a great flood, but so do other legends of the region where the ancient Hebrews dwelt. Understanding where Genesis fits among the similar stories found in Near and Middle Eastern legends became an urgent task when it was realised that, historically speaking, the matter needed tidying up. If there was here an indication that the Hebrew and these other traditions had a common ancestry, what did that say about the Old Testament's standing as a sacred text?[40]

Parts of the Genesis creation story resemble the creation myths of ancient Mesopotamia. The closest of these is this episode of the Flood, in which an angry God drowns the world, rescuing only his faithful servant Noah and his family and paired specimens of living creatures, so that they can make a fresh start. There is still uncertainty as to the interrelationship of these Middle Eastern flood legends. The Sumerian civilisation flourished in the fourth and third centuries BC and for a period it was dominated by Semitic peoples. Sumerian religion recognised many gods, with a pantheon of senior gods, including a god of heaven and a goddess of earth. Their cosmos was a flat earth with a dome of sky or heaven above it, and a gloomy underworld 'below' into which the dead descended for a depressing eternity.

Into a reality structured in this way came, as a matter of history, either episodic floods of the rivers Tigris and Euphrates, or perhaps some great and particularly notable flood, devastating enough to enter into myth. Colourful details about the boat vary in different versions, but this is always a 'salvation by starting again' creation story. The earliest record of the Sumerian Flood story survives in the Sumerian creation myth from about two millennia BC, on a tablet known as the Eridu Genesis. This includes the story of the gods creating a race of people. Gods are said to have made the animals and human beings and to have sent down kings to establish and rule cities on earth. There is a missing passage. When the story continues, it seems a flood is imminent. The Flood is sent as a warning to misbehaving mankind. The gods choose not to save mankind. The legend has a 'Noah' figure who builds an ark in which humans and animals survive to make a fresh start and build a new relationship with the gods. In other versions a plan is formed in which a hero is to be saved by his own efforts in building a great ship and filling it with creatures. There is a terrible storm, but eventually the waters subside and the creatures are able to leave the ship and return to the earth. The 'Noah' figure is rewarded with eternal life by the grateful gods.

The *Epic of Gilgamesh* tells a Flood story too. Gilgamesh is a hero of legend with hints of divine ancestry, and possibly also a real Sumerian king of the early third millennium BC. The *Epic of Gilgamesh* is a story of great deeds and long journeys. The Flood story occurs on Tablet XI of the set of tablets recording the tale, where it may be an importation.[41] Here too there is the building of a great boat with a rescue mission, a storm, the receding of the flood and the gods' rewarding of the hero with immortality.

The important difference between Genesis and the Mesopotamia Flood is that in the Genesis story only one god is involved and he is supreme. There is no uncertainty about his intentions. He causes the Flood. It is entirely under his control. He brings it for a purpose, which is to punish mankind. He chooses Noah as his instrument and tells him what to do. The 'reward' at the end of the story is the promise that never again will the earth suffer such a flood, with the rainbow as the sign and token of that assurance. One of the important legacies of this version of the story was the strengthening of the belief in a Creator who is not only one and supreme and good, but intolerant of bad behaviour and unable to allow evil to flourish. His is a moral universe.

18. The *Gilgamesh* tablet

Several of the South American peoples seem to have had a creation-related Flood myth, though the morals of these tales vary. Sometimes the Flood takes the form of a covering of ice and snow which melts, possibly recording some memory of an earlier glacial period which could possibly fit with the eras of inward migration into the Americas. In one such story, the snow god Kun decided to punish humans for their arrogance by covering the whole of creation with snow. Once the human race had been wiped out in this way, fertility gods were able to send eagles to make new people, the people who are to be found to this day near Lake Titicaca and are called the Paka-Jakes. In another version, a speckled ibis, annoyed with humanity, caused it to snow until the whole earth was covered, and when the snow melted the floodwaters covered the whole earth except a few mountain tops and destroyed all life.[42]

The Flood stories of the Middle East may be linked by such borrowing of one another's legends, but those of South America (see Chapter 1 (i)) and the Indian Ocean and Pacific are less easy to explain in this way. Among the Pacific Islands there is a story of two fishermen. They tried to fish in waters which were sacred to the god of the sea. But they caught the god himself and as they drew him out of the water, with his seaweed hair trailing, he bellowed at them because they had woken him from his sleep. In retribution he swore to drown their islands. One island alone he would save, because its princess was his faithful worshipper.[43]

A polytheistic flood story may include descriptions of transmutations between plant and animal states, or accounts of the changes amphibians experience. The instigator of the flood may be divine – or a mere creature – feeling irritation with the behaviour of mankind. Many flood stories are about punishment of misbehaving humanity. They tend to include a rebirth or new creation to replace the unsatisfactory old one. Characters in the stories sometimes became gods in the course of the events described. It is a commonplace of polytheistic systems that such deifications may happen. Gods have not always been gods.

In a Venezuelan story, people were punished by Kuamachi, for allowing themselves to be persuaded by a jaguar to kill and eat a girl. He invited the people to pick fruit with him and he dropped a fruit whose juices flowed into a flood. Kuamachi and his grandfather were safe in a canoe, from which they shot at the offending people, who were trying to save themselves by climbing into trees. Kuamachi climbed a ladder of arrows into heaven, where he became the evening star.[44]

Warnings occur. In a story from Quechua a depressed llama would not eat. When asked why, this South American Eeyore explained that the world wanted to come to an end and this was making it miserable. The animal creation all knew about the imminence of a great flood, but the humans did not. The llama's human owners set off to take refuge on a mountain and there they found many animals already assembled. The flood came, and the human beings who survived began to breed again only afterwards.

In a story from Bolivia, there is also a 'warning' which saves a particular person. Two boys noticed their food was being stolen. They suspected it was being taken by a snake. They lit a fire, which duly drove the snake out of its hiding place. It fell into the fire and was cooked and one of the boys ate it. Driven by thirst, he went to drink in a lake. He turned into a frog, then into a lizard, then into a snake, which swelled to an enormous size. The waters of the lake were displaced and overflowed and in the end the world was flooded. The boy-snake warned his brother and he climbed to the top of a palm tree and waited until the waters subsided, then he went to collect his brother. The rest of humanity perished and vultures ate their rotting bodies when the waters went down. Another version of the flood story featuring a snake also survives from the Andes.[45]

A flood story may not describe the destruction and re-creation of a previously completed creation, but something closer to a stage in a creation story which involves a process. The Creator in that case is not necessarily all-powerful or fully in control of events. In a story from Guyana, the divine Creator Makunaima and his brothers cut down a tree, from which flowed water. Makunaima took the opportunity to create some fish. But the flow of water ran out of control and the whole earth was flooded. Mayuruberu, Creator of the Ipurina people who lived in what is now Brazil, was a stork. He made a vessel of water which was boiling in the sun overflow onto the earth. In this case it was plant life which was destroyed, with the exception of the cassia plant. So agriculture had to be restarted with the creation of many new plants. The great divine stork ate people who would not work in this new agriculture.[46]

The Fall and the rescue

From a Christian point of view, the Flood remedy did not work.[47] Human beings continued to misbehave. The Creator's righteous indignation was not, in the long term, appeased. Saving creation needed a more radical work of restoration, involving the incarnation of the Son of God.

In Book VII of Milton's *Paradise Lost*, Adam asks the Archangel Raphael to tell him how the world came to be. Milton's version makes a bold innovation. Genesis does not explain when the angels were created, and theologians had suggested it was probably when light was separated from darkness. The belief that there was first a period when there were angels but possibly no human beings was 'constructed' in early Christian theology from various oblique references in the scriptures. The apocryphal book of Enoch describes the fall of the angels (6–11). Luke 10:18 speaks of Satan as falling from heaven like lightning. Revelation 12:3–4 has stars falling from the heavens.

When the angels 'fell', the Creator had to do something about it, unless his intentions for creation were to be frustrated. Anselm of Canterbury discusses this problem at length in his book *Why God Became Man* (*Cur Deus Homo*). He argues that God could not simply pick up the fallen angels and restore them to heaven having learned their lesson, because that would not be fair to those who had not rebelled. For the same reason he could not just make some more angels and slot them into the empty places; they would not misbehave because they would know that the consequences would be and they would therefore not love God with the same pure and disinterested ardour as the original unfallen angels. He could not forget the missing numbers and allow the universe to continue. If he had created the perfect number, that would be to acknowledge weakness or failure, which is not, Anselm considers, even to be thought of. The only option 'reason' can see was for the Creator to fill up the spaces in heaven left vacant by the fallen angels with a new creature, rational but not pure spirit. These body–spirit hybrids were humans.

Milton also makes the creation of the world as we know it God's second thought. After some of the angels rebelled against him, and Satan and his armies were cast out of heaven, Milton says, God made a new world with new creatures in it:

> Another World, out of one man a Race
> Of men innumerable.[48]

But this explanation has to be modified if it is to be believed that the Creator was not taken by surprise. The Christian position has been that when he made the angels he knew what would happen because he is omniscient. He planned and foresaw that he would need to create human beings later on, and he also foresaw the Fall of Adam, and the need for the incarnation of his Son, the Logos, who would rescue fallen humanity. Creation was thus an event with a second stage.

Christian theologians realised that the decision to rescue mankind but not the fallen angels also needed explaining. The Creator made a heaven with exactly the right number to dwell in it in the eternal bliss of his presence. When some of the angels fell, it left an incomplete 'perfect number'. That number had to be made up in some way.[49]

In *Why God Became Man*, Anselm of Canterbury suggested the lapsed angels could not be rescued and restored to their places without making it 'easier' for the fallen than for the unfallen to love God in future, which would be unfair. The fallen would naturally feel gratitude for their rescue and would know the dreadful consequences of any further lapses. Angels were not designed to have offspring, so the good angels could not multiply to make up the number. The solution was to create human beings, rational spiritual beings with bodies, who can breed. God knew that they too would sin, but there would be scope for them to multiply so as to fill the vacant spaces in heaven with individuals the Creator chose for the purpose (Augustine, Calvinists) or who were justified in his sight by their faith (Lutherans) or who lived sufficiently virtuous lives (Roman Catholics), depending on various schools of Christian thought and belief.[50]

And there had to be an explanation for a further puzzle. An omnipotent Creator could have ensured that there could be no 'falling'. Why did he allow this muddled and damaging unfolding of events? The answer was that he gave his rational creatures freedom of choice. Anything else would have made them mere puppets.

Satanic opposition: the ultimate challenge to the Creator's omnipotence?

Challenge to the omnipotence of the Creator has come in many stories through the actions of an adversary 'power', the devil, who – even if he is not the full 'equal and opposite' eternal power of dualism but merely an angelic creature gone wrong – can cause a great deal of trouble:

... Eblis[51] watched
The Seven Soils slow moulded into Man,
And feared the living clay God made his lord ...
'Tis writ the angels shuddered when they heard
Clamour and lamentation through the dark;
Cries of huge beasts whom Eblis slew to make
His Man more perfect; thunders from the Pit
And voices of the Devils and the Djinns
Rejoicing[52]

In this dramatic poem, Rudyard Kipling rehearses an episode from the Qur'an in which Eblis (Satan) tried to 'better' Allah's creation.[53] Eblis, like the Christian Satan, is a creature, but a powerful one, who rebels against God and spends eternity trying to seduce human beings to be his followers.

There is modern life in the old stories of the war of good and evil. C.S. Lewis was the author of a science fiction trilogy: *Out of the Silent Planet* (set on Mars), *Perelandra* (set on Venus) and *That Hideous Strength*. The hero meets Eldila, angels and a Venusian Adam and Eve and discovers that on these planets there has been no Fall. On earth, meanwhile, the evil angels are in charge, but they have been confined to the sublunar sphere until the last novel in the series, where a war of good and evil is played out on earth.

Christianity tended to see the devil and his demons always at work trying to capture souls. The idea was that the Creator allows this because it is spiritually educational.[54] Demons lack the tranquillity of God. They have feelings very like ours, sharing our unworthiest and unhappiest emotions. They get cross, feel irritation, can be vengeful, are easily flattered and bribed. In *The City of God*, Augustine wrote about the demons as spirits always busy doing harm.[55] They have real powers, though they use them capriciously and for deceitful and trivial purposes. They are the beings which provide the information sought by augurs and appear in dreams and make the tricks of magicians work.

As Daniel Defoe commented many centuries later, devils know a lot about creation and what happened next. Satan was there at the beginning. As 'Author of *all things,* by originally creating and giving them being ... *Father of the Universe ... from* whom all things derive their existence ... the *Angels* rejoiced and praised God at the time of the creation of the visible world':[56]

What a fine history might this old Gentleman [Satan] write of the Antediluvian world, and of all the weighty affairs, as well of state as of religion, which happen'd during the fifteen hundred years of the patriarchal administration. Then, who like him, could give a full and compleat account of the deluge, whether it was a meer vindictive, a blast from heaven, wrought by a supernatural power in the way of miracle?[57]

In *The Screwtape Letters,* C.S. Lewis published a correspondence between a senior devil and a junior one who is not making much headway with his task of tempting a human being. This is written on a presumption that devils are more purposeful than Augustine's vain and silly spirits. They are engaged in warfare. They want to win souls for Satan so that the forces of evil can grow and in the end achieve a great victory by defeating the good. The devils' problem, as Lewis seeks to show, is that they cannot understand generous impulses, only the seeking of advantage:

When the creation of man was first mooted and when, even at that stage, the Enemy freely confessed that he foresaw a certain episode about a cross, Our Father very naturally sought an interview and asked for an explanation. The Enemy gave no reply except to produce the cock-and-bull story about disinterested love which He has been circulating ever since. This Our Father naturally could not accept. He implored the Enemy to lay His cards on the table, and gave Him every opportunity. He admitted that he felt a real anxiety to know the secret; the Enemy replied 'I wish with all my heart that you did.'[58]

Incarnation and redemption

Now they began to wonder and ask one another what would be the best thing to give him. And one said, 'Fifty bags of cocoanuts!' And another – 'A hundred bunches of bananas! – At least he shall not have to buy his fruit in the Land Where You Pay to Eat!'[59]

In Hugh Lofting's *The Story of Dr. Dolittle* the monkeys of Africa are indignant to discover that Britain is a land where food must be worked for and paid for. Genesis describes a post-lapsarian world in which the ground no longer yields food without human effort. There are thistles and other inconveniences. Adam has to work for a living.

From the doctrine of the Fall follows the whole sequence of further reasoning. The fallen humans who were born of Adam and Eve and their offspring have all inherited the taint of 'original sin'; none of them can act rightly without help. Their free will now works only in the direction of doing the wrong thing.

Christianity sought to explain why the Creator sent the Logos to earth as a human being, to die in order to put things right. This is the 'certain episode about a cross' mentioned in the *Screwtape Letters* just quoted. There has been a great deal of discussion down the centuries about the way this act of selfless generosity could have mended what was wrong with the universe, why God could not just have made the necessary adjustments, why he himself had to suffer and how he *could* suffer, being impassible. The theory may depend on the view that sacrifice can placate or in some other way make up for an offence. It may also assume that the Creator is a just God who cannot allow his honour to be tarnished by just forgiving and forgetting, or that the universal order requires what has gone wrong to be put right in this way (as Anselm argued). Some thinkers – for example, Peter Abelard (1079–1142)[60] – preferred to put the emphasis on the idea that Jesus simply showed people how to live rightly, since they had not been able to do it unaided. He set an 'example'. But the Christian explanation of everything that seems to have gone wrong or to be imperfect in the universe is that, fundamentally, it has now been put right, though there are still consequences to be worked through.

Punishing the creature for the Creator's failure to ensure that things could not go wrong

Inseparable from the discussion of the nature and origin of evil was the question of what happened to the damaged, morally bruised and consequently misbehaving creatures who did not respond to the Creator's efforts to restore them. For it is obvious that the cosmic putting-right did not change human behaviour. People still sin. There is still suffering in the world. Bad things still happen.

Did a righteous and angry Creator punish these recidivist wrongdoers by consigning them to some place under the earth and, if so, when did he make this place of suffering? Was there hell, or an underworld, from the beginning of the world or did it have to be invented to hold those who did wrong and had to be punished?

The Fall described in Genesis made human beings mortal. It did not, to Christian thinking, mean that they were thus annihilated. Where do dead people go? Hell is not a well-developed idea in Genesis, which only hints at a 'place' for the dead to dwell.[61] In Numbers, there is a description of a pit into which God cast those who rebelled against the leadership of Moses and Aaron. They went into it alive with all their households, and the earth closed over them.[62] In Deuteronomy 32:22 there is a description of a place, often translated as 'hell', in which God's anger will burn like fire, and there are other hints of hell in the Old Testament. Jesus also spoke of a hell of punishing fire (Matthew 5:22).

Many myths and culturally local stories do not describe the underworld as a place of punishment, merely a gloomy place without hope. Classical Greek and Roman mythology describes an underworld, though it is more a repository than a place of punishment.

An appendix to Sahagun's sixteenth-century *History of Ancient Mexico* discusses the beliefs of the Mexicans he asked about life after death. The souls of the departed in this version of the created world went to one of three different places. 'One was hell, where a devil or demon lived whose name was Mictlantecutli,' and also a goddess, 'who was the wife of Mictlantecutli'. To hell went people of all sorts, high and low, who had died of a disease. Those left behind would say the following: hell 'is very large, and there will be no memory left of you'. It is a sombre place 'which has neither light nor windows, and you never will return or get out of there'.[63]

The second place where the dead might go was the earthly paradise. This is a place called Tlacocan, where they say 'there is much rejoicing and coolness (comfort also) and without any suffering. There they never lack green corn (ears of corn), calabash, wild amaranth seeds, green pepper, tomatoes, green beans and flowers.' Those who go there are those 'killed by lightning, those who are drowned, the lepers, those afflicted with pustules, the mangy, the gout-stricken, and those with dropsy'.[64]

The third place where the dead might go is heaven, 'where the Sun lives'. 'Those who went to heaven were those killed in war and the captives who had died . . . at the hands of their enemies . . . also those who died from having had torches tied all over their bodies which, being lighted, burned them to death,' presumably the human sacrifices.

After four years, when the souls of these dead went on, they changed into different kinds of birds of rich plumage, of fine hues, and they flew off to drink honey from all flowers as well in heaven as on the earth, as do the . . . humming birds.[65]

These ideas contrast strongly with the Christian doctrine of hell as a punishment. In this alternative mythology, the eternal dwelling place is determined by the manner of someone's death.

Common to many mythologies is an 'underworld' of the dead, whose chief defining feature, apart from its gloom and tendency to be full of monsters, is the difficulty of getting out of it. The Roman poet Virgil described in his epic poem about the founding of Rome how Aeneas went down into hell in the knowledge that it is easy to get there but not at all easy to leave (*Facilis est descensus averno*).[66]

The underworld Aeneas visits takes him into some of the worst nightmares of existence:

> On they went, hidden in solitary night, through gloom,
> through Dis's empty halls, and insubstantial kingdom,
> like a path through a wood . . .
> Right before the entrance, in the very jaws of Orcus,
> Grief and vengeful Care have made their beds,
> and pallid Sickness lives there, and sad Old Age,
> and Fear, and persuasive Hunger, and vile Need,
> forms terrible to look on, and Death and Pain:
> . . . many other monstrous shapes of varied creatures,
> are stabled by the doors, Centaurs and bi-formed Scylla,
> and hundred-armed Briareus, and the Lernean Hydra,
> hissing fiercely, and the Chimaera armed with flame,
> Gorgons, and Harpies, and the triple bodied shade, Geryon.[67]

Living in this eternal realisation of their worst fears are miserable crowds of the dead.

Is this an ultimate consequence for human beings of their own mistakes, or of mistakes not their own but the Creator's?

Minor adjustments: magic and miracle

Can the process of creation and the running of the created world be interfered with? If so, can creatures interfere or only the Creator himself, making adjustments as he pleases? Could there be ways of changing the orderly running of things and achieving the extraordinary?

Magic got a bad press in the ancient world partly because its practitioners were seen to act for their own ends (such as making a profit), were deceitful and swindled their victims. Roman law took magic seriously. It included provisions against such behaviour as stealing a growing crop by moving it from one field to another by magic.

Roman opinion was sometimes less damning and there was awareness that there might be some more dignified realms of magical practice. Pliny calls Zoroaster the inventor of magic, although little of the extensive writing in this area was attributed to him or survives with his name attached.[68] The considerable ancient literature of the magical arts had many putative authors and was partly 'secret' and for initiates only. That was another reason for mistrusting it.

Christian theology inherited this mistrust of magic, along with a paradoxical willingness to believe it worked. Augustine of Hippo thought magic was the work of evil spirits. He confidently believed in such beings. Even in an officially Christian late Roman Empire, Europe and North Africa were still full of pagans who worshipped many little local gods. Augustine accepted their reality, simply categorising them as 'fallen angel' demons turned malevolent. Indeed, he took it for granted that the air was full of them. Their willingness to allow themselves to be bribed and their alleged fondness for theatrical performances of a decadent kind were to his mind clear indications of their debased tastes.[69] (He had his own problems in controlling a love of the wrong kind of theatre.)

Augustine was prepared to accept the reality of magical practices partly because he knew many of his readers and listeners did so, and their beliefs had to be accommodated if he was to win them over to Christianity. It was right that such spiritual beings gone wrong should be believed in by Christians. Despite their damaged state, they were powerful and could make things happen. It was one thing to pray for divine or saintly aid, quite another to appeal to demons for help.[70] The question was not whether magic worked, but whether it was appropriate conduct for a Christian to try to use it.

The *Clementine Homilies* blamed Zoroaster for the invention of magic, perhaps because of the belief that Zoroaster belonged among the Babylonians, who were reputed to be magicians.[71] In the same Christian tradition of mistrust of magic, Robert Grosseteste, in the Proemium to his commentary on the six days of creation in Genesis, stresses the undesirability of the operations of Magi and magicians, who get their name from *malefici* ('workers of evil').[72]

Miracles

Magic interferes with the proper running of things, but so does a miracle. Why is a magic trick not a miracle? If the world had a Creator who made the rules for the universe, can he break them when he likes? Why would he? Is the breaking of creative rules a sign of weakness or of strength in a Creator?

> If we by analogy call God 'the Creator' we are thereby admitting that it is possible for Him to work miracles; but if we examine more closely the implications of our analogy, we may be driven to ask . . . how far it is really desirable that he should do anything of the kind.[73]

For many centuries the Christian tradition thought well of miracles. Miracles, in contrast to magic, are deemed to be a 'good' breaking of the rules of expected order. Augustine's discussion of miracles in *The City of God* describes them as deliberate educational acts of God, designed to surprise and thus to prompt faith.[74] He says miraculous acts have happened since the beginning of the world and Christ's resurrection and ascension are the supreme examples.

He himself has seen more than one miracle. When he was lecturing in Milan, he witnessed a blind man's sight being restored by the 'virtue' or miraculous power inhering in the bodies of two martyrs, Protasius and Gervasius, whose location had appeared to Bishop Ambrose in a dream. At Carthage, he also saw a cure by impassioned prayer of a man whose chronic illness physicians had failed to cure, although he had been operated on many times. A catalogue of examples follows, mostly cures by saints or their relics, or by martyrs, but also miraculous dispossession of devils which had been occupying individuals and raisings from the dead. The list becomes lengthy and Augustine regrets that even so he cannot find space to tell of all the miracles he knows of personally.

Miracles of these small personal sorts are, suggests Augustine, testimonies of faith, an extension of the faith which took the martyrs to their deaths and left merit over for others to gain miraculous benefits through their own faith. They keep the believer in touch with the Creation and its processes and leave him wondering in admiration at the way God intervenes, even perhaps through powers entrusted to miracle-workers, or through the good offices of angel-messengers, as well as by direct intervention. It is important to ensure that although the divinely inspired thaumaturges (miracle-workers) may be honoured they should not be worshipped.[75]

It remained the firm conviction of authors of medieval histories and hagiographies (which regularly contain miracle stories) that miracles are of evidential value and teach about the Creator and his works. In the case of the lives of saints the miracle stories are regularly used as evidence of sanctity. Unless the miracle is linked with the saint and in some way 'done' by him, he is not a genuine saint at all.

7

Creation as a system: initiation followed by a process of planned development?

I. A PROCESS WITH BUILT-IN MECHANISMS FOR IMPROVEMENT?

People are not statues in a landscape

The world certainly does not seem to be a static creation. In many religions and cultures, creation is seen as a process, a working model. It is not obvious in all creation stories that the beginning time was the best. Could a 'Whig theory' of creation involving a process of unfolding or development be plausible?

In mythologies where the first beings are Titans or giants, the behaviour of these entities tends to be violent and destructive. In earliest Greek mythical time, Chronos killed his father Uranus and when he learned of the prophecy that his own children would eventually kill him in their turn he swallowed each as it was born. Virgil writes in his fourth *Eclogue* of a restoration, with a Golden Age to come, a new reign of Saturn, a new breed of men.

Laws of natural growth or a confusion of transformations?

It is, of course, possible to argue, as we saw earlier (see Chapter 1 (i)) that the laws which govern evolution are themselves the Creator's laws, built into an initial creative act:

Ask of thy mother earth, why oaks are made
Taller or stronger than the weeds they shade?[1]

The act of creation is sometimes thought of as resembling the sowing of a seed. Like an acorn growing into an oak, the world unfolded and 'became' fully itself. The plan or programme for doing this was already inside it. It could only become what it was designed to become. An acorn does not turn into an elephant or a baby elephant into an oak tree.

This assumes orderliness and a Creator powerful enough not only to set all this in motion but also to build in control of the process and maintain order. That more than one power was and remains involved in the creation and overseeing its unfolding is logically possible but organisationally more difficult to envisage.

Diodorus Siculus identified two main opinions about the origins of humanity.[2] One view is that there have always been people and always will be. The other is that the universe had a beginning and so did humanity. Those who think the world had a beginning say it began undifferentiated, heaven and earth mingled together. Then the elements separated and order appeared. Each element behaved in its own way. Air blew as wind. Heat rose. Earth and water sank downwards and resolved themselves into land and sea by gathering themselves as two different elements. They did not do this smoothly. The earth boiled and swelled into hillocks and bumps, and where membranes of earth contained liquid there grew inside them all sorts of creatures, which developed and matured and then burst forth to cover the earth with living things. Warmth imparted life and moisture nourishment. Those which had benefited from most warmth rose into the air to fly as birds. Those most earthy crept and walked on land. Some, partaking more of water, took up residence in the water. And once there were living creatures they began to breed and multiply.

Diodorus quotes the view of Euripides, in the now fragmentary *Melanippe*:

'Tis thus that the heav'n and earth were once one form;
But since the two were sundered each from each,
They now beget and bring to life all things,
The trees and birds, the beasts, the spawn of sea,
And race of mortals.[3]

Diodorus then moves on to discuss the lives of human beings.[4] Here he postulates a social evolution. The first men behaved like beasts. But in order to survive amongst the other beasts, they learned to cooperate to protect themselves. That led them to develop language and writing. (However, social groups sprang up independently all over the world, which is why they do not all speak the same language.) Humans found they needed more than this primitive alliance. They had to learn to store food against hard times and to eat in winter, to build shelters and make clothing, and that led to the cultivation of the arts, to education and the development of civilisation as we know it.

Diodorus acknowledges the problem of finding evidence for what happened before the invention of writing and the appearance of the first historians. He also knows that it is not only the Greeks who make claims to be the first of the human race, and to be aboriginal to their lands and the inventors of these features of advanced human life. Barbarians do too. So he resolves to try to give a balanced account of some of these claims to antiquity.

The Egyptians claim the origin of the gods is to be discovered in Egypt and that Egypt is where the stars were first observed. They say that it was the Nile which was the reason why human being first came to be in Egypt.[5] The Nile encourages fertility and thus human beings could be fed. They point to the rumoured spontaneous local generation of mice, which emerge from the ground with their front ends fully formed but still earth behind.

The Egypt story as told by Diodorus includes the Flood in its Deucalion version. In the Greek myth, Deucalion was the son of Prometheus. When an angry Zeus, chief of the gods, flooded the world to 'cleanse' it, the two of them built a box in which to float until the waters subsided. The Egyptians can claim to have survived better than most because the southern part of the area is without rain and would have been less affected. Or if all living things perished in the Flood it would be in Egypt that they could most easily come forth from the ground again. This impression that spontaneous generation was a real possibility was readily derived from observation of the annual flooding of the Nile, the transformation of desert to fertility as the flood rose and receded.

The Egyptians also drew inferences from watching the skies, says Diodorus. They saw the sun, which they called Osiris, and depicted her as a cow because a cow has horns. These horns oversee the seasons and the cycling of the year. They are complementary, importing fire and spirit or air (sun) and dry and wet (moon).

These are the constitutive elements of the universe. They are all there is.

But, having identified forces and constituents of nature, the Egyptians made them gods. Diodorus says that the Egyptians have a conception of 'first gods', the primal powers and entities and sources, the originators. The source of spirit and life could also be thought of as a father. Fire as a separate element becomes the god known to the Greeks as Hephaestos. Earth is a mother goddess. And this assimilative process made syncretism easy too, as equivalent or counterpart gods would be identified in the pantheons of other races and localities and nations in the way the Romans encouraged as their Empire spread. The developing gods could also be linked to animals, which enabled them to be portrayed visually in distinctive and easily recognised ways. But the essential feature of these primal gods for the Egyptians, says Diodorus, is that they are from eternity. They also recognise secondary gods, some of them mortals – but mortals who had been outstanding during their lives. Naturally this included kings (some of these, confusingly, have the same names as the primal and eternal gods).

Pliny makes the suggestion that this 'being and becoming' of the world is not so much an act of the Creator as a process in the Creator himself. He is both the work of nature and himself Nature:[6]

> I liked his description of the creation of the world. You know, how everything is really a part of this giant man, and that we're somewhere around his waist. Of course, Mahavira's geography is not what we've been taught at school, but I did like all those different circles of oceans. There is one of milk and one of clarified butter and one of sugar cane.[7]

To move from traditions of thought developed in the West from Greek and Roman philosophical roots to Eastern traditions is to encounter different assumptions about process and orderliness. Eggs, seeds and orderly arrangement may look different there:

> The emperor is a living reflection of heaven, that ghostly residence of a line of emperors which extends back to the Yellow Ancestor, who created all things when he pushed apart a sort of cosmic egg, whose upper half became heaven while the lower became earth.[8]

Some creation stories (for example, Hindu Vedic ones of India) begin with a cosmic egg or a seed – something which contains the starting point of all the multiplicity of created things. Some envisage a womb belonging to an earth mother, from which the present world and its peoples were 'born', sometimes with the aid of a midwife, as in some North American Indian myths.

In some stories there are 'parents', who became polarised into male and female or otherwise divided (and offspring sprang from their tearing apart), or who formed a union from which offspring were born. Some narratives begin from darkness or chaos, from which the Creator brings 'order'. In Genesis a God who is himself without beginning brings chaos 'without form and void' to a new mode of existence as a cosmos, separating darkness and light, eternity and time, as day follows day and God makes a succession of creatures, culminating with human beings. The essential element in these versions of Creation is the emergence of what we can now recognise as 'order' in things.

Other stories describe a being such as a bird or a frog, which dives down into a watery chaos, a primeval ocean, and brings up the world. North American Indians have such myths, as does the mythology of the Finnish peoples and speakers of the cognate group of languages of the Baltic region and of the Turkish (Tatar) peoples.

In such elaborately constructed sequences of events, the hypothesis that the creation evinces order and shows evidence of the Creator's planning does not necessarily run counter to ideas of the infinite mutability of things, their capacity to turn into one another, the sheer lack of rules and norms about change which are vivid in the mythologies of many peoples, and which Pliny also refers to when he describes how seeds falling down, especially into the sea, generate monstrous shapes.[9]

Human social and religious development: a possibility?

Thomas More sketched in fictional form a process of growth and realisation in a population in his *Utopia:*

> There are several sorts of religions, not only in different parts
> of the island, but even in every town; some worshipping the
> sun, others the moon or one of the planets: some worship such
> men as have been eminent in former times for virtue or glory,
> not only as ordinary deities, but as the supreme God: yet the

greater and wiser sort of them worship none of these, but adore one eternal, invisible, infinite, and incomprehensible Deity; as a being that is far above all our apprehensions, that is spread over the whole universe, not by His bulk, but by His power and virtue; Him they call the Father of All, and acknowledge that the beginnings, the increase, the progress, the vicissitudes, and the end of all things come only from Him; nor do they offer divine honours to any but to Him alone. And indeed, though they differ concerning other things, yet all agree in this, that they think there is one Supreme Being that made and governs the world, whom they call in the language of their country Mithras. They differ in this, that one thinks the god whom he worships is this Supreme Being, and another thinks that his idol is that God; but they all agree in one principle, that whoever is this Supreme Being, He is also that great Essence to whose glory and majesty all honours are ascribed by the consent of all nations.

By degrees, they fall off from the various superstitions that are among them, and grow up to that one religion that is the best and most in request; and there is no doubt to be made but that all the others had vanished long ago, if some of those who advised them to lay aside their superstitions had not met with some unhappy accident, which being considered as inflicted by heaven, made them afraid that the God whose worship had like to have been abandoned, had interposed, and revenged themselves on those who despised their authority.[10]

Geology and fossils, classification, evolution: some nineteenth-century perceptions

From the fifteenth and sixteenth centuries, the study of geology and fossils was prompting awkward questions, because it was hard to see how the fossil record tallied with the Old Testament narrative. Leonardo da Vinci (1452–1519) puzzled in his *Notebooks* over the groupings of fossil shells found inland. He reasoned that if they had been carried there by the Flood, there would have been other remains mixed in with them and the shells of different creatures would have been mixed up and not found in single-species clusters. Moreover, observation of the strata revealed in the sides of the 'cuttings' made by rivers show distinct layers of deposits and that seems to suggest that if the deposits were the result of floods, there must have been not one but many floods.[11]

The Danish scientist Nicholas Steno (1638–86), who grew up a Lutheran but became a Roman Catholic, proposed natural laws to account for the formation of fossils. One was that fossils were laid down in a succession of layers, with the top layer at any one time being fluid and then becoming solid, before another layer formed on top. Another was that a layer would normally be level all across the world at a given date, unless it was formed in some separate structure like a cup of rock. So his ideas laid the foundations for the argument that instead of all creatures having been made on the 'day' of creation on which they are mentioned in Genesis, some must have come into existence after others.

Robert Hooke (1635–1703) combined an interest in optics with an interest in geology. He studied fossils with the aid of an early microscope and noticed the correspondences between the minute forms of the fossil molluscs and those of living molluscs. This made him bold enough to reject Aristotle's explanation that fossils somehow grew inside the earth and 'imitated' living things. He proposed the opposite: that they had originally been living things and had become mineralised by some fossilising process which must be regarded as geological. Some lectures he gave in 1667–9 became a book, *Lectures and Discourses of Earthquakes and Subterraneous Eruptions. Explicating the Cause of the Rugged and Uneven Face of the Earth; and What Reasons May be given for the Frequent Findings of Shells and Other Sea and Land Petrified Substances, Scattered over the Whole Terrestrial Superficies.*

In the first examination Charles Darwin had to take as an undergraduate at Cambridge in 1830, one of the set books was William Paley's *Evidences of Christianity*. This had been published only in 1794, but within a generation it was in the syllabus and focusing the minds of students on what can be known about the way the world began, and how we know it.

It was not uncontroversial. Adam Sedgwick preached a critical sermon to the university and its students on Paley's arguments. Geological evidence does not counter Genesis. He claims that though we now know that a 'thousand ages' have passed in geological time, it is still possible to argue that man 'was called into being within a few thousand years of the days in which we live – not by a transmutation of species . . . but by a provident contriving power'.[12]

In his Preface to the *The Voyage of the Beagle*, Darwin explained that he had seen his role on the ship as that of a scientist:

it was in consequence of a wish expressed by Captain Fitz Roy, of having some scientific person on board, . . . that I volunteered my services, which received, through the kindness of the hydrographer, Captain Beaufort, the sanction of the Lords of the Admiralty.[13]

Darwin felt he had come close on that voyage to the moment of creation:

both in space and time, we seem to be brought somewhat near to that great fact – that mystery of mysteries – the first appearance of new beings on this earth.[14]

This newness struck him especially forcefully as betokening the aboriginal, the freshly created:

The natural history of these islands [the Galapagos] is eminently curious, and well deserves attention. Most of the organic productions are aboriginal creations, found nowhere else; there is even a difference between the inhabitants of the different islands.

He expressed amazement at the sheer multitude of 'aboriginal' creatures in such a small area: 'Considering the small size of the islands, we feel the more astonished at the number of their aboriginal beings, and at their confined range.'

It still came naturally to this Victorian scientist to ask questions about the geology:

Seeing every height crowned with its crater, and the boundaries of most of the lava-streams still distinct, we are led to believe that within a period geologically recent the unbroken ocean was here spread out.[15]

Also natural to a Victorian scientist was an interest in the application of systems of classification. Various apparently settled scientific notions became unfixed as Darwin studied his specimens. Chapter 9 of *The Voyage of the Beagle* discusses the coral found in the Falklands. Are these plants or animals, Darwin wonders:

What can be more remarkable than to see a plant-like body producing an egg, capable of swimming about and of choosing a proper place to adhere to, which then sprouts into branches, each crowded with innumerable distinct animals, often of complicated organizations? The branches, moreover, as we have just seen, sometimes possess organs capable of movement and independent of the polypi. Surprising as this union of separate individuals in a common stock must always appear, every tree displays the same fact, for buds must be considered as individual plants. It is, however, natural to consider a polypus, furnished with a mouth, intestines, and other organs, as a distinct individual, whereas the individuality of a leaf-bud is not easily realised; so that the union of separate individuals in a common body is more striking in a coralline than in a tree.[16]

Darwin's eventual conclusion that living things have evolved rather than being made in a single creative act at one time was not entirely original (see Chapter 1 (i)), but it was the publication of his mid-century *Origin of Species* which caused a lasting furore, partly because it proposed mechanisms or natural laws by which evolution occurs without requiring direct intervention by the Creator to make modifications or new species.

Charles Kingsley (1819–75) gave an inaugural lecture as Regius Professor of Modern History in Cambridge in 1860, entitled 'The limits of exact science applied to history'. He published his allegorical children's story *The Water Babies* in 1862–3. It contains references to the issues Darwin had been raising. In Chapter 6 he teasingly describes the 'development history' of mankind, from its first happy innocence, through stages of increasing sophistication. In the end the way people live begins to affect the way they look, just as Darwin argued happens in all evolving species:

'But there is a hairy one among them,' said Ellie.

'Ah!' said the fairy, 'that will be a great man in his time, and chief of all the tribe.'

And, when she turned over the next five hundred years, it was true.

For this hairy chief had had hairy children, and they hairier children still; and every one wished to marry hairy husbands, and have hairy children too; for the climate was growing so damp that none but the hairy ones could live: all the rest coughed and sneezed, and had sore throats, and went into consumptions, before they could grow up to be men and women.

Then the fairy turned over the next five hundred years. And they were fewer still.

'Why, there is one on the ground picking up roots,' said Ellie, 'and he cannot walk upright.'

No more he could; for in the same way that the shape of their feet had altered, the shape of their backs had altered also.

'Why,' cried Tom, 'I declare they are all apes.'

Kingsley slips in here a reference to the Hermetic tradition, with its ancient warning that those who behave like animals will grow more beastly:

'Yes!' said the fairy, solemnly, half to herself, as she closed the wonderful book. 'Folks say now that I can make beasts into men, by circumstance, and selection, and competition, and so forth. Well, perhaps they are right; and perhaps, again, they are wrong. That is one of the seven things which I am forbidden to tell, till the coming of the Cocqcigrues; and, at all events, it is no concern of theirs. Whatever their ancestors were, men they are; and I advise them to behave as such, and act accordingly. But let them recollect this, that there are two sides to every question, and a downhill as well as an uphill road; and, if I can turn beasts into men, I can, by the same laws of circumstance, and selection, and competition, turn men into beasts. You were very near being turned into a beast once or twice, little Tom.'[17]

So despite the reaction against the theory of evolution, which continues to be strong, where it is felt to conflict with a literal reading of Genesis, evolution has had the effect of encouraging a strong sense that the Creator's role would not be diminished if he had in a single or serial act of creation built in a potential for development within certain rules and norms. There have been disagreements with Darwin which allow other possibilities of creation taking place in some successive way.[18] This understanding of the matter could allow the Creator to create and then stand away and let creation 'roll' on its way.

II. CREATION AS A SYSTEM WITH THE CREATOR AS SUPERVISOR

Is the Creator still involved in these possibilities of development and if so, how? Did he make the world, set the ball rolling and continue to watch what happened, giving the world a push now and then to keep it going? The story told in the Old Testament book of Job depicts a Creator who takes an active interest in the world he has made, but who seems confident that everything will work out as he intends; indeed, he knows it will. He behaves confidently in allowing experiments. In the book of Job, beings sometimes translated as 'the sons of God', though traditionally thought of as angels, are described as having conversations with the Creator. One of them, who is called Satan, has been looking round the earth to see what is happening there. God asks him whether he has noticed Job. Job is a good man.

Of course he is, answers Satan. God has been good to him and made him flourish. But if God takes away his blessings, he will curse God. Try it, says God (Job 2:6). So Satan tests Job and Job loses his home and family and health, and all his neighbours encourage him to curse God. But he will not, and God is shown to have foreseen his reaction accurately. In the end, Job gets back all he has lost and more and once again he flourishes. Here is the Creator watching events and allowing situations to be adjusted in the confidence that they will turn out as he foresees.

Two contrasting narratives are found in creation stories in which standards in creation change. One describes a decline from the high standards of the world as first created, a decline both moral and physical, with an enticing possibility of climbing back by better behaviour. The other describes a progression upwards, a development which may be seen as built in to the Creator's original design, so that things get better and better. This can have the look of a mere mechanism, not involving the Creator's active intervention, as in the machineries discussed in the previous chapter. Or it can depend on a Creator who holds the rudder or steering-wheel and corrects the trajectory of creation if it seems to be heading for a collision.

A process of decline from a Golden Age and a last chance to retrieve lost glory?

> I particularly liked his description of the first cycle of creation, when everyone was six miles high . . . and there was no work for anyone to do because there were ten trees on which grew everything you would ever want . . . pots and pans . . . food, already cooked, . . . clothes . . . palaces.[19]

Good times, according to the Hindu epic Mahabharata, are times when there is peace and plenty, with social equality and no worldly desires, with no greedy and ruthless people trying to seize all the wealth for themselves, and no disease or suffering. A similar picture of a Golden Age (*gullaldr*) appears in Old Norse legends when the gods build a new city on the ruins of Asgard. In Christianity this age of innocence was the time in the Garden of Eden, when Adam and Eve by their own action ended their time of unreflective 'living for the moment' in quiet enjoyment.

Stories of a Golden Age usually involve gloomy talk of an 'old age of the world' in which standards have slipped and there is decay, getting worse from age to age from that 'golden' time to the present age:

> Such will be the old age of the world, irreligion, disorder, confusion of all goods . . . then . . . God . . . [will annihilate] then he will bring back the world to its first beauty, so that . . . God also, creator and restorer . . . may be glorified . . . That is what the rebirth of the world will be; a renewal of all good things.[20]

The Greeks set the Golden Age in Arcadia, though real Arcadia was merely a poor rural area. Hesiod described the downhill path from the Golden Age in his *Works and Days:*

> Golden was the race of speech-endowed human beings which the immortals . . . made first of all . . . just like the gods they spent their lives, with a spirit free from care, entirely apart from toil and distress. Worthless old age did not oppress them, but . . . they delighted in festivities, lacking all evils, and they died as if overpowered by sleep.[21]

These beings had no need to work to live. The food they needed just grew; it did not need to be cultivated.

This Golden Age ended when Prometheus, one of the Titans, gave fire to mankind and taught humanity various skills in the arts. Zeus, king of the gods, punished Prometheus by chaining him to a rock, where an eagle pecked at his liver for all eternity. Human beings then set about causing trouble. Then came a second age, when a 'silver' race was born, a more foolish race still. After that came a 'bronze' race, in which emerged beings given to acts of violence. Then emerged the demigods, including some human heroes. We modern humans are the fifth race.[22]

Plato adopts and adapts this tale in his *Cratylus*.[23] He mentions that Hesiod says the first race of men were a 'golden race' (*Chrusoun genos*).[24] 'Golden was the race of speech-endowed human beings which the immortals . . . made first of all. Then silver, bronze and iron, then a fifth race, made by Zeus, Cronus' son.'[25]

Virgil's *Georgics* borrow from Hesiod, telling of a time when:

> Fields knew no taming hand of husbandmen
> To mark the plain or mete with boundary-line.
> Even this was impious; for the common stock
> They gathered, and the earth of her own will
> All things more freely, no man bidding, bore.[26]

Ovid in the *Metamorphoses* simplified the story by describing only four ages, gold, bronze, silver and iron.

Bewailing the 'old age of the world' and the way standards had slipped became a *topos* in medieval literature.[27] A modern version of all this, the Green Movement, began in the 1970s[28] and has more recently developed into a warning that 'global warming' caused by human activities will make the planet uninhabitable. Whether or not its concerns prove to be well founded, the present 'global warming' scare is another of the 'doom stories' about the loss of creation's first glories which recur down the centuries. These tend to include moral censure and the hypothesis that what is happening is a 'punishment' for human misbehaviour. They also encourage humans to repent and change their habits, with the modern pressure to reduce one's carbon footprint replacing earlier proposed reforms of personal conduct. This is the other face of the idea that the world was made for mankind and that human beings are superior to the animal creation and in charge of it.

Providence: creation as an unfolding process with an unsafe outcome?

> The Gods are happy.
> They turn on all sides
> Their shining eyes . . .
> They see the Centaurs
> In the upper glens
> Of Pelion . . .
> They see the Indian

Drifting, knife in hand; . . .
They see the Scythian
On the wide stepp, unharnessing
His wheel'd house at noon . . .
They see the Heroes
Sitting in the dark ship.[29]

In this picture, sketched by the nineteenth-century poet Matthew Arnold, creation is not something that has happened and is done with. It is all present before the eyes of the gods, who see with the gaze of eternity and as though all the cosmos extended below them because their view stretches an infinite distance. The gods can see before and behind and survey everything as if it is 'now' and 'here'. For to them all things are present in both time and space.

Matthew Arnold's gods in the poem look on in eternal tranquillity. Whether they *cared* about the physical and temporal world and what became of it was a topic of enormous interest in the world of Greek and Roman antiquity and for some centuries afterwards. They could 'foresee', but did this 'providence' (*providere*, seeing ahead) prompt them to ensure that things worked out as they wished? And did they have power to make that happen? And was that power self-justifying, so that whatever it did was right?

That to the highth of this great Argument
I may assert Eternal Providence
And justifie the wayes of God to men.[30]

The Creator could have made the world like a great building or a statue, as a monument. It could have been static. But he made something which moves and changes, for that is inherent in life as we know it. He could have made it like a clockwork toy, wound it up and stood back. He could then have watched it run down and stop, picked it up, rewound it, and watched it once more as it ran down to a stop. He apparently made it as a more complex system, full of entities capable of repairing and reproducing themselves. But how far did he allow these freewheeling entities to act as they chose and what was the plan for the system as a whole? Did the Creator regard it as an experiment, whose outcome he would watch with a detached interest before perhaps setting up a different experiment? Or did he treat this as a project whose good end he would ensure?

If so, did he plan in detail, with every event foreseen and fore-ordained? Did he foresee but not foreordain, and if so, how would

that be possible? Did he merely give things a push and stand ready
to correct the trajectory if something went wrong and the little
cart containing the created world threatened to overturn?

But that could mean he did not foresee what would happen,
so he is not omniscient. Or it could mean he did foresee what
would happen and chose to allow things to go wrong in the
interests of giving his creatures freedom, knowing he could
intervene like a caring parent and put things right even if the
mistakes were serious. Did the Creator just set things going but
watch to see what happened and make adjustments? Christians
believe he made an enormous adjustment which required him
to enter the world he had made and die on the cross as a human
being to mend things.

A process of improvement under secure providential guidance?

> Who finds not Providence all good and wise,
> Alike in what it gives, and what denies?[31]

Alexander Pope is here proposing a very 'accepting' idea of a
providential governance of the universe by its Creator. Things are
as they should be, and are indicators of the Creator's goodness,
even if they are not what we as creatures like. Many creation stories
depict the Creator as all-powerful, the beginning of everything.
Some claim the power was needed only at the beginning, as in the
'big bang' theory of how things began; some that the Creator has
to exercise continuing omnipotence to keep creation in existence.
Some attach to their high view of an omnipotent God a number
of other attributes which seemed to follow: for example, power
to punish creatures or to reward them according to principles of
justice inherent in the Creator himself.

Providence was a subject of great interest in late antiquity.
There was a wide spectrum of opinions about how much the
Creator could do and how much he cared to involve himself in
the afterlife of the world he had made. As an influential author
in the Western tradition, Augustine describes a Creator whose
power not only brought the world into existence but maintains
it in being.[32]

Augustine wrote a good deal about the operation of providence
in his book *On the City of God*, in which he was trying to win round
pagans with philosophical educations who had taken refuge in

North Africa as the Roman Empire fell to barbarian invaders. They complained that the Christian God of a now officially Christian Empire had scarcely shown himself to be powerful enough. Augustine's argument in response was that the critics were not seeing things on a large enough scale. In the great span of the world's history, the fall of Rome was of no real importance. The Creator's plans were bigger than that and ultimately he would have his way. Augustine sees no force in the argument that different gods are needed to take care of different parts of the universe, as the polytheists believe. Those who think small and worship little gods are resigning themselves to a life of fear, he claims.[33]

Predestination, foreknowledge, grace and free will

> Practically speaking, if [the] vision of an inexorable immutable creation were to prevail, the result would lead to a complete breakdown of human society.[34]

In Buddhism and Hinduism (where the Vedas suggest that to do good is to experience good things), the idea that the will to do an act can have an influence on events is part of the theory of *karma*. The shaping of destiny includes good works which bear fruits, and acts of unkindness and wickedness which have evil consequences. These consequences are not always experienced in this life but eventually the individual's 'account' will balance. The individual soul builds up an accumulated *karma* of consequences over several lifetimes. The individual human will is thus thought to participate in a universal process in which actions prompt similar reactions and causes have effects. In this enormous and complex system there are various views on the degree to which divinities or supernatural forces control or intervene. In some forms of Hinduism a single personal supreme being such as Shiva or Vishnu is in ultimate charge of events and their outcomes. In some explanations a god or a guru intervenes to make adjustments for the individual or undertakes action for him.

So even in a system of explanation less relatively unified than that of Christianity it has not been possible to settle on a single consistent explanation for a fundamental paradox: if creatures are more than robots, the Creator cannot have decided in advance exactly what they will all do. There is 'process' in creation and it is dynamic. And unless the omnipotent Creator was content to make his creatures mere toys, it introduces a set of very difficult questions, already familiar to ancient thinkers.

The ancient world had various ideas about the 'determinist' notion that the world was made like a clockwork toy, which once wound up would run as it was designed to do until the spring ran down and it stopped. Some thinkers personalised the winder-up of the toy and called it Fate – with, some thought, a fierce goddess playing the part of Fate.

Classical mythology is full of stories of Fate getting its way despite human efforts to thwart it. When Paris was born, his father Priam was warned that he was fated to bring the land to destruction. He accordingly had him exposed as an infant so that he might die. But he did not die. He was found and taken home and brought up by a concerned shepherd and he grew up strong and brave and married the nymph Oenone, who was the child of Kebren the river god. Nevertheless, he did not avoid his 'fate'. Zeus, the king of the gods, appointed him to be judge in the affair of the beauty contest between three goddesses, and there were ensuing adventures. In the end he fell in love with Helen of Troy, with all the political consequences which followed from that.[35]

Others saw determinism as Fortune, another goddess, but this time a capricious one, who enjoyed playing with her victims, making them feel successful only to knock them off their pedestals and cast them down again into ruin.[36] Fortune is given to turning things round in ways humans cannot control and deciding the outcome. This is why it seemed apt to Boethius to describe Fortune as like a wheel. The individual finds himself carried helplessly round and round, sometimes at the top of its rotation and sometimes at the bottom.

Was it worth desperate creatures seeking to placate these powers and forces? That depended. Epicurus wrote:

It were better, indeed, to accept the legends of the gods than to bow beneath destiny which the natural philosophers have imposed. The one holds out some faint hope that we may escape if we honour the gods, while the necessity of the naturalists is deaf to all entreaties. Nor does he hold chance to be a god, as the world in general does, for in the acts of a god there is no disorder; nor to be a cause, though an uncertain one, for he believes that no good or evil is dispensed by chance to people so as to make life happy, though it supplies the starting-point of great good and great evil. He believes that the misfortune of the wise is better than the prosperity of the fool. It is better, in short, that what is well judged in action should not owe its successful issue to the aid of chance.[37]

Other thinkers – and the Christian tradition – saw in 'this scene of man', 'A mighty maze! but not without a plan'.[38]

There was, though, a difference between believing in a Providence which is impersonal and believing in a Providence which cares. Boethius' Providence is not merely one of the watching gods, or a committee of such gods. It is a higher power, essentially abstract not personal.[39] Augustine's Christian Providence cares.

A medieval Christian analogy offers an image which brings the nature of this Christian providential caring alive. Peter Abelard, explaining Genesis, suggests the Spirit of God 'brooded over the waters', 'in the manner of a bird which sits on an egg, so as to warm and vivify it'. He describes the structure of the egg, its shell and inner membrane, its white and its yolk:

> Hence just as the bird sitting on the egg and applying itself to it with the utmost affection, warms it with its heat so that thence, as was said, the chick is formed and vivified so also divine goodness, which is understood to be the Holy Spirit, . . . somehow makes warm by its heat that as yet fluid and unstable mass . . . said to pre-exist as waters so that from then on it might produce living things.[40]

The underlying questions, as Abelard would have been the first to recognise, remained philosophical as well as theological. The problem is that if Providence 'cares' and has allowed scope for creation and creatures to make choices, as Christians came to believe, there can be nothing mechanical about what happens. Yet an omniscient Creator must know what will happen. And an omnipotent Creator cannot be mistaken. So how can I possibly have the freedom to choose to do something which will result in a different outcome? And if I do not have that freedom, am I anything more than a robot? And if the Creator foresees what will happen and I do not have the capacity or wish to do my part, can he override or assist my feeble will and make sure I do it, without compromising my freedom?

Towards the end of his *On Interpretation* (*De Interpretatione*), Aristotle discusses the difficulties of constructing arguments when the statements from which a conclusion is to be drawn are in the future tense and do not state something which must necessarily be the case but appear to be conditional on certain other things happening which may or may not occur. It may be true that a sea fight will take place tomorrow or it may not. But the truth of the matter cannot be known until tomorrow.[41]

For some Christians it seemed obvious that if an omnipotent God knew in advance what was going to happen, it would follow that that future happening was predestined. The creature could have no choice in the matter.

Augustine was one of the most influential early Christian authors who wrote about this problem. He took it as a certainty that God chooses whom he will ultimately allow to enter heaven and who will be consigned to hell and that the elect and the damned can do nothing about it. His justification for this hard line is that God would be entitled to condemn everyone to hell. All are sinners. All have offended him. It is an act of enormous generosity that he should select a few to enjoy heavenly bliss.

The fortunate elect do not know that they are chosen. They live in ignorance. In the ordinary passage of events, any appearance that things are not fixed in advance is illusory. Augustine says (following Romans 8:28–9) that God can make even unpromising events and things which appear to be contrary to his will work out as he would wish. And when it seems that God's will has changed, it is simply that we perceive things differently and the same will of God appears to us in a different guise.[42]

Augustine's extensive treatment did not conclude the discussion by any means. It was revived in the Carolingian period, when it was debated whether a wholly good God could be the author of an eternity in hell for sinners, which looks like a bad thing for them. It was argued that they take themselves to hell and he is not responsible. When John Calvin took up the debate in the sixteenth century he would have no truck with that. He thought not only that the Creator created as he chose – some for hell and some for heaven – but also that those who were saved for heaven had an assurance that this was to be their future.

C.S. Lewis, in his a series of 'letters' from a senior devil to a junior one, instructing him in the skill of seducing souls offers some notes on the problem of time and eternity in this context. The 'Enemy' is the Creator. The junior devil is reminded that the human being he is working on, supposes that the Enemy, like himself, sees some things as present, remembers others as past, and anticipates others as future; or even if he believes that the Enemy does not see things that way, yet, in his heart of hearts, he regards this as a peculiarity of the Enemy's mode of perception – he doesn't really think (though he would say he did) that things as the Enemy sees them are things as they are!

The senior devil explains that God treats human prayers as 'one of the innumerable coordinates' with which he 'harmonises the weather of tomorrow':

creation in its entirety operates at every point of space and time . . . the Enemy does not foresee the humans making their free contributions in a future, but sees them doing so in His unbounded Now. And obviously to watch a man doing something is not to make him do it.[43]

Did the Creator plan the whole scheme at the outset? Setting the machine going and letting it run allows a good deal of scope for upsets. A clockwork toy or a wireless-controlled one may bump into the furniture and be overturned. It may be trodden on by a careless paternal foot. In the progress and development of a full-grown plant from a seed, the process may be affected by weather, or the descent of a bovine foot in a pasture crushing the seedling. A plant may grow different shapes and sizes but still be recognisably an oak not a cabbage, but if the oak never produces acorns has it really fulfilled itself and its purposes as an oak tree? Such teleological questions had been addressed philosophically by Aristotle but they had extra dimensions when considered theologically. The Christian accepted that every bruised leaf and every aborted foetus was foreseen and part of the divine plan.

If the Creator knows and can never be wrong, *knowing* what will happen amounts to *deciding* what will happen. If everything that happens is already fixed, creatures seem mere puppets. Determinism becomes predestination. Free will and free choice appear impossible. Even God does not interfere with his own fixed plan for it was always and always will be the best plan.

Alexander Pope described it:

Of systems possible, if 'tis confest
That Wisdom infinite must form the best,

... 'tis plain
must be somewhere, such a rank as man:
And all the question (wrangle e'er so long)
Is only this, if God has plac'd him wrong?[44]

Does the Creator care about his creatures and want the best for them?

Any theory of creation involving a doctrine of a benevolent Providence assumes the Creator 'cares'. This might not mean he 'cares' in the sense of having any feelings as we understand them about the fate of the world. Most of the 'schools' of philosophers of the ancient world thought it was inappropriate for a supreme being[45] to experience emotions, though it was accepted that lower deities were often angry and revengeful and liked to have their feelings mollified with gifts and even sacrifices. The ideal was tranquillity, but that went with order and rational behaviour. Indeed, so remote was the supreme held to be that even 'being' might not be attributable to him.

This meant that a Creator could be thought to take an interest in the orderly conduct of a created world which had been set up so as to be orderly. It also meant that those creatures designed by the Creator to be capable of rational thought might be able to observe and understand the working of the process. So the philosophers' task of inquiry and comment itself became clear and fitted in nicely.

Philosophy's advice to Boethius when he consults her in his condemned cell is to think big. He ought to place these events in their proper scale in cosmic events. One of the *Consolation*'s poetic interludes depicts God as maker of the sphere of the stars, spinner of the circling heavens, sitting on his throne.[46] In her role as counsellor Philosophy asks Boethius probing questions so as to diagnose what is wrong with him and recommend the right cure. Does he believe the world is run by chance or that it is directed by reason? What is the purpose of things (*rerum finis*) and the *intentio* towards which all nature progresses? She assures him that Providence protects the outcome and it does so for an ultimate and certain good.[47] This is the New Testament hypothesis of Romans 1:25–6: that for those who believe, all things fall into a pattern for good.

A person facing bad times ought to take comfort from this certainty and remember that his circumstances merely represent a turn of Fortune's wheel. Boethius has enjoyed good times, honours, positions of importance in affairs of state, but he never had a right to such good fortune, so why now repine at bad luck? As a rational animal he should not depend for his satisfactions on such ultimately unimportant ups and downs.[48] Life itself is a matter of cycles, in which fortunes can go up and down.

III. THE 'PHOENIX' THEORY OF CREATION

> About time, too. He's been looking dreadful for days; I've been telling him to get a move on.[49]

In the 'Harry Potter' novels, Dumbledore expresses satisfaction as his phoenix, Fawkes, bursts into flames and is reborn from the ashes as a chick. The legendary phoenix was a bird subject to periodic conflagrations. It appears in different forms in mythologies all over the world. The Greek historian Herodotus admits he has not actually seen one of these beautiful red and gold birds, because he is told they make very rare appearances, perhaps only every five hundred years. But they are reputed to appear from time to time in Heliopolis in Egypt, where they bring with them the ashes from which they themselves sprang.[50]

The phoenix is an archetype of a creation which repeatedly renews itself, after a catastrophic destruction. The Stoic philosophers were particularly attracted by the role of fire in such a process. Fire seemed to them the element best fitted to cause change and to destroy. Some, including Zeno, postulated a repeating cycle of destruction of the universe in a great conflagration, followed by a rebirth of the world just as it had been before.

There are many theories of creation which describe backsliding from better times, followed by recovery, sometimes over and over again, so that creation becomes a process with built-in cycles.

Individual reincarnation and return

Virgil envisaged the possibility that the dead might live again once they have been cleansed of the wrongdoing of their lives:

> So they are scourged by torments, and pay the price
> for former sins: some are hung, stretched out,

to the hollow winds, the taint of wickedness is cleansed
for others in vast gulfs, or burned away with fire:
each spirit suffers its own: then we are sent
through wide Elysium, and we few stay in the joyous fields,
for a length of days, till the cycle of time,
complete, removes the hardened stain, and leaves
pure ethereal thought, and the brightness of natural air.
All these others the god calls in a great crowd to the river Lethe,
after they have turned the wheel for a thousand years,
so that, truly forgetting, they can revisit the vault above,
and begin with a desire to return to the flesh.[51]

Virgil was not the only Greek or Roman thinker to entertain
this possibility but it was not central to contemporary religious
belief, as it has been in many world religions.

There are accounts of creation in which the same soul is
reborn repeatedly in a succession of new beginnings, sometimes
progressing to a higher level of being, sometimes sinking to
a lower one as a consequence of bad behaviour in the previous
life. The idea that some states of being are lower or higher than
others belongs with hierarchical theories of creation, but with the
difference that in reincarnation a soul may re-enter 'life' at a new
place in the hierarchy. So a belief in reincarnation could mean
that 'remaining human' is not a certainty for any human being
living now.

These ideas have a central place in Hinduism, Buddhism and
Sikhism, and they were held by some philosophers among the
ancient Greeks, notably Pythagoras. They are also found in some
African tribal religions, where it is believed that an ancestor
may come back in a newborn child, or as a spiritual guardian
dwelling within the child to give it the benefit of the spirit's
accumulated learning from its own many previous lives. Native
American religions often include a belief in reincarnation. Small
groups and individuals in Islam and Judaism and Christianity
say they believe in reincarnation, though for Christians the idea
is incompatible with the doctrine that the individual lives one
life, on the basis of which he or she is irrevocably committed to
heaven or to hell.

This 'cycling' or metempsychosis is not generally regarded
as enjoyable for the soul. The process is driven by excessive
attachments and desires. The enlightened soul wants to be
liberated from reincarnation and reach a state of lasting rest. This

is usually understood as a reunion with the Creator, a return to the source of the soul's being (and of all being). In the Upanishads can be found the theory that all human individuals have their essence from Brahman and that they will not reach their appointed end and fulfilment until they are reunited with him. A human being who has become free of the cycles of rebirth through which all must pass in the process of literally 'realising' themselves, making themselves real – that is, becoming what they were created to be – can be seen as somehow 'becoming Brahman'.

Hindu cycles are immensely long, lasting millions of years (or in a shorter version, 24,000 years). Brahman teaching similarly depicts lengthy cycles, with golden, silver and bronze or copper and iron ages following one another in a downward lapse, at the end of which a new Golden Age begins.

Such 'cycle' theories in Buddhism as well as Hinduism teach that human beings are reincarnated until they reach a state where they may step off the recycling process and rest. This makes the cycling process an unfortunate and undesirable phenomenon. The aspiring soul cries, 'Stop the world; I want to get off':

> There is neither beginning nor end. We are fated to continue from level to level, up or down, as we have always done and will always do until this cycle of the world ends.[52]

Natural cycles, following natural laws?

It is easy to see why the ancient Egyptians should have seen creation in terms of cycles of flood and dryness. The river Nile flooded each year. That was a reassuring pattern of events because it made the valley fertile and enabled the Egyptian people to grow food. There were other beliefs in the ancient world, in which the cycles follow settled laws. In *On Generation and Corruption* (*De Generatione et Corruptione*), Aristotle discusses whether the processes of 'coming to be' and passing away or 'ceasing to be' constitute 'alteration'. He lists the views of earlier philosophers, who mostly say this is not the case. This concept of alteration as something involving growth or diminution seemed appropriate to Aristotle because he was thinking about 'magnitudes'. Growth is an increase of a magnitude which already exists. It does not necessarily change the something into something else. If I am small and 'come to be' larger, I do not cease to be myself but something has happened to my substance.[53]

When Aristotle tries to apply his ideas about growth and change in the *De Generatione et Corruptione* to the universe he finds himself wrestling with the way the distinct 'elements' (fire, water, earth and air) could be understood to emerge from primal matter and with the need to postulate a void in which there is room for movement of things as they grow or shrink, the void filling the pores in the expanding growing things.[54]

Spring cycles and the mystery religions

> April is the cruellest month, breeding
> Lilacs out of the dead land, mixing
> Memory and desire, stirring
> Dull roots with spring rain.[55]

Common, too, are 'cyclical' theories in which creation dies into winter and is reborn each year in spring. A very ancient celebration of 'initiation' into the mysteries of the annual death of vegetation and its rebirth each spring, probably going back to the first millennium BC, were the ancient Greek Eleusinian mysteries held at Eleusis each year. This cult had at its centre the story of Demeter (the Roman goddess Ceres) and Persephone (Roman Proserpina), the goddess of the harvest and her daughter the goddess of the spring. Persephone was carried off by Hades, the god of the underworld and went down into the underworld with him, but each year she returns with the spring. So here was an explanation of the cycles of the seasons, microcosm of a cycle of creation itself.[56]

In the classical Greek myth of Persephone, one version of the tale begins with the defeat of the Titans by Zeus (Jupiter) and his fellows in the new pantheon. The Titans were banished to Tartarus and then arose the giants. They too were defeated and buried under Mount Etna. Their struggles to escape caused earthquakes and volcanic eruptions and their fiery breath comes up through cracks in the ground. Then Pluto emerges from his realm under the earth to inspect the damage and satisfy himself that his kingdom is not being destroyed:

> Pluto, King of the Underworld, found all this disturbance worrying in case his underground kingdom might be laid open to the air. He made a tour in his chariot 'to satisfy himself of the

extent of the damage'. Venus saw him and send her son Cupid
to fire a dart into his heart.

Thus exposed to falling in love:

Pluto saw beautiful Proserpina, daughter of Ceres, playing with
her companions in a flowery meadow, snatched her and carried
her off to his kingdom where he made her his queen.

Her grieving mother sought her everywhere, and legend
tells of adventures on the way. Eventually she learned where
her child was. She went to Jupiter and asked him to order the
return of her child. Jupiter granted her wish, on condition that
Proserpina had not eaten during her captivity. But she had. She
had taken a few seeds of a pomegranate given her by Pluto, and
that meant that each year she must pass the winter in Hades,
while her mother, goddess of fertility, grieved, but could return
in spring, when her happy mother caused flowers and crops to
grow again.[57]

The god who dies and is resurrected

> Peace, peace! he is not dead, he doth not sleep
> He hath awakened from the dream of life.[58]

Another strand in such cyclical re-creation stories is the sacrifice
of a god who dies and is resurrected or reborn. This has some
obvious similarities with the Christian doctrine that the son of
God died on the cross and was resurrected to save mankind. J.G.
Frazer, writing in *The Golden Bough,* commented on the way the
Spaniards were struck by finding natives 'sacrificing the human
representative of a god' when they:

conquered Mexico in the sixteenth century, and whose curiosity
was naturally excited by the discovery in the this distant region
of a barbarous and cruel religion which presented many curious
points of analogy to the doctrine and ritual of their own church.[59]

The Greek and Phoenician god Adonis, the Mesopotamian
Tammuz, appears in various forms in the Middle Eastern legends.
Adonis is a vegetation god, and he is born again or resurrected
each year. He is a male counterpart of Persephone, and was even,

in some versions of the story, entrusted as a baby to Persephone to look after, by Aphrodite, who had fallen in love with him. Persephone did not want to give him back. Jealous quarrels led to Zeus ruling that each should have him for a third of the year and he should choose with whom he spent the remaining third. More jealous quarrels led to his being killed by a wild boar, sent by a vindictive god or goddess (the identity varies).

The Fisher King

A variety of stories are associated with the Fisher King. The idea echoes that of the dying divinity who takes the world down with him or her into winter but is rescued or reborn and brings the spring. This legend seems first to have been told by Chrétien de Troyes towards the end of the twelfth century, in connection with the 'King Arthur' stories. This may derive from older Celtic tales in which a king or hero has a vessel or cauldron which is capable of bringing the dead back to life, though in some versions only as silent presences. In the Fisher King stories this 'cauldron' appears as the Holy Grail, the cup in which Jesus' blood was caught as he hung on the cross at the crucifixion, and also as the chalice used in the Christian eucharist where the wine 'becomes' the blood of Christ. The connecting thread is that when the Fisher King is ill or wounded, his country suffers with him, the crops fail, the cattle die. When he is brought back to life and health as a result of a successful quest for the Holy Grail, his kingdom recovers too.

The mystery religions and the cults of personal salvation

The 'mystery cult' which probably began in Thrace, but was more widespread in Greece by the fifth century BC, had a cyclical basis. Initiation for individual disciples or adherents carried assurances that spring would return each year and there would be a harvest once more, but the primary purpose of becoming a member of the cult was to seek personal salvation. Initiates into the mystery practised ascetic rituals in the belief that they might thus be able to get off the rotating wheel of recurring events and join the gods.

Secrecy has historically had its attractions for religious groups with exclusivist tendencies. In such religious communities, only initiates may know the mysteries – there is a *disciplina arcani*. The *disciplina arcani* in early Christianity reflected the preference for protecting the inner mysteries of the faith. But the secrets of the faith were taught to the would-be initiates before their baptism and were declared in the creeds in the context of worship.

The pagan mystery religions brook no mingling of ideas and beliefs. The Roman imperial conquerors found that their habit of comfortable syncretism did not really work in the case of the oriental mystery religion, with locked-in cults persisting (through secrecy, distinctiveness and commitment) to Isis and Cybele, Baal, Mithra and others.[60] Such cults made proselytes and, although the cults had a strong 'local' character, they turned out to be portable across the immensity of the Roman Empire. Initiates were found spread across vast distances, as far as modern Germany at least. Initiation ceremonies were an important feature. Initiates knew they were 'joining' something and that the joining might be painful and costly. Once joined together, members of the group had a strong sense of solidarity and community, which might be celebrated in communal sacred meals.

Mithraism tended to be a 'soldiers' religion' in ancient Rome. Votaries of Mithra took an oath on joining (*sacramentum*) and were branded with a hot iron (imposing on them an indelible stamp or *character*), and when they reached the third level of initiation into the mystery, they became *milites*, members of the god's army, fighting in his war on evil.[61] The Mithraic cult began at the time when Christianity began and it was the subject of comment by early Christian writers, who may or may not have been well informed and were anxious to debunk this rival religion. Mithraism was a particularly successful ancient mystery religion, but so successful was it in keeping its secrets that they are hard to recover now. Mithraism had its temples, usually constructed underground and containing depictions of figures and activities whose meaning remains uncertain.

Phrygia the Great Mother entered the Roman pantheon in 205 BC when the oracles, the Sibyls, were consulted about the way to drive the invading Hannibal from Italy at last. The Sibyls were an importation from Asia Minor and they said that Hannibal would finally be vanquished if the Great Mother was brought to Rome. A black stone embodying her was brought to Ostia and carried to the Palatine Hill. Hannibal was indeed vanquished and the Great Mother became established as a goddess in Rome.[62] This was a matriarchal religion in which the Great Mother was the mistress of the animals and in a union or partnership with the male god of

19. Fragment of a mosaic with Mithras, the Persian god of creation

vegetation, Attis. The religion attracted women who might have wished to join the initiates of Mithra but whose sex did not allow them to do so.

The particular conception of divinities indwelling a living world, where their worshippers could blend or merge with them when snatched 'out of themselves' in an extremity of rapture, was formed in local landscapes of mountain and forest, through which worshippers worked themselves up into ecstasies, as they rampaged through the forests after the goddess, playing musical instruments. Something approaching 'deficiation' or unification with the divine was experienced.

The poet Catullus (84–54 BC) wrote of Attis, out of his mind in the grove of the goddess, cutting off his genitals, and singing a wild song as the blood drips to the ground.[63] Blood sacrifice, with the initiate united with the sacrificial victim as the blood falls upon him, or as he is smeared with it or drinks it, is an archetypal belief in primitive religions. It was readily associated with dying and rebirth and also with fertility and thus with cycles of creation and with 'new' or 're-creation'.

Some features of these cults were 'oriental', adopting the ideas of those oriental religions which offered a prospect of eternal bliss.

The Persians were probably the immediate source of the idea of the belief of the 'Mazda' affiliates that mankind could live for ever. In Mazdaism the bull is the god, the creator, the author of the universe. To descend into the pit was to enact one's burial. There the bull's blood dripped down and gave renewal of life and one was reborn, possibly given eternal life. To be reborn in eternal life (*in eternum renatus*) was an attractive possibility. The advantage of entering the mystery is that you benefit in the life to come, for this forms a link.[64] Prudentius (348–405/13) describes a *Taurobolium* of this sort in his *Peristephanon*.[65]

The theory underlying all this is that the universe is a great organism or system in which an endless exchange and interaction is going on.[66] The question remains: did a Creator set it all in motion and then rest for ever or is he in some way involved in or ultimately controlling what is happening?

8

The search for a key

I. IS THERE A SINGLE UNDERLYING METHODOLOGY?

Making sense of all this, to finite human minds, has meant looking for pattern and consistency, to try to reduce the stories and explanations described in this book to a single system. One approach has been methodological: a search for consistent underlying rules which can be seen to inform a multitude of apparently quite different events and entities. Reviewing responses to his *The Origin of Species* for the third edition, Charles Darwin stresses that others before him had written about 'the introduction of new species' as 'a regular, not a casual phenomenon',[1] or, as Sir John Herschel expresses it, 'a natural in contradistinction to a miraculous, process'.[2] Darwin particularly approved of the way Baden Powell and others had looked for coordinating principles in the rules by which creation runs, so that: 'even the most seemingly monstrous and incongruous forms of animated existence in past times are all, without exception, constituted according to regular modifications of a common plan.'[3]

Geology presented a difficulty to the would-be architects of a single system because of the fossils, which did not seem to fit with the story in Genesis. Baden Powell rebutted the contemporary suggestion that geology was somehow an exception to the rule that everything could be subject to the same rules of study and analysis because it deals with the remote past which cannot be directly observed or experimented upon. On the contrary, he says:

> at the present day, it exhibits to us, preserved in their stony sepulchres, the successive varieties of organised structures, as they lived and worked in the same world, subject to the same immutable laws, mechanical, optical, and physical, uninterruptedly in operation through all the incalculably vast periods of past time.[4]

There have been floods and earthquakes. Do these extraordinary events challenge the contention that creation began and proceeds by the same rules? Georges Cuvier (1769–1832) said these explain the changes which the fossil record seems to show and why whole species are no longer to be found on earth. Charles Lyell (1797–1875) disagreed. He published three volumes on the *Principles of Geology* (1830–3), in which he saw these forces of change in the earth's surface as more gradual, and chiefly involving such processes as soil erosion and decomposition of living matter, which could also explain the end of certain species. James Hutton (1726–97) favoured the view also embraced by Baden Powell that whatever these processes had been, they had followed essentially the same fundamental rules.

Auguste Comte (1798–1857) identified three stages by which human beings have come to understand creation.[5] Primitive humans expected a supernatural power to be responsible for the creation and running of the world. More advanced humans moved on to philosophy and looked for abstract principles to explain phenomena. Now, in the third stage, mankind is learning to study by observation the laws and rules by which the world runs, but the rules have always been there; it has just taken time for human beings to grow sophisticated enough to realise it.

Would the theory that creation is all governed by a single system of rules still work if there should be more worlds than this? What can we know of 'the existence of organised life in the heavenly bodies'? Modern astronomers using telescopes have revealed 'great diversities of form and species' of 'nebulous matter' in the heavens. Nineteenth-century scientists considered 'the possibility of intelligent beings inhabiting those distant worlds' the planets. They knew this was not a new notion. Plutarch 'gives arguments for and against the moon being inhabited', Giordano Bruno 'declares not only for a plurality of worlds, but that the earth is inhabited in its interior as well as its exterior', commented Baden Powell.[6] Despite this great enlargement of the scope of the things which would need to be explained by a single set of laws, he still felt sure it could be done.

What kinds of explanation are respectable?

How far can this optimistic notion that it is all one story be stretched to accommodate different approaches and different disciplines and the mindsets of a variety of religions and philosophies? Those with a taste for magical arts which invite interference with creation and the Creator's intentions have often sought to know the future. Roman culture took such things seriously. The Romans favoured divination by studying the behaviour of birds – for example, their direction of flight – or by killing sacrificial animals and inspecting their entrails (*haruspex*); or by genethlialogy (casting birth dates),[7] though these practices were growing less fashionable by the beginning of the Christian era. There were also oracles, for example the Greek ones at Delphi and Epidaurus, who could be consulted by individuals or statesmen wanting guidance. In all these the hand or the voice of a god was perceived, indicating either foreknowledge or power to change the future. Ptolemy's *Tetrabiblos* treats astronomy and astrology as though they were branches of the same discipline. First the student must become familiar with the stars and planets and their motions and relationships and positions in the heavens Then he must learn how they influence events.[8]

Isaac Newton made special studies of the book of Daniel and the book of Revelation, which were brought together and published in his name after his death by his nephew Benjamin Smith, with the title *Observations Upon the Prophecies of Daniel, and the Apocalypse of St. John* (1733). Newton claims in the introduction to the book of Daniel, where he tried to fix the date when it was written, that 'the books of *Moses, Joshua,* and *Judges,* contain one continued history, down from the Creation to the death of *Sampson*' and accepts the authorship of Moses. He discusses the time of composition of Revelation in a similar way in the second half of the book.[9]

Here was an early modern scientist, a pioneer of the formulation of principles and concepts which have given him a key position in the history of science, who was by no means an orthodox Christian, willing to conjure with a mixture of types of evidence. History, he seems to be saying, obeys the same deep rules as science or mathematics. Like many of his contemporaries, he found prophecy as intellectually respectable as alchemy; he took a lively interest in both. These areas of his work, which he was still busy with when he died, now look jejune and naive. His scientific work still stands as respected 'Newtonian' physics. Newton himself saw the comparison in very different terms. Both seemed to him valid and complementary routes to understanding how creation began and how it works.

Can cataloguing and classification show that there are consistent underlying rules?

The 'key to all mythologies', painstakingly sought by Newton in reality and by the fictional Mr Casaubon in George Eliot's *Middlemarch* two centuries later, was realised in a limited way a generation later still in a multivolume attempt by Antti Aarne to bring order to the innumerable versions of myths and legends by classifying their themes and narrative patterns.[10] Stith Thompson brought the work up to date in the twentieth century in a sequence which begins with the Creator and his identity. There follows a series covering the sun god, the grandfather, the stone woman, the Brahma as Creator, then various multiple creators and pairs, and the first mother as Creator. Then come reasons for creation, and the descendants of the Creator. Then he considers what kind of being the Creator is (invisible, hermaphrodite, animal, particular animals – cow, bird, raven, eagle, insect, spider, beetle, snake, worm). Then there are stories in which the Creator is a craftsman or an angel. There is a sequence of story-types about where the Creator came from: from the sky, from chaos, from the underworld or the ocean, the East, an egg. There are stories classified according to the Creator's family members or companions in the creative process, including animal companions, sun and moon and angels. There are stories involving angels and devils and the war of good and evil.[11] D.L. Ashliman's *A Guide to Folktales in the English Language* includes many examples of an overlap between folk-tales and creation legends. Eve complains to God when he gives her children different blessings and treats them unequally.[12] There are many stories in which the devil appears, frequently to be cheated of his prize. Often the unfolding of events as predicted is frustrated by a clever trick by the hero of the tale.

Is all this anything more than a housewifely tidying of the contents of the drawers and cupboards of mythology? Can this sorting and classifying exercise provide the 'key' the fictional Mr Causabon was looking for and which was evidently a notion which made sense to the novelist? It is apparent from much earlier attempts to reconcile the varieties of myths and legends that people recognised that something deeper could be looked for.

II. CAN 'COMPARATIVE RELIGION' PROVIDE A UNIFYING PRINCIPLE?

J.G. Frazer, author of *The Golden Bough*, was a Mr Casaubon, searching among the myths and religions of the world for analogous beliefs and practices, but focusing on the motif of the dying and resurrected god and the theme of the growth of the human soul. He did this not out of piety but out of a scepticism about the special claims of Christianity as they were presented in the English society of his time. He was a secularist and his objective was to shrink the Christian story to a relatively minor position in a vast complex of similar beliefs.[13]

The urge to make such 'comparisons' of religions is much older than these nineteenth-century examples and the early modern attempts to make sense of the apparent confusions of mythologies. Olaus Magnus compared religious practices such as the religious significances of the colour red among Lapplanders and in Herodotus and Pliny, the horns of stag-beetles (comparing the significance Egyptians gave to scarabs), giants in Norse myths (Harthben) and in Deuteronomy 3, the description of the enormous Og, King of Bashan.[14]

> All the Gallas are heathens. Or rather, are neither Christians, Moors nor heathens, for they have no idols to worship and take very little account of God. Yet after they inhabited the territories of the empire [invaded Ethiopia] and lived among the Christians . . . they began to be circumcised, more as a national custom than as a sign of religion.[15]

On the whole, 'comparative religion' as understood by Olaus Magnus and others at this early stage simply looked for likenesses:

> From a primeval age, when there were giants in the northern lands, long, that is, before the Latin letters were invented and before Carmenta reached the mouth of the Tiber from Greece and set foot with Evander on Roman soil, drove out the Aborigines, and taught manners and literacy to the ignorant and wholly rustic people, the kingdoms o fthe North had a script of their own . . . If anyone doubts that this was accomplished by the strength of giants in very early times, let him go there.[16]

Richard Eden (*c.*1520–76) was a student at Cambridge, and he acquired patrons who could offer him access to men in prominent positions in public life such as Roger Ascham, the tutor of the young princess who was to become Queen Elizabeth I – men of strong intellectual interests but also able to get him an entry to court circles and a post in government. Eden took up alchemy on behalf of one of these patrons. Another, the Earl of Northumberland, was keen to foster discovery of new lands for English trade, but by sailing east not west. The obliging Eden produced a book on the 'New India' in 1553 and another on the 'New World or West India' in 1555, together with translations of works of related interest which were being published elsewhere.[17]

'Credulous, imaginative, unscientific, and very much influenced by classical and Biblical tradition'.[18] This mid-twentieth-century editorial comment on Richard Eden's narratives about voyages to Guinea is a reminder that the observer's or commentator's time and place offers a vantage-point of its own. It is not easy to be completely detached about religious belief, and the 'observer' is likely to have his own views. What looked 'credulous, imaginative, unscientific' in 1942 was the last word in intellectual adventurousness in the 1550s and 1560s.

Today the study of 'comparative religion' sees itself as more scientific. It involves trying to look objectively at features of different systems of religious belief and practice so as to identify similarities and borrowings where one has drawn something from another. It assumes respect for alternative 'systems'; sneering at them as primitive is no longer as acceptable as it once was. The idea is not to take any religion as representing the only truth, but to make comparisons with the same sort of detachment as would be applied to comparing apples and oranges. That detachment makes it difficult for the study of comparative religion to satisfy the urge to have an answer which can be embraced as a way of life.

Was there an 'original true religion of the human race'?[19]

Ad fontes, 'back to the sources', is a call which assumes that the oldest evidence is the best evidence. Renaissance and Reformation thinkers tended to take that view, but it has earlier antecedents. Much earlier attempts to discover common ground are noticeable in the many links made by classical authors between systems of thought and explanations known to them. Strabo makes comparisons with the ideas of gymnosophists, who he says are to be found in India,[20] and compares other views he has learned about in distant cultures. Plutarch notes in his *Life of Alexander* that Alexander the Great met gymnosophists in northern India.

Olaus Magnus regrets the loss of information which occurs when there is a failure to write things down or to keep the records:

> A great many excellent memorials from men of the earliest times would therefore still be in our possession for the instruction of the present age, if those people, born for eminent feats, had left for their successor writings as extensive as their deeds were glorious.[21]

But they sing the stories 'spiritedly in rhythmical melodies'.

III. LOOKING INWARD FOR AN ANSWER?

The only viewpoint from which to look back to creation remains that of someone standing on the earth, and the only interpreter of that limited evidence is still the human mind, which we have seen struggling with its options. Perhaps it is simply not big enough.

> But of this frame the bearings, and the ties,
> The strong connections, nice dependencies,
> Gradations just, has thy pervading soul
> Look'd through? or can a part contain the whole?[22]

Is the search for a key overconfident? Alexander Pope's rousing verses are the work of a satirist:

> Go, wondrous creature! mount where science guides,
> Go, measure earth, weigh air, and state the tides;
> Instruct the planets in what orbs to run,
> Correct old time, and regulate the sun;
> Go, soar with Plato to th' empyreal sphere,
> To the first good, first perfect, and first fair;
> Or tread the mazy round his follow'rs trod.[23]

Buddhism favours an exploration in which intuition and reflection play a significant part. It is by this route that the soul frees itself from suffering and enters the state of Nirvana, which transcends ordinary understanding and resembles the heavenly rapture of Christianity. Inward contemplation of the knowable territory of the soul itself is the 'know thyself' method of making sense of creation which gave rise to both the Greek and the Latin aphorisms:

> Know then thyself, presume not God to scan;
> The proper study of mankind is man.[24]

So perhaps there is another method or route altogether to discovering an explanation of creation. How far is it possible to get by inward contemplation? Each person's ideas about the origins of the world he finds himself in are likely to be a blend of the direct and very 'local' perceptions of the young child, the explanations the child is given as he or she grows, and a varying amount of education, which may or may not set a context and enable him or her to discuss the ideas he has and place them in the conspectus of ideas of other races, other times. All this sits in a cradle of cultural norms and assumptions.

Augustine and Anselm point out that nothing which is completely new can be discovered by the human artist or inventor or inquirer. Human creativity can only mirror and adapt God's ideas. This, if correct, must apply to ideas about how the world began. They are a synthesis, but of what?

'Puritan' Christians from the sixteenth or seventeenth centuries, wishing to join a community of believers, might be expected to relate before the congregation their personal stories or experiences, their struggles with sin and their acceptance of divine grace.[25] So Puritans have seen personal experience of God as 'evidence'. They are not the only ones. In his *Meditations*, Descartes made an attempt to 'inspect' his own inner knowledge:

> The belief that there is a God who is all powerful, and who created me, such as I am, has, for a long time, obtained steady possession of my mind. How, then, do I know that he has not arranged that there should be neither earth, nor sky, nor any extended thing, nor figure, nor magnitude, nor place, providing at the same time, however, for [the rise in me of the perceptions of all these objects, and] the persuasion that these do not exist otherwise than as I perceive them? And further, as I sometimes think that others are in error respecting matters of which they

believe themselves to possess a perfect knowledge, how do I know
that I am not also deceived each time I add together two and
three, or number the sides of a square, or form some judgment
still more simple, if more simple indeed can be imagined?
But perhaps Deity has not been willing that I should be thus
deceived, for he is said to be supremely good. If, however, it were
repugnant to the goodness of Deity to have created me subject
to constant deception, it would seem likewise to be contrary to
his goodness to allow me to be occasionally deceived; and yet it
is clear that this is permitted.[26]

He adds:

And, in truth, it is not to be wondered at that God, at my creation,
implanted this idea in me, that it might serve, as it were, for the
mark of the workman impressed on his work; and it is not also
necessary that the mark should be something different from
the work itself; but considering only that God is my creator,
it is highly probable that he in some way fashioned me after
his own image and likeness, and that I perceive this likeness,
in which is contained the idea of God, by the same faculty by
which I apprehend myself, in other words, when I make myself
the object of reflection, I not only find that I am an incomplete,
[imperfect] and dependent being, and one who unceasingly
aspires after something better and greater than he is.[27]

20. Large Hadron Collider in CERN, Geneva

Conclusion

The end-game

Creation stories are kaleidoscopic. A shake, and the colourful scraps settle into another pattern. It is hard to fix principles on which to consider one of these ephemeral pictures more 'true', 'beautiful' or 'meaningful' than another. And creation stories do not all depict the universe as a fixed device in which little bits of colour and detail such as human beings and their earth can shift about.

When Aristotle asked what was the *telos* or purpose of things, he looked both at the acorn and at the oak, at the foal and at the grown-up stallion. The 'final' (ultimate) cause of both was both the initiator and the end. The Creator has been seen as both Alpha and Omega.[1]

Completions and perfectings of a beginning, after which a great deal has happened (and is still happening), are to be found in many world religions. Hinduism looks forward to a time when creation's struggle and change will all be over, an end of creation, with a return of all created things to their Creator. In the book of Revelation, the Christian tradition looks towards a final dénouement and the beginning of an everlasting happy state of things in which there will be no more change. The fortunate who have been chosen for heaven are to spend a contented eternity in worship of the Creator, of their own free choice and with no further desire for any other occupation or distraction than enjoying the Creator's presence:

> Then I saw 'a new heaven and a new earth', for the first heaven and the first earth had passed away, and there was no longer any sea. I saw the Holy City, the new Jerusalem, coming down out of heaven from God, prepared as a bride beautifully dressed for her husband. And I heard a loud voice from the throne saying, 'Look! God's dwelling place is now among the people, and he will dwell with them. They will be his people, and God himself

will be with them and be their God. He will wipe every tear from
their eyes. There will be no more death or mourning or crying
or pain, for the old order of things has passed away. He who was
seated on the throne said, I am making everything new!'[2]

This is a lovely and comforting conclusion to one religion's
creation story, but it is only one of many. There is no single unifying
version of the end any more than there is of the beginning. If there
once was, it seems to have disappeared beyond retrieval:

That race is now so intermingled with other races that our
original religion is quite forgotten or confused.[3]

Notes

Preface

1 Douglas Adams, *The Hitchhiker's Guide to the Galaxy* (London, 1979); and Douglas Adams, *The Original Hitchhiker Radio Scripts*, ed. Geoffrey Perkins (London, 1985).

2 George Eliot, *Middlemarch*, ed. David Carroll (Oxford, 1986), p. 23.

3 Isaac Newton, *Chronology of Ancient Kingdoms Amended* (London, 1728).

4 Sonu Shamdasani, *A Biography in Books* (London and New York, 2012), pp. 49–61; and see C.G. Jung, *The Red Book*, ed. Sonu Shamdasani, tr. Mark Kyburz and John Peck (London and New York, 2009).

5 Lisa Appignanesi (ed.), *Free Expression is No Offence* (London, 2005), p. 201.

6 Ibid., p. 202.

Introduction

1 John Donne, 'Sermon 3, on Whitsunday, 1629, at St. Paul's', in John Donne, *Sermons*, ed. Evelyn Simson and George R. Potter (Berkeley, 1959), Vol. IX, p. 92.

2 Charles Kingsley, *The Heroes*, republished in S.H. McGrady (ed.), *Legends and Myths of Greece and Rome* (London, 1936), p. 51.

3 Pope, *Essay on Man*, Epistle One, I.21–34.

4 Rose Tremain, *Trespass* (London, 2010), Chapter 1.

5 Francis Bacon, *Instauratio Magna, III: Historia Naturalis and Historia Vita. The Oxford Francis Bacon, Vol. XII*, ed. Graham Rees and Maria Wakely (Oxford, 2007), p. 7.

6 Opinions differ on the date of Homer, but the process of writing which produced the two epics probably took place in the eighth century BC.

7 Clement of Alexandria, *Miscellanies*, Book I, 15.71.

8 Pope, *Essay on Man*, Epistle One, V.131–4.

9 Ibid., Epistle One, V.16.

10 John Bunyan, *Holy War*, ed. T.H. Jenkins (Darlington, 2003), and www.ccel.org/ccel/bunyan/holy_war.iv.html (accessed 23 May 2013).

11 Phillip Pullman, *The Amber Spyglass* (London, 2000), p. 382.

12 Ibid., p. 33.

13 Augustine, *City of God*, XI.4–6.

14 John Donne, 'Sermon preached to the King at Court in April, 1629', in Donne, *Sermons*, Vol. IX, p. 47.

15 Joseph Butler, *Analogy* (London, 1896), Part I, Chapter I, 'Of a future life', 72, www.ccel.org/ccel/butler/analogy.toc.html (accessed 23 May 2013).

16 C.S. Lewis, *Perelandra* [1943] (London, 1953).

17 Robert Grant, *Hymns Ancient and Modern* (Norwich, 1984).

18 David Hempton, *The Church in the Long Eighteenth Century* (London, 2011), p. 59.

19 John Milton, *The History of Britain*, in John Milton, *The Works of John Milton* (New York, 1932), X, p. 3.

20 Pedro Sarmiento de Gamboa, *History of the Incas*, tr. Clemens Markham, Hakluyt Society, Series II, Vol. 22 (Cambridge, 1907), p. 20 ff.

21 Elizabeth Barrett Browning, 'A musical instrument', in Elizabeth Barrett Browning, *Poems*, ed. Karen Hill (London, 1994), p. 570.

22 A.J. Church, 'Heroes and kings', in McGrady, *Legends and Myths of Greece and Rome*, p. 152 ff.

23 Charles Lamb, 'The adventures of Ulysses: heroes and kings', in McGrady, *Legends and Myths of Greece and Rome*, p. 148.

24 Edward Brooks, 'The story of the Aeneid', in McGrady, *Legends and Myths of Greece and Rome*, p. 181.

25 Kingsley, *The Heroes*, pp. 38–9.

26 C. Witt, 'The myths of Hellas', in McGrady, *Legends and Myths of Greece and Rome*, p. 79.

Chapter 1

1 Garlandus Compotista, *Dialectica*, ed. L.M. de Rijk (Assen, 1969), p. 26.

2 E. Vailati, *Leibniz and Clarke* (Oxford, 1997), pp. 123–5.

3 H.G. Alexander (ed.), *The Leibniz–Clarke Correspondence* (Manchester, 1956), Leibniz, third letter to Clarke, 5.

4 Ibid., Clarke, third letter, 2 and 5.

5 Vailati, *Leibniz and Clarke*, pp. 123–5.

6 H.G. Wells, 'The time machine', in H.G. Wells, *Tales of Space and Time: The Short Stories of H.G. Wells* (London, 1927), pp. 9–11 and Chapter 3.

7 Francis Bacon, *Parasceve ad historiam naturalem*, republished in Francis Bacon, *The Instauratio Magna Part II, Novum Organum and Associated Texts. The Oxford Francis Bacon, Vol. XI*, ed. Graham Rees and Maria Wakeley (Oxford, 2004), pp. 456–7.

8 Ibid., pp. 456–7.

9 Ibid., pp. 458–9, 16–17 and 104–5.

10 Ibid., pp. 16–17.

11 Francis Bacon, *The Instauratio Magna Part III, Novum Organum and Associated Texts. The Oxford Francis Bacon, Vol. XII*, ed. Graham Rees and Maria Wakeley (Oxford, 2007), pp. 6–9.

12 Bacon, *Instauratio Magna Part II, Novum Organum and Associated Texts*, pp. 458–61.

13 Particularly in the English universities, which added his inductive method to the logic syllabus.

14 François Marie Arouet de Voltaire, *Letters on the English* (Cambridge, MA, 1909–14), Letter XIV and XVII, www.bartleby. com/34/2 (accessed 23 May 2013).

15 Aethelweard, *The Chronicle of Aethelweard*, ed. A. Campbell (Londo, 1962), p. 3.

16 Richard S. Westfall, 'Isaac Newton's *Theologiae Gentilis Origine Philosophicae*', in W. Warren Wagar (ed.), *The Secular Mind* (New York and London, 1982), pp. 15–34, p. 17.

17 Ibid., p. 18.

18 Ibid., pp. 19 and 21.

19 Isaac Newton, *The Chronology of Ancient Kingdoms amended* (London, 1728), pp. 15, 10, 3, 5, 265 and 8.

20 Charles Williams, *Many Dimensions* (London, 1931), p. 133.

21 Augustine, *City of God*, XI.4–6.

22 Ibid.

23 Ibid.

24 Pope, *Essay on Man*, Epistle Two, 43.

25 Ibid., Epistle Two, 31–4.

26 Williams, *Many Dimensions*, p. 262.

27 Hesiod, *Theogony*, ed. Glenn W. Most (Cambridge, MA, 2006), Vol. I, pp. 116, 123 and 126.

28 Plato, *Timaeus*.

29 Ibid.

30 Catherine Delano Smith, 'The emergence of "maps" in European rock art: a prehistoric preoccupation with place', *Imago Mundi*, 34 (1982), pp. 9–25, p. 21.

31 H.G. Wells, 'The star', in Wells, *Tales of Space and Time*, pp. 644–5.

32 E.S. Kennedy and Imad Ghanem (eds), *The Life and Work of Ibn al-Shatir* (Aleppo, 1976). His work came close in its conclusions to the theory of Copernicus.

33 www.esotericarchives.com/solomon/sphere.htm (accessed 28 May 2013).

34 A hymn of John Chadwick (1864).

35 The Latin is *animus* (mind) not *anima* (soul).

36 Cicero, *Republic*, VI.9ff, 'Somnium scipionis', VI.15.

37 Ibid., VI.16.

38 Ibid., VI.17.

39 Ibid., VI.20 and VI.26. From: Oliver J. Thatcher (ed.), *The Library of Original Sources* (Milwaukee, 1907), Vol. III, pp. 216–41.

40 Cicero, *Republic*, VI.16 and VI.19.

41 Pliny, *Natural History*, II.iii.6.

42 Ovid, *Metamorphoses*, I.48.

43 Virgil, *Georgics*, I. 233–4.

44 He explains the difference between the eight cosmic spheres which Aristotle identified and the nine favoured by the *astrologi* or astrologers of his own time.

45 Pliny, *Natural History*, VI.xxxix.211–18.

46 Herodotus, *Histories*, IV.8.

47 Plutarch, *On the Face in the Moon*.

48 C.R. Beazely, *The Dawn of Modern Geography* (London, 1897), Vol. I, p. 274–81.

49 Exodus 36:8–39:43.

50 Beazely, *Dawn of Modern Geography*, Vol. I, pp. 294, 292.

51 Pierre d'Ailly, *Imago Mundi* (Paris, 1930), Book I, Chapter i; and see Beazely, *Dawn of Modern Geography*, Vol. I, p. 274–81.

52 Augustine, *City of God*, XIV.9; and Isidore, *Etymologiae*, ed. C.C.J. Webb (Oxford, 1911), XIV.5.17. See 2 Esdras 6:42, on God commanding the waters to be gathered together on the third day of creation.

53 As in British Library MS, BL Cotton Tiberius B V, see V.I.J. Flint, *The Imaginative Landscape of Christopher Columbus* (Princeton, 1992), p. 31.

54 www.fordham.edu/halsall/source/urban2-5vers.html#Fulcher (accessed 28 May 2013).

55 Ibid.

56 August C. Krey, *The First Crusade: The Accounts of Eyewitnesses and Participants* (Princeton, 1921), pp. 33–6; www.fordham.edu/halsall/source/urban2–5vers.html#balderic (accessed 28 May 2013).

57 Ezekiel 5:5 has Jerusalem set in the 'centre' of the nations and in Ezekiel 38:12 Jerusalem is set in the 'centre' of the earth.

58 Christopher Columbus, 'Letter to the sovereigns on the third voyage, 18 October, 1498', in Christopher Columbus, *Journals and Other Documents on the Life and Voyages of Christopher Columbus*, tr. and ed. Samuel Eliot Morison (New York, 1963), p. 287.

59 Ibid., p. 284; Flint, *Imaginative Landscape of Christopher Columbus*, p. 153.

60 Ibid., pp. 13–15.

61 Catherine Delano Smith, 'Cartographic signs on European maps and their expansion before 1700', *Imago Mundi*, 37 (1985), pp. 9–29, p. 9, quoting translation by J. Schultz, 'Jacopo de Barbari's view of Venice', *Art Bulletin*, 60 (1978), pp. 435–74, from MS. Vat. Lat. 1960, f. 13.

62 Martin Luther, 'Lectures on Genesis', in Martin Luther, *Luther's Works* (St Louis, 1958), Vol. I, pp. 87–91, 97–101.

63 Elizabeth M. Ingram, 'Maps as readers' aids: maps and plans in Geneva Bibles', *Imago Mundi*, 45 (1993), pp. 29–44. See also Catherine Delano Smith, 'Maps as art and science: maps in sixteenth-century Bibles', *Imago Mundi*, 42(1990), pp. 65–83, pp. 69, 75.

64 William Worcestre, *Itineraries*, ed. John H. Harvey (Oxford, 1969), lists islands off Africa, pp. 371–3.

65 Cicero, *Republic*, VI.xx.21.

66 Beazely, *Dawn of Modern Geography*, Vol. I, p. 294.

67 Pierre d'Ailly, *Imago Mundi*, Book I, Chapter vii.

68 And they could not have had known about Christ because no one could have preached the Gospel to them (*notitia predicationis Christi*). See Augustine, *City of God*, XVI. 36–7.

69 Daniel Defoe, *A General History of Discoveries and Improvements* [1725-6], in W.R. Owens and P.N. Furbank (eds), *Writings on Travel, Discovery and History by Daniel Defoe* (London, 2001), Vol. IV, pp. 74–5.

70 William Carey, *An Enquiry into the Obligations of Christians to Use Means for the Conversion of the Heathens* (Leicester, 1792).

71 H.G. Wells, 'The crystal egg', in Wells, *Stories of Space and Time*, pp. 638–9.

72 Gore Vidal, *Creation* (London, 1993), p. 209.

73 Augustine, *City of God*, XVI.9.

74 Job 37:7 describes how the 'morning stars sang together and all the sons of God shouted for joy'.

75 Beazely, *Dawn of Modern Geography*, Vol. I, p. 294.

76 E.M.W. Tillard, *The Elizabethan World-Picture* (London, 1998).

77 John Hayward, *David's Tears* (London, 1623).

78 Dorothy Sayers, *The Mind of the Maker* [1941] (London, 1994), p. 38.

79 Milton, *Paradise Lost*, VII.519–24.

80 Pope, *Essay on Man*, Epistle One, V.131–4.

81 Ibid., II.43–50.

82 John Locke, *Two Treatises on Government* (London, 1764), I.3.15, www.lonang.com/exlibris/locke/loc–103.htm (accessed 28 May 2013), I.3.16.

83 Ibid., I.3.19.

84 Mill, *Theism*.

85 Jean Jacques Rousseau, *Contrat Social* (Paris, 1986).

86 1 Corinthians 12:12–31.

87 Hayward, *David's Tears*.

88 Hugh Lofting, *The Story of Dr. Dolittle: Being the History of his Peculiar Life at Home and Astonishing Adventures in Foreign Parts Never Before Printed* (London, 1920), www.pagebypagebooks.com/Hugh_Lofting/The_Story_of_Doctor_Dolittle (accessed 28 May 2013).

89 Herodotus, *Histories*, IV.13.1.

90 J.B. Friedman, *The Monstrous Races in Medieval Art and Thought* (New York, 2000); and see Pliny, *Natural History*, II.iii.6 and Book VII on what is man and what is monster.

91 Pliny, *Natural History*, VII.ii.

92 Friedman, *Monstrous Races*, p. 95 on the Rabbinic tradition.

93 Syllacio translated his letters into Latin ('in the style of Lucian') and printed them at Pavia 1494/5 in an edition dedicated to the duke of Milan.

94 Columbus, *Journals and Other Documents*, p. 236.

95 Friedman, *Monstrous Races*, p. 1.

96 Macrobius may have invented the term.

Chapter 2

1 John Donne, 'Sermon 1', in John Donne, *Sermons*, ed. Evelyn Simson and George R. Potter (Berkeley, 1959), Vol. IX, p. 48.

2 Moses.

3 Milton, *Paradise Lost*, I.6–10.

4 Romans 1:19–20 (NIV).

5 'Knowledge is human or divine. Divine knowledge is that which *Deo auctore hominibus tradita est*, even if it is written down by human agency (*humano ministerio*)', Robert Kilwardby, *De Ortu Scientarum*, ed. Albert G. Judy (London 1976), Vol. I, Chapter 1.1, p. 9.

6 Aquinas, *Summa Theologiae*, I, q.1, a.5.

7 Roger Bacon, *Opus Maius*, ed. John Henry Bridges (London, 1900), Vol. I, Part II, Chapter VIII.

8 Ibid., Vol. I, Part II, Chapter IX.

9 Matthew Tindal, *Christianity as Old as the Creation* (London, 1730).

10 Gilbert Burnet (ed.), *A Defence of Natural and Revealed Religion, Being an Abridgement of the Sermons Preached at the Lecture Founded by Robert Boyle* [1737] (London, 2000), includes nearly two dozen preachers (originally published in four volumes), beginning with Richard Bentley.

11 Ibid., p. 3.

12 Ibid., pp. 9–10, 12, 14–15.

13 In particular, cultural diversity with respect to religious beliefs could no longer be ignored. As Edward Herbert wrote in *De Religione Laici*, ed. and tr. Harold R. Hutcheson (New Haven, CT, 1944), p. 87: 'Many faiths or religions, clearly, exist or once existed in various countries and ages, and certainly there is not one of them that the lawgivers have not pronounced to be as it were divinely ordained, so that the Wayfarer finds one in Europe, another in Africa, and in Asia, still another in the very Indies.'

14 David Hume, *A Dissertation on the Passions: The Natural History of Religion*, ed. Tom L. Beauchamp (Oxford, 2007), pp. 44, 45.

15 Ibid., p. 46

16 Ibid., p. 44.

17 Ibid., p. 48.

18 Ibid., pp. 52, 47, 49.

19 William Paley, *Natural Theology* (Oxford, 1802), Chapter 1.i. Equally influential was Paley's *Evidences of Christianity* (1794).

20 Paley, *Natural Theology*, Chapter 1.i.

21 Mill, *Theism*, p. 449.

22 Joseph Butler, *Analogy of Religion* (London, 1896), 'Introduction', para. 9, p. 11.

23 Ibid., 'Introduction', para. 10, p. 11.

24 Ibid., 'Introduction', para. 12, p. 12.

25 Ibid., I.iii.28, p. 86.

26 Mill, *Theism*, p. 169.

27 Baden Powell, *Essays on the Spirit of the Inductive Philosophy, the Unity of Worlds, and the Philosophy of Creation* (London, 1855), p. 41.
28 Ibid., pp. 42–3.
29 Ibid., pp. 18–19.
30 Ibid., pp. 19, 21.
31 Ibid., p. 21.

Chapter 3

1 Pope, *Essay on Man*, Epistle One, III.99–102, 110–12.
2 www.fordham.edu/halsall/mod/1000Vinland.html (accessed 29 May 2013).
3 Olaus Magnus, *Description of the Northern Peoples*, ed. Peter Foote and tr. Peter Fisher, Hakluyt Society, Vol. 182 (London, 1996), pp. 149, 148.
4 John Locke, *Essay Concerning Human Understanding* (London, 1741) mentions the Indian who said the world was on an elephant which was on the back of a tortoise.
5 Bertrand Russell, 'Why I am not a Christian' (1927), http://users. drew.edu/~jlenz/whynot.html (accessed 29 May 2013).
6 Pope, *Essay on Man*, Epistle Two, I.3–18.
7 Ficino's contemporary Lodovico Lazzarelli (1447–1500) also made translations, which he did of his own motion from another manuscript and these were printed in 1507.
8 John Hayward, *David's Tears* (London, 1623).
9 Hermes Trismegistos, 'Poemandres', in Hermes Trismegistos, *Corpus Hermeticum*, ed. A. Festugière and A.D. Nock (2nd edn, Paris, 1960–72).
10 Ibid., pp. 24–5.
11 Hermes Trismegistos, 'The sacred sermon', in Hermes Trismegistos, *Corpus Hermeticum*, ed. A. Festugière and A.D. Nock (2nd edn, Paris, 1960–72).
12 Hermes Trismegistos, 'To Asclepius', in Hermes Trismegistos, *Corpus Hermeticum*, ed. A. Festugière and A.D. Nock (2nd edn, Paris, 1960–72).
13 Lactantius, *Divine Institutes*, tr. Mary Frances Macdonald (Washington, 1964), II.5.
14 Augustine, *City of God*, VIII.23–4.
15 Hermes Trismegistos, 'Though unmanifest God is most manifest', in Hermes Trismegistos, *Corpus Hermeticum*, ed. A. Festugière and A.D. Nock (2nd edn, Paris, 1960–72).

16 Frances Yates, *Giordano Bruno and the Hermetic Tradition* (London, 1964), p. 238, describing the account of creation in the *Koré Kosmou* (*Minerva Mundi*), first published 1591.

17 Their belief that Hermes was a contemporary of Moses allowed them to argue that the Hermetic tradition had influenced the Old Testament and Plato, rather than the other way round. Ibid., pp. 40–3.

18 The two Genesis accounts describe a different order of the creation of plants.

19 Genesis 2:19–20.

20 Abu Nasr al-Farabi, *On the Perfect State,* ed. and tr. Richard Walzer (Oxford, 1985).

21 Ibid., Chapter 1, p. 71, Chapter 2, pp. 89–90 and Chapter 5, p. 109.

22 Ibid., Chapter 2, pp. 89–90.

23 Ibid., Chapter 3, p. 101 and Chapter 4, p. 107.

24 Ibid., Chapter 10, p. 165.

25 God has no gender.

26 Fernando Cervantes, *The Devil in the New World* (New Haven, CT, 1994), p. 109.

27 Genesis 2–3.

28 Franz Cumont, *The Mysteries of Mithra,* tr. James J. McCormack (London, 1903).

29 Porphyry, *On Abstinence from Animal Food,* I.4, www.ccel.org/ccel/pearse/morefathers/files/porphyry_abstinence_00_eintro.htm (accessed 29 May 2013).

30 C.R.C. Allberry (ed.), *A Manichean Psalm Book* (Stuttgart, 1938).

31 Augustine, *Against the Fundamental Epistle of Mani* (Nicene Fathers), www.biblestudytools.com/history/early-church-fathers/nicene/vol–4-saint-augustin/anti-manichaean-writings/against-epistle-of-manichaeus-called-fundamental–1.html (accessed 29 May 2013).

32 Ibid., XII.14, XII.15 and XII.16.

33 Philip Pullman, *The Amber Spyglass* (London, 2000), p. 33.

34 John Donne, 'Sermon 3, on Whitsunday, 1629, at St Paul's' in John Donne, *Sermons,* ed. Evelyn Simson and George R. Potter (Berkeley, 1959), Vol. IX, p. 92.

35 Ibid., p. 99.

36 Ibid., p. 100.

Chapter 4

1 Macrobius, *Saturnalia,* ed. Robert A. Kaster (Cambridge, MA, 2011).

2 Milton, *Paradise Lost,* VII.225–44.

3 Catherine Osborne, *Dumb Beasts and Dead Philosophers* (Oxford, 2007).

4 Porphyry, *Life of Pythagoras,* in David R. Fideler (ed.), *The Pythagorean Sourcebook* (Grand Rapids, MI, 1987), p. 12.

5 Cicero discusses some of these theories in his *On the Nature of the Gods.*

6 Works of Aristotle of particular relevance for cosmology are *On the Heavens* and parts of *Physics* and *Meteorology.*

7 Aristotle, *On the Heavens,* I.3.

8 The contents of this book were adopted more or less wholesale by Boethius and it became a textbook for the European study of arithmetic and its philosophical basis for many centuries.

9 Aristotle, *On the Heavens,* 5, 6, 8.

10 Aristotle, *Metaphysics,* XII.5.

11 Aristotle, *Physics,* 258b.

12 Aristotle, *Metaphysics,* XII.2.

13 Plato, *Timaeus.*

14 Ibid., 27C.

15 Ibid., 30B.

16 Ibid., 30C.

17 Charles Williams, *Many Dimensions* (London, 1931), p. 230.

18 Plato, *Timaeus,* 32C–D.

19 Ibid., 33B.

20 Ibid., 31B.

21 Ibid.

22 Swami Krishnanani, 'Second Brahmana: The Creation of the Universe', www.swami-krishnananda.org/brdup/brhad_I-02.html (accessed 29 May 2013).

23 Cicero, *On the Nature of the Gods,* I.i.1.

24 Ibid., I.i.2 and I.ii.3.

25 Ibid., I.ii.4.

26 Ibid., I.x.24 and I.xi.27.

27 Ibid., I.viii.19 and I.ix.20–1.

28 Ibid., I.viii.19.

29 Boethius, *Consolation,* II.

30 Cicero, *On the Nature of the Gods,* I.viii.18 and I.viii.19.

31 Cicero, *Academica,* I.vii.26–8

32 Gore Vidal, *Creation* (London, 1993), p. 204.

33 Cicero, *De Finibus* I.vi.19.
34 Lucretius, *On the Nature of Things*, V.146–8.
35 Ibid., V.181–6 and V.195–9.
36 Ibid., V.235–9.
37 Ibid., V.240–6 and V.517–23.
38 Ovid, *Metamorphoses*, I.5–9.
39 Ibid., I.17, I.21–3, I.25. I.34. I.76, I.89 and I.151–5.
40 Pliny, *Natural History*, II.i.1, II.vi.27 and II.i.3.
41 Ibid., II.iv.12, II.v.14; II.v.18, II.v.15 and II.v.16; II.v.19 mocks the tendency to call men by the names of gods, Jupiter, Mercury and so on. II.v.21 speaks of counting gods on fingers and mocks sacrificing to find auspicious days to marry etc.
42 Ibid., II.v.21–5, II.vi. 27–9 and II.vi.26.
43 Robert Grosseteste, *On the Six Days of Creation*, tr. C.F.J. Martin (Oxford, 1999), V.x–xi, pp.170–1, and see Chapter 6 (i).
44 Epicurus, *Principal Doctrines*, tr. R.D. Hicks, http://classics.mit. edu/Epicurus/princdoc.html (accessed 29 May 2013).
45 Seneca, *Natural Questions*, Book I, Preface, 16, Book I, Preface, 14, 15, 16.
46 Seneca, *On Providence*, tr. Aubrey Stewart (1900), I–II, http:// en.wikisource.org/wiki/Of_Providence (accessed 29 May 2013).
47 Peter Comestor, *Liber Genesis, Historia Scholastica*, CCCM, 191, p. 7.
48 Henry Chadwick, *Early Christian Thought and the Classical Tradition: Studies in Justin, Clement, and Origen* (Oxford, 1966), pp. 66–94.
49 Justin Martyr, *Dialogue with Trypho*, 2–8.
50 Ibid., 1.
51 Justin Martyr, *Apologies*, II.12.
52 Clement of Alexandria, *Miscellanies*, Book II, 1.15. The topic of 'despoiling the Egyptians' was something of a favourite among the Fathers of the Church. See, for example, Augustine, *On Christian Doctrine*, II.xl.60.
53 Clement of Alexandria, *Miscellanies*, Book II.
54 Eusebius, *Ecclesiastical History*, ed. and tr. G. Bardy (Paris, 1952), VI.25.7.
55 Origen, *On First Principles*, Preface, I.4.
56 Ibid., Preface, I.4 and I.1.
57 Basil of Caesarea, *Hexameron*, www.newadvent.org/fathers/32011. htm (accessed 29 May 2013), I.1.
58 Ibid., I.2.
59 Ibid., I.3.
60 Ibid., I.8, quoting Isaiah.

61 Ibid., I.9.
62 Ambrose, *Hexameron*, I.i.1.
63 Augustine, *Confessions*, VI.3.
64 Augustine, *On Genesis against the Manichaeans*, I.iv.7.
65 Augustine, *City of God*, XI.4, XII.10 and XIII.16.
66 As he gazed at the letter theta (for *thanatos*, death) on his condemned-prisoner garments.
67 Boethius, *Consolation*, I, Prose 4.
68 Boethius, *Theological Tractates*.
69 Boethius, *Consolation*, V, Prose 6; Boethius, *Theological Tractates*.
70 Augustine, *City of God*, VIII.1.
71 Gregory the Great, *Morals*, II.iii.3, II.xii.20, II.iii.3 and II.xx.34.
72 Bede *Hexameron*, Preface, 'To Bishop Acca Hagustaldensis'.
73 Bede, *Opera Didascalica*, p. 192.
74 This clause was added by the West but rejected by the Eastern Christians and formed one of the points of disagreement in the schism of 1054.
75 This is the modern ecumenical version, http://en.wikipedia.org/wiki/English_versions_of_the_Nicene_Creed_in_current_use (accessed 31 May 2013).
76 www.ccel.org/creeds/apostles.creed.html (accessed 31 May 2013).
77 Robert Grosseteste, *On the Six Days of Creation*, ed. C.F.J. Martin (Oxford, 1999), 'Proemium', pp. 22, 23. Robert Grosseteste, *Hexameron*, tr. C.F.J. Martin (Oxford, 1996).
78 Grosseteste, *On the Six Days of Creation*, Chapter VIII.iiiff, p.59; Grosseteste, *Hexameron*.
79 Grosseteste, *On the Six Days of Creation*, I.x, p. 63; Grosseteste, *Hexameron*.
80 Grosseteste, *On the Six Days of Creation*, I.xvi, pp. 70–1; Grosseteste, *Hexameron*.
81 Virgil, *Aeneid*, VI.724–51.
82 Charles Williams, *Many Dimensions* (London, 1931), p. 139.
83 Dorothy Sayers, *The Mind of the Maker* [1941] (London, 1994), p. 70.
84 Justin Martyr, *Apologies*, II.13.
85 Justin Martyr, *Dialogue with Trypho*, 56, 129.
86 Tatian, *Address to the Greeks*, in Tatian, *Writings*, ed. M. Dods (Edinburgh, 1883), V.
87 Milton, *Paradise Lost*, VII.163–79.

Chapter 5

1 Charles Darwin, *The Origin of Species* (London, 2009); and see M.G. Brock and M.C. Curthoys (eds), *A History of the University of Oxford* (Oxford, 1997), Vol. VI, pp. 657–9 for references to the numerous conflicting accounts of what was said.

2 Charles Darwin, *The Origin of Species*, 'Preface to Third Edition', www.talkorigins.org/faqs/origin/preface.html (accessed 31 May 2013).

3 Ibid.

4 See Darren Curnoe et al., 'Human remains from the Pleistocene-Holocene transition of Southwest China suggest a complex evolutionary history for East Asians', *Plos One*, published online 14 March 2012, www.plosone.org/article/info%3Adoi%2F10.1371%2Fjournal.pone.0031918 (accessed 31 May 2013).

5 'African bushmen creation myth', www.cs.williams.edu/~lindsey/myths/myths_14.html (accessed 31 May 2013).

6 Hugh Lofting, *The Story of Dr. Dolittle: Being the History of His Peculiar Life at Home and Astonishing Adventures in Foreign Parts Never Before Printed* (London, 1920), www.pagebypagebooks.com/Hugh_Lofting/The_Story_of_Doctor_Dolittle/ (accessed 28 May 2013).

7 John William Blake (ed. and tr.), *Europeans in West Africa*, Hakluyt Society, Vol. 87 (London, 1942), pp. 340, 341, 338, 340.

8 M.A. Tolmacheva, 'Ptolemy's East Africa in early medieval Arab geography', *Journal for the History of Arabic Science*, 9 (1991), www.medievalists.net/2009/03/11/ptolemys-east-africa-in-early-medieval-arab-geography/ (accessed 31 May 2013).

9 Ibn Battuta, *The Travels of Ibn Battutah*, ed. Tim Mackintosh Smith (London, 2002), p. 262.

10 Ibid., p. 231.

11 Ibid., p. 235.

12 Ibid., p. 217.

13 Ibid., p. 248.

14 Wendy James, Gerd Baumann and Douglas H. Johnson (eds), *Juan Maria Schuver's Travels in North East Africa, 1880–83*, Hakluyt Society, Vol. 184 (London, 1996) pp. 33–4.

15 Ibid., pp. 33–4.

16 Ibid., p. 283.

17 With the formation of the London Missionary Society, the enterprise began to have more success.

18 Daniel Defoe, *Captain Singleton* [1720], in W.R. Owens and P.N. Furbank (eds), *The Novels of Daniel Defoe* (London, 2008–9), Vol. V, pp. 54–5, 83.

19 Daniel Defoe, *A General History of Discoveries and Improvements* [1725–6], in W.R. Owens and P.N. Furbank (eds), *Writings on Travel, Discovery and History by Daniel Defoe* (London, 2001), Vol. IV, p. 21, p.176.

20 William Carey, *Enquiry into the Obligations of Christians to Use Means for the Conversion of the Heathens* (Leicester, 1792), pp. 3ff.

21 Henry Stanley, 'How I found Livingstone', in Tim Youngs (ed.), *Nineteenth-Century Travels, Explorations and Empires: Writings from the Era of Imperial Consolidation, 1835–1910* (London, 2004), Vol. VII, pp. 25–58, 153–215.

22 David Livingstone, 'Missionary travels and researches in south Africa', in Youngs, *Nineteenth-Century Travels*, Vol. VII, pp. 37, 40.

23 Ibid., p. 43.

24 Verney Lovett Cameron, *Across Africa* [1877, 2 vols], in Youngs, *Nineteenth-Century Travels*, Vol.VII, pp. 239ff (in Vol. II of original edition).

25 Richard Burton, *A Personal Narrative of a Pilgrimage to El-Medinah and Meccah* (London, 1855–6), 3 vols, made Burton famous and became a classic of travel literature (later republished as *A Secret Pilgrimage to Mecca and Medina*, ed. Tim Macintosh-Smith (London, 2004)). See also Burton's entry in *Dictionary of National Biography*.

26 Richard Burton, *The Lake Regions of Central Africa* (London, 1860), 2 vols. The lakes were Lake Tanganyika and Lake Victoria.

27 Richard Burton, *A Secret Pilgrimage to Mecca and Medina*, ed. Tim Macintosh-Smith (London, 2004), p. 36.

28 Published in *Blackwoods Magazine*, and as a short novel in 1903.

29 Joseph Conrad, *Heart of Darkness* (London, 1991), Chapter 2, para. 29.

30 Sanford H. Bederman, 'The Royal Geographical Society, E.G. Ravenstein, and *A Map of Eastern Equatorial Africa – 1877–1883*', *Imago Mundi*, 44 (1992), pp. 106–19.

31 Ruth Kark, 'The contribution of nineteenth-century Protestant missionary societies to historical cartography', *Imago Mundi*, 45 (1993), pp. 112–19.

32 Pierre d'Ailly, *Imago Mundi* (Paris, 1930), Book I.

33 Christopher Columbus, *The Book of Prophecies*, ed. Roberto Rusconi, tr. Blair Sullivan (California, 1997).

34 Ibid., pp. 31, 77.

35 Ibid., p. 67.

36 Ibid., p. 75.

37 V.I.J. Flint, *The Imaginative Landscape of Christopher Columbus* (Princeton, 1992), p. xii.

38 Pedro Sarmiento de Gamboa, *History of the Incas*, tr. Sir Clemens Markham Hakluyt Society, Series II, Vol. 22 (Cambridge, 1907), p. 28.

39 Ibid., p. 24.

40 Ibid., p. 26.

41 Ibid., pp. 27, 28, 29.

42 Ibid., p. 29.

43 Thomas More, *Utopia*, http://oregonstate.edu/instruct/phl302/texts/more/utopia-I.html (accessed 31 May 2013).

44 Richard Hakluyt, *The Principal Nauigations, Voyages, Traffiques and Discoueries of the English Nation* (London, 1589), dedication to Sir Francis Walsingham.

45 Richard Hakluyt, *Hakluyt's Voyages: A Selection*, ed. Richard David (London, 1981), pp. 64–5.

46 Ibid., pp. 66, 162.

47 Ibid., pp. 162–3, 164, 208.

48 Samuel Puchas, *Purchas his Pilgrimes* (Glasgow, 1905), Vol. I, pp. 135, 136.

49 Ibid., Vol. I, pp. 150–2, 153.

50 Ibid., Vol. I, pp. 156, 159.

51 *Hadis-i nev Tarig-i garbi*, in Thomas Goodrich, *The Ottoman Turks and the New World* (Wiesbaden, 1990), p. 71.

52 Ibid., pp. 74, 71–2.

53 Ibid., pp. 77ff.

54 James Cook, *The Journals of Captain Cook. Vol. I, The Voyage of the Endeavour, 1768–1771*, ed. J.C. Beaglehole (Cambridge, 1955), p. cclxxx.

55 Ibid., p. cclxxxii.

56 James Cook, *The Journals of Captain James Cook. Vol. II, The Voyage of the Resolution and Adventure, 1776–80*, ed. J.C. Beaglehole (Cambridge, 1969), p. 763.

57 George Augustus Robinson, *The Port Phillip Journals of George Augustus Robinson (1842–3)*, ed. I.D. Clark (Monash, 1988), pp. 8–9, 11.

58 From Kaye Price, *Our Land: Our Living History*, rev. edn (Hobart, forthcoming).

59 Nahuatl is the indigenous language common to many Central America tribes but originally the language of the Aztecs.

60 Twins also appear in Aryan legends. 'Of course, the Aryans say that once upon a time, as the beginning, there were twins – a man and a woman . . . But then, who made the twins?', Gore Vidal, *Creation* (London, 1993), p. 184.

61 William Weber Johnson, *Cortés* (London, 1977), pp. 48–51.

62 Paul Gallez, 'Walsberger and his knowledge of the Patagonian giants, 1448', *Imago Mundi*, 33 (1981), pp. 91–3.

63 Friar Bernardino de Sahagun, *A History of Ancient Mexico*, ed. Carlos Maria de Bustamente, tr. Fanny R. Bandellier (Nashville, 1932, republished Detroit, 1971), pp. 21–3.

64 Ibid., pp. 190ff.

65 *Laws of Burgos* (1512), http://faculty.smu.edu/bakewell/ BAKEWELL/texts/burgoslaws.html (accessed 24 June 2013).

66 Darwin, *Voyage of the Beagle*, Chapter 16.

67 Ibid, Chapter 16.

68 Ibid., Chapter 21. Spain was often seen as more exotic than the rest of Europe; see Fernando Cervantes, *The Hispanic World in the Historical Imagination* (London, 2006).

69 William Dampier, *Dampier's Voyage Round the World*, ed. Robert Steele (London, 1893), pp. 8–10.

70 Ibid., pp. 71, 74, 76, 79.

71 Ibid., pp. 88, 95.

72 Ibid., p. 71.

73 Ambrose Evans, *The Adventures and Surprizing Deliverances of James Dubourdieu and his Wife* (London, 1719), pp. 77, 80.

74 Ibid., pp. 88–9.

75 Ibid., pp. 92–3.

76 And see Daniel Defoe, *A General History of Discoveries and Improvements* [1725–6], in W.R. Owens and P.N. Furbank (eds), *Writings on Travel, Discovery and History by Daniel Defoe* (London, 2001), Vol. IV, p. 176.

77 Ibid., pp. 230–1.

78 Ibid., pp. 231, 29ff. On the spoiling of the Egyptians, see Chapter 5 (iv).

79 Ibid., pp. 68ff. and see p. 176 on ignorance of Africa, and see Daniel Defoe, *An Essay upon Literature; or An Enquiry into the Antiquity and Original of Letters; Proving [that] Tablets on Mount Sinai, Written by God Was 'The First Writing in the World' and All other Alphabets Derive* [1726], in W.R. Owens and P.N. Furbank (eds), *Writings on Travel, Discovery and History by Daniel Defoe* (London, 2001), Vol. IV, p. 227.

80 By 1724 there were at least three more female 'Robinsonades' and by 1731 there were German examples.

81 Jonathan Swift, *Gulliver's Travels*, Chapter 1, www.online-literature. com/swift/gulliver (accessed 31 May 2013).

82 Ibid., Chapter 2.

83 Ibid., Chapter 3.

84 Ibid., Chapter 12.

85 Ibid., Chapter 23.

86 Ibid., Chapter 24.

87 Richard Burton, *The Book of the Thousand and One Nights*, 6 vols, ed. Isabel Burton (London, 1885–6), vol. VI, story 120.

88 Thomas Daniell, William Daniell and Samuel Daniell, *An Illustrated Journey Round the World by Thomas, William and Samuel Daniell*, ed. Katherine Prior (London, 2007), pp. 115, 147.

89 Thomas Jefferson, American Declaration of Independence, www. ushistory.org/declaration/document (accessed 3 June 2013).

90 Daniel Defoe, *Robinson Crusoe* (Basingstoke, 2007).

91 Thomas Coke, *A Farther Continuation of Dr. Coke's Journal: In a Letter to the Rev. J. Wesley* (London,1787).

92 Mungo Park, *Travels in the Interior of Africa* [1860] (London, 2005), Chapter 22.

93 Ibid., p. 25.

94 Ibid., p. 37.

95 Ibid., p. 85.

Chapter 6

1 Augustine, *On Genesis Taken Literally*, I.2.

2 Ibid., I.2.

3 Robert Grosseteste, *On the Six Days of Creation*, tr. C.F.J. Martin (Oxford, 1999), V.xii–xiii, pp. 174–5; I.ii, pp. 48–9; I.iii, p. 50.

4 Ibid., IV.i, p. 124.

5 Ibid., IV.ii; IV.iii; IV.iv; IV.i, p. 47; IV.ii, p. 125.

6 Mill, *Theism*.

7 Pope, *Essay on Man*, VI.190–5.

8 Cited in E.M.W. Tillyard, *The Elizabethan World Picture* (London, 1943), pp. 24–5.

9 Ibid.

10 Pope, *Essay on Man*, Epistle One, VIII.241–6, 251–5.

11 Cited in Tillyard, *Elizabethan World Picture*, p. 26.

12 C. Wade Savage, 'The paradox of the stone', *Philosophical Review*, 76.1 (1967), pp. 74–9.

13 Pope, *Essay on Man*, Epistle One, V.143–4, 145–6.

14 Mill, *Theism*.

15 Milton, *Paradise Lost*, VII.86–94.

16 Matthew Tindal, *Christianity as Old as the Creation* (London, 1730).

17 Ibid., Chapter 1.

18 Augustine, *City of God*, V.10.

19 Anselm of Canterbury, *Proslogion*, ed. F.S. Schmitt, in Anselm of Canterbury, *Anselmi Opera Omnia* (Rome and Edinburgh, 1938), Vol. I, VII.

20 Thomas Aquinas, *Summa Theologica*, www.ccel.org/a/aquinas/summa/FP/FP025.html (accessed 31 May 2013), Section I, Question xxv, Articles 2 and 3.

21 René Descartes, 'Letter to Arnauld, 29 July, 1648', in René Descartes, *Philosophical Letters*, tr. and ed. Anthony Kenny (Minneapolis, 1970), p. 236.

22 Pope, *Essay on Man*, Epistle One, X.290–4.

23 Isaac Newton, *The Correspondence of Isaac Newton*, ed. H.W. Turnbull, J.F. Scott, A. Rupert Hall and Laura Tilling (Cambridge, 1959–77), Vol. III, pp. 233–54.

24 Isaac Newton, *Four Letters from Sir Isaac Newton to Doctor Bentley. Containing Some Arguments in Proof of a Deity* (London, 1756), pp. 2–3.

25 On this term, see Joseph Addison, *Spectator*, 565 (July 1714).

26 Isaac Newton, '*Optics*, Query 28 (Appendix A)', in H.G. Alexander (ed.), *The Leibniz–Clarke Correspondence* (Manchester, 1956), p. xv.

27 Ibid., p. xvii.

28 Ibid., p. 184.

29 Gottfried Leibniz, *Die Werke von Leibniz*, ed. O. Klopp, (Hanover, 1884), Vol. XI.

30 Newton, '*Optics*, Query 28 (Appendix A)', p. 188.

31 Dorothy Sayers, *Whose Body* (London, 1968), Chapter 1.

32 Augustine, *City of God*, XI.4–6.

33 Mill, *Theism*.

34 Pope, *Essay on Man*, Epistle Two, IV.208.

35 Mill, *Theism*.

36 For the origin of the 'butterfly' topos, see Edward Lorenz, '*Predictability: Does the Flap of a Butterfly's Wings in Brazil set off a Tornado in Texas?*, American Association for the Advancement of Science (Washington, 1972).

37 'Philosophia est rerum divinarum humanarumque cognitio cum studio bene vivendi coniuncta', Robert Kilwardby, De Ortu Scientarum, II, ed. Albert G. Judy (London, 1976), Vol. II, quoting Isidore, Etymologiae, ed. C.C.J. Webb Oxford, 1911), I.24.9.

38 Roger Bacon, Opus Maius, ed. John Henry Bridges (London, 1900), Vol. I, Part II, Chapter xvii; Vol. I, Part II, Chapter xviii.

39 Sanskrit, the language in which religious thought and belief was expressed in parts of Asia, was not studied by Western readers until the early modern period. The same period, from the mid-sixteenth to the eighteenth centuries, was also an important period for the development of a distinctive Indian intellectual culture. That came to an end with the colonial dominance of the region by the West. Some Western scholars knew Persian and, once a translation was available from Sanskrit into Persian, it became possible for Hindu texts to be put into Latin by Anquetil du Perron in 1802. His translation had a considerable influence.

40 Leonard W. King, 'Legends of Babylon and Egypt in relation to Hebrew Tradition', The Schweich Lectures (1916), www.sacred-texts. com/ane/beheb.htm (accessed 31 May 2013).

41 The Epic of Gilgamesh, www.ancienttexts.org/library/mesopotam ian/gilgamesh (accessed 31 May 2013).

42 'South American Flood myths', Mythhome, www.mythome.org/ fludmytc.html (accessed 31 May 2013).

43 Compare with the story of Sodom and Gomorrah described above.

44 'South American Flood myths', Mythhome.

45 Ibid.

46 Ibid.

47 Noah's Ark appears in both Genesis and the Qur'an.

48 Milton, Paradise Lost, VII.155–60.

49 On the logic of the perfect number see D.P. Henry, The Logic of St. Anselm (Oxford, 1967).

50 Anselm of Canterbury, Cur Deus Homo, Opera Omnia, ed. F.S. Schmitt, 6 vols (Rome and Edinburgh, 1938–68), Vol. II.

51 An important demon in Islamic mythology, the counterpart of the Christian Satan.

52 Rudyard Kipling, 'Poem in India', in Rudyard Kipling, Early Verse, ed. Andrew Rutherford (Oxford, 1986), p. 310.

53 Qur'an 7.11–18.

54 Fernando Cervantes, The Devil in the New World (New Haven, CT, 1994), pp. 105–13.

55 Augustine, City of God, VIII.16.

56 Samuel Clarke, 'Sermon XX', in Samuel Clarke, *Works*, (London, 1738), Vol. I, p. 124, God as the Father of Mankind.

57 Daniel Defoe, *The Political History of the Devil* [1726], ed. John Mullan, in W.R. Owens and P.N. Furbank (eds), *Satire, Fantasy and Writings by Daniel Defoe*, Vol. VI, (London, 2005), p. 42.

58 C.S. Lewis, *The Screwtape Letters* (London, 2001), and http://xa.yimg.com/kq/groups/20904922/838225067/name/screwtape.pdf, Letter XIX (accessed 24 June 2013).

59 Hugh Lofting, *The Story of Dr. Dolittle: Being the History of His Peculiar Life at Home and Astonishing Adventures in Foreign Parts Never Before Printed* (London, 1920), www.pagebypagebooks.com/Hugh_Lofting/The_Story_of_Doctor_Dolittle (accessed 28 May 2013).

60 Peter Abelard, *Commentary on Romans*, CCCM, 11, pp. 117ff.

61 Genesis 37:35; 42:38; 44:29 and 31; and see Psalms 9:17.

62 Numbers 16:33, which describes a 'pit' into which it was possible to 'descend'.

63 Friar Bernardino de Sahagun, *A History of Ancient Mexico*, ed. Carlos Maria de Bustamente, tr. Fanny R. Bandellier (Nashville, 1932, republished Detroit, 1971), pp. 193–4.

64 Ibid., p. 193.

65 Ibid., p. 194.

66 Virgil, *Aeneid*, VI.126 on the entrance to Hades.

67 Ibid., VI.264–88.

68 Pliny, *Natural History*, XXX.ii.3.

69 Augustine, *City of God*, VIII.19.

70 Ibid., VIII.19.

71 *Clementine Homilies*, ed. A. Robert and J. Donaldson (Grand Rapids, 1995), IX.4–5.

72 Grosseteste, *On the Six Days of Creation*.

73 Dorothy Sayers, *The Mind of the Maker* [1941] (London, 1994), p. 63.

74 Augustine, *City of God*, XXI.8.

75 Ibid., XXI.9, XXI.10.

Chapter 7

1 Pope, *Essay on Man*, Epistle One, II.39–40.

2 Diodorus Siculus, *Histories*, I.1–7.

3 Ibid., I.1.

4 Ibid., I.8.

5 Ibid., I.10.
6 Pliny, *Natural History*, II.i.2.
7 Mahvira is a Jain deity. Gore Vidal, *Creation* (London, 1993), p. 272.
8 Ibid., p. 428.
9 Pliny, *Natural History*, II.iii.7–8.
10 Thomas More, *Utopia*, Book II.
11 I.A. Richter (ed.), *The Notebooks of Leonardo da Vinci*, (Oxford, 1998), pp. 27–8.
12 Adam Sedgwick, *A Discourse on the Studies of the University* [1833 version], intr. Eric Ashby and Mary Anderson (Leicester, 1969), pp. 49, 22–3.
13 Darwin, *Voyage of the Beagle*, Preface.
14 Ibid., Chapter 17.
15 Ibid., Chapter 17.
16 Ibid., Chapter 9.
17 Charles Kingsley, *The Water Babies* (London, 1961).
18 Louis Agassiz, *Contemplations of God* (Cincinnati, 1851) and *Principles of Zoology* (Boston, MA, 1870), wrote in favour of successive creation without agreeing with Darwin.
19 Vidal, *Creation*, p. 272.
20 Frances Yates, *Giordano Bruno and the Hermetic Tradition* (London, 1964), p. 41.
21 Hesiod, *Works and Days*, p. 109.
22 Hesiod, *Works and Days*, pp. 127, 143, 156, 174.
23 Plato, *Cratylus*, 397E.
24 Hesiod, *Works and Days*, pp. 109–10.
25 Plato, *Cratylus*, 401E.
26 Virgil, *Georgics*, I.125–8.
27 James Dean, *The World Grown Old in Later Medieval Literature* (Cambridge, MA, 1997).
28 Aldous Huxley, 'The politics of ecology' [1963], in Cecil E. Johnson (ed.), *Eco-crisis* (California, 1970), pp. 24–33.
29 Matthew Arnold, 'The strayed reveller', in S.H. McGrady (ed.), *Legends and Myths of Greece and Rome* (London, 1936), pp. 13–17.
30 Milton, *Paradise Lost*, I.24–6.
31 Pope, *Essay on Man*, VI.205–6.
32 Augustine, *City of God*, IV.
33 Ibid., I–II on Providence, IV.10, VIII on small gods and a life of fear.
34 Vidal, *Creation*, p. 192.
35 Boethius, *Consolation*, IV, Prose 6.

36 Boethius, *Consolation*, IV, Prose 6.

37 Epicurus, *Letter to Menoeceus*.

38 Pope, *Essay on Man*, Epistle One, 5–6.

39 Boethius, *Theological Tractates*, pp. 357–71.

40 Peter Abelard, *An Exposition on the Six-Day Work (34)*, tr. Wanda Zemler-Cizewski, CCCM in Translation, 8 (Turnhout, 2011), Section 34, p. 39; Peter Abelard, *Expositio in Hexaemeron*, ed. M. Romig, C. Burnett and D. Luscombe, CCCM, 15 (Turnhout, 2004), Section 34.

41 Aristotle, *De Interpretatione*, IX.19a.

42 Augustine, *City of God*, XXII.2.

43 C.S. Lewis, *The Screwtape Letters* (London, 2001), and http://xa.yimg.com/kq/groups/20904922/838225067/name/screwtape.pdf (accessed 24 June 2013), Letter XXVII.

44 Pope, *Essay on Man*, Epistle One, II.43–50.

45 E. Vailati, *Leibniz and Clarke* (Oxford, 1997), p. 127.

46 Boethius, *Consolation*, I, Verse 5.

47 Ibid., I, Prose 6.

48 Ibid., II, Prose 1.

49 J.K. Rowling, *Harry Potter and the Chamber of Secrets* (London, 1998), Chapter 12.

50 Herodotus. *Histories*, II.73.

51 Virgil, *Aeneid*, VI.724–51.

52 Vidal, *Creation*, p. 205.

53 Aristotle, *On Generation and Corruption*, 320b, 317a.

54 Ibid., 325b.

55 T.S. Eliot, *The Waste Land*, in T.S. Eliot, *The Complete Poems and Plays of T.S. Eliot* (London, 2004), I.1-4.

56 In the story of Orpheus, too, Orpheus goes to the underworld to try to rescue Eurydice and wins her release on condition he does not look back as he leaves. He cannot bear the suspense; he looks back and loses her for ever as she falls away into the underworld again.

57 Arnold, 'The strayed reveller', pp. 24–30.

58 Percy Bysshe Shelley, *Adonaïs* (Pisa, 1821), http://www.bartleby.com/41/522.html (accessed 24 June 2013), pp. 343–4.

59 J.G. Frazer, *The Golden Bough*, ed. Robert Fraser (Oxford, 1994), p. 97.

60 Franz Cumont, *Oriental Religions in Roman Paganism* (New York, 1956), p. 22.

61 Ibid., p. xix.

62 Ibid., pp. 46–7.

63 Catullus, Poem 63, in J.W. Mackail (ed.), *Lyric Poetry: Catullus* (Cambridge, MA, 1913).
64 Cumont, *Oriental Religions in Roman Paganism*, pp. xxiii, xix.
65 Prudentius, *Peristephanon*, ed. H.J. Thomson (Cambridge, MA, 1953), www.thelatinlibrary.com/prud.html (accessed 3 June 2013), pp. 295–9.
66 Cumont, *Oriental Religions in Roman Paganism*, p. 171.

Chapter 8

1 Charles Darwin, *The Origin of Species*, 'Preface to Third Edition', www.talkorigins.org/faqs/origin/preface.html (accessed 31 May 2013). Referring to Baden Powell, 'Essay on the Unity of Worlds', in Baden Powell, *Essays on the Spirit of the Inductive Philosophy, the Unity of Worlds, and the Philosophy of Creation* (London, 1855).
2 C. Babbage, *Ninth Bridgewater Treatise* (London, 1838), letter from Herschel to Lyell, 20 February 1836, pp. 226–7.
3 Powell, *Essays*, p. 337.
4 Powell, *Essays*, pp. 52–3.
5 Auguste Comte, *Positive Philosophy* (London, 1832), Introduction and Chapter 1.
6 Powell, *Essays*, pp. 183, 185, 174–5, 176–7.
7 Franz Cumont, *Oriental Religions in Roman Paganism* (New York, 1956), pp. 162ff.
8 Ptolemy, *Tetrabiblos*, tr. J.M. Ashmand (1822), www.sacred-texts. com/astro/ptb/index.htm (accessed 3 June 2013).
9 Isaac Newton, *Observations upon the Prophecies of Daniel, and the Apocalypse of St. John* (London, 1733), www.isaacnewton.ca/ daniel_apocalypse (accessed 3 June 2013). His interest seems to have been motivated by his belief that the theology of the Trinity was a great heresy or apostasy. He argues that the doctrine of the Incarnation too was a corruption of the true faith which had been held by the sons of Noah. In the early 1680s Newton went beyond mere Arianism in his most important theological composition, *The Philosophical Origins of Gentile Theology* (*Theologiae Gentilis Origines Philosophicae*).
10 Antti Aarne, *Verzeichnis der Märchentypen*, enlarged by Stith Thompson (Helsinki, 1910).
11 Stith Thompson, *Motif-Index of Folk Literature* (Copenhagen, 1955), Vol. I.

12 D.L. Ashliman (ed.), *A Guide to Folktales in the English Language* (New York, 1987), p. 758.

13 J.G. Frazer, *The Golden Bough*, ed. Robert Fraser (Oxford, 1994).

14 Olaus Magnus, *Description of the Northern Peoples*, ed. Peter Foote and tr. Peter Fisher, Hakluyt Society, Vol. 182 (London, 1996), pp. 150, 233.

15 C.F. Beckingham and G.W.B. Huntingford (eds), *Some Records of Ethiopia, 1593–1646*, Hakluyt Society, Vol. 97 (London, 1954), pp. 136–7.

16 Magnus, *Description of the Northern Peoples*, p. 77.

17 Richard Eden, *A Treatyse of the Newe India* (London, 1553).

18 John William Blake (ed. and tr.), *Europeans in West Africa*, Hakluyt Society, Vol. 87 (London, 1942), pp. 254–5.

19 Gore Vidal, *Creation* (London, 1993), p. 185.

20 Strabo, *Geography*, ed. H.L. Jones (Cambridge, MA, 1917), XVI.I.60.

21 Magnus, *Description of the Northern Peoples*, p. 78.

22 Pope, *Essay on Man*, Epistle One, I.21–34.

23 Ibid., Epistle Two, 19–25.

24 Ibid., Epistle Two, I.1–2.

25 Charles Lloyd Cohen, *God's Caress: The Psychology of the Puritan Religious Experience* (Oxford, 1986), pp. 137–61.

26 Descartes, *Meditations*, tr. John Veitch (Chicago, 1939), and www. wright.edu/cola/descartes/mede.html (accessed 3 June), I.9.

27 Ibid., III.38.

Conclusion

1 NIV, Revelation 1:8, 21:6, 22:13.

2 Revelation 21:1–5, NIV.

3 Gore Vidal, *Creation* (London, 1993), p. 185.

Texts and abbreviations

Note on texts: Some of the classical and other texts cited are available in many different editions and forms. Unless otherwise stated, the versions used are normally those of the editions or online versions cited below. References to these texts are made using the standard book, chapter and line format so that readers can also use other translations or originals.

Ambrose, *Hexameron*	Ambrose, *Hexameron*, ed. C. Schenkl, CSEL, 32 (Vienna, 1896).
Aquinas, *Summa Theologia*	Thomas Aquinas, *Summa Theologiae* (Rome, 1962).
Aristotle, *De Interpretatione*	Aristotle, *De Interpretatione*, ed. and tr. Hugh Tredennick (Cambridge, MA, 1949).
Aristotle, *Metaphysics*	Aristotle, *Metaphysics*, ed. and tr. Hugh Tredennick (Cambridge, MA, 1933).
Aristotle, *On Generation and Corruption*	Aristotle, *On Generation and Corruption*, ed. E.S. Forster (Cambridge, MA, 1955).
Aristotle, *On the Heavens*	Aristotle, *On the Heavens*, ed. and tr. W.K.C. Guthrie (Cambridge, MA, 1939); and tr. J.L. Stocks, http://classics.mit.edu/Aristotle/heavens.html (accessed 29 May 2013).
Aristotle, *Physics*	Aristotle, *Physics*, ed. Philip Henry Wickstead and Francis M. Cornford (Cambridge, MA, 1927).
Augustine, *City of God*	Augustine, *De Civitate Dei*, tr. Henry Bettenson (London, 2003); Augustine, *De Civitate Dei*, ed. E. Hoffmann,

CSEL, 40.1 (Vienna, 1888); and www. newadvent.org/fathers/1201.htm (accessed 23 May 2013).

Augustine, *Confessions* — Augustine, *Confessiones,* ed. L. Verheijen, CCSL, 27 (Turnhout, 1981); and tr. H. Chadwick (Oxford, 1998).

Augustine, *On Christian Doctrine* — Augustine, *De Doctrina Christiana,* ed. and tr. R.P.H. Green (Oxford, 1995).

Augustine, *On Genesis against the Manichaeans* — Augustine, *De Genesi contra Manichaeos,* ed. D. Weber, CSEL, 91 (Vienna, 1998).

Augustine, *On Genesis Taken Literally* — Augustine, *De Genesi ad Litteram,* CSEL, 28 (Vienna, 1895).

Bede, *Hexameron* — Bede, *Hexameron,* ed. C.W. Jones, CCSL, 118 (Turnhout, 1967).

Boethius, *Consolation* — Boethius, *Consolation of Philosophy,* in Boethius, *Theological Tractates,* ed. H.F. Stewart, E.K. Rand and S.J. Tester (Cambridge, MA, 1973).

Boethius, *Theological Tractates* — Boethius, *Theological Tractates,* ed. H.F. Stewart, E.K. Rand and S.J. Tester (Cambridge, MA, 1973).

CCCM — Corpus Christianorum Continuatio Medievalis.

CCSL — Corpus Christianorum Series Latina.

Cicero, *Academica* — Cicero, *Academica,* ed. and tr. H. Rackham (Cambridge, MA, 1979).

Cicero, *De Finibus* — Cicero, *De Finibus Bonorum et Malorum,* ed. and tr. H. Rackham (Cambridge, MA, 1961).

Cicero, *On the Nature of the Gods* — Cicero, *De Natura Deorum,* ed. and tr. H. Rackham (Cambridge, MA, 1979).

Cicero, *Republic* — Cicero, *De Re Publica,* ed. and tr. C.W. Keynes (Cambridge, MA, 2000).

Clement of Alexandria, *Miscellanies*	Clement of Alexandria, *Stromateis, 1–3*, tr. John Ferguson (Washington, DC, 1991); and Book I at www.newadvent.org/fathers/02101.htm (accessed 23 May 2013) and Book II at www.earlychristianwritings.com/text/clement-stromata-book2.html (accessed 29 May 2013).
CSEL	Corpus Scriptorum Ecclesiasticorum Latinorum.
Darwin, *Voyage of the Beagle*	Charles Darwin, *The Voyage of the Beagle*, ed. and abbr. Janet Browne and Michael Neve (London, 1989); and www.literature.org/authors/darwin-charles/the-voyage-of-the-beagle (accessed 31 May 2013).
Diodorus Siculus, *Histories*	Diodorus Siculus, *Histories*, ed. and tr. C.H. Oldfather (Cambridge, MA, 1933).
Epicurus, *Letter to Menoeceus*	Epicurus, *Letter to Menoeceus: The Extant Remains*, ed. Cyril Bailey (Oxford, 1926); and tr. R.D. Hicks, http://classics.mit.edu/Epicurus/menoec/html (accessed 3 June 2013).
Gregory the Great, *Morals*	Gregory the Great, *Moralia in Job*, ed. M. Adriaen, CCSL, 143 (Turnhout, 1979); and tr. J.H. Parker; J. Rivington, www.lectionarycentral.com/GregoryMoraliaIndex.html (accessed 30 May 2013).
Herodotus, *Histories*	Herodotus, *Histories*, ed. A.D. Godly (Cambridge, MA, 1982).
Hesiod, *Works and Days*	Hesiod, *Works and Days*, ed. and tr. Glenn W. Most (Cambridge, MA, 2006).
Justin Martyr, *Apologies*	Justin Martyr, *Apologies*, ed. D. Minns and P. Parvis (Oxford, 2009).

Justin Martyr, *Dialogue with Trypho* — Justin Martyr, *Dialogue with Trypho*, ed. L.A. Williams (London, 1930); and www.earlychristianwritings.com/text/justinmartyr-dialoguetrypho.html (accessed 29 May 2013).

Lucretius, *On the Nature of Things* — Lucretius, *De Rerum Natura*, ed. and tr. W.H.D. Rouse (Cambridge, MA, 1924); and tr. W.E. Leonard, http://classics.mit.edu/Carus/nature_things.html (accessed 29 May 2013).

Mill, *Theism* — John Stuart Mill, *Theism* ed. J.M. Robson, in John Stuart Mill, *Works. Vol. X* (Toronto, 1969); and http://oll.libertyfund.org/?option=com_staticxt&staticfile=show.php%3Ftitle=241&chapter=21523&layout=html&Itemid=27 (accessed 23 May 2013).

Milton, *Paradise Lost* — John Milton, *Paradise Lost,* ed. David Loewenstein (Cambridge, 2004).

NIV — New International Version (of the Bible).

Origen, *On First Principles* — Origen, *De Principiis,* tr. G.W. Butterworth, from P. Koetschau, ed. (New York, 1966).

Ovid, *Metamorphoses* — Ovid, *Metamorphoses,* ed. Frank Justus Miller, tr. Frank Justus Miller (Cambridge, MA, 1984).

Philo of Alexandria, *On the Making of the World* — Philo of Alexandria, *De Opificio Mundi,* ed. L. Cohn (Vratislava, 1889).

Plato, *Cratylus* — Plato, *Cratylus,* ed. H.N. Fowler (Cambridge, MA, 1983).

Plato, *Timaeus* — Plato, *Timaeus,* ed. and tr. R.G. Bury (Cambridge, MA, 1981); and tr. B. Jowett, www.gutenberg.org/files/1572/1572-h/1572-h.htm (accessed 23 May 2013).

Pliny, *Natural History*	Pliny, *Natural History*, tr. H. Rackham (Cambridge, MA, 1983–95).
Plutarch, *On the Face in the Moon*	Plutarch, *De Facie in Orbe Lunae*, tr. F.C. Babbitt (Cambridge, MA, 1957).
Pope, *Essay on Man*	Alexander Pope, *An Essay on Man*, ed. Mark Pattinson (Oxford, 1969); and http://rpo.library.utoronto.ca/poem/1637.html (accessed 29 May 2013).
Seneca, *Natural Questions*	Seneca, *Naturales Quaestiones*, ed. and tr. Thomas H. Corcoran (Cambridge, MA, 1971).
Virgil, *Aeneid*	Virgil, *Aeneid, Books I–VI*, ed. R.D. Williams (London, 1972); and tr. A.S. Kline (2002), www.poetryintranslation.com/PITBR/Latin/Virgilhome.htm (accessed 31 May 2013).
Virgil, *Georgics*	Virgil, *The Georgics*, ed. and tr. H. Rushton Fairclough and G.P. Goold (Cambridge, MA, 1999); and The Internet Classics Archive, http://classics.mit.edu/Virgil/georgics.html (accessed 3 June 2013).

Select Bibliography

Aarne, Antti, *Verzeichnis der Märchentypen*, enlarged by Stith Thompson (Helsinki, 1910).

Abelard, Peter, *An Exposition on the Six-Day Work*, tr. Wanda Zemler-Cizewski, CCCM in Translation, 8 (Turnhout, 2011).

Adams, Douglas, *The Hitchhiker's Guide to the Galaxy* (London, 1979).

—— *The Original Hitchiker Radio Scripts*, ed. Geoffrey Perkins (London, 1985).

Addison, Joseph, *Spectator*, 565 (July 1714).

Aethelweard, *The Chronicle of Aethelweard*, ed. A. Campbell (London, 1962).

Agassiz, Louis, *Contemplations of God* (Cincinnati, 1851).

—— *Principles of Zoology* (Boston, MA, 1870).

d'Ailly, Pierre, *Imago Mundi* (Paris, 1930).

Alexander, H.G. (ed.), *The Leibniz–Clarke Correspondence* (Manchester, 1956).

Ambrose, *Hexameron*, ed. C. Schenkl, CSEL, 32 (Vienna, 1896).

Appignanesi, Lisa (ed.), *Free Expression is No Offence* (London, 2005).

Aquinas, Thomas, *Summa Theologiae* (Rome, 1962)

Aristotle, *Physics*, ed. Philip Henry Wickstead and Francis M. Cornford (Cambridge, MA, 1927).

—— *Metaphysics*, ed. and tr. Hugh Tredennick (Cambridge, MA, 1933).

—— *On the Heavens*, ed. and tr. W.K.C. Guthrie (Cambridge, MA, 1939).

—— *De Interpretatione*, ed. and tr. Hugh Tredennick (Cambridge, MA, 1949).

—— *On Generation and Corruption*, ed. E.S. Forster (Cambridge, MA, 1955).

Arnold, Matthew, 'The strayed reveller', in S.H. McGrady (ed.), *Legends and Myths of Greece and Rome* (London, 1936).

Augustine, *De Civitate Dei*, ed. E. Hoffmann, CSEL, 40.1 (Vienna, 1888).

—— *Contra Manichaeos*, ed. J. Zycha, CSEL, 25 (Vienna, 1891–2).

—— *De Genesi ad Litteram*, CSEL, 28 (Vienna, 1895).

—— *Quaestiones in Genesim*, ed. J. Zycha, CSEL, 28 (Vienna, 1895).

—— *Confessiones,* ed. L. Verheijen, tr. H. Chadwick, CCSL, 27 (Turnhout, 1981).

—— *De Doctrina Christiana,* ed. and tr. R.P.H. Green (Oxford, 1995).

—— *De Genesi Contra Manichaeos,* ed. D. Weber, CSEL, 91 (Vienna, 1998).

—— *De Civitate Dei (On the City of God)*, tr. Henry Bettenson (London, 2003).

Bacon, Francis, *Parasceve ad Historiam Naturalem,* in Francis Bacon, *The Instauratio Magna Part II, Novum Organum and Associated Texts. The Oxford Francis Bacon, Vol. XI,* ed. Graham Rees and Maria Wakely (Oxford, 2004).

—— *The Instauratio Magna Part III: Historia Naturalis and Historia Vita. The Oxford Francis Bacon, Vol. XII,* ed. Graham Rees and Maria Wakely, (Oxford, 2007).

Bacon, Roger, *Opus Maius,* ed. John Henry Bridges (London, 1900).

Beazely, C.R., *The Dawn of Modern Geography* (London, 1897).

Beckingham, C.F. and G.W.B. Huntingford (eds), *Some Records of Ethiopia, 1593–1646,* Hakluyt Society, 97 (London, 1954).

Bede, *Hexameron ,* ed. C.W. Jones, CCSL, 118 (Turnhout, 1967).

Bederman, Sanford H., 'The Royal Geographical Society, E.G. Ravenstein, and *A Map of Eastern Equatorial Africa – 1877–1883'*, *Imago Mundi,* 44 (1992), pp. 106–19.

Blake, John William (ed. and tr.), *Europeans in West Africa,* Hakluyt Society, Vol. 87 (London, 1942).

Boethius, *Consolation of Philosophy,* in *Theological Tractates,* ed. H.F. Stewart, E.K. Rand and S.J. Tester (Cambridge, MA, 1973).

—— *Theological Tractates,* ed. H.F. Stewart, E.K. Rand and S.J. Tester (Cambridge, MA, 1973).

Brock, M.G. and M.C. Curthoys (eds), *A History of the University of Oxford* (Oxford, 1997).

Brooks, Edward, *The Story of the Aeneid,* in S.H. McGrady (ed.), *Legends and Myths of Greece and Rome* (London, 1936).

Bunyan, John, *Holy War,* ed. T.H. Jenkins (Darlington, 2003).

Burnet, Gilbert (ed.), *A Defence of Natural and Revealed Religion, Being an Abridgement of the Sermons Preached at the Lecture Founded by Robert Boyle* [1737] (London, 2000).

Burton, Richard, *A Personal Narrative of a Pilgrimage to Al-Madinah and Meccah* (London, 1855–6).

—— *The Lake Regions of Central Africa,* 2 vols (London, 1860).

—— *A Secret Pilgrimage to Mecca and Medina,* ed. Tim Macintosh-Smith (London, 2004).

Butler, Joseph, *Analogy of Religion* (London, 1896).

Cameron, Verney Lovett, 'Across Africa' [1877], in Tim Youngs (ed.), *Nineteenth-Century Travels, Explorations and Empires: Writings from the Era of Imperial Consolidation, 1835–1910* (London, 2004), Vol. VII.

Carey, William, *An Enquiry into the Obligations of Christians to Use Means for the Conversion of the Heathens* (Leicester, 1792).

Cervantes, Fernando, *The Devil in the New World* (New Haven, CT, 1994).

—— *The Hispanic World in the Historical Imagination* (London, 2006).

Chadwick, Henry, *Early Christian Thought and the Classical Tradition: Studies in Justin, Clement, and Origen* (Oxford, 1966).

Comte, Auguste, *Positive Philosophy* (London, 1832).

Church, A.J., 'Heroes and Kings', in S.H. McGrady (ed.), *Legends and Myths of Greece and Rome* (London, 1936).

Cicero, *De Finibus Bonorum et Malorum*, ed. and tr. H. Rackham (Cambridge, MA, 1961).

—— *Academica*, ed. and tr. H. Rackham (Cambridge, MA, 1979).

—— *De Natura Deorum*, ed. and tr. H. Rackham (Cambridge, MA, 1979).

—— *De Re Publica*, ed. and tr. C.W. Keynes (Cambridge, MA, 2000).

Clarke, Samuel, *Sermons*, in Samuel Clarke, *Works* (London, 1738), Vol. I.

Clement of Alexandria, *Stromateis, 1-3*, tr. John Ferguson (Washington, DC, 1991).

Clementine Homilies, ed. J. Donaldson (Edinburgh, 1870).

Cohen, Charles Lloyd, *God's Caress: The Psychology of the Puritan Religious Experience* (Oxford, 1986).

Coke, Thomas, *A Farther Continuation of Dr. Coke's Journal: In a Letter to the Rev. J. Wesley* (London, 1787).

Columbus, Christopher, *Journals and Other Documents on the Life and Voyages of Christopher Columbus*, tr. and ed. Samuel Eliot Morison (New York, 1963).

—— *The Book of Prophecies*, ed. Roberto Rusconi, tr. Blair Sullivan (California, 1997).

Cook, James, *The Journals of Captain Cook. Vol. I, The Voyage of the Endeavour, 1768–1771*, ed. J.C. Beaglehole (Cambridge, 1955).

Cumont, Franz, *The Mysteries of Mithra*, tr. James J. McCormack (London, 1903).

—— *Oriental Religions in Roman Paganism* (New York, 1956).

Dampier, William, *Dampier's Voyage Round the World*, ed. Robert Steele (London, 1893).

Daniell, Thomas, William Daniell and Samuel Daniell, *An Illustrated Journey Round the World by Thomas, William and Samuel Daniell*, ed. Katherine Prior (London, 2007).

Darwin, Charles, *The Voyage of the Beagle*, ed. and abbr. Janet Browne and Michael Neve (London, 1989).

—— *The Origin of Species* (London, 2009).

Defoe, Daniel, *A General History of Discoveries and Improvements* [1725–6], in W.R. Owens and P.N. Furbank (eds), *Writings on Travel, Discovery and History by Daniel Defoe*, (London, 2001), Vol. IV.

—— *The Political History of the Devil* [1726], ed. John Mullan, in W.R. Owens and P.N. Furbank, *Satire, Fantasy and Writings by Daniel Defoe* (London, 2005), Vol. VI.

—— *Robinson Crusoe* (Basingstoke, 2007).

—— *Captain Singleton* [1720], in W.R. Owens and P.N. Furbank (eds), *The Novels of Daniel Defoe* (London, 2008–9), Vol. V.

Delano Smith, Catherine, 'Maps as art and science: maps in sixteenth century Bibles', *Imago Mundi*, 42(1990), pp. 65–83.

Descartes, René, *Meditations*, ed. and tr. John Veitch (Chicago, 1939).

—— 'Letter to Arnauld, 29 July, 1648', in René Descartes, *Philosophical Letters*, ed. and tr. Anthony Kenny (Minneapolis, 1970).

Diodorus Siculus, *Histories*, ed. and tr. C.H. Oldfather, 10 vols (Cambridge, MA, 1933).

Donne, John, *Sermons*, ed. Evelyn Simson and George R. Potter (Berkeley, 1959).

—— *Poetical Works*, ed. H.J.C. Grierson (Oxford, 1971).

Eden, Richard, *A Treatyse of the Newe India* (London, 1553).

Eliot, George, *Middlemarch*, ed. David Carroll (Oxford, 1986).

Epicurus, *Letter to Menoeceus: The Extant Remains*, ed. Cyril Bailey (Oxford, 1926).

Evans, Ambrose, *The Adventures and Surprizing Deliverances of James Dubourdieu and his Wife* (London, 1719).

al-Farabi, Abu Nasr, *On the Perfect State*, ed. and tr. Richard Walzer (Oxford, 1985).

Flint, V.I.J., *The Imaginative Landscape of Christopher Columbus* (Princeton, 1992).

Frazer, J.G., *The Golden Bough*, ed. Robert Fraser (Oxford, 1994).

Friedman, John Block, *The Monstrous Races in Medieval Art and Thought* (New York, 2000).

Gallez, Paul, 'Walsberger and his knowledge of the Patagonian giants, 1448', *Imago Mundi*, 33 (1981), pp. 91–3.

de Gamboa, Pedro Sarmiento, *History of the Incas*, tr. Clemens Markham, Hakluyt Society, Series 2, Vol. 22 (Cambridge, 1907).

Garlandus Compotista, *Dialectica*, ed. L.M. de Rijk (Assen, 1969).

Gregory the Great, *Moralia in Job*, ed. M. Adriaen, CCSL, 143 (Turnhout, 1979).

Grosseteste, Robert, *Hexameron* , tr. C.F.J. Martin (Oxford, 1996).

—— *On the Six Days of Creation*, ed. C.F.J. Martin (Oxford, 1999).

Hadis-i nev Tarig-i garbi, in Thomas Goodrich, *The Ottoman Turks and the New World* (Wiesbaden, 1990).

Hakluyt, Richard, *The Principal Nauigations, Voyages, Traffiques and Discoueries of the English Nation* (London, 1589).

—— *Hakluyt's Voyages: A Selection*, ed. Richard David (London, 1981).

Hayward, Sir John, *David's Tears* (London, 1623).

Hempton, David, *The Church in the Long Eighteenth Century* (London, 2011).

Herbert, George, *De Religione Laici* (London, 1645).

Hermes Trismegistos, *Corpus Hermeticum*, ed. A. Festugière and A.D. Nock (2nd edn, Paris, 1960–72).

Herodotus, *The Histories*, ed. A.D. Godly (Cambridge, MA, 1982).

Hesiod, *Works and Days*, ed. and tr. Glenn W. Most (Cambridge, MA, 2006).

Hume, David, *A Dissertation on the Passions: The Natural History of Religion*, ed. Tom L. Beauchamp (Oxford, 2007).

Huxley, Aldous, 'The politics of ecology' [1963], in Cecil E. Johnson (ed.), *Eco-crisis* (California, 1970).

Ingram, Elizabeth M., 'Maps as readers' aids: maps and plans in Geneva bibles', *Imago Mundi*, 45 (1993), pp. 29–44.

Ibn Battuta, *The Travels of Ibn Battutah*, ed. Tim Mackintosh-Smith (London, 2002).

Isidore, *Etymologiae*, ed. C.C.J. Webb (Oxford, 1911).

James, Wendy, Gerd Baumann and Douglas H. Johnson (eds), *Schuver's Travels in North East Africa, 1880–83*, Hakluyt Society, Vol. 184 (London, 1996).

Johnson, William Weber, *Cortés* (London, 1977).

Jung, C.G., *The Red Book*, ed. Sonu Shamdasani, tr. Mark Kyburz and John Peck (London and New York, 2009).

Justin Martyr, *Dialogue with Trypho*, ed. L.A. Williams (London, 1930).

—— *Apologies*, ed. D. Minns and P. Parvis (Oxford, 2009).

Kark, Ruth, 'The contribution of nineteenth-century Protestant missionary societies to historical cartography', *Imago Mundi*, 45 (1993), pp. 106–19.

Kennedy, E.S. and Imad Ghanem (eds), *The Life and Work of Ibn al-Shatir* (Aleppo, 1976).

Kilwardby, Robert, *De Ortu Scientarum*, ed. Albert G. Judy (London, 1976).

King, Leonard W., 'Legends of Babylon and Egypt in relation to Hebrew tradition', *The Schweich Lectures* (London, 1918).

Kingsley, Charles, *The Heroes*, in S.H. McGrady (ed.), *Legends and Myths of Greece and Rome* (London, 1936).

—— *The Water Babies* (London, 1961).

Kipling, Rudyard, *Kipling's Early Verse*, ed. Andrew Rutherford (Oxford, 1986).

Klopp, O. (ed.), *Die Werke von Leibniz, Vol. XI* (Hanover, 1884).

Krey, August C., *The First Crusade: The Accounts of Eyewitnesses and Participants* (Princeton, 1921).

Lamb, Charles, 'The adventures of Ulysses: heroes and kings', in S.H. McGrady (ed.), *Legends and Myths of Greece and Rome* (London, 1936).

Lewis, C.S., *Perelandra* [1943] (London, 1953).

—— *The Screwtape Letters* (London, 2001).

Livingstone, David, 'Missionary travels and researches in South Africa', in Tim Youngs (ed.), *Nineteenth-Century Travels, Explorations and Empires: Writings from the Era of Imperial Consolidation, 1835–1910* (London, 2004), Vol. VII.

Locke, John, *Two Treatises on Government* (London, 1764).

Lofting, Hugh, *The Story of Dr. Dolittle: Being the History of his Peculiar Life at Home and Astonishing Adventures in Foreign Parts Never Before Printed* (London, 1920).

Lucretius, *De Rerum Natura*, ed. and tr. W.H.D. Rouse (Cambridge, MA, 1924).

Luther, Martin, 'Lectures on Genesis', in Martin Luther, *Luther's Works* (St Louis, 1958), Vol. I.

Macrobius, *Saturnalia*, ed. Robert A. Kaster (Cambridge, MA, 2011).

Magnus, Olaus, *Description of the Northern Peoples*, ed. Peter Foote and tr. Peter Fisher, Hakluyt Society, Vol. 182 (London, 1996).

Mill, John Stuart, *Theism*, ed. J.M. Robson, in John Stuart Mill, *Works. Vol. X* (Toronto, 1969).

Milton, John, *The History of Britain*, in John Milton, *The Works of John Milton* (New York, 1932), Vol. X.

—— *Paradise Lost*, ed. David Loewenstein (Cambridge, 2004).

Morison, Samuel Eliot (tr. and ed.), *Journals and Other Documents on the Life and Voyages of Christopher Columbus* (New York, 1963).

Newton, Isaac, *Chronology of Ancient Kingdoms Amended* (London, 1728).

—— *Observations upon the Prophecies of Daniel, and the Apocalypse of St. John* (London, 1733).

—— *Four Letters from Sir Isaac Newton to Doctor Bentley. Containing Some Arguments in Proof of a Deity* (London, 1756).

—— '*Optics*, Query 28 (Appendix A)', in H.G. Alexander (ed.), *The Leibniz–Clarke Correspondence* (Manchester, 1956).

—— *The Correspondence of Isaac Newton*, ed. H.W. Turnbull, J.F. Scott, A. Rupert Hall and Laura Tilling (Cambridge, 1959–77).

Origen, *Contra Celsum*, tr. Henry Chadwick (Cambridge, 1953).

—— *De Principiis Book*, tr. G.W. Butterworth from Koetschau, ed. (New York, 1966).

Osborne, Catherine, *Dumb Beasts and Dead Philosophers* (Oxford, 2007).

Ovid, *Metamorphoses*, tr. G.P. Goold, Frank Justus Miller (Cambridge, MA, 1984).

Park, Mungo, *Travels in the Interior of Africa* [1860] (London, 2005).

Peter Comestor, *Liber Genesis, Historia Scholastica*, CCCM, 191 (Turnhout, 2005).

Philo of Alexandria, *De Opificio Mundi* (*On the Making of the World*), ed. L. Cohn (Vratislava, 1889).

Plato, *Timaeus*, ed. and tr. R.G. Bury (Cambridge, MA, 1981).

—— *Cratylus*, ed. H.N. Fowler (Cambridge, MA, 1983).

Pliny, *Natural History*, tr. H. Rackham (Cambridge, MA, 1983–95).

Plutarch, *De Facie in Orbe Lunae* tr. F.C. Babbitt (Cambridge, MA, 1957).

Pope, Alexander, *An Essay on Man*, ed. Mark Pattinson (Oxford, 1969).

Powell, Baden, *Essays on the Spirit of the Inductive Philosophy, the Unity of Worlds, and the Philosophy of Creation* (London, 1855).

Puchas, Samuel, *Purchas his Pilgrimes: Microcosmus, or, The Historie of Man* (Glasgow, 1905).

Pullman, Philip, *The Amber Spyglass* (London, 2000).

Reitan, E.A., 'Expanding horizons: maps in the *Gentleman's Magazine*, 1731–1754', *Imago Mundi*, 37 (1985), pp. 54–62.

Richter, I.A. (ed.), *The Notebooks of Leonardo da Vinci* (Oxford, 1998).

Robert Grosseteste, *On the Six Days of Creation*, tr. C.F.J. Martin (Oxford, 1999).

Robinson, George Augustus, *The Port Phillip Journals of George Augustus Robinson* [1842–3], ed. I.D. Clarke (Monash, 1988).

de Sahagun, Bernardino, *A History of Ancient Mexico*, ed. Carlos Maria de Bustamente, tr. Fanny R. Bandellier (Detroit, 1971).

Savage, C. Wade. 'The paradox of the stone', *Philosophical Review*, 76.1 (1967), pp. 74–9.

Sayers, Dorothy, *The Mind of the Maker* [1941] (London, 1994).

Schultz, J., 'Jacopo de Barbari's view of Venice', *Art Bulletin*, 60 (1978), pp. 435–74.

Sedgwick, Adam, *A Discourse on the Studies of the University* [1833 version], intr. Eric Ashby and Mary Anderson (Leicester, 1969).

Seneca, *Naturales Quaestiones*, ed. and tr. Thomas H. Corcoran, 10 vols (Cambridge, MA, 1971).

Smith, Catherine Delano, 'The emergence of "maps" in European rock art: a prehistoric preoccupation with place', *Imago Mundi*, 34 (1982), pp. 9–25.

Stanley, Henry, 'How I found Livingstone', in Tim Youngs (ed.), *Nineteenth-Century Travels, Explorations and Empires: Writings from the Era of Imperial Consolidation, 1835–1910* (London, 2004), Vol. VII.

Tatian, *Address to the Greeks*, in Tatian, *Writings*, ed. M. Dods (Edinburgh, 1883).

Thatcher, Oliver J. (ed.), *The Library of Original Sources* (Milwaukee, 1907), Vol. III.

Thompson, Stith, *Motif-Index of Folk Literature* (Copenhagen, 1955), Vol. I.

Tillyard, E.M.W., *The Elizabethan World-Picture* (London, 1943).

Tindal, Matthew, *Christianity as Old as the Creation* (London, 1730).

Tolmacheva, M.A., 'Ptolemy's East Africa in early medieval Arab geography', *Journal for the History of Arabic Science*, 9 (1991).

Tremain, Rose, *Trespass* (London, 2010).

Vailati, E., *Leibniz and Clarke* (Oxford, 1997).

Vidal, Gore, *Creation* (London, 1993).

Virgil, *Aeneid, Books I–VI,* ed. R.D. Williams (London, 1972).

Virgil, *The Georgics*, ed. and tr. H. Rushton Fairclough and G.P. Goold (Cambridge, MA, 1999).

de Voltaire, François Marie Arouet, *Letters on the English* (Cambridge, MA, 1909–14).

Walbridge, J.T., 'Explaining away the Greek gods in Islam', *Journal of the History of Ideas*, 59 (1998), pp. 389–403.

Wells, H.G., *Tales of Space and Time: The Short Stories of H.G. Wells* (London, 1927).

Westfall, Richard S., 'Isaac Newton's *Theologiae Gentilis Origine Philosophicae*', in W. Warren Wagar (ed.), *The Secular Mind* (New York and London, 1982).

White, V.S., *Atlantic Sailings prior to 1492* (Wheathampstead, 2006).

Whymper, Edward, *Travels amongst the Great Andes of the Equator* (London, 1891).

Williams, Charles, *Many Dimensions* (London, 1931).

Witt, C., 'The myths of Hellas', in S.H. McGrady (ed.), *Legends and Myths of Greece and Rome* (London, 1936).

Worcestre, William, *Itineraries*, ed. John H. Harvey (Oxford, 1969).

Yates, Frances, *Giordano Bruno and the Hermetic Tradition* (London, 1964).

Index

References to illustrations are denoted in italics